ROTORBOYS

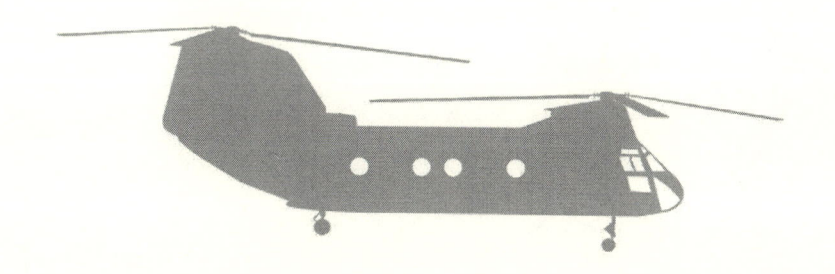

ROTORBOYS

Larry Carello

Braveship
BOOKS

Aura Libertatis Spirat
San Diego

ROTORBOYS

Copyright © 2013, 2018 by Larry Carello

All rights reserved. No part of this book may be used or reproduced by any means, graphic, electronic, or mechanical, including photocopying, recording, taping or by any information storage retrieval system without the written permission of the author or publisher, except in the case of brief quotations embodied in critical articles and reviews.

Braveship Books
San Diego, CA

www.BraveshipBooks.com

This is a work of fiction. Names, characters, places or incidents are either the product of the author's imagination or are used fictitiously, and any resemblance to actual persons, living or dead, business establishments, events or locales is entirely coincidental and beyond the intent of either the author or the publisher.

About the Cover Artist

Depicted on the cover is "Sideflare 65," painted by Emmett Lancaster, an award-winning commercial artist who worked in charcoal, pastels, oil, and acrylic. His service as a B-26 pilot during World War II and later with the Arizona Air National Guard imbued him with a love of aviation. He created numerous aviation-themed paintings, including this one of an H-46 with the first detachment deployed from the newly-commissioned VERTREP squadron, HC-11, based at N.A.S. North Island, California.

ISBN-13: 978-1-64062-051-3
Printed in the United States of America

AUTHOR'S NOTES

Rotorboys is a work of military fiction, inspired by my time flying the CH-46 helicopter in the Western Pacific Theater. All characters are fictional; resemblance to any real people or actual events is purely coincidental.

References to historical military and political figures are accurate to the best of my knowledge, except for the meeting depicted in Chapter 26 between Ferdinand Marcos and two naval officers. That event, of course, never really happened.

The U.S. Navy retired the last of its CH-46s in 2004, capping off the aircraft's forty-year span of service to the fleet. U.S. Marines continued flying this splendid machine until 2015.

— Larry Carello

For those who know how to hover

Prologue

The nightmare always began the same way. Bud Lammers set down his Huey gunship in a grassy clearing during a raging tropical storm. He was the only soul on board – his copilot and door gunner had vanished. He keyed his mike and called their names, but heard only static in his headset. Bud twisted the helicopter's engine throttle to its idle position, unstrapped and stepped from the aircraft's landing skid onto the soggy Vietnamese soil. His flight boots sank ankle-deep as he struggled across the clearing searching for his crew. About one hundred meters away, he saw images of men as they emerged from the bush. Bud shielded his eyes from the downpour and focused on the images. They were a team of American fighters. The men sighted the helo and began running toward it. Bud tried to pivot and return to his aircraft, but the quagmire had risen to his knees and he was stuck in place. A rifle shot tore through the wet air, then another, and another. Bud turned to see a throng of black-clad rebels in pursuit of the Americans. He fumbled for his sidearm, but the holster latch was jammed; he couldn't open it. He stood helplessly and, for the countless time, watched the surreal tragedy unfold. The enemy's bullets found their targets; the first American fell to the ground. One after another they dropped, until the team's leader was fighting alone, refusing to surrender. Ultimately, a flurry of lead shredded the valiant warrior's legs and he toppled face first into the mud. With their last foe eliminated, the rebels turned toward Bud and took aim.

Lammers bolted awake and raised his head from the damp pillow. His heart raced as he grappled in the dark for the reading lamp suspended above his bunk. He found it and flicked on its switch. Cold, grayish light illuminated the tiny stateroom. A chill ran through him as frigid air from a ceiling vent blew against his sweat-soaked T-shirt. Bud saw his flight suit hanging from the corner of a locker door. It swayed ominously, like a pendulum, as USS *San Angelo* began taking some moderate rolls. He checked his watch; still a few minutes to compose himself before today's launch. He took a deep breath and then reached for his cigarettes.

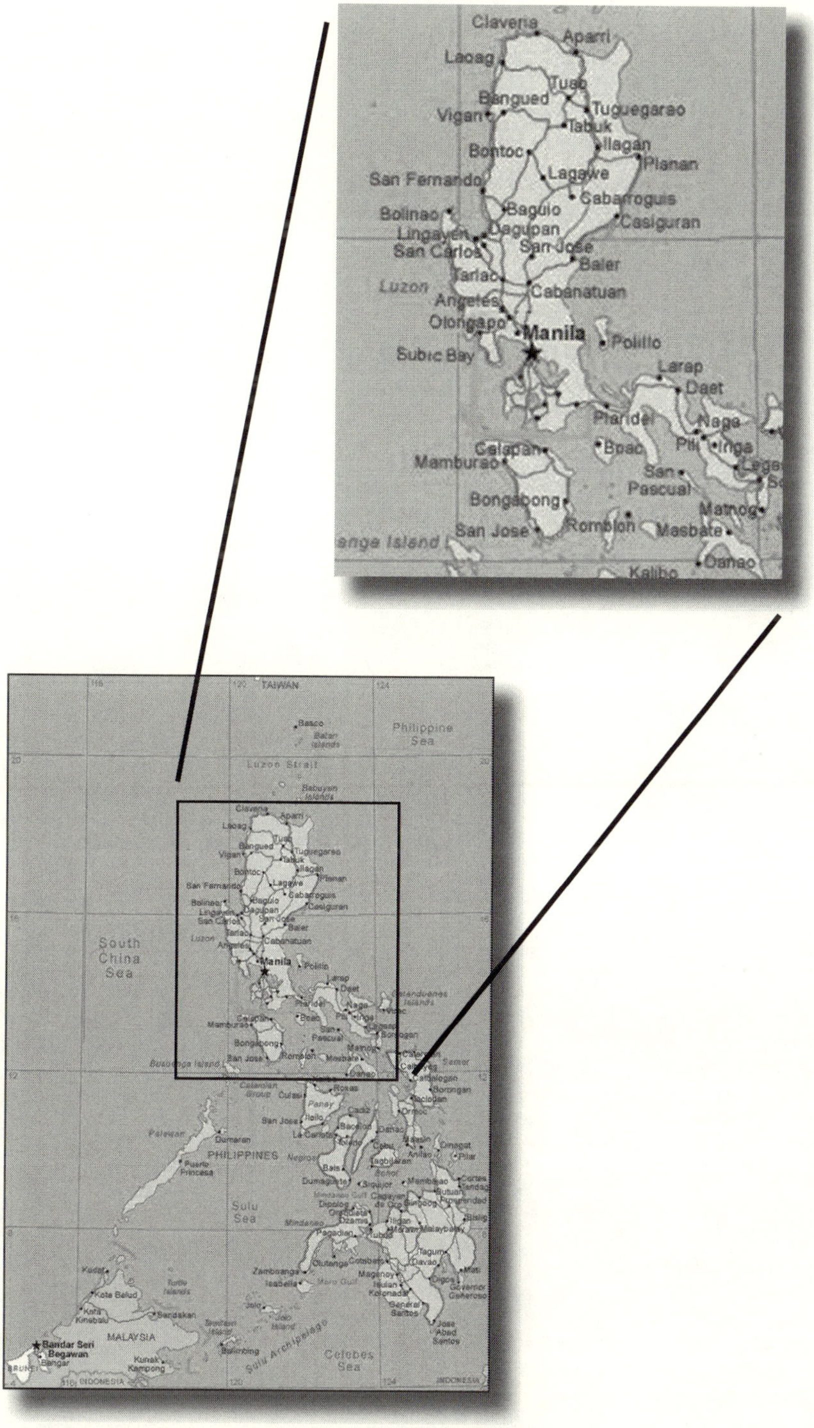
Claveria
Aparri
Laoag
Tuao
Bangued
Tuguegarao
Vigan
Tabuk
Bontoc
Ilagan
Palanan
San Fernando
Lagawe
Cabarroguis
Bolinao
Baguio
Casiguran
Lingayen
Dagupan
San Carlos
San Jose
Baler
Tarlac
Luzon
Cabanatuan
Angeles
Olongapo
Manila
Polillo
Subic Bay
Larap
Daet
Pandel
Naga
Calapan
Boac
Pili
Iriga
Mamburao
San Pascual
Bongabong
Matnog
San Jose
Romblon
Masbate
Kalibo
Danao
TAIWAN
Basco
Batan Islands
Philippine Sea
Luzon Strait
Babuyan Islands
South China Sea
Palawan
PHILIPPINES
Sulu Sea
Celebes Sea
MALAYSIA
Bandar Seri Begawan
BRUNEI
INDONESIA
Sulu Archipelago

Chapter 1

Flying a helicopter isn't easy. Its whirling, twirling mass of moving parts makes it inherently unstable. Piloting a helicopter, low-level over the water at night, is one of the most challenging jobs that any aviator can ask of himself.

Bud Lammers hated to fly over the open ocean after dark. He was an experienced helo pilot with combat under his belt. He'd been shot at and had seen just about every emergency that his aircraft's complicated systems could throw at him. But in the course of a two-hour nighttime flight, he'd burn a dozen smokes and chew half a pack of gum to keep himself calm. Forget about eating; he'd skip dinner in the officers' wardroom, preferring instead to scrounge something from the cooks after landing.

"Sideflare Zero-One, wind steady at zero-two-zero, eight knots. Green deck," said the voice in Bud's headset.

"Roger, Tower, copy green deck."

Bud rolled the H-46 smoothly to wings-level, shifted his eyes from the warm security of his flight instruments and found the ship, about a mile ahead. A smattering of dim lights on *San Angelo's* flight deck twinkled on this moonless night in the South China Sea. At his altitude of two hundred feet, he'd have only a few seconds to get his line-up squared away before he started a gradual, constant-angle descent to the ship's flight deck. Unlike his fixed-wing brothers flying their sexy machines to the carriers, he had no visual guidance, or "ball" as they called it. No angle-of-attack indicator or landing signal officer to talk him down.

"Looks good, Boss. Speed ninety knots, descent rate five hundred," said his copilot, Ron Carbone. The ship's landing pad grew larger in their windscreen. The aircraft buffeted as it passed though the twisting air that funneled around *San Angelo's* superstructure, prompting Bud to make some quick corrections to stay on course. Now, less than one hundred feet above the water, the fluorescent glow of the ship's churning wake filled the clear chin bubble between the pilots' feet. Somehow, no matter how black the night was, that aqua-green glow could always be seen from above, signaling a silent, frothy "welcome home."

"Fifty feet," Carbone said.

Bud located the orange wands of the ship's enlisted landing signalman, or LSE, on the deck below. Forward, forward, add power and come to a hover above the landing spot. The signalman's wands were extended straight out from his shoulders, parallel to the deck as the helo floated in suspension. He lowered his arms slowly, telling Bud "land now." Bud pushed the collective down gently with his left hand, flattening the pitch of all six rotor blades. One short nudge of the stick to compensate for the ship's roll and *thump*, Sideflare Zero-One was on deck. The chock and chain gang swarmed the aircraft, securing it down.

"Hey Carbs, great to be done, huh?" Bud said.

"You know it, Boss," the burly Bostonian answered, already loosening his helmet's chinstrap and easing the tension on the five-point shoulder harness that had strapped him in for the last several hours.

"Tower, Zero-One to disengage rotors," Bud requested over the radio. Like Carbone, he'd slackened his straps and harness lock. Stopping the bird's rotors and killing fuel to the engines was just a formality now. A quick reading of the shutdown checklist and the two pilots' work would be over. *San Angelo's* two helicopters had moved more than one hundred eighty tons of freight to seven other ships by a method called vertical replenishment, or VERTREP. The ships had ranged in size from an aircraft carrier down to a small frigate.

"Tower, say again, request permission to—"

"Zero-One, stand by, Bridge is tracking a close-in surface contact and may have to execute a breakaway. Be ready to get airborne if needed," the control tower operator said.

"WTF, Brightness?" Carbone blurted out, breaking from standard radio discipline. The wisecracking former enlisted sailor was low on patience. He looked up, trying to sight the air control officer, or "Tower Flower." Tonight, that job fell to an off-duty pilot, Ensign Robert Bright, call sign

"Brightness." The radio was silent. Carbone leaned his head from the helo's side window and threw his hands up, begging a response from the Tower Flower. Still poised outside of the rotor path, the LSE crossed the wands in an "X," telling the flight crew to hold. Carbone watched as he shuffled the wands into one palm and pressed his free hand against the headset he wore, which linked him to the control tower's intercom. He nodded toward the tower, and then gave the signal for chocks and chains to be removed.

"Hey, Tower, what gives?" Bud asked.

"Standby..." Brightness answered.

"Looks like the party's not over yet, Boss," Carbone said. Both pilots cinched-up their harnesses.

"Yeah, I got it," Bud said, grabbing the controls again. Two young sailors ran back out to the helo, disconnected chains from the bird's stubby winglets and removed a pair of chocks that hugged the main wheels. *San Angelo* began to take on some heavier rolls and light rain misted over the helicopter's windscreen. Carbone glanced at the ship cruising in tight formation off *San Angelo's* port side, still attached by a jungle of cargo transfer lines and refueling rigs. Distance markers glowed like a string of Christmas lights. The two massive vessels were only a hundred feet apart, steaming in unison at twelve knots and in the last stages of their replenishment evolution.

Bud started to key his mike again when *San Angelo's* whistle belched five thunderous blasts, signaling an emergency breakaway. Within seconds, all lines connecting the two vessels were severed. Lammers and Carbone watched as the destroyer eased ahead of them, gaining speed steadily as her boilers went to flank power. *San Angelo* continued straight ahead for a few seconds and then began a hard turn to starboard. The helicopter's parking brake and nose steering were locked, but the centrifugal force generated by the ship's turn, combined with the rolling deck, was too much. Bud jammed down the helo's collective, hoping to pin her to the deck, but the aircraft started creeping as it lost traction. Spinning blades dipped perilously toward the deck and the two rotor heads pounded against their mechanical stops. Bud needed to get airborne, and fast, to avoid losing control.

"We gotta get off this deck, Tower!" he shouted into his mike. He flashed the helo's nose light three times and prepared to lift off. The LSE looked up and over his shoulder at the array of lights next to the Tower — still all red. Obeying his orders, he kept the wands crossed, signaling the helo to remain on deck. Wind and rain picked up as *San Angelo* entered a squall and continued to accelerate while turning. The scene suddenly looked like a newsreel from a hurricane; small hailstones pelted the flight deck as the LSE braced himself to hold his footing.

The nose wheel broke free first, followed by the two main tire assemblies as the aircraft leapt sideways, bounced, and began sliding toward the deck edge. Bud couldn't wait for a green deck: he yanked an armful of collective and jerked the craft into the dark sky. He pulled back on the control stick, placing the helo in a stable hover, fifty feet above the water, aft of the fantail. As he did, the Tower Flower pressed a button switching off the red lights and turning on the green ones, clearing the crew for lift-off.

"Well... OooKaay..." Carbone said sarcastically over the radio. The LSE figured out what was going on and sheepishly raised his wands to the hover position. He scanned both directions, circled the wands above his head and gave a "clear to go" signal.

"Tower, you heard anything from Zero-Two?" Bud asked. "I'm not crazy about blasting through this weather blindly without knowing where my playmate is."

"Last time they checked in, they said they were a couple miles off the port side after making a drop," Tower responded. "Oh, maybe two minutes before everything hit the fan."

"Yeah, I remember McGirt saying they were gonna extend downwind while we made our approach. They're out there somewhere," Carbone said.

"OK. We'll hold over here on starboard side for a while," Bud said. He pitched the helo's nose over and added power. The rain let up, enabling him to climb to a few hundred feet and remain in the clear. He switched on the autopilot and reversed course, keeping *San Angelo* in sight as they flew downwind. He was too whipped to hand-fly the machine right now, and with more than four thousand flight hours, there was no reason to prove his "stick and rudder" skills. Besides, he needed a cigarette.

"Looks like we're coming out of the crud, Tower. I can see some stars peeking through. That was some nasty stuff," Carbone said.

"Copy, Zero-One. Just hold a starboard delta 'til we sort this all out."

"Roger, starboard delta," Bud said, acknowledging the holding pattern on the ship's right side. "Hey, Brightness, hand the mike over to Rayburn, will ya?"

"Can't do that, Boss, he's not here." Bud remembered that he'd reluctantly endorsed Rayburn's request to be on the Bridge for the last couple hours of tonight's event. His Assistant Officer in Charge had blindsided him with the proposal during a briefing in the ship's wardroom earlier in the day. Rayburn had presented such an altruistically convincing argument to the ship's executive officer that Bud would have looked foolish not to go along with his request. He regretted that decision now.

"You gotta be shittin' me! Brightness is running this circus by himself?" Carbone said.

"You take it, Carbs, I gotta burn one," Bud said. Carbone acknowledged with a waggle of the stick and assumed control. Bud pulled out a pack of unfiltered Pall Malls and lit up. *Another lousy habit from the war,* he thought to himself. He sucked down a couple deep draws and tilted his helmet back, onto the top of his seat. Carbone monitored the autoflight system and guided them into gentle right turns while they held abeam of the ship. Bud reached up and slid open the Plexiglas window by his side. The fresh air felt good against his sweaty flight suit.

Tower came up on the radio again. "Sideflare Zero-Two, Tower, radio check."

No answer.

"Hey guys, where you at?" Brightness asked. It wasn't unusual for the helo's crew not to respond. If the bird was several miles away, over the horizon and at low altitude, its UHF radio would be out of range.

"Zero-One, Zero-Two's not answering," Tower said.

"Yeah, we got that, Brightness." Light rain started up again as they entered another squall. Bud closed his window and turned on the wipers in order to keep the ship in sight. Despite all the spectacular, sunny days that the Pacific had to offer, when the weather turned bad, it turned really bad. Tonight seemed to be one of those times.

"Hey Tower, you boys out there somewhere?" piped a familiar voice over the radio. Johnny Jack McGirt's soft Kentucky twang was unmistakable. "Sounds like ya'll been right busy for a while."

"Welcome back, Zero-Two," Tower answered.

"Thought we'd stay out of the fracas and hold off to port while things got sorted out. Any paint get swapped between us and that small boy?" McGirt asked.

"Negative," Tower said. "Bridge had to do some maneuvering, but we're ready to recover you and Zero-One. Say fuel state."

"Well, glad you asked," McGirt said. "We're a little low on gas and need to get on back to home plate. We got maybe... make 'er two-zero 'til splash."

Tower answered, "Copy Zero-Two, twenty minutes until splash. Stand by."

Bud didn't wait for Brightness to make a decision. With only twenty minutes of fuel in his tanks, McGirt had to get aboard. Both helos had eaten up extra fuel during the emergency breakaway, plus McGirt and his crew had done most of the heavier loads and traveled farther between ships to make their drops. It hadn't been planned; it had just worked out that way tonight.

"Tower, we're fat on gas with three-zero till splash. Better get Zero-Two aboard first," Bud said.

"Got it, Boss," Tower replied. "Break... Sideflare Zero-Two, wind zero-five-zero at eight, green deck." *San Angelo* had settled into a northeasterly track, the reverse of what it had held before the breakaway. The ship traveled in and out of light showers, but the worst of the weather seemed to be behind them now, to the south.

"Bridge will continue on this course for recovery."

"Appreciate that, Tower. We just passed over a little guy. Fishin' boat or something. Did he try cuttin' in on our dance with that tin can?"

"Zero-Two, we'll brief you when you get on deck. Call us in sight," Tower said.

"Roger that. Entering some heavier squalls now. Wind musta pushed us a bit — gauges say we're ten miles out. We'll call the deck in sight," McGirt said.

Bud and Carbone remained in their holding pattern to starboard while Zero-Two began its approach. Bud hacked the helo's clock and lit another Pall Mall. All eyes on the flight deck focused aft, searching for Sideflare Zero-Two to emerge from the dark mist. The LSE had removed his goggles, wiped the raindrops away, then peeled off the cranial headgear everyone on the flight deck wore: a combination of lightweight helmet and sound protectors. Zero-One was a mile or so forward in a lazy holding pattern. The *thump, thump, thump* of its rotor blades faded out as it flew upwind from *San Angelo*. The wind began gusting again as the LSE donned his gear and illuminated the wands. The deck crew waited, eager to wrap up the night's work and climb into their bunks.

Bud tossed his half-burnt smoke out the window. He raised his helmet's visor, hoping to pick up the reassuring sight of the other aircraft's lights as it came to a hover over the deck. Carbone switched off the autopilot and guided the bird around some low-hanging clouds. A gust of wind buffeted the airframe, causing them to lose altitude, as they waited.

***

Lammers' playmate, Sideflare Zero-Two, had maneuvered clear of the scene after hearing the Tower's warning of the impending emergency breakaway. Inside the helicopter's cabin, two enlisted aircrew prepared the aircraft for its final landing. The senior of the two – a big Louisianan named LaRue– ambled forward to the cockpit and crouched down, wedging himself between the two pilots' seats.

"Mr. McGirt, we gotta put a fix on that dang cargo hook," LaRue said over the interphone. "It's been a pain in the ass all night."

"It can wait," McGirt replied without turning his head. "We're done hauling loads for the night. The maintenance guys can handle it after we land." His eyes were glued on the bird's dimly lit flight instruments as he flew the aircraft at a precise speed of one hundred knots. The needle of his radar altimeter gauge was pinned at exactly two hundred feet. After months of intense nighttime ops, McGirt felt confident flying low-level above the Pacific's black, foamy wave tops.

LaRue swiped a flight glove over the chewing-tobacco drool on the corner of his mouth then asked, "With all due respect, sir, why waste time?" He jerked his head toward the rear of the aircraft and laughed. "I got my pet monkey, Lincoln, on it as we speak."

McGirt swiveled his head slowly and faced LaRue. "I warned you about that language, LaRue. Knock it off," he said. "Secure the hell-hole and prepare for landing."

"Aye, aye, Lieutenant," LaRue answered innocently. He stood up and began walking aft into the darkened cabin. He made no attempt to hide the sneer that had crept over his face.

As the aircraft went into a turn, LaRue gripped a handrail that ran along the helicopter's sidewall. He heard the pilots saying something about bad weather, but their words were muffled by the high-pitched whine of the machine's engines and transmissions. LaRue grinned as he watched the shadowy image of Lincoln in mid-cabin. The younger sailor was seated over an open, three-foot-square hatch that housed the aircraft's cargo hook assembly. Lincoln's legs dangled freely in the windstream as he struggled to repair the jammed release mechanism that had plagued the crew all night.

LaRue felt the aircraft's bank angle steepen. He squeezed harder on the handrail as G-forces pressed against the soles of his boots. He peered out a cabin window and saw the reflection of the helicopter's beacon as its pulsing light bounced off the water. A sinking feeling welled inside his gut as he watched the reflection grow brighter and the angry sea zoom up at him. He heard McGirt shout something over the interphone, then the aircraft rolled rapidly in the other direction and pitched up violently. LaRue lost his grip and crumpled to the deck.

Chapter 2

San Angelo's bridge crew had spent a hectic eight hours during tonight's replenishment event. They were tired and wanted to hit the rack — all except for one sailor: Lieutenant Thomas Rayburn III. He'd taken a quick bathroom break, wolfed down a ham sandwich from a tray on the quartermaster's table, and then guzzled a can of diet soda. He was more energized now than when he'd left the Tower. With the VERTREP going smoothly, he'd felt comfortable leaving Bright alone. Rayburn strutted onto the dimly lit Bridge and received a briefing from the officer of the deck, a crusty fifteen-year veteran named Johnson. When he was ready, Rayburn adjusted his ball cap, stood tall and declared for all to hear, "This is Mr. Rayburn and I... have... the con." It was important that he said those time-honored words in the most appropriate way, slowly and in a slightly louder, more forceful tone than he normally spoke. He'd actually practiced his delivery in front of the mirror, a couple minutes ago, while alone in the officers' head. At six-foot two inches in height and blessed with square-jawed handsomeness, Rayburn projected the image of a natural leader. Taking control, or "the con" as it was commonly known at sea, was a feather in the cap for Thomas Rayburn III as he climbed another rung on the promotional ladder.

Over the last six months, he'd worked diligently to establish himself a cut above his fellow pilots by pulling double duty: flying the H-46 and pursuing his Surface Warfare Officer designation, or "water wings" as everyone called them. Rayburn's goal was to be the youngest aviator ever to achieve the feat of earning both qualifications. He was well on his way to pinning the shiny new insignia on his starched khaki shirt, just below the aviator wings.

Rayburn walked outside the Bridge to the port lookout wing. Alongside, about one hundred feet from his ship, was the hulking silhouette of another vessel, the last of seven ships *San Angelo* would service tonight. The two ships appeared to be loosely hinged together by a collection of lines and hoses that dipped and rose as the vessels glided through the rolling seas at a lazy twelve knots. Over the wind noise and sound of rushing water below, Rayburn heard the muted thwapping of rotor blades as his squadron mates approached the ship's helo landing spot, several hundred feet aft. As light rain resumed, he returned to the Bridge.

"Sir, Combat reports contact alpha at ten thousand yards, three-three-zero degrees relative and closing."

"Very well," Rayburn replied. The Combat Information Center had been following the surface target with its radar for the last hour. Earlier, on his way back to the Bridge, Rayburn had visited CIC for an update on the unidentified small vessel, now only a blip on *San Angelo's* big radar screen.

"I'd guess a small, mongrel freighter, churning its way toward Manila," the CIC watch officer had told him. The officers stared down at the green speck on the radar console. "She's been moving on an erratic course. Hard to predict really, possibly a steering casualty. Considering the kinds of derelicts I've seen in these waters, though, maybe the helmsman fell asleep at the wheel." Both officers chuckled at the thought of that old cliché actually being the case. "Anyway, for the last thirty minutes she's been on a constant course, decreasing range. We'll keep you advised."

"OK, Mr. Rayburn, what do you think?" said a voice to his side.

Rayburn turned to the OOD. "Well, sir, I recommend we make a broadcast in the blind on channel sixteen stating where we are and what we're doing. With these rain squalls and limited visibility, there's a good chance they can't see us. It's questionable whether they even have radar on board. I understand that our lookouts on the signal bridge reported seeing some spotty lights, confirming what Combat's painting on their scope."

"Good choice. I can see you've been doing your homework," the OOD said. He dialed up channel sixteen, the emergency frequency, and made the transmission, hoping to raise the stray contact on radio. Rayburn grinned confidently and glanced over toward the ship's captain, Walt Lugansky, who sat in a big, barber shop-like chair, reading from a clipboard. The "Old Man" had propped up his feet and seemed blasé about the activities around him.

Earlier in the evening, Rayburn had successfully brought *San Angelo* alongside the lead vessel, an aircraft carrier, in a textbook display of seamanship. As junior officer of the deck, he'd used his keen ship handling skills, or "conning," to maneuver into position, closely abeam the giant "bird farm." With *San Angelo* now the lead vessel, it was the destroyer's responsibility to maintain the course and speed that Rayburn chose to set during the replenishment event. Not much different than flying an aircraft in formation, he'd concluded.

Unlike flying his helicopter, however, Rayburn didn't use a control stick and collective, but rather the knowledge in his head that gave him the ability to control the lumbering vessel through commands directed at others. There was a helmsman, who actually steered the ship, and another sailor who relayed signals to the engine room to fine-tune the ship's propeller, regulating its speed. Rayburn had seen these same maneuvers before, on a much smaller scale, at the Naval Academy, where he'd studied in Luce Hall and practiced guiding Yard Patrol training boats in the Chesapeake Bay. The process was tedious and boring in the eyes of most aviators, and absent the instant gratification pilots felt after a slick shipboard landing or a precision cargo drop on a black-ass night.

But Thomas Rayburn III was a different breed of aviator, "the complete naval officer," as he liked to think of himself. Being able to con a ship was just another square to fill on his race to the top.

The rain and wind intensified as the formation passed through another squall line. No one on the bridge wing bothered donning their foul weather gear; the cool droplets felt good against their skin. They'd been dealing with bad weather all evening: short bursts of sideways precipitation lasting two or three minutes at a time. After several hours of this routine, the foul weather was more of a nuisance than a hazard.

Captain Lugansky set down the telephone next to his chair. "Officer of the Deck, we'll execute an emergency breakaway if contact alpha closes to four thousand yards," he said. "Pass the word to the destroyer and all work stations."

"Aye aye, Captain," the OOD acknowledged.

Rayburn's heart rate picked up. He'd only conned the ship once during an emergency breakaway, and that had been during a training event in daylight with perfect weather, about five months ago. Combat had calculated a closing rate of twenty knots with the freighter. With only six thousand more yards to lose, Rayburn guesstimated another ten to twelve minutes until the formation would be at the captain's execute point, four thousand yards.

He took a deep breath and reviewed the emergency procedures in his head. This would be a defining moment in his career and he had all the confidence and the knowledge to handle it like he always did: perfectly.

"Tower, Bridge, heads-up for a possible emergency breakaway," the OOD said over the intercom. "Say position of the two choppers, over."

"Bridge, Tower, Zero-One just landed and Zero-Two is off the port side. Last transmission, McGirt said that they were extending downwind to avoid some clouds."

On the Bridge was a speaker that monitored UHF radio communications between the Tower and the ship's two helicopters. The chatter, however, had blended in with the rest of the cacophony inside the cramped Bridge, packed with watch standers.

The OOD turned to a string of young, dungaree-clad sailors standing against the Bridge's aft bulkhead and said, "Phone talkers, pass the word to all stations to prepare for breakaway and be ready for heavy seas while turning." The seamen repeated his words verbatim and spoke into an apparatus known as a sound-powered telephone, which permitted conversation without the use of electricity. This was an essential feature if anyone along the network were to lose power. The talkers passed the word to all work stations, most importantly the deck crews, who handled fueling lines and cargo, CIC, and the engineering spaces that controlled the ship's boilers. Lugansky rose quietly from his chair and stood next to the OOD, who was on the telephone with the CIC officer.

"Skipper, Combat has contact alpha now at three-three-zero, fifty-five hundred yards, still closing at twenty knots," the OOD said. "We're on a direct collision course."

Rayburn remained on the port wing. He still had the con. A phone talker stood dutifully at his side. Rain started pouring down at a forty-five degree angle. Both Rayburn and his talker grabbed their yellow slickers and slipped the gear on over their already-wet uniforms. The two ships began taking bigger rolls, the shallower-drafted destroyer leaning hard on her side in the ten-foot swells. Lugansky joined Rayburn on the wing and looked below at the deck handlers struggling to do their jobs. Refueling lines and cargo transfer rigs slackened and then drew taut again as the vessels plowed forward in unison through the worsening weather. On the ships' main decks, platoons of sailors controlled the lines' tension manually, in essence forming a long tug-of-war between the two vessels. In calm seas, this was a moderately easy task, but not tonight. The crews whipped fore and aft across the wet deck, gamely trying to compensate for the ship's motion. One handler stumbled and tripped, causing another half dozen sailors to cascade over him like dominoes. Unable to get to their feet, the entire group was dragged across the deck, refusing to let go.

"Captain, contact now at forty-five hundred yards and closing," the OOD reported.

Lugansky didn't hesitate. "That's enough!" he said. He moved halfway back onto the Bridge and shouted, "This is the captain — I have the con! Execute emergency breakaway. Sound five blasts on the ship's whistle. Maintain present course and speed."

The helmsman and engineman echoed his commands. Talkers barked the order through their microphones. Lugansky returned to the port wing and watched as the scene unfolded. *San Angelo* stayed on her present course. Systematically, lines and hoses connecting the two ships dropped into the water. Fluorescent lights, attached as distance markers, sprang from the waves like illuminated flying fish as the lines bounced wildly off the whitecaps. One by one, lines were reeled back aboard. The destroyer eased forward of *San Angelo,* steadily gaining speed. Black smoke spewed from her stacks as her OOD ordered maximum turns from the engine room.

The agile destroyer continued accelerating rapidly, now well ahead of *San Angelo.* "Right full rudder, all ahead full," Lugansky commanded. He added forty-five degrees to the ship's last heading, turned toward the helmsman and added, "Continue right to course two-seven-five degrees."

"Let's go look for this guy," Lugansky said to the OOD at his side. The air of tension began to dissipate as the escape maneuver unfolded, separating the ships from impending disaster. The captain and OOD rejoined Rayburn on the port wing. With the speedy destroyer already well clear, the threesome had a good view of what would have been the closest point of approach between them and the errant vessel, which refused to give way. Through the steady rain shower, they got a glimpse of a small craft, its running lights bobbing erratically in the high seas. Slowly it began to come around, turning on a southerly track.

The OOD raised a set of binoculars and found the vessel's profile in the darkness. "Looks like a small freighter, Skipper. She has no business in these waters tonight," he added rhetorically.

The captain grabbed the railing in front of him and gazed at the tiny vessel's fading lights. "Jesus Christ, all this for that little piece of crap?" He shook his head and walked back onto the Bridge. "OOD, take back the con. Slow us down to twelve knots, maintain present course."

The OOD acknowledged and assumed control of the ship. The captain added, "Let's get both birds on deck and sort this out. I'll be in Combat with the XO."

The ship's navigator came forward and interrupted. "Pardon me, Captain, but you may not have heard the tower over the radio. They report Sideflare Zero-One never disengaged rotors during the breakaway. The crew got airborne and is holding in starboard delta. We've lost comms with their playmate."

The skipper walked out onto the starboard lookout wing and saw the helo's position lights as it circled, a few hundred feet above the water.

"What? They had a red deck. Now they're up again?" The Old Man seemed peeved.

"Appears so, Captain. It all happened in the middle of the breakaway."

Chapter 3

"Whoa," Carbone said, adding power to maintain altitude as Zero-One continued in its holding pattern. "The navigator said we'd be in and out of this crap all night. Guess he was right."

Bud had grown edgy when McGirt hadn't answered Tower. He gripped the cyclic to key his mike when a shout rang out over the radio.

"In the water! In the—"

"Say again, Zero-Two," Bud transmitted before Tower had a chance.

Something unintelligible came across the radio, followed by static and then nothing. Bud and Carbone glanced at each other, stunned, hoping their ears had played a trick on them. A few more radio queries went out from Tower, Bridge, and Zero-One, but still no response.

Bud shuddered at the specter of losing anyone from his unit. He drew a couple deep breaths before he spoke. "Carbs, we have to rig for rescue and go look for them." But before Carbone could acknowledge, a voice from the back of the helo answered on the intercom.

"We heard you, Commander. We're on it." Bud turned and looked over his left shoulder, and saw his lead crewman, Norris, give a nod. "Ready in two minutes, sir," he added.

Standing beside Norris was a skinny kid from New Jersey, Sartelli. He was already out of his green Nomex flight suit and, with the help of Norris, slipping into the wet suit and gear of a rescue swimmer. Bud made eye contact with the youngster, whose expression was a mixture of determination and pure terror. The crewman's hands trembled visibly, but he flashed a "ready to go" thumbs-up at Bud.

The rest of the crew of *San Angelo* had settled down after the successful emergency breakaway. Some went straight to bed; others drifted down to the mess deck for midnight rations, hoping to unwind before turning in. When the officer of the deck triggered the helo crash alarm, it was met with wide-eyed expressions and "WTF" looks. Tired sailors grumbled and bitched, but doubled-timed it to their duty stations. One critical group, a crew of boatswain mates, readied a motorized rescue boat, all the while wondering how on earth they'd control their small craft at night in rough seas, if given the order to launch from the ship's skipper.

The OOD radioed ahead to the aircraft carrier, now spraying a rooster tail at flank speed toward liberty in Subic Bay. Except for the lagging destroyer that had participated in the breakaway, the flattop and her escorts had already put over thirty miles between themselves and the supply ship. *San Angelo's* OOD knew that the carrier had one asset onboard that might be key to the rescue: the H-3 helicopter. With its sophisticated automatic Doppler hovering system, the H-3 Sea King was the Cadillac of nighttime search and rescue. Without this automated feature, Bud and Carbone in their H-46 would be in a fifty-foot manual hover above rolling seas, guided only by basic verbal commands from the hoist operator and their own "seat of the pants" skills. Plus, with Sartelli in the water, they'd have one more body to pull from the drink, assuming there were in fact any survivors. Not an impossible feat, but one that would test Bud and his crew mightily, especially on the heels of a long, arduous mission.

"Tower, we're starting a search pattern a few miles to port, in the area Zero-Two reported that civilian small boy," Bud announced.

Before Tower could respond, CIC came up on frequency and said, "Zero-One, Combat here, breakaway was initiated to avoid a slow-moving surface target. She's not talking with anyone. Last contact I had was two-seven-zero degrees at eight miles. We had a faint radar return with Zero-Two in that same area just prior to his distress call. Radar is down now. Expect to have it up in a few minutes."

"Thanks, Combat, that helps," Bud replied. Carbone rolled the bird into a steep bank and took up a westerly heading.

"Eight miles... we'll be there in less than five minutes," Bud said.

Carbone held the aircraft at two hundred feet and one hundred twenty knots, relying solely on the primary flight instruments to navigate. They were flying through moderate rain and turbulence, but Carbone kept the helo rock-steady, on course and altitude. His eyes scanned rapidly, back and forth between gauges: attitude gyro, compass, altimeter and airspeed. Interrupting the pattern for a split second, he checked the aircraft's fuel quantity.

"Hey, Bud, hate to bring this up, but we're getting skosh on gas ourselves."

Bud did what most pilots would do in the same situation; he tapped the fuel gauges a couple of times, then pressed the "reset" button, wishfully thinking the instruments might recalibrate themselves to a higher value. Sadly, they didn't.

"Damn, you're right," he said. The last thing he wanted to do was put a swimmer in the water and then flame out his own aircraft before they could make a pickup and return to the ship. "But we have to give it a shot. With these seas, it'll take the rescue boat a good half hour to get in the water and motor to their position. If we can't make a fast pickup, we'll mark the spot with a flare and drop them a raft."

Bud glanced back into the cabin to see how things were progressing. After helping Sartelli suit up, crew chief Norris had rigged the rescue boom and tested its electric hoisting wench. Sartelli stood barefoot, clad in a full-body wetsuit. A mask and snorkel were perched at parade rest on his forehead. Under one arm, he held a pair of long, sleek fins.

"Crew chief, about four minutes till we're on station. Let Sartelli know, will ya?" Bud said over the intercom.

"Got it, sir," Norris replied. He pushed the mike away from his mouth, held up four fingers and screamed into Sartelli's ear, "Four minutes, Guido!" Sartelli caught Bud's eye and flashed a calm, confident grin. The shakiness had subsided as his training kicked in and helped quell the initial adrenaline rush. This was what he had volunteered to do for a living and he was ready.

"Zero-One, Tower, Combat tells me there's an H-3 doing 'buster' to us. Should be on scene in about twenty minutes." Bud felt some relief at knowing they'd have a backup soon. The H-3 was making its best speed with a fresh crew and full load of fuel.

The clouds had crept down to one hundred feet above the surface and visibility was less than a quarter mile. Rain pelted the aircraft's windshield as the crew of Sideflare Zero-One pressed on. Carbone flew with his eyes glued to the flight instruments; Bud scanned outside for any sign of survivors. Sartelli came forward and squatted between the two pilots in the narrow entry to the cockpit, prepared to help Bud as a lookout. The crew chief leaned out the helo's side entry door, looking as well.

Bud checked his clock and noted the mileage from the ship's TACAN signal. "We should be there in about a minute," he said. Carbone slowed to forty knots and descended to fifty feet.

"Take it up to seventy-five, Carbs; that little freighter's out here somewhere," Bud said. "Light's coming on." He slid his left hand to the top of the collective and found the searchlight switch.

Carbone bore-sighted the flight instruments as Bud swiveled the beam back and forth over the wave tops. Light reflecting off the fog and rain illuminated the cockpit with an eerie glow. Bud knew his partner was forcing himself to stay focused inside, fearing he'd develop vertigo if he shifted his sights outside, even for a second.

"Commander, over there on the right! I see some lights!" Norris exclaimed. Using only instruments for guidance, Carbone gently fed in some right rudder, pointing the helicopter's nose in that direction. The aircraft held a perfect hover, motionless.

"Tell me when, Bud," Carbone said.

"OK, that's a good heading. Stop. Continue forward," Bud said.

The lights grew brighter. It was the freighter. She bobbed and rolled in the rough seas. Bud flicked on the searchlight again: black waves and blowing sea foam were all he saw — no sign of aircraft wreckage. McGirt and his crew would have an arsenal of devices inside their survival vests to signal rescuers: pencil flares that could be fired high into the air; another brighter, handheld flare, and lastly, a powerful strobe light that could be affixed atop of their helmets. That was, of course, assuming anyone had survived the crash and then managed to wriggle free of the helo before it sank to the bottom.

"Boss, we're guzzling gas hovering around out here," Carbone said. His tone was composed but wary.

"Sir, standing by," Norris said. Bud looked back and saw Sartelli, at the doorway and in position. The crew chief held a hand firmly on the youngster's shoulder, ready to give him three quick pats — the signal to jump. Bud made eye contact with Sartelli and saw the fearful look had returned to his face, but he raised his arm and gave a trembling thumbs-up.

Bud checked the fuel gauges one more time. They were down to the minimum safe reserve. This wasn't going to work; they'd have to return to *San Angelo* and land. He shook his head and said, "We gotta go. The H-3 should be here in a few minutes. Crew, secure from rescue ops and prepare for landing."

Bud and his crew headed back to home plate. He figured that by the time they finished refueling, the H-3 would have arrived on station and assumed control of the search. He'd heard them check in on *San Angelo's* radio frequency during Carbone's approach back to the ship. Nonetheless, there was no way that Bud Lammers was going to sit this one out. After a quick shutdown, refuel, and cup of black coffee, he'd be ready to get back into the air. He'd polled his crew, asking if anyone wanted to get off after over ten hours on duty. Not a single man chose to quit.

The ship's radar was still down, so Carbone executed a homemade approach, using *San Angelo's* radio beam to guide them in. As they descended to fifty feet, Bud picked up the glow of the churning wake about a half-mile out.

"Carbs, I've got the wake. Stay on the instruments until I call the deck."

"Roger that," Carbone acknowledged as they flew in and out of rain showers. He lowered the collective and began to bleed off airspeed when Bud called the flight deck in sight. The rain eased up a quarter mile out.

"I'm visual, Boss," Carbone said.

"Green deck, cleared to land," Bud replied.

Carbone guided the aircraft into a constant-angle descent, arriving over the deck in a ten-foot hover. The LSE gave them the "land" signal with his wands. Carbone lowered the collective a notch, but then yanked it back up when the flight deck unexpectedly rolled to the left.

"Aw, fuck it!" he said. Frustrated, he pressed the collective down and planted the aircraft roughly on deck. "Sorry, Bud, I don't have the patience to play around with it," he said.

The chock and chain crew did their thing; Tower cleared Sideflare Zero-One to disengage rotors. Bud pulled the engine condition levers to stop, killing fuel to the turbines, then reached up and pressed the rotor brake switch. The helicopter's two transmissions and six blades came to a smooth, firm stop. Bud and Carbone unstrapped.

"Let's refuel, do a quick engine wash, and get back into the air," Bud said. After several continuous hours of flying in the salt-laden environment, the aircraft's turbines were subject to fouling. Their intakes needed to be sprayed with fresh water to flush away salt encrustation.

The ship maintained a rolling motion as the fueling crew dragged a thick hose across the flight deck. Halfway to the aircraft, they stopped, dropped the hose and looked up. Despite still wearing their helmets, both pilots heard the thump, thump, thump of rotor blades — not the smoother, fanlike sound of an H-3, but the unmistakable beat of an H-46. The helo was close enough that Bud and Carbone felt the pounding vibrations in their seat cushions. Sartelli had deplaned, peeled down his wetsuit to the waist, and joined the gawking fueling crew. All eyes were fixed off the ship's fantail.

Bud removed his helmet and poked his head out the cockpit's side window. There, like a ghostly mirage, a helicopter emerged from the misty darkness. The ambient lighting from the flight deck lit the surroundings enough for him to make out the numerals on the nose: "02."

Carbone crawled over the center console and crammed his head out the opening next to Bud. In unison, they let out a wild whoop at what they saw. McGirt and his crew were still airborne!

Bud and Carbone scrambled out of the helo and joined the rest of the crew to get a better look. However, as their feet hit the nonskid deck, it became obvious that something was seriously wrong with Zero-Two. She couldn't hold a stable hover and gyrated erratically in all three axes.

A loud, boyish voice boomed over giant speakers above the flight deck. "Zero-Two's got to be almost out of fuel, Boss. We have to get you in the barn so they can land." Lost in the excitement, Bud had forgotten that McGirt's aircraft would be even lower on gas than his bird. He spun around and waved his arms back at Brightness, signaling that he understood.

"All hands, prepare to move aircraft into the hangar. Now!" Brightness ordered over the speakers. A crowd of sailors, wearing a variety of different colored jerseys, exploded onto the flight deck from all directions, surrounding Bud's aircraft — firefighters and ordinance handlers clad in red; the "purple gang" of fuelers; the launch and recovery crew in green, plus a collection of mechanics and "lookey-loos" unable to sleep, milling around the hangar.

"Carbs, I'm going up to the Tower. I want you to take charge here while they push her in the barn," Bud said to his copilot. "These guys look pretty fired up — don't let anyone get hurt."

Carbone nodded. He knew exactly what his boss was getting at. Sadly, a lot of blood had been shed over the years by the crews of distressed aircraft, as well as by the well-meaning folks trying to help. Adrenaline and bravery frequently won out over good sense while attempting to save a shipmate.

Bud hurled himself up the steep steel ladder that led to the Tower, two stories above the flight deck. Once topside, he grabbed the compartment's hatch and felt the handle being twisted from the other side. He backed away as a series of latches spun around and the three-hundred-pound slab of iron rotated on its hinges. A massive man stood in the entryway, nearly filling the big, oval-shaped opening. In the darkness, all that Bud recognized was a khaki uniform and the prominent white eyeballs of the black-skinned sailor, Chief Petty Officer Irvis Jenks.

"I'm up here helping the ensign, sir," Jenks shouted. He backed away from the hatch, making room for another body. Once inside, Bud battened down the weather-tight door. With it secured, the tiny observation tower became nearly silent. The air inside was sweltering and smelled like a locker room.

"A.C. musta crapped out, Boss," Jenks said loudly. He pulled out a white handkerchief and mopped his glistening face. He took his voice down a few decibels once it registered that the door was shut. "We tried opening the hatch for a breeze, but the noise got bad. Couldn't hear you or the Bridge."

Seated at the Tower's control station was Ensign Robert Bright. The short, slightly built officer held a phone receiver to his ear and a round microphone in the other hand. His light blond hair was plastered down with sweat.

"Understand, Bridge, we're pushing her in now. Green deck for recovery at my discretion," Bright said. He placed the phone against his chest, put the mike to his mouth and said, "Cleared to move aircraft — let's go, guys!" Inside the snug tower, without the amplification of a P.A. system, the officer's tinny voice came across like that of a male cheerleader, pumping up the crowd at a high school ball game. All three men stood up and looked below to the flight deck. Someone had already begun the process of folding the aircraft's rotor blades. A swarm of bodies leaned into the helicopter, pushing against the machine's stubby winglets that housed fuel cells and its landing gear. Bright reached overhead and flicked on a set of wipers to clear the Tower's windows. In less than a minute, the helicopter disappeared into the hangar bay beneath the tower.

With that situation under control, Bud turned his attention to McGirt's aircraft, which had maneuvered directly off the stern, ready to set down. Its crew struggled to keep her in a decent hover, wobbling in all directions and unable to communicate over the radio.

"Brightness, where's Rayburn?" Bud asked. He instinctively pulled out a crumpled pack of smokes from a pocket in his flight suit.

"Not sure, Boss, probably still on the Bridge." Bud saw anger in the young officer's eyes. "I think he wanted to work on his OOD qualifications tonight during the UNREP. Chief Jenks came up to help when the shit hit the fan."

Bud looked out at the helicopter dangling precariously off the tail end of the ship, reassuring himself that they were still airborne. "All right, we don't have time to track him down," he said. "McGirt's gotta be down to only a few minutes of gas."

The tower hatch opened and Rayburn hurried inside.

"Where the hell have you been?" Bud asked.

Rayburn brushed the rainwater from his face and said earnestly, "They needed me on the Bridge. What can I do to help?"

Bud shook his head in disgust. "Nothing, now. Brightness has things under control without you," he said. Rayburn slinked to the back of the tower cab like a scolded child. Below, the LSE ran out to the center of the flight deck and waved his wands at the Tower, signaling that Bud's aircraft was out of the way and the deck was clear for McGirt's landing.

"OK, give them a green deck... let's get this fiasco wrapped up," Bud said.

Before Bright could switch the deck status lights, Zero-Two ignored the LSE's hold signal and lurched forward over the small landing spot.

Chief Jenks was the first to spot the helo's damage. "Christ, the nose gear's missing! And what's that hanging down from the hell-hole?"

Simultaneous with Jenks' revelation, Carbone burst from the hangar bay and grabbed the wands from the LSE, who robotically continued giving the flight crew a "land" signal. Carbone positioned himself squarely in the center of the flight deck and crossed the wands. Zero-Two jerked backwards, placing the helicopter's ass end hanging off the fantail and over the water. As it did, something fell from the bird's underside and into the wire safety nets that surrounded the deck edge. It was one of Zero-Two's crewmen. Two deck hands ran toward the nets and dragged the limp body across the flight deck and into the hangar.

"What the?" Jenks shouted. He and Bud ran outside, hoping to get a better look at the bizarre scene unfolding before them.

Carbone stood defiantly in the center of the flight deck, blocking any chance of Zero-Two setting down. Its crew flashed its landing lights frantically, signaling for him to move so that they could land.

"They can't set down like that, Chief!" Bud hollered into Jenks' ear. "Without the nose strut, they'll go into ground resonance." The aircraft's nose and two main gear struts were similar to shock absorbers on a car. If a landing were made missing any one of the three, the helicopter's rotor system could become dynamically unbalanced and the machine would essentially thrash itself to pieces. Bud walked to the deck railing, pulled a flashlight from his survival vest, and beamed it at the hovering aircraft. The LSE joined Carbone at center deck, and also shined a light on the bird's underside. The helicopter's nose strut had been ripped completely off. In the area where the nose gear had been, the bird's aluminum skin was peeled back as if someone had taken a can opener and plied at it haphazardly. Wires and cables hung from the gaping hole.

"Chief, we've got two options: find a way to brace the nose when they set down or order a ditch," Bud said. Jenks stared back at his boss, speechless. The odds of recovering the helicopter after an open ocean ditching were slim to none. With the present sea state and the aircraft's inherent top-heaviness, once the rotors stopped turning, she'd flip over in seconds. The crew would have a fair chance of escaping, but the helo would be destined for Davey Jones' locker, miles beneath the surface.

Jenks stood tall and hollered back above the noise. "We're not going to lose that aircraft, Commander, not on my watch! Let's go back inside. I got an idea." Bud and Jenks hurried back into the Tower with Bright. The air conditioning had come back on, lowering the temperature from stifling to merely hot and muggy.

"Boss, Bridge is up to speed with what's going on," Bright said. "I calculate they've got about seven minutes of fuel in their tanks." On the table was an aircraft manual opened to the "fuel burn" charts. Next to the manual was a standard Navy-issue green notebook. Bud glanced down at its page and saw that the young officer had kept a meticulous log of the events as they'd unfolded: times, verbatim radio transmissions, calls to the Bridge, everything.

"Thanks for writing this all down, Brightness; we'll need that when we try to put this all together," Bud said. He picked up the phone and punched a button that linked him to *San Angelo's* Bridge. While he did, Jenks and Bright huddled together over the notebook.

"Yeah, Bridge, Lammers here in the Tower. I need to speak with the captain." Bud never considered using the chain of command and going though the OOD. He knew the ship's skipper would be on the Bridge now, running the show.

"Captain, Bud here. Zero-Two is hovering over the fantail but can't land. It appears that they hit the water and tore off the aircraft's nose gear. Without support under the nose, she'll have to ditch or crash land onto the deck. Our other option might be to conduct a HIFR." Bud was referring to Helicopter Inflight Refueling, also known as "hi-drink."

"How much time we got?" Lugansky asked.

"Six, seven minutes, tops," Bud said.

The captain didn't hesitate. "Get a fuel hose inside that aircraft and buy some time," he ordered. "I'll get the ball rolling from this end."

"Copy, sir," Bud said. He hung up the phone and turned to Jenks. "Hi-drink, Chief."

Jenks stared at the flailing aircraft an instant then said, "Ensign's working on a plan, sir. I'm going down to get the word to the crew about fueling them."

Jenks ran out of the Tower and down onto the flight deck, where the LSE had taken back his wands and relieved Carbone, maintaining the "hold" signal. Jenks went to the hangar's maintenance office and searched for something big to write on. Attached to the steel bulkhead above his desk was a blackboard. He grabbed a piece of chalk, held it on its side and wrote in bold print, "NOSE GEAR GONE – DON'T LAND! HI-DRINK." Then he yanked on the board, busting it loose from its fasteners one corner at a time. He ran through the hangar and out on to the flight deck, where a gaggle of sailors had already pulled out an extra length of fuel hose and waited.

Jenks joined the LSE on deck and held the blackboard above his head. He could see McGirt at the controls, wrestling with the bucking machine as it oscillated. McGirt inched the bird closer, then turned on the searchlight and rotated it directly at Jenks.

The chief turned his head to the side, blinded by the spotlight. He felt the blackboard begin to buckle from the rotor wash and prayed that McGirt could read his writing before the board snapped. Then McGirt blinked the light a few times, indicating that he understood, and backed off.

A crewman appeared at the side door and gave the chief a thumbs-up. Slowly, the aircraft's rescue winch swiveled into position and began to pay out cable. A hook at the end of the cable contacted the deck as the crewman un-spooled another few feet of slack. The LSE gave the fueling gang the sign to run the hose out to the middle of the flight deck, where one of the crew attached the hose's nozzle to the hook on the cable's end. The crew chief winched in the line, lifting the thick hose from the deck. The fueling crew then stood off to the side in a line, cradling the hose in their arms, much like firefighters, allowing it to roll off of its reel and up, into the aircraft. Inside, Zero-Two's crew chief located the quick-disconnect fitting along the helo's sidewall and attached the hose. He flashed the OK signal to the cockpit crew, who relayed it outside to the LSE. Another sign was given to the pump station operator, who turned on the spigot. A few seconds later, the crew chief reappeared at the door, clapped his hands together and gave a jubilant double thumbs-up. The aircraft's fuel gauges began to rise.

Bud called the Bridge again. "Captain, tell the fuel gang to give them fifteen hundred pounds; that'll give us about an hour." He hung up and rubbed a hand across the top of his head. His thinning hair was soaked in sweat. Brightness handed him a paper towel to dry off. Bud sank down in the empty chair next to the junior officer and said to himself, *Now what?*

Bright slid the green notebook across the table and said. "Boss, take a look at this. The chief and I have an idea."

Chapter 4

Salipada Menadun hadn't really wanted to go on this voyage. His last two weeks at home, he'd started to feel halfway normal: decent food, clean clothes and a warm Filipino woman lying next to him every night — well, almost every night. He'd spent the last of his pesos three days ago and watched as his little harem had disappeared one by one.

"No money, no honey, Sali-boy," the last of the mahogany-skinned hard bodies had told him as she'd slammed the door in his face. *You'll change your mind as soon as I get paid,* he'd thought. When his boss, Eduardo Borco, had called and offered him the nine-day run to Manila, Sali, broke and lonely, had jumped at the opportunity.

The first day out of Cotabato City, his job as *Jolo*'s first mate couldn't have been easier: calm seas and sunny skies. The old freighter, loaded with rattan, coconut oil and hardwoods, handled well on the placid waters. After a day and a half, the ship had made a brief stop in Sabah, west of Mindanao, before beginning its "money trek" to Manila. During the ten-hour port call, more goods were brought on board and crammed into the vessel's already teeming holds. But equally significant, for some reason known only to the shipping company, was the departure of *Jolo*'s regular captain. A new skipper, Santos, had taken his place. Sali had never worked with this new man, who, according to shipmates, had the personality of a loose fart and didn't say much.

Jolo was on a northeasterly track, paralleling the coast of Palawan, when Sali relieved the ship's helmsman. At this hour, he was the lone person on the Bridge and, most likely, the only crewmember awake. The ship's other topside watch stander, a lookout, was curled up and asleep on the bow. Sali glanced at his wristwatch: 23:30. Four more monotonous hours steering the ship before his relief would show up. He looked forward to getting off his feet, finding a peaceful spot on the fantail, and doing a joint before getting some shuteye. The one he'd smoked before coming on duty was wearing thin.

Prior to turning in for the night, the captain had mapped out a course and given Sali blunt running orders: "Keep us on course and wake me if something important happens," he'd said. Sali gave a nod and Santos retired to his sea cabin, downed a tumbler of cheap scotch and drifted off in a stupor. The middle-aged seaman had made these runs scores of times, and despite having never worked with Sali, he figured that if the shipping company had confidence in his first mate, that was good enough for him. Before getting under way from Sabah, he'd noted in the weather forecast a storm brewing over the Sulu Sea. Using some optimistic calculations, he figured if *Jolo* maintained its present track, west of Palawan, they'd outrun the worst of the weather. After thirty years sailing these waters, there wasn't much he hadn't seen, and this trip was no different from all the rest. *Deliver the goods, reload and head home with a nice bag of cash.* He'd be back at his Sulu beach house in no time.

Sali, bored and restless, picked up the Bridge phone and dialed the engine room, hoping to find someone to talk with. The phone rang a dozen times with no answer. *Those maggots are all deaf anyway, probably can't hear it even if they're still awake,* he thought as he hung up.

He looked down at the compass: still rock-steady on the northeasterly course the captain had ordered. The flat seas they'd glided across earlier in the day had given way to moderate swells once *Jolo* had ventured into the South China Sea. The vessel rocked gently as the breeze picked up, offering some relief from the Bridge's stale, humid air. Sali let his body relax with the rhythm of the waves and closed his eyes for a few seconds. The short reprieve felt enticing to his weary brain. His head snapped back as he caught himself fading off. Startled, he checked the compass again — still steady on course. The old freighter was making his job easy tonight, requiring few, if any, corrections at the helm.

Sali let go of the wheel and walked the few feet across the tiny bridge. He found a folding chair tucked behind a table where the captain had plotted the ship's track, and then reached up to lower the volume on the radio transmitter that hung down a few inches above his head. *Nothing but static tonight. No need to listen. We're a little ship and it's a big ocean*, he rationalized. He opened the chair and set it down behind the wheel. The swells started building, but *Jolo* stayed glued to her course as if attached to submerged rails. With the vessel loaded to its gunwales and at her maximum draft, she held her own against the ocean's power. Sali sat his tired body on the chair, resting his forehead against the wheel. He followed up by draping his arms through the wheel's spokes to hold it in place. He felt the tension release from his neck and shoulders as he slumped over and closed his eyes.

When Sali had showed up for work the other day, he'd noticed a fragile-looking youngster sitting on a rusty capstan outside of the shipping company's office. The boy was dressed in clean, pressed work clothes and wore a delicately knitted *kufi* atop his head. The light-colored cap contrasted sharply with the teen's dark skin and brown eyes. A tiny set of wire-rimmed glasses rested snugly on the bridge of his nose.

The boy had looked up from his prayer book and smiled. If not for his short hair and skullcap, Sali could have easily mistaken the lad for a young girl. The kid had a peaceful, angelic look that caused Sali to wonder what the teen was doing alone on the busy wharf. He'd smiled back, butted his cigarette on the pavement and opened the office door.

"Who's the kid outside? Did you father another illegitimate bastard, Eduardo?" Salipada asked. He let out a demented laugh at his own joke. Over the last ten years, he'd delighted in swapping insults with the tubby little dispatcher. "Why don't you share some of that with me, fatso?" Sali added as he reached over the counter, aiming for the pile of sweet rice cakes on Eduardo's desk.

"Keep your filthy Moro hands off my *merienda*," Eduardo said. He grabbed the paper plate full of treats and held them away at arm's length.

"Ah, relax, you can have them all for yourself. I don't want to turn into a lard butt like you, anyway," Sali said. Eduardo looked down at the plate in front of him and frowned. He slipped on a pair of reading glasses, gathered some documents and shoved them into a folder.

"Here, take these and lead the boy over to your boat. He's going with you to Manila," Eduardo said.

Sali walked around the counter. He sat on the edge of Eduardo's desk, took the folder and opened it. The top sheet was a manifest that listed the boy as a "minor passenger," with Sali's name as his guardian for the voyage.

"What, I'm a babysitter now?"

Eduardo removed the glasses and tucked them in his shirt pocket. He leaned back and reached for another rice cake.

"He's seventeen years old. He'll be OK by himself; just make sure he gets on and off the ship safely," he mumbled between mouthfuls. "And don't let those slobs onboard give him any crap — he's just a kid."

"So I *am* the babysitter, aren't I?"

Eduardo brushed some powdered sugar off his chest and stood up to adjust the air conditioner that creaked from a window above his head. "I'm doing his father a favor and letting him travel in the vacant cabin, behind the skipper's stateroom."

Sali laughed smugly. "So you owe his old man some money — I get it. Still losing your ass at the cockfights, fat man? Thought you promised that old hag of yours you'd give it up." He filched a rice cake before the dispatcher could sit down. Eduardo's face reddened.

"That's not it, Sali," he said. "His dad's a farmer, upriver. We grew up together. Like I said, I owe the guy a favor."

"Yeah, that's the least you and your pack of thieves could do," Sali said sarcastically.

Like thousands of Christian families, Eduardo's clan had migrated from the Philippines' northern provinces when he was a child, as part of the government's campaign to "civilize" Mindanao and other distant islands of the archipelago. In the process, they'd finagled themselves into some of the region's choicest jobs. Most of Eduardo's brothers and cousins had cushy positions with the Hong Kong-based shipping company here in Cotabato.

"Christ, you'd think he could at least buy the kid a ticket on a decent ferry boat. It's gonna take us four or five days to get up there."

Eduardo thought about explaining the story to Sali, but decided against it; he was hopelessly behind with the paperwork strewn across his desk and needed to get back to work.

"That's all you need to know about it," he said, pointing to the papers in Sali's hand. "I could've called a half dozen other guys to do this run, but I called you."

The arrogant grin left Sali's face and he nodded gratefully. Unable to resist life's decadent temptations, his financial state tended to vary widely — either flush with cash, or broke. "I was just busting your balls," Sali said. He patted Eduardo on the shoulder affectionately. "I'll bring you back some good smokes from Manila. There's usually some GIs in port willing to smuggle me a few cartons off the military base."

"That'd be great." Eduardo took the cigarette from his mouth and held it up disgustedly. "These things taste like the corn husks we used to puff on when I was a teenager."

Sali left the cool confines of Eduardo's office and walked back outside. The young Muslim boy hadn't moved from his spot along the pier. He sat peacefully in the blazing sun, head lowered in deep prayer.

As Sali got closer, the boy rose from his seat and extended a small, soft hand. His dark eyes glowed with joy. "You must be Mr. Menadun," he said in a gentle voice. "My name is Malik Abbas."

* * *

When Sali came to, the first sounds that he heard were the thunderous blasts of a ship's whistle. The first thing he saw was the half-naked torso of *Jolo*'s skipper as he stumbled onto the bridge and ran to the helm. His bulbous gut shook loosely above his sagging boxer shorts as he fought to untangle Sali's arms from the wheel.

"You moron!" Santos shrieked, his voice a full octave higher than normal. He pushed Sali out of the way and kicked the chair across the bridge with his bare foot. Sali landed with a thud, banging his head on the damp deck. He lay there stunned and speechless as the skipper spun the wheel furiously to regain control of the vessel. Sali got up and attempted to make his way back toward the helm, only to be halted by Santos' glare.

"Get away from me, you!" he growled. Sali stood immobilized, hanging his head in shame. He knew instantly how serious this was. He'd been caught committing the cardinal sin — the one that, throughout the ages, seamen would never tolerate from one another, for any reason: he'd fallen asleep at the helm.

Sali's cocky veneer melted as he paced aimlessly from one side of the bridge to the other. The skipper, thankful that *Jolo* had avoided the collision, took a deep breath and slackened his death grip on the wheel. He grabbed the bridge phone, dialed the engine room and barked some orders to the watch stander there. That sailor, alerted by the vessel's violent turn, obeyed and cranked up power to the ship's two diesels. The increased speed helped Santos maneuver *Jolo* around to a new course.

By now, several crewmen had gotten up and stood half-dressed in the narrow passageway that led to the bridge. Not one of them dared set foot inside the ship's tiny control station. Their eyes were frozen on their captain as he stood stoically at the helm. Realizing that his crew was there, Santos collected himself and stood more erect despite his state of undress. He nonchalantly wiped the sweat from his dripping brow.

"Mr. Menadun, leave the bridge and go below," he said. His deep, authoritative voice evoked both fear and relief in the crewmen. They whispered nervously amongst themselves, grateful that the ship had avoided disaster.

Sali walked off the bridge as the men pressed themselves up against the bulkhead to make way. He kept his eyes down, ashamed to face them. As he cleared the throng, he shifted his sights up from the floor and made his way along the dimly lit passageway that led below. A few meters ahead, he saw what looked like a ghost in the shadowy light: a tiny person wearing a long, linen nightshirt, standing motionless and silent before him.

Sali braced himself against the steel bulkhead as the ship took a steep roll. He rubbed his eyes and looked again. The image steadied itself against the vessel's motion and began to move toward him. As it came forward, Sali finally recognized the delicate figure: it was Malik.

Chapter 5

San Angelo had sent a message to the carrier group detailing the airborne crisis with Sideflare Zero-Two. The carrier, with its parking lot-sized flight deck, volunteered to turn around and offer assistance. After some discussion back and forth between the ships' captains, it was determined that there really wasn't any advantage to landing on the flattop. McGirt's aircraft was still missing its nose gear, and having a larger space to set down would, in effect, only provide a bigger area over which to spread the wreckage of parts if he screwed up. The H-3, with its fresh crew and extended endurance, remained on the scene.

With McGirt's crippled bird gassed up and able to stay in the air, Bud had bought them all some time to regroup and put a plan together. Captain Lugansky, a career "boat driver" with limited aviation knowledge, had delegated the recovery operation to Lammers and his crew. Luckily, the OOD had found a reasonably smooth stretch of ocean in which to loiter. The sea state was still moderate, but by steaming directly into the wind, *San Angelo* had settled into an acceptable roll and pitch to allow McGirt to put down. Bottom line: unless the crew of Zero-Two was willing to stay in a hover off the fantail, refueling every couple hours until the ship could get closer to land, they'd have to make a shipboard landing. Jenks, Bud and Carbone crowded into the Tower with Bright while Zero-Two bobbled in a hover off the fantail.

"Boss, the chief and I came up with an idea," Bright said.

"Yes sir, we made a little drawing," Jenks added. He leaned his six-foot six-inch frame over Bright's head and grabbed hold of the green notebook on the desk. Perspiration dripped from his chin and onto the page as he spoke. "We get some wooden pallets from the Supply boys, stack 'em about yea high, then pad 'em with some mattresses. Lieutenant McGirt sets her down nice and soft. Soon as he does, he cuts the rotors and my guys strap the bird down good and tight, so she don't slide." Jenks looked up at the three officers crowded around him. "We can do it, Commander, I know we can," he said.

Bright nodded in agreement. "Chief's right. This is our best chance."

"Let's do it, Bud," Carbone added.

Bud agreed and the plan was set in motion. After he called the Bridge and relayed the message directly to the skipper, the OOD had the duty quartermaster on the Bridge pass word to all hands via the ship's PA system (1MC):

"All hands not on watch, remove mattresses from bunks and lay same to the hangar deck. Break, break. All Supply personnel, locate all empty pallets and lay same to the hangar deck as well. I say again...."

Jenks and Carbone made their way back down to the hangar deck. By the time they got below, the empty half of the hangar bay was already piled high with dozens of mattresses. Eager sailors, many barefoot and in their underwear, were lined up in the passageway, lugging their bedding and wanting to help. Likewise, a mountain of wooden pallets had appeared, spilling out on to the flight deck.

"OK, guys, that's enough... that's enough!" Jenks shouted above the rotor noise. "We got it from here. You can go back to your bunk rooms." Some retreated with disappointed looks on their faces, but a large number stayed behind, anxious to see exactly what would unfold.

"Somebody call the Bridge and tell them we got enough and ain't got no room for more," the chief said, shaking his head with amazement. He found Carbone across the hangar, talking on a phone to the Tower. "Sir, you think McGirt's got any idea of what we're trying to do?" Jenks asked.

Carbone hung up, turned to the chief and said, "That's what I was talking to the boss about. Let's start building the pedestal for the nose. McGirt will figure it out."

Jenks barked out orders to anyone in earshot, picked up a wooden pallet with one hand, and marched out onto the flight deck. Brightness saw him and turned up the floodlights, which were usually dimmed down during flight ops. Jenks surveyed the deck markings, and with Carbone at his side, determined the spot where the helo's nose gear would normally be positioned on deck. He dropped the pallet and turned back toward the throng assembled in the hangar bay, motioning with both arms and beckoning the group toward him. Sailors ran out, dragging pallets and mattresses. A couple petty officers, under Jenks' supervision, began stacking and strapping: several layers of pallets, then topping the pallets with mattresses. Once Jenks was satisfied with its height, the entire mass was anchored down with nylon cargo straps, hooked into pad-eye fittings recessed in the flight deck. It took less than ten minutes to complete the task. Jenks walked around the stack, tugging at it with his big hands.

"That ain't going nowhere," he said confidently. "OK, let's get this show on the road!"

All hands cleared the flight deck except for the LSE. McGirt edged back over the flight deck and turned on the helo's nose light as the LSE guided him closer, over the jury-rigged pedestal. He flashed the light a few times, signaling that he understood the plan. The lone crewman still onboard drooped his head out the hell-hole and shined a flashlight along the aircraft's underside as it came to a hover over the landing spot. The aircraft continued gyrating back and forth across the deck as McGirt searched for the sweet spot for the nose to set down. Finally, he found it and eased off on the collective, allowing the main landing gear to kiss the deck. As he did, he maintained backpressure on the stick, holding the nose section several feet above the pedestal. The helicopter looked like a giant preying mantis, ready to pounce.

Slowly, McGirt applied forward pressure to the stick and the aircraft's nose settled closer to the stack. Four feet, three feet, two... everything looked perfect until the ship entered a roll to port and the flight deck pitched left, then up. The aircraft's nose section came down abruptly, hit the pedestal squarely and slid to one side. Jagged aluminum tore through the top mattress, scattering shredded stuffing across the deck and into the rotor wash. The aircraft's unsupported nose continued to fall toward the deck, its forward rotor blades carving a deadly swath. Disaster was imminent as blades passed less than six feet above the flight deck. The main wheels broke free and the machine skidded forward. The LSE and deck crew ran for their lives. McGirt finally wrested back control and jerked the crippled beast into the air. He fought with it and stabilized into a hover off the fantail once more.

The flight deck was now barren except for two items: the ragged mattress pedestal and one brave soul: Chief Irvis Jenks. Jenks had sprawled on his belly with his arms wrapped around his head. Once the helo had cleared, he rolled to one side and grabbed the two wands the LSE had dropped when he'd bolted. Jenks staggered to his feet and looked up to the Tower for guidance: still a green deck.

Personnel returned cautiously to their stations. Some had fled to the hangar bay while others had jumped into the safety nets surrounding the flight deck. Jenks didn't bother looking for the LSE. He marched out to the center of the flight deck, pointed both wands at the nose pedestal, then backed off to guide the bird in for another try. A piece of the airframe dropped from the right side of the helo and crashed to the deck. McGirt had jettisoned his escape door, allowing him to bend his upper body out of the cockpit and get a better view of the landing site. Jenks continued to give him signals, but McGirt ignored him, choosing instead to get the job done with a pilot's two most valuable assets: his own eyes and the seat of his pants. He switched on the bird's nose light again and leaned farther out of his seat. He sighted the pedestal and inched forward, centering the nose section over it as best he could.

McGirt held a steady hover and waited for the ship's rolling and pitching to dampen out. When the flight deck appeared to be the most stable, he shoved down the collective. The helicopter slammed to the deck in a three-point landing. All six rotor blades drooped momentarily from the impact. Simultaneous with the helo touching down, McGirt's copilot chopped the throttles and hit the rotor brake switch. The helicopter's two giant fans came to a jarring stop. A thin plume of smoke rose from the forward head, where the rotor brake assembly was housed.

"Strap her down, strap her down!" Brightness hollered over the loud speakers. A swarm of sailors attacked the aircraft and quickly chained the two main gear to the deck. The damage, however, had sheared the tie-down fittings from the nose section. There was nowhere for the crew to hook their chains.

"Everybody get over here and brace the nose until we can get a strap through the cockpit!" Jenks yelled.

A dozen sailors engulfed the aircraft's nose section, bracing their arms and shoulders against its sides. The airframe teetered as the ship rolled, but the nose stayed put on the mattresses. Jenks hoisted himself into the cabin through the side entry door and reached across the chest of Ensign Paul Uker, McGirt's copilot.

"Pardon me, sir," he said. "Somebody catch this door!" Jenks shouted out the side window as he pulled the release handle and watched Uker's escape door break loose from its hinges. It fell into waiting arms.

"Welcome home, gentlemen," Jenks said to McGirt and Uker. "With all due respect, sirs, get the hell outta here. We gotta tie this sucker down good and tight."

The two pilots unstrapped and got out, and Jenks grabbed a couple cargo straps from the cabin. With the help of the crew chief, he fed the straps across the empty pilot seats and onto the deck. The crew outside took the ends of the straps and secured them to the flight deck, cranking them down tight as violin strings.

Brightness powered up the floodlights. Everyone squinted as their eyes adjusted from night vision. *San Angelo* seemed to be coming out of the storm, for good this time. A warm, soft breeze swept across the flight deck as the ship rocked lazily from side to side. The angry skies began to clear, gradually revealing the unmatched, brilliant display of stars that only can be viewed while on the open ocean.

What minutes ago had been a scene filled with noise and chaos was now a peaceful evening on the South China Sea. Muted laughter filled the air as tension and fear gave way to relief.

McGirt and Uker solemnly inspected the scarred underside of their machine. Ripped chunks of metal, severed wires and twisted cables protruded out from between the helo and the compressed mattresses. Bud Lammers and a cadre of officers emerged from the hangar bay and picked their way through the crowd. Behind them, rescue personnel peeled off their heavy fire suits and leaned up against the hangar's bulkhead or slumped to the deck.

The boatswain's whistle sounded over the 1MC, followed by a calm, baritone voice: "Men of the USS *San Angelo*, this is the captain. I think we've had enough excitement for one evening. Secure from flight quarters."

* * *

Freddy Lincoln couldn't stop shivering. When the two hospital corpsmen had carried him down to Sickbay, he'd guessed that the shakes had been brought on by nerves, following his jump from the damaged helo, or fatigue. His knees and hands shook uncontrollably. But now, twenty minutes later and wearing only his skivvy-shorts, he was just plain cold.

"Step on the scale, please," the corpsman ordered. Freddy obliged. He wasn't sure what his weight had to do with the gouges on his wrist and shin, but the corpsman was two full ranks higher than him — a petty officer first class. Freddy wasn't about to question his authority.

"One-thirty-eight. Boy, you a real lightweight! We got to get some meat on them bones. How you gonna have the strength to pick cotton all day back in 'Bama when you show up looking like a stick man?" He snorted a laugh at his own joke.

Freddy didn't take kindly to the crude humor. The petty officer had noticed the keychain ornament that Freddy wore on a pocket zipper that read "Sweet Home Alabama." Upon seeing it, the short, chubby petty officer had announced proudly that he was "born 'n raised in Georgia, right next door. We'z almost family!" Freddy thought to himself, *Just what I need, some cracker Georgia peach wanting to be my new friend.*

The Peach had been helpful though, when he'd bandaged up Freddy after his jump from the helicopter. *San Angelo's* doctor, Bill Williams, had given him a quick initial examination in the hangar and declared the injuries "superficial, nothing broke." He'd delegated the rest to the Peach, who, after tending to Freddy's leg and wrist, had him carted below for a thorough examination, head to toe.

After the weigh-in and taking of vital signs, the Peach led Freddy to a small exam room adjacent to Sickbay's main office. He'd instructed Freddy to lie face down on a chrome-plated examining table.

"Just checking for subsequent damage and abrasions," the corpsman said. His stubby fingers moved slowly across Freddy's shoulder blades. The man's sweet-smelling cologne reminded Freddy of his Aunt Lucille. Freddy heard the door to Sickbay open and close, followed by footsteps across the tiled floor.

"That'll be fine, Hauser, I'll take it from here," Doc Williams said as he entered the tiny, lime-green colored space and pulled up a chair next to Freddy.

"Yes, sir," the Peach said. He gave Lincoln a soft pat on the head, left the room and quietly closed the door behind him. Williams shook his head and frowned as the corpsman left.

"Petty Officer Lincoln, I apologize for not coming back sooner, but I needed to be on the flight deck when they recovered your aircraft."

"Everybody OK, sir?" Lincoln asked. He rolled to his side and sat up.

"Yup, the crew did a great job. The aircraft's banged up pretty good, but you're our only injury." Williams took Freddy's wrist in his hands and examined the Peach's work approvingly. Freddy winced when the doc rolled his bandaged leg from side to side.

"I'll give you something to help with the pain. You'll be grounded for a while. Come by in the morning so I can take another look." Williams set his clipboard on the examining table, then slid his chair across the floor to a cabinet and pulled out a gray blanket.

"Here, cover up, you look like you're freezing," he said. "Sickbay's air conditioning has two settings, ice cold and off," he added with a smile. He studied the skinny young sailor's face as Freddy unfolded the blanket and draped it over his shoulders.

"People will want to know what happened up there tonight. They'll ask you to give an official statement, probably first thing in the morning. Anything that you'd like to talk about now, son, off the record?"

Freddy wrapped himself up snugly in the coarse, woolen blanket, and finally stopped shivering for the first time since jumping into the safety nets. His eyes began to well up as he recalled the event.

"Sir, all I could think about when I was hanging out the hell-hole was, if I lost my grip, the sharks were gonna eat me." Lincoln choked up but recovered, refusing to give in to his emotions. His leg started to throb and he felt a burn from the solution that the Peach had used to clean the wound.

Williams edged his chair closer to Freddy, patted his shoulder and said, "Yeah, sailor, but you didn't let go and you're still here."

Freddy continued, "LaRue had me go back to try and unjam the cargo hook release. It'd been giving us trouble all night. I couldn't figure why he wanted me to fix it right then — we'd made our last drop and were heading back to Saint Angie to call it a night. I was just sitting there on the edge of the hell-hole, working on the release switch with a screwdriver. I think Ensign Uker was flying and we must've gone into a steep bank because my ass — I mean my buttocks — was pressed down hard to the floor. Last thing I remember hearing was Lieutenant McGirt shouting on the intercom, 'too low, pull up' or something like that. Next thing I know, I was all wet and hanging out the hell-hole. I think my arm got hung up on the cable I was fixing. LaRue tried to pull me back in but I was afraid to let..." Freddy gasped, a short, painful cry, before he caught himself and stifled his tears.

The doctor interrupted and patted his uninjured arm. "We've got a bed for you in Sickbay, if you'd like."

"No, sir, I want to get back to the guys. I'd rather sleep in my own bunk tonight."

"Yeah, I can understand that," Williams said. Freddy stood up and collected his flight gear from the corner of the room. He pulled on his wet flight suit.

"Son, hold up for sec," Williams said. "You're the first black aircrew member that I've treated. Can't be too many of you guys, huh?"

Lincoln mustered an impish grin, lowered his head bashfully and answered, "Guess not, sir. I ran into a black pilot in San Diego and another one in P-cola. That's Pensacola, Florida."

Doctor Williams chuckled and said, "Yeah, I know Pensacola." He smiled, leaned back and listened intently as the young sailor started to open up about himself.

"I had a bunch of brothers in my boot camp class down in Orlando. None of us knew how to swim so they put us in a special group with a Navy SEAL. Hard-ass dude. But damned if he didn't teach everybody how to swim. Told us that we had two options: swim or drown; he wasn't gonna let us quit."

They chatted for a while longer, giving Freddy plenty of time to compose himself. Finally Williams scribbled on a form, tore off a copy, and handed it to Freddy. "You're on light duty. You can skip reveille and sleep in today."

Freddy glanced over the doctor's shoulder at a picture on his desk — a pretty young woman hugging a couple of children dressed in bright Christmas sweaters. The older one, a girl, smiled gleefully despite missing her two front teeth.

"Nice family, sir. I'm single, myself," Freddy said as he opened the door to leave.

"Yes, they are. Thanks."

After the door closed, Williams kept his eyes fixed on the photo and wondered how much the kids had grown since he'd said good-bye, six months ago.

Chapter 6

Bud Lammers had been inside the captain's stateroom only once, the day before *San Angelo* had set sail for the Western Pacific from Naval Station Alameda, California. The skipper and executive officer had welcomed him and his pilots aboard at a casual meeting where the captain's personal steward served the group coffee and freshly baked cookies. The eight of them had exchanged enthusiastic small talk as they prepared for their half-year voyage to the other side of the globe and back. The skipper had asked Bud to stay behind after the group was dismissed.

"Bud, we're looking forward to working with you fellas. Those two choppers are a terrific asset during an UNREP," Walt Lugansky said, referring to the common acronym for the underway replenishment of vessels at sea. "This should be an outstanding cruise for *San Angelo* — plenty of work and some great liberty to boot." Like the rest of the ship's crew, the two officers were eager to visit the exotic ports in Asia, especially Singapore. As the commanding officer had shaken Bud's hand at the conclusion of that initial meeting, he'd held his firm grip a little longer than expected, looked Bud straight in the eye and said, "I want you to know that I spoke with your squadron commander the other day. He had some good words to say about your detachment, and he's expecting great things from you guys."

Six months later and nearing the conclusion of their cruise, those words were stuck in Bud's head as he climbed a final set of ladders and walked down the narrow passageway leading to the captain's stateroom. The gray-painted steel door bore an unadorned, black plastic nameplate. Its white lettering read "W. P. LUGANSKY, CAPTAIN."

Bud paused and glanced down at his flight suit. He'd lost over twenty pounds during this cruise and the coveralls looked too big on his gaunt frame. He squared his appearance the best that he could, knocked on the door and said, "Permission to come aboard, Skipper?"

"Door's open. Come on in, Bud," replied a deep voice from the other side.

The captain's private space was about the same size as the standard room at a Holiday Inn, and not much fancier. Compared to the ship's other quarters, however, it was like the Taj Mahal. A twin-sized bed, not a bunk, sat in the corner. The captain's personal steward made it up each morning. The bed could be cordoned off from the rest of the space with a beige partition whenever Lugansky received civilian guests or dignitaries. Tonight the divider was wide open, revealing a neatly folded black and gold blanket that bore the emblem of the skipper's favorite team, the Pittsburgh Steelers. In the center of the room was a rectangular table that was large enough to accommodate eight for dinner. At sea, however, it was capped with a green Naugahyde cover and used mainly for meetings.

Walt Lugansky had insisted on only one luxury when he'd taken command of *San Angelo*. He'd brought his own desk aboard — a prized teak rolltop model that he'd bought while still a bachelor. He'd purchased another one, twenty-two years ago, for his wife, but this piece of furniture held a special place in his heart. As the boot ensign on his first cruise to the Western Pacific, he'd spent a month's pay on the desk when his ship had tied up in Taiwan. Lugansky loved the old rolltop, not just for the nostalgia, but for its functionality. He was a horribly sloppy paper-pusher, and the desk allowed him to tidy up with the simple flick of a wrist to lower the rolltop and hide his mess. Tonight, he made no attempt to be neat; the desktop was buried in forms, clipboards holding important messages, and a half-full styrofoam cup of coffee.

"Grab a seat," Lugansky said, motioning to the side of the stateroom with a leather sofa and matching chair. Bud chose the chair.

"Coffee?"

"No, sir," Bud said. "I've probably had a half dozen cups since we suited up for the launch tonight, and I'm pretty wired. Doubt if I'll be able to sleep."

"I've sent the JOOD down to fetch McGirt," Lugansky said. "I wanted to see how you guys are doing. Doc's looking in on Uker and the aircrewmen as we speak. He tells me that young fella, Lincoln, got a little scraped up, but he'll be OK."

Bud nodded. Lugansky rose from the desk, groaned quietly and rubbed his back. Bud heard something crack as the Old Man took a slow, deep breath and stood erect. He reached toward an array of buttons next to a speaker. He pressed one marked "executive officer" and spoke. "XO, Skipper."

After a few seconds, the efficient voice of Tom Latimer came across the intercom. "Yes, sir, go ahead."

"I'm in my stateroom meeting with the two pilots. We'll be kicking back for a while."

"Got it, Skipper. FYI, I'm drafting a follow-up to our Immediate OPREP message. Should be ready for your chop in a few minutes." Latimer had overseen all communications and messages that were required after the helicopter mishap. Due to the gravity of the matter, Captain Lugansky would have the final look, or "chop," before the message was sent out over the Navy's teletype message network.

"Take your time, XO, we're not going anywhere."

"Roger, sir."

Lugansky plunked himself down on the sofa near Bud. He reached to his side and opened the door to what Bud had thought was an end table.

"Not much to choose from tonight — Coors or whiskey? I'm having some Jack," Lugansky said. He reached deep into the small refrigerator and pulled out a nearly full bottle of Jack Daniels.

Well, now I know what the Old Man meant when he told the XO that we were "kicking back," Bud thought. The two "blackshoe" sailors had their own code words for when one wanted a little break from the tensions of his job.

Bud's face reddened. He'd heard of alcohol being occasionally doled out by the ship's doctor for medicinal purposes, and there were the infamous sea stories of the jet jocks stashing hooch in their staterooms. He never, however, expected to be offered a drink by the commanding officer while underway. Unlike the navies of many countries, like Britain, U.S. sailors were barred from drinking alcohol at sea.

"I'll... have the same as you, sir," Bud answered.

Lugansky broke open an ice tray from the fridge's tiny freezer, tossed a few cubes into a couple tumblers and poured. Bud waited for the captain to take the first sip and followed his lead. The Tennessee sour mash burned his throat going down, but tasted damn good. Within seconds, Bud started to feel the drink's numbing effects.

Lugansky shifted his husky body on the sofa and relaxed. "I don't have to tell you that we're in a dangerous business, Bud," he said. "I lost a man from my division when I was a junior officer. Night UNREP, like this one, but before we had the helos." He took a deep draw from his glass, shifted his weight and grimaced, eventually finding a comfortable position. "Young kid got whacked in the head by a swinging cargo boom and fell overboard. We stayed on station until after sunrise. Put two boats in the water looking for him. All we found were some busted-up pieces of plastic from his hard hat. He probably got sucked into the screws. I always prayed that the smack on his head knocked him cold and he never knew what hit him." Lugansky drained his glass and reached for the bottle. "As skipper, I haven't had to write a letter to a dead sailor's mother yet. We were lucky tonight."

"Yes, sir, we were," Bud said. In their numerous encounters over the last six months, Bud had never seen the skipper like this. The Old Man appeared almost melancholy.

"I guess you guys do a fancy investigation when these things happen. We're waiting on a message from the carrier. Looks like they're sending a couple of JAG officers over first thing in the morning. They'll be looking pretty hard at all of us."

"Yes, sir, they will," Bud replied. After fourteen years as a naval aviator, he'd witnessed his share of accidents and knew what it meant to the Officer In Charge of a detachment, like himself, when a mishap occurred. The deployment had gone flawlessly until this point and Bud was in line for an outstanding fitness report —something that his career needed desperately.

A slightly awkward period of silence followed as the two officers sat waiting for McGirt to join them. The fiery drinks had done their job and mellowed them both. Soon two sharp knocks rang out from the skipper's door and roused them from their thoughts.

"Lieutenant McGirt reporting as requested," a voice said from the other side of the door.

"Come on in, Lieutenant," Lugansky replied.

Johnny Jack McGirt, aircraft commander of Sideflare Zero-Two, walked slowly into the captain's stateroom. Like Bud, he still wore his green flight suit. McGirt had the sinewy look of a gymnast: broad shoulders and chest, tapering down to a narrow, boyish waist. His closely cropped blond hair, a throwback to the 1950s butch cut, set him apart from most everyone else of his generation. A thin, jagged scar on his chin stood out from an otherwise unblemished face.

"Good to see ya, Johnny Jack, find a seat and join us," Lugansky said warmly. "Something to drink?"

McGirt's eyes found Bud's, silently asking for guidance on what to say. Bud shrugged his shoulders.

"Just some coffee for me, thanks," McGirt said. He started walking toward the pot next to Lugansky's desk, but the skipper beat him to it. The senior officer found a gold-rimmed, white china cup and filled it.

"Black's fine, sir, thank you," McGirt said. He moved across the room gingerly and took a seat on the sofa. Lugansky joined him and set the cup on the glass-topped coffee table in front of them.

The skipper began the conversation. "Helluva night for you guys."

McGirt cut right to the chase. "Sir, when do you expect the JAGs to arrive?"

They all knew that a comprehensive investigation lay ahead. It would be conducted by a team of Navy lawyers with backgrounds in aviation.

"Still waiting on the message from the carrier, Lieutenant," Lugansky said.

"Well, Skipper, it's pretty simple: I fucked up. Puker... rather, Ensign Uker was flying at the time 'cause my knee cramped up and I gave him the stick for a spell. Nonetheless, as aircraft commander, it was my responsibility."

Bud interrupted. "J. J., you sure you want to get into the details right now?"

McGirt set his cup down and said, "What the hell's the difference? We're all on the same team, aren't we?" He faced the skipper as he spoke.

"Well, Mr. McGirt, you're correct: we are all on the same team," Lugansky replied. "But there's a methodology to these things, and the less I hear from you about your accident at this time, the better. That's why the Navy wants an independent team to handle the fact-finding." The warmth left the room as Lugansky deftly changed hats, from father figure back to commanding officer of a United States Navy warship.

"Yes, I know, sir. I'm just pissed." McGirt sat back and shook his head. Thick veins on his neck pulsed as he clenched his jaw. "Bud, I know this was about the last thing you needed. We had a great cruise going until tonight."

Neither Lammers nor Lugansky had much to add. They'd allowed McGirt to vent his frustrations, but now it was time to move on with the ship's business. Fatigue and the effects of the whiskey were catching up with Bud. His eyes drooped and his head bobbed. He caught himself dozing as the captain wrapped up his remarks about what he expected to happen in the next several hours.

"Commander Lammers, get some shuteye. I'll have the XO call you when we have a definite plan." Bud stood up and McGirt followed.

"Lieutenant, I'd like a few words with you," Lugansky said as Bud exited the room. It was more of an order than a request. "I really don't want to hear the details of what happened in your helicopter tonight, but I've got a few questions that I've wanted to ask you for a while." Lugansky went over to the rolltop and pulled out a folder. "I see from your service record that you claim Long Beach as your home of record, but you sound like you're from down south someplace. What's up with that?"

"Well, sir, I finished college at Long Beach State. When I was young, we moved around a lot. Spent my early years in Kentucky. Then my dad went north to find work in the sixties, a place in Michigan called Ypsilanti."

"I've heard of Ypsilanti. My sister married a guy from Detroit who worked there for a while," Lugansky said.

McGirt flashed a relaxed smile, something he wasn't accustomed to doing in the company of such a senior officer. "Don't meet too many folks who've heard of Ypsi. Detroit and Ann Arbor, maybe." McGirt cut himself off abruptly, thinking that he may have spoken on a too-familiar basis with the Old Man. Lugansky picked up on this and decided to press on, intrigued with the junior officer's background.

"If you don't mind me asking, I also see that Johnny Jack is your given name. A bit unusual, if you don't mind me saying. Is that common in Kentucky?"

"No, I can't say I've met another one. See, my folks each wanted to name me after their daddies. One was Johnny, the other Jack. Guess just calling me John was too simple, so I was christened 'Johnny Jack' at a Baptist church outside of Louisville. Didn't seem to matter much to folks in the south — lots of odd names down there. Once we came north, though, people thought it was pretty strange. Guess I just got used to it over the years."

Lugansky listened intently as McGirt talked. He hadn't said more than a dozen words to the soft-spoken pilot since the cruise had started. After thirty years of experience, working with all kinds of people, he'd become a decent judge of character. There was something that he liked about Johnny Jack McGirt — he wasn't sure what it was, but there was something.

"One more thing," the captain said. "I noticed you rubbing your knee and you're limping now. Is that from tonight or an old football injury?"

McGirt bit his bottom lip and stared down at the floor. A pained look crossed his face for a split second before he answered, "No problem, sir; nothing that some aspirin and a sack of ice can't fix."

"Well, Lieutenant, let's call it a night." Both men stood up.

"Thanks for the coffee, sir," McGirt said as he closed the door behind him.

Captain Lugansky resumed his duties at the rolltop desk. He thought about catching a few moments of sleep, but instead reached over to pour himself a cup of coffee. His ship would be receiving orders soon: either continue on to Singapore or steam in the opposite direction, back to Subic Bay, Philippines. He glanced at the clock above his head. In another hour, reveille would sound and the ship would come to life.

* * *

McGirt's right knee pounded with pain. The weather had cleared as the cluster of storms that had raised havoc last night headed northwest toward the coast of China. Thankfully, *San Angelo* had settled into a gentle rolling rhythm that made it easier for him to walk away from the skipper's cabin. He navigated the last set of ladders and hobbled down a narrow passageway to the officers' wardroom. He opened the door and found the brightly lit room empty.

His senses were accosted by the sounds and smells of breakfast. Either fried potatoes and onions or corned beef hash, he couldn't tell the difference. It all pretty much smelled the same at this hour, greasy and sizzling. In the kitchen, two Filipino cooks chatted about something in their native language while they prepared the morning meal.

Johnny Jack poked his head through the narrow pass-through between the dining room and kitchen. "Hey, fellas, can ya'll spare some ice?" he asked. He rested his forearms on the stainless steel countertop and took in the pungent aromas floating up from the grill.

"Morning, Mista McGut, you say you want a glass of ice?" one of the cooks asked him.

"Naw, more than a glass full, Petty Officer Estrada. I need a whole bag. Can you help me out?"

"Sure, no problem, sir," Estrada said. He shouted something in Tagalog to the other cook and pointed to the stove. His partner waved his hands feverishly in agreement, turned down the heat and began flipping the steamy hunks of fried potatoes before they burned. Estrada slid a plastic bag full of ice across the counter to McGirt. "This OK, sir?" he said.

"Yeah, that'll do. Thanks."

McGirt unzipped a breast pocket on his flight suit, pulled out a small container of aspirin, and popped three into his mouth. He washed them down with a glass of fruit punch.

"Good bug juice today, Petty Officer," he said. "What is it, grape or raspberry?" McGirt and the kitchen staff had a running bet that he could correctly guess the flavor of the drink whirling around inside the dispenser — always some sort of fruity concoction with a sweet, indistinguishable taste.

"Passion pear-blueberry-apple," Estrada shot back.

McGirt bowed his head in mock defeat, acknowledging that once again he'd been outsmarted. The game had gone on nearly every day for months, with the same result: McGirt always lost. The two cooks giggled and high-fived each other.

McGirt crossed the dark-paneled compartment, ignoring the chairs placed carefully around a half dozen round eating tables. He found a tattered couch in the small sitting area adjacent to the dining room, where he sat down and propped up his bad leg on a coffee table. On the table was an acey-deucey board, used to play the sailors' bastardized version of backgammon. He draped the ice pack over his knee, sat back and sipped his bug juice.

"You want fresh pastry, Mr. McGut?" Estrada appeared holding a silver serving platter, piled high with Danish pastries, right out of the oven. Their sugary frosting was still warm and gooey.

"Can't turn down one of those," McGirt said.

Estrada took two pastries off the serving tray and placed them on a small china plate. He moved the dice and chips aside and set the plate on the game board. He took off the white paper cap from his head.

"I walked down to see your helicopter when I got up this morning, sir. It looked pretty smashed up," Estrada said. "Glad you and Mr. Puker OK."

McGirt finished the first Danish and started on the second, this one with a dollop of apricot in the center.

"Thanks. Yeah, we were pretty lucky last night," he said without looking up from his plate.

"Anything else I can get you, sir?"

"No thanks. Nice job on the Danish."

The little Filipino steward put the paper cap back on and retreated to the kitchen, where he resumed giving orders to his coworker in their sing-song native tongue. McGirt slouched back on the couch and gave in to exhaustion after being awake all night. The doping effect of the aspirin reached his brain, his chin fell to his chest and he dozed off. He awoke to the booming voice of the Detachment's Assistant Officer in Charge, Lieutenant Thomas Rayburn.

"I'll take the usual, and try not to bust the yolks like you did yesterday," Rayburn said to the cooks. Seated across the table from Rayburn was the ship's junior ensign, Eddie Bishop, who always seemed to be in tow of the lieutenant. Rayburn lowered his voice and said to the young officer, "Christ, you'd think after all this time the little Flips could get it right."

McGirt repositioned his leg on the table and adjusted the ice pack. The pain was replaced with cold stiffness — a fair trade in his mind. He shoved a throw pillow under his head and tried to fall back to sleep. A half wall separated him from the two officers eating breakfast. Slouched below the wall, he was out of their sight.

"Well, so long Singapore, hello Subic," Rayburn said to his protégé between mouthfuls. Estrada came back into the dining area and set a stack of glasses next to the juice machine.

"Bet that'll make you boys happy, huh?" Rayburn said to the steward.

Estrada went back inside the kitchen without answering.

"I hear that Singapore is great liberty, Lieutenant," Bishop said.

"Yeah, a real gem of a place. Some of the best buys in WESTPAC: jewelry, ivory, you name it. When McGirt's bird hit the water last night, though, that changed everything. Hey back there, we could use some more coffee." Rayburn turned toward the kitchen and held up his cup.

Estrada reappeared and set a fresh pot on the table. McGirt gave up on going back to sleep, checked his watch and removed the ice bag. He stood up and put weight on his leg, gingerly testing the bad knee joint. It felt good now — completely numb and pain-free.

"Didn't see you over there, John," Rayburn said. He smiled nervously, gathered up the papers he'd spread on the table and tucked them inside a thick manual. "Bud told you the plan yet?"

"Nope."

"Well, I don't have time to fill you in on the details right now." He pointed to the pile of folders and manuals in front of him and shrugged his shoulders. "But we're steaming back to Subic to offload the wreck. Not sure what's after that."

"I'll talk to Bud," McGirt said as he walked to the door. He dropped off the half- melted ice bag on the counter and said, "Hey, fellas, can you toss this for me? And thanks for the Danish."

"You've probably figured it out by now, John, but you and Uker are grounded until further notice," Rayburn said to McGirt's back. McGirt threw a glare at him, opened the door and left.

"You got Danish today?" Rayburn hollered over his shoulder. "Why aren't they on the table?"

Chapter 7

Of all the dirty jobs that Rolio had done, this was the lowest. He wasn't prepared for how bad it would be. When he'd gotten his orders from Angeles City, he hadn't bothered to pack anything; he had only the thin clothes on his back and a few pesos for the two-hour ride on the Victory Liner bus. Commander Sumulong's gang would get him whatever he needed, he'd thought. But now, submerged deep below the surface like a rat, he felt something Filipinos seldom experience — the sensation of being cold.

Get the goods, pay the money and someone will be there to pick you up was all he'd been told. He had no reason to think otherwise. After a couple decades of stealing and running dope, he had a job and was making some good money. Maybe he could finally move out of the dump where he lived and find a decent place.

Rolio had relieved himself thirty minutes before he'd shimmied into the shaft, but after an hour lying on the damp earth, felt the need again. He thought about unzipping and sending a stream down the tunnel but quickly nixed the idea: he'd have to crawl through it on his way back out. He pulled a small flashlight from his jeans pocket and shined it at his watch — 3:50 a.m. His mule should have been here five minutes ago. Rolio felt a thud and heard a rumble above. It was time.

He slithered up the slope toward the opening. The dirt tunnel was no more than a few inches wider than his shoulders. He struggled as the inclined steepened. The dank air grew warmer as he neared the top and he soon stopped shivering. Rolio heard a motor shut off and a mechanical latch click as the vehicle's door opened. He felt the urge to bolt forward the last few feet but held his place, ready to snake his way out backwards if the person at the top wasn't who he was supposed to be.

Rolio heard a clank as the hatch above him was moved away. A man's head and shoulders were silhouetted against the starlit sky at the end of the shaft, making it appear as if Rolio were looking through a long, dark telescope. The head and shoulders leaned into the opening, blotting out what little ambient light there was. Rolio heard the sound of a man clearing his throat followed by three quick, clicking sounds: *"Thit, thit, thit."*

Rolio tucked his tongue against the roof of his mouth, just behind his front teeth, and returned the signal: *"Thit, thit."* The man above eased a little farther inside the tunnel and replied, an echoing *"thit, thit."*

Rolio raised himself onto his elbows and crawled the last few feet. As he approached the opening, a big hand reached down and grabbed him by the bicep, yanking him to the surface as if he were a sack of chicken feathers. He felt himself briefly suspended in the air. As his feet hit the ground, he backed off and instinctively grabbed the switchblade stashed in his sock.

"Where's ma money?" the soldier demanded.

Rolio held the knife to his side and said, "Where's my package?" He backed away farther to size up his adversary, a big GI, over a foot taller and close to three times Rolio's own weight.

"Oh, Ah got yer Ma Deuce, little man." He spoke so slowly that Rolio had trouble deciphering his words. Rolio's English was passable, but this guy's accent threw him off.

He could see the soldier's face well enough to recognize that he was young and white. Must be one of those characters they call "shit-kickers," from Texas or someplace in the American South. He'd met a few of them outside the hillbilly bars on Fields Avenue and in Subic Bay's sailor town, Olongapo. They weren't very bright, and could be meaner than hell when they got drunk.

"Ah was told you'd gimme a little bonus if Ah'd be on time." He leaned up against the vehicle, nodded his head and laughed in a goofy way. "Well, here Ah is!"

Rolio stood motionless, taking in everything around him. The GI stayed in place, mumbling something unintelligible to himself. Behind him was a tall fence topped with concertina wire. The fence butted up against dense trees. Directly in front of them was an open field with tables and swing-sets — a picnic area. Farther in the distance, Rolio saw tall light poles illuminating the flight line and hangars of Clark Air Force Base. The airbase was quiet; still a few hours to go before the morning launch.

"I don't know anything about your bonus, friend. I got cash inside the bag, that's all," Rolio said.

The GI lunged forward and knocked Rolio off his feet, causing him to drop the switchblade. He patted him down and yanked out a small canvas bag that Rolio had tucked inside his pants waistline. As he got up, Rolio read the letters stenciled on the armband attached to the GI's fatigues: MP. Strapped to the man's side was a revolver. Rolio's knife would be useless against an armed soldier anyway.

"Hey, let's get this done and go our separate ways, OK?" Rolio said. He tried to muster up some friendliness, but his voice sounded nervous and strained. The MP pulled a flashlight from his belt and shined its red-filtered light into the bag.

"Hey, there's no stuff in here!" he said loudly. "The guy said you'd have—"

Rolio interrupted, "Let's quiet down, OK?" He needed to end this and end it fast. The MP became more agitated and continued digging through the bag, then held it out and shook his head. "No dope, no package."

Rolio looked past the MP and saw a patrol car on a deserted road, a couple hundred yards away. A searchlight beamed from side to side ahead of its path.

"I'll tell our guy that he owes you one," he said desperately. "Besides, you got plenty of cash in there to buy whatever you want — hookers, booze, you name it."

Another goofy laugh as the GI nodded in agreement. Without saying another word, he went to the back of the Jeep and dropped its tailgate. He grabbed hold of a long crate and slid it out of the vehicle, onto the ground. He then gripped one handle and pulled the crate across the grass to the base of the fence, parking it next to some rocks that had been piled there.

"Get your little ass over here, monkey-man," the MP said. The slowness in his speech had vanished magically, as if his brain had been injected with adrenaline. He was all business now.

The MP opened the crate and lifted out a sleek metal contraption, bound together with tape. He aimed his flashlight at the box. Rolio could read a series of numbers and letters that meant nothing to him except for the two largest ones, M-2, stenciled in white on the dark green box. Commander Sumalong's people had told him "M-2" and "50 cal" — he remembered that. The MP returned to the Jeep, pulled out a long black case and stuffed the piece inside. "Tripod's taped to it," he said. "Now help me with these."

Together they filled the box with the rocks that had been measured out ahead of time to a precise weight. Satisfied, the MP latched the crate, dragged it back to the Jeep and heaved it onto the tailgate.

No further words were needed. Rolio lifted the case. It was much heavier than it had appeared when the big American had held it. He pulled it along the ground to the tunnel opening, maneuvered his body over the bundle, and pulled it in behind him. He felt the hatch hit the soles of his shoes as the MP set it in place and resealed the entry.

Rolio propped himself on his elbows. He reached for the flashlight in his pants pocket, hoping to light his way for the crawl back. He fumbled with it, unable to drag the case and hold the light at the same time. Frustrated, he tossed the flashlight aside. Inching deeper and deeper under the security fence, the return trip seemed much longer. After concluding that he'd reached the tunnel's midpoint, he stopped to rest for a moment before starting the upward trek. It took only a few yards of crawling before his body became soaked in perspiration and he lost his breath. He felt the dirt caking into mud on his wet, scraggly beard as he labored upslope, inch by inch. The air grew warmer as he neared the surface. He grunted and blindly lugged the dead weight the last few feet, until his head struck the exit hatch. He rolled on to his back, exhausted. His heart felt as if it would burst through his chest. *I'm too old for this,* he thought.

It was pitch black inside the tunnel, and without his flashlight, he couldn't check the time. His breathing and heart rate settled down as he lay there motionless. He'd dozed off for a few seconds when the hatch popped open without warning.

"Ah, my brother Rolio! So nice of you to join me tonight."

Rolio scrambled out of the hole, thankful to be free. "No time for humor, Rafael. Help me with this," he said. The men leaned into the tunnel to retrieve their prize.

"*Christo*, this is heavy!" Rafael said. "What'd you put in here, rocks?" Rolio chuckled at the irony of Rafael's comment.

"I almost didn't make it," Rolio said while they dragged the case over to a small pickup truck. Its cargo bed was topped with a fiberglass camper cover. Rafael pulled down the tailgate and together they heaved the load inside.

"They need to find some better mules, ones not so stupid and who show up on time. This big redneck started hollering about not getting some dope and almost blew it for us."

Rolio closed the tailgate, set the tunnel's hatch in place and covered it with dirt. He joined Rafael in the truck's cab. As he sat down, he smelled a sweet mix of perfume and alcohol. He turned and saw a young woman squatting behind them in the truck bed. The window between the cab and the truck bed had been removed.

"What the hell is this?" Rolio said. The girl came forward, placed a hand on his shoulder, and held up a flask.

She giggled and said, "We have good pills, too." Rolio grabbed the flask from her hand and tossed it out the window. It hit the chain link fence with a clink.

"Rafael, you know the rules! Who is this little *puki*?"

"Calm down," Rafael said. "She's OK. We're staying together at the mountain camp and she's been through all the lectures." The girl leaned on Rafael and stroked his face.

Rolio shook his head. "I don't have time to deal with this right now." He pointed his finger at the girl. "You sit down and stay out of sight. You're out as soon as we can find a place to dump you. And keep quiet!"

The girl put her hand across her mouth and rolled her eyes mockingly. Rolio looked at the truck's dashboard clock. It read 4:05.

"Curfew's over, let's go," he said.

Rafael maneuvered the truck, without headlights, along a path that Sumalong's guys had carved through the dense vegetation. The jungle canopy obscured the faint moonlight, making their drive nearly as dark as Rolio's crawl through the tunnel. They paralleled the perimeter fence for a couple hundred meters before coming to a dirt road that led into the village.

Rolio turned in his seat to see the girl perched in the opening between the cab and the cargo bed. She was pretty and appeared no more than twenty. *Probably another bored college kid from Manila*, he thought. Her olive-drab t-shirt and pants hung loosely on her petite frame. Atop her head was an oversized ball cap that looked comical above her small face and her big eyes that beamed back at him like an alley cat's. He stared her down until she looked away. "Who the hell are you and where do you live, *puki*?"

Rafael spoke first. "It's OK, Rolio. I told you, she's been to the mountains and heard all the talks. She's with us."

Rolio shot them both a fierce look. The girl said, "I'm ready to do whatever's necessary to stop the imperialist pigs from ruining our homeland." It was more of a decree than a mere statement. She held her ground defiantly, face to face with Rolio, and then settled back.

"I'll bet you had a good time with her, Rafael. She smells loaded."

Rafael turned to him and smiled. "We'll get you some later. You could use a little. You're too tense."

"Keep your eyes ahead," Rolio said. They came to the end of the path and made a left turn onto a two-lane paved highway. Rafael flicked on the headlights and they accelerated up to the speed limit as they entered the outskirts of the town at the north end of the airbase. Shopkeepers had already opened their shutters and *balut* vendors were hawking their delicacies to early risers. Rafael slowed down as they came to an intersection. As they passed through, a car turned onto the street behind them and approached rapidly. Its headlamps flooded the truck with light. As it zoomed forward, the driver flashed its lights feverishly and turned on a rotating red beacon on the vehicle's rooftop.

"Mother of God!" Rolio exclaimed. "Floor it — we're dead men if they catch us!"

Rafael made a sharp right turn and pounded the gas pedal down. A dull thud came from the truck bed as the girl and their payload slid back and smashed against the tailgate. The car's headlights disappeared for a second, but came back into view as it pulled into the passing lane and raced after them. Rafael held the pedal to the floor as the truck's four-cylinder engine groaned and knocked, trying to answer the call. It was, however, no match for their pursuer.

Rolio looked back and saw the girl sprawled out, holding her head. After a moment, she caught her breath and let out a wail. She crawled forward and grabbed Rafael's arm through the opening, causing him to swerve off the road and onto the shoulder.

"Let me out!" she pleaded. The ball cap was off, revealing long black hair that had been tucked inside. Her bangs were matted slick against her forehead and blood flowed freely down onto her t-shirt. Rafael got the truck under control, only to have her lunge at him again.

"Please!" She was crying hysterically now, groping at the wheel.

Rolio shoved her away. "Shut up, you stupid bitch!"

Rafael turned off the boulevard onto a narrow alleyway filled with pedestrians and motorbikes. The headlights reappeared in the rearview mirror, cautiously weaving through the crowd in pursuit but falling back a few hundred meters.

"I'm not sure where I'm going," Rafael said.

"Go! Just keep moving!" Rolio ordered.

Rolio focused his attention on the road ahead. He felt the girl at his back. This time she forced her hands between their shoulders and started to climb awkwardly into the cab. Her backside pressed up against Rolio's head and pushed his body sideways, pinning him against the door. Rafael elbowed her in the ribs, trying to push her away, but she was determined. Rolio freed himself and pulled her off Rafael as she clawed at them both, screaming like a banshee. Rolio tried to dodge her nails gouging at his face. He braced his body against the dashboard, held her head with both hands, and then jammed her through the window opening, back into the cargo bed. First her head and shoulders, then her legs and butt. Facing aft, Rolio saw the police car closing in on them as he crawled into the truck bed with her. He was sweating and out of breath. His hands were slippery with her blood.

"Get back on the main highway and head north," he ordered.

"Which way is north?" Rafael asked.

"There, I can see Mount Arayat ahead. We have to go north," Rolio said. Traffic in the alley had thinned out. The police car chasing them had a clear path and roared toward them, closing the gap.

"When we get to the highway, turn right, that should take us to Concepcion Road," Rolio added. Rafael held the pedal down, forcing the truck to its maximum speed. The little vehicle shuddered under the strain.

"Stay down, you!" Rolio said to the girl. She nodded meekly and sobbed, appearing ready to give up the fight. Rolio eased his grip on her and leaned forward, into the cab. As he did, she made a last desperate attempt to free herself, latching onto his arm and clamping down with her teeth.

Rolio cried out. "That's it, no more!" Holding her head with one hand, he smashed his fist flush on her nose and followed up with another powerful blow. Her body went limp. He then grabbed the payload and moved it forward to a more secure position.

"What are you doing?" Rafael asked. His eyes were filled with confusion and panic as he alternated between watching the road ahead and the scene behind him.

"Drive!" Rolio shouted.

Rafael made the next right turn without braking, slid across the intersection and sideswiped a parked jitney. The pursuing car slowed as it negotiated the turn.

Rafael begged, "Don't hurt her, please." His voice was weak and quivering.

"Too late," Rolio replied.

They entered a long straightaway with some traffic heading in the other direction. Rolio kept his hold on the girl as she moaned incoherently.

"Raffy, slow down a little and let them gain on us."

"But—"

"Just do it!"

Rolio dragged the girl by the arms and pressed her body against the tailgate. The lights from the police car beamed on his face as it zoomed toward them.

"When I tell you, floor it and turn down a side street."

"Which one?"

"I don't care, any one, just make a turn!"

Rafael let up on the gas. Immediately, the pursuing car sprang closer, as if reeling them in on a line. One hundred meters, fifty, twenty... Rolio stared directly into the car's blinding lights, now only a few meters away.

"Go... now!"

Rafael shifted to a lower gear and mashed the accelerator. As he did, Rolio unlatched the tailgate and shoved the girl out. He saw the police car's front tires lift off the road when it hit her. It weaved wildly and then veered to its left into oncoming traffic. Rolio watched as it struck a motorbike, flinging its rider in the air and onto the car's windshield, then jerked to a stop as the biker fell to the pavement.

Rafael made a sharp left, turned down a dirt path and came up to Concepcion Road, where he made another left and headed north.

Rolio crawled back into the passenger seat. Traffic on the highway was light going in their direction. Jitneys, buses and bikes began to fill the other lane, carrying workers to their jobs on the airbase.

They were silent as they drove the posted speed limit another couple kilometers before turning onto a tree-lined dirt road. Mount Arayat rose from the landscape to the southeast, silhouetted against the orange-red dawn.

Another half kilometer east, they turned onto an elevated path between two rice paddies. It was barely wide enough for the truck's wheels. As they approached a fenced-in farmhouse, a man appeared from the shadows to open a metal gate. Rafael guided them onto the gravel driveway and forward into an open barn, where he parked next to a *telyadora* machine. The barn door closed quietly behind them.

Rafael turned off the motor and slumped forward onto the steering wheel. The barn was humid, and smelled of hay and chicken dung. Rolio opened his door and stood up. His entire body ached from the tunnel crawl and his bout with the girl. He walked over to a window and looked south, toward Mount Arayat. The rising sun peeked over the horizon, illuminating the valleys and mountains of central Luzon. He felt a throbbing in his gut. He remembered that, over an hour ago, he'd needed to relieve himself, but never did. He turned away from the truck and did his business on the barn's dirt floor.

"You violated our rules with that poor young girl," he said, and heard Rafael start to cry. "We have no room for those mistakes, my friend. Never again."

Chapter 8

San Angelo's bow peeled back the calm Pacific water, churning it into white foam as she steamed at flank speed toward Subic Bay Naval Base, northwest of Manila. With last night's storm rolling its way toward China, the late morning sun shined down through clear skies onto glasslike seas. It was a perfect day for a high-speed run.

The ship had received orders to reverse course and head back to the place it had departed just a few days prior. By the time a messenger had shuttled the dispatch to the skipper's stateroom, directing a return to Subic, word had already leaked out from the ship's radio room where the teletype had been first received. When Captain Lugansky picked up a microphone to make the "all hands" announcement, about the only sailors on board who hadn't already gotten the word were the "snipes" in the engine room. They lived in the grimy world of hot, roaring machinery, oblivious to most everything around them other than keeping *San Angelo's* power plant running. Good news traveled fast through the crew of nearly five hundred; bad news traveled even faster. This was bad news; the long-awaited port call to Singapore was cancelled.

Making the high-speed run was Lugansky's idea. Sensing the crew's disappointment, the Old Man had a hunch that firing up all three of the ship's boilers and "letting the big dogs eat," as he liked to say, might lift everyone's spirits — or at least direct their minds away from the change in itinerary. Although *San Angelo* was barely making twenty knots, the vessel pulsated with energy as her single screw propelled the bulky cargo ship at its maximum speed.

Singapore, along with British-controlled Hong Kong, was considered one of the best ports of call in WESTPAC. Four months had passed since the ship had anchored in Hong Kong harbor. A jaunt to Singapore, with its glamorous Eurasian women and inexpensive treasures, would have been a fitting reward for the crew's hard work and productive deployment. Unfortunately, plans had changed when McGirt's helicopter had pancaked off the water twelve hours ago.

McGirt awoke from a brief, fitful sleep. He sat up slowly in the lower bunk, set his feet on the deck and tested the knee: the swelling had subsided, but it hurt again, the same as when he'd left the captain's stateroom. The sleep deprivation made him feel groggy, so he got to his feet and stood under the single air vent that flowed into the windowless quarters that he shared with Bud Lammers. The frigid air helped to clear his head.

A few feet across from the bunks was a steel-gray wall unit where he and Bud stored their uniforms, civvies, and a handful of personal possessions. Built into the unit were two small, fold-down tables that the officers used for desks. McGirt turned on the fluorescent lamp above his desk and saw a neatly stacked pile of mail. Someone, probably Bud, had slipped in while he was dozing and left it there. He got out of his soggy, reeking flight suit and tossed it into a dirty clothes bin.

The desk lamp cast a dank, shadowy light across the closet-sized space. Stripped to his t-shirt and briefs, McGirt sat down and went through his mail: a letter from his mom in Florida; a round, brightly decorated package from his sister at college in Michigan; a couple of bills and three back issues of *Sports Illustrated* magazine. He tapped the package from his sister and smiled. It sounded like a tin can beneath the colorful wrapper, most likely containing a batch of pink cherry cookies that she knew he liked. He gently removed the paper, cracked open the container, and dug into the sweet-smelling delicacies. His sister was the only family member who'd been able to duplicate his grandmother's prized recipe for them. Normally a holiday treat, she'd sent him a fresh supply, every month without fail, since *San Angelo* had set sail.

McGirt sat back and read the short note inside while eating. He laughed out loud at his sister's zany cartoon drawings depicting his life at sea. Palm trees, helicopters and dolphins adorned the handmade greeting card. He set the letter from his mom aside for later and picked up one of the sports magazines, hoping to find some news about the upcoming football season. He settled back into his chair when he found an article entitled "Preseason Picks."

The cookies and magazine offered a brief reprieve from the stress of last evening. After a few minutes, though, he found his thoughts drifting back to the incident. He'd almost killed himself and three other crewmen, and now it was time to face the music. He set down the magazine, and grabbed his bathrobe and shaving kit. In a few hours he'd be eye-to-eye with the Navy lawyers investigating the crash.

As he departed the stateroom for the showers, he saw one lone piece of mail on Bud's desk. No colorful drawings or decorative handwriting there; just a plain, business-style envelope. He got closer to read the sender's address. Printed in black, bold capitals, it read, "JILL LAMMERS, BONITA, CALIFORNIA."

* * *

Bud slid his finger down the clipboard. "Sir, Supply shows thirty-five pallets left over for that loner small boy," he said. During last night's evolution, one of the group's destroyers had suffered an engineering casualty and fallen behind the carrier. Her skipper had to break off from the formation and steam independently until repairs were made. "Should take about an hour and a half with our one bird."

"Well, better late than never," Tom Latimer said. The XO's demeanor hadn't changed since the ship had left Alameda, months ago. Stress-weary from the never-ending "crisis de jour" at sea, the forty-something officer wore a permanent frown, reminiscent of a man nursing a bad case of indigestion. Rail-thin and blunt, he was a complete contrast to Captain Lugansky's big, welcoming persona. "Anything else?" he asked.

"No, sir," Bud answered. McGirt sat quietly and wished he'd respectfully turned down the XO's invitation to join the meeting: he felt useless. He took a slow, deep breath and sat back in his chair. As he did, he caught a glance of the white envelope he'd seen earlier on Bud's desk. It protruded from Bud's pocket, one corner raggedly torn open.

"Fine," Latimer said. "I'll call you when I know what the plan is to get your wreck off-loaded." He grabbed an apple from a bowl on the wardroom table and left. Bud flipped through some other documents on the clipboard and looked at his watch.

"Brightness and I will fly," he said. "I'd like you and Puker to work the Tower today."

"No problem," McGirt answered. He'd never before been removed from the flight schedule, and already the feeling didn't set right. Nonetheless, he put on the facade of a team player. He and Bud were alone for a few minutes before the cooks would return to start the noon meal.

"Boss, I'm sorry I dropped this pile of shit on your head," McGirt said. Bud took a deep drag from his Pall Mall, held the smoke in and exhaled through his mouth, off to one side.

"Yeah, well, what are you gonna do?" he said. "That's the breaks of Naval Air, I guess. Some things are more important — we got you guys back aboard last night."

McGirt knew that as the Detachment's Officer In Charge, this tour would likely make or break Bud's career. Regardless of the investigation's findings, his mishap came down on the OIC's watch, staining the unit's otherwise flawless record.

"You've been up all night. You sure you're OK to fly? Where's Rayburn, anyway?"

"I just saw Doc in the passageway. He handed me a grounding chit for Lieutenant Rayburn. Sinus block."

"What? He hasn't been in the air for over a week," McGirt said. He knew that the Assistant Officer In Charge had logged the least flight time during the cruise, less than half the average of the other five pilots. McGirt liked to compare Rayburn to a seagull: someone who squawks a lot and won't fly until you throw a rock at him.

"I've got him and Jenks getting our maintenance and training records together for the JAGs." Bud fidgeted in his seat, bent down and pushed the envelope deep into the pocket above his flight boot. "Between meeting with Supply, XO and the skipper, I've been bouncing around like a ping-pong ball this morning. Managed to zonk out for a few minutes on the couch. I'll be OK."

McGirt looked over at the wardroom's empty lounge area, where he'd iced his knee. He was dog-ass tired and marveled at Bud Lammers' endurance and drive. He'd heard the scuttlebutt about how Bud had left Vietnam in a less than honorable way. Nonetheless, he found it difficult to understand how such a hard-working officer and war vet could have been skipped over for promotion.

"To tell the truth, I'd rather get back up in the air for a while and clear my head," Bud added. "Know what I mean?" He tossed a Zippo lighter on the table and ran both hands over his head. He slouched, resting his head on the chair top, and stared absently at the ceiling tiles. "I got a letter today from Jill. She said she's leaving San Diego and going back to Norfolk."

"Probably just lonely? Wanted to see her family or something?" McGirt asked.

"Naw... this time it's for real. Can't say that I blame her — it's been pretty shitty between us for the last few years. Nothing's been right since I got sent back from 'Nam."

Bud's face reddened and his neck muscles tightened. He reached for the lighter and rolled it between his fingers. During the last several months, the two men had shared a space no bigger than a walk-in closet. They'd experienced one another's ups and downs, joked and laughed, and gagged on each other's flatulence. Through the hours of tedious boredom at sea, they'd talked about family, friends and their pasts. But Bud Lammers never got past the surface when he talked about his wife. Now, it seemed, he was ready to open up.

"Things have been on shaky ground for a while. She's sick of moving every three years and trying to make new friends. Guess when I canned her trip over here last month, it must've put her over the edge."

"I thought she just changed her mind and didn't feel like making the long flight to Manila." McGirt said.

"No, that wasn't it. I would've had to take leave and be away from the ship for a few days. I was afraid it would look bad, like I was slacking off, so I called from Cubi Point and told her to cash in the ticket." Bud took the crumpled envelope from his flight suit, pulled out a picture and handed it to McGirt. "This probably didn't help matters," he added.

McGirt studied the photo. It had been taken a few months ago at a squadron party in Olongapo City, off base. The crew had posed behind tables covered with food and drink. Smiling faces of sailors and bar girls filled the frame. At the bottom of the picture sat McGirt and Bud, hoisting their drinks, each with a dark-skinned cutie on his lap.

"Aw, come on, Bud — we were all clowning around. This was just a joke."

"Well, whoever gave this to her didn't think it was so funny. Read the back." McGirt flipped over the picture and read out loud: "Lammers and McGirt having a grand time with the mothers of their future offspring."

"Jesus Christ!" McGirt exclaimed. "Who's the asshole that sent this to the States? You don't ever send something like this home! I'll call Jill when we get into port and set the record straight."

"Don't bother. It's been building up for a long time. This was just the straw that broke the camel's back," Bud said.

"You sure I can't help?" McGirt volunteered.

An angry, defeated look spread over Bud's face. "Naw, she's gone," he said.

McGirt reached over and gave Bud a friendly squeeze on the shoulder. "Hang in there, Boss, things will get better," he said. With nothing else to say, McGirt left the wardroom.

Bud sat alone with his thoughts. He felt embarrassed after letting down his guard and spouting off about his marital problems. He'd never been a quitter, however, he felt hopeless now, as his marriage seemed to be crumbling before his eyes. He'd known Jill since high school and he didn't want to lose her. He knew that he'd have to do something to save the relationship, but in an hour, he'd strap in and get back in the air. Once again, his personal life would have to take a back seat.

Chapter 9

Jill Lammers rolled over and shielded her face from the California Dream. The cheap curtains she'd hung up were no match for the bright sunrays filling the room. She opened one eye and focused on the alarm clock, propped herself up onto an elbow and took a few deep breaths to clear the cobwebs. Her head still buzzed from last night's going away party, where the laughs and margaritas had flowed freely. She and a few gal pals from the office had made the rounds, hitting all of their favorite watering holes before finally settling in at a grungy surfer bar in Pacific Beach. They'd pushed away a couple of tanned beach bums who'd come on to them, and then giggled like schoolgirls about it while walking to their cars. Why in the hell their group of thirty-something ladies had descended on that place, she didn't know. Thank God one of the girls had taken her keys, gotten her home in one piece and put her to bed.

She'd hardly made a ripple in the king-sized bed during the night. Bud's side of the large mattress remained unwrinkled, the same way it had been every morning for the last six months. The big bed had been Bud's idea; he was a restless sleeper. At times, he would wake literally knotted up in the covers from a fitful night. Jill teased him, saying that it seemed as if he were running a marathon or manning the controls of a helicopter. Bud could never remember what he'd dreamed about – at or least that's what he always told her.

The restless nights became more of a nuisance to Jill as the years passed. At times she selfishly looked forward to Bud leaving, so that she might spend uninterrupted nights by herself in the big bed. But it hadn't always been like this. Jill had loved Bud since she was seventeen years old. Their futures had seemed so bright and limitless. They'd each earned a college degree and married right after graduation; they had decided to hold off starting a family for a few years in order to devote time to themselves.

Bud was commissioned as a naval officer after attending the University of Virginia on an ROTC scholarship. Jill had looked forward to the thrill of traveling to exotic places and meeting new people. At first, their lives had been exactly what they'd dreamt about: flight training in Florida and then assignment to a squadron in Norfolk. Bud's career as a naval aviator seemed the perfect choice for the young newlyweds. They purchased their first property – a brick rambler in Virginia Beach – not far from Jill's mother and sister. The cozy house had served as home base for the couple while Bud deployed to the Mediterranean. Jill made several trips overseas to visit him during port calls. It was a happy and exciting time for the both of them.

Everything changed, however, when Bud volunteered for a tour in Vietnam. The gregarious, hard-charging officer she'd admired returned from the war a sullen, high-strung man. After that, a series of dull, less than career-enhancing duty assignments had followed. The couple began to grow further and further apart. After fourteen years of being a Navy wife, Jill was tired and bitter. When their orders to San Diego came through, Bud did his best to steer her back to a more positive mindset. He'd told her that this job was his last chance to "right the ship" and get his career back on track. By then, Jill considered those words more of the "same-old-same-old."

She'd thought about getting a dog or cat to keep her company, but pets weren't permitted in the complex. So with her husband overseas again, Jill Lammers lived by herself in the two story, two-bedroom condominium. It looked identical to the other one hundred forty-four units in the development: standard "Navajo white" painted walls, beige carpet and popcorn-textured acoustic ceilings. When the brand-new units had gone on sale last fall, Bud had sat in line on a lawn chair all night with a couple dozen other eager buyers.

Another Skippy Murdoch Development! the billboard had read. Beneath the bold lettering was the smiling face of a sandy-haired man, who almost single-handedly was transforming this arid California landscape into a vibrant community. Shopping centers, schools and playgrounds dotted the roadsides as acre after acre of new homes, condos and apartments sprang from the hard-packed adobe soil.

Jill stumbled groggily into the kitchen to make coffee. Her heart sank when she opened the can of Folgers to find only a smidgeon of grinds and dust at the bottom. She ran her finger along the bottom of the can, picked up a few morsels and pressed them to her lips, as if the act would magically arouse her senses. With coffee no longer an option, she split an English muffin, dropped the slices in the toaster and walked out to the front step to get the newspaper.

"Padres win in 14 innings, details on page C1" was the first headline that she read in the upper left corner of the *San Diego Union*. Beneath that, the lead story was about sewage from Tijuana polluting the shores across the border in Imperial Beach. Jill flipped through the pages, found the lifestyle section, and threw the rest of the paper into the trash. She'd plopped down onto the sofa with her muffin and paper when the phone rang.

"Hi, is this Jill?" asked the perky voice on the other end.

"Yes, it is."

"Great! This is Maddy Rayburn from the Wives Club. We haven't heard back from you yet about the wine and cheese tasting party this weekend. Are you coming?" Maddy's bubbliness was overpowering at this hour. Jill set down the newspaper and took a deep breath.

"Well, Maddy, this is the first I've heard about it."

"Oh, darn, someone was supposed to call you earlier in the week! I—"

Jill cut her off. "Look, I work during the day, but I've been home most every night. One of your girls must have dropped the ball," she said, making no attempt to hide her indignation. Confident that even a dolt like Maddy would get the point, she prayed that the little twit would simply apologize and say goodbye. Jill was nearly ten years older than Maddy and had been a Navy wife since she was twenty-three. It hadn't taken her much time in the system to learn to detect bullshit.

Defiant, but clinging firmly to her Southern charm, Maddy retorted, "Well, some of us have children and don't have time to keep calling people all day! I'm sorry that you weren't home to take the call, but that's not my fault."

So that's what it is again, Jill thought, *the kid thing*. Bud was the only married lieutenant commander in the squadron without children and the other squadron wives had shunned her as if she had the plague since she'd arrived. Jill chose to take the high road, ignoring the girl's disingenuous babble. She didn't have the time or the patience for this.

"Listen, dear," she said, "You and the other girls have fun tasting your wine and cheese, but I've made other plans."

"Well, thanks for understanding, and have a nice day!" Maddy said cheerfully. Jill visualized the air-brain snapping her gum and tossing her hair girlishly, never catching a drop of Jill's sarcasm.

"You too," Jill said. She hung up the phone and walked back into the bedroom to pack for her trip. As she passed through the living room, she was struck by her reflection in the hallway mirror. Unconsciously, her slender body drifted closer to the image until she could see only her face, a few inches away. Crow's feet ran out from the corners of her puffy eyes and, seemingly overnight, more gray hairs had sprouted by her temples. She knew that these signs of age were inevitable, but for the first time in her life, she realized that she was starting to look old. Not just mature, but tired and haggard like her mother and aunts back home. The years of marriage to a Navy pilot were finally taking a toll. Jill stepped back and forced herself to look away, frightened by the woman staring back at her.

Although she'd been planning this road trip for weeks, she hadn't yet bothered to pack a single thing; she'd done it so many times before, it wouldn't take long. She grabbed the two biggest suitcases from the closet and began making a mental inventory of what she'd need. The usual necessities like underwear, socks and toiletries were easy enough, but fall was approaching back east and that presented a challenge. She'd adapted easily to the year-round, spring-like weather of southern California and had long ago stashed all of her winter clothing in the garage. Bud had piled the boxes high on shelves he'd built above the garage door. There was precious little extra space in the condo, but her husband had a knack for locating every unused crevice in a room where shelves or hooks could be placed. Jill didn't feel like climbing a stepladder and maneuvering the big boxes at the moment, and besides, her head was throbbing, absent its morning caffeine fix. She'd be OK with a jacket and a couple sweaters. Whatever else she needed, she'd borrow from her sister and mom.

It took her less than an hour and a half to pack, shower and dress. She unplugged the kitchen appliances, TV and stereo. Bud had always cautioned her to do this back east where thunderstorm-induced power surges could damage electronics. Jill couldn't remember a single storm since they'd moved to San Diego; in fact, she could count on one hand the number of times that it had rained in the last twelve months. Nonetheless, she followed the usual routine and unplugged everything.

She lugged her suitcases out to the garage, brushing up against the tarp draped over Bud's Corvette in the process, accidentally pulling the cover halfway off. She set down the bags and put it back in place. Other than a once-a-week drive around the block to exercise its parts, the sports car had sat idle since her husband shipped out. She struggled getting the overstuffed bags into the trunk of her Camaro. Bud usually took care of the heavy lifting. She'd have to become better at doing these sorts of things living on her own, she thought. Climbing into the driver's seat, she smelled the ashtray crammed with cigarette butts from the night before, and took a moment to empty it.

She backed out of the driveway and paused for a second to make sure that the garage door closed fully. Despite her disdain for the sterile, cookie-cutter complex, the powered garage opener was a new convenience that she loved. *Standard feature with all Skippy Murdoch homes,* the sales brochure had said.

Jill maneuvered though the neighborhood and onto Otay Mesa Road. She looked up and saw a glint of sunlight reflect off an airliner as it lined up for a landing at the San Diego airport. A sudden jolt of fear filled her senses when she realized what she was actually doing — walking out on her husband. Her eyes began to well up with tears, but she brushed them away stoically and pressed on.

Chapter 10

Hashim Abbas turned his face toward the sun, raised his arms and thanked Allah for all that he had. Several seconds passed before he lowered his eyes and gazed out at the wide, green land that for centuries had been occupied and nurtured by his ancestors. The refreshing breeze from the river valley below touched his skin, providing a calming reassurance that this would be a good day.

Hashim knew that the coolness would not last very long: the stifling late summer heat of the southern Philippines would build as the sun rose higher into the cloudless morning sky. Nonetheless, it would take more than the baking sun to change his mood. He'd spent several restless nights, worried about today and all that it meant. His thoughts and dreams had been troubled with the spirits of his father and grandfather, the ones who'd taught him to live from the land, the only home that he'd ever known. But it was if they were speaking to him now in a silent way to let him know this was right. Hashim nodded to himself. He felt their strength deep inside his body.

He could not recite how far back into time his family had claimed this fertile soil. But what did that really matter anyway? Could a mere piece of paper or map erase the history of his people?

As he limped across the dirt, his steps startled a flock of roosters and hens pecking crumbs from beneath the porch of his *nipa* hut. Their soft clucking sounds brought joy to his heart. He remembered how his son, Malik, had treasured the chickens and other small animals that waited patiently for morsels to drop through the gaps between the rough-cut floor planks. Hashim eased himself into his favorite chair and breathed a relaxed, grateful sigh: Allah had finally brought to him a restful night of sleep and he was blissful.

While he waited for his destiny, his creaky rocker picked up speed. "Hashim, the man told you he would be here at ten," his wife, Ilham, called out to him. "Be patient and have faith." Hashim acknowledged her words with silence in a way that only a man and woman who've been together for a lifetime can. Obligingly, he sat back and waited.

Barely five feet tall and less than one hundred pounds, Hashim's brown, leathery body had been pounded by decades of tortuous farm labor, wringing a living from the land. Weary, errant swings of the harvesting machete had claimed two fingers while hacking down coconuts and corn stalks. Scars and permanent bruises covered his tiny frame from clearing brush. It was his right leg, however, gnarled and depleted, that caused his painful, slow shuffle. His hand instinctively rubbed at its small calf muscle, an ugly reminder of the dreadful day when his daughter had died. For the last seventeen years, since Malik had "descended from heaven," Hashim had devoted his own life to living in a way to honor her memory.

"I'm making the *merienda* for our guests; would you like to come taste?"

"No, thank you, I'm fine right now," he replied. Ilham was preparing a snack of tea, rice cakes, and Hashim's favorite, a concoction of flour, sugar and coconut milk called *bibingka*. Normally, *merienda* would be served in the afternoon; however, on this glorious Saturday morning, Hashim had asked his wife to break from tradition out of respect for their visitors. The beauty of this day and all that it meant should be recognized, and they should honor their guests.

Hashim had stood up to glance inside at the house's only clock when he heard the distant, muffled sound of a car's engine. He shaded his eyes from the bright sunlight and peered across the land toward the sound. Ironically, despite the ravages that time and grueling labor had taken on him, Hashim had retained the sharp, perfect vision of his youth. When Malik was a child, the two of them would compete to see who could spot a bird or wild boar first, while hunting. More often than not, Hashim would win their friendly game.

There they were. Over three kilometers away, along the line of construction machines and trucks, he sighted a small yellow vehicle working its way up the dirt path that led to his home. Its driver proceeded slowly, avoiding the deep potholes and fissures that last night's heavy rains had carved out. During the dry season, clouds of billowing dust would have obscured the approaching vehicle.

"They are coming now!" Hashim announced. Ilham ran to his side; a fearful groan came from her lips and she scurried back into the house. Hashim heard the rattle of glasses and plates as she hurriedly put together the tray.

Unable to contain his excitement, Hashim once more hobbled down the steps. A tight feeling of anxiety crept over him. He'd never negotiated a transaction larger than three or four hundred pesos for cartloads of fruits and vegetables with the merchants downriver. He had rehearsed this many times in his mind: how he would stand firm for his price and convince the buyers of the value of his land with its mature trees and rich soil. The yellow vehicle was now clearly distinguishable as a covered jitney. It jerked and canted as it reached a badly pitted stretch of road, less than one hundred meters from the house. Hashim saw heads sway side to side as the driver struggled to make the ride bearable for its occupants.

As he waited, his thoughts drifted back to his son. The image of the young boy always brought him peace and confidence. After Malik had learned of his scholarship to the university, time had passed too quickly. The day when the boy had informed them of the news, he'd also brought home a large map from school and proudly unfurled it on the floor. He wanted his parents to see for themselves where he was going: Manila.

Malik had attempted to teach them to read when he was only eight years old and already singled out as the brightest student in his class. Intrigued at first, Hashim had tried earnestly to grasp the symbols on the paper, but became discouraged and embarrassed as he struggled to make sense of it all. He eventually found other things to do. Ilham persevered, however, and had mastered this new and enlightening skill — first with simple children's stories, then magazines, and finally textbooks and novels. Now, she read nearly every day.

The day that Malik had showed them the map of their country, Hashim eagerly recognized a few words printed on the large island that rested at the far edge of the paper: Mindanao, and in smaller print Cotabato City and the Pulangi River. Malik had traced his finger gently across the map, first from a blank spot where they lived along the Pulangi, then to Cotabato, and finally out to sea and northward.

"Luzon," his son had said, slowly and phonetically, much like Hashim and Ilham had done when they'd taught Malik and his older sister to say "mama" or "itay."

"Manila, on Luzon!" Hashim had repeated loudly. His face beamed proudly at the accomplishment.

As the jitney grew closer, Hashim's heart filled with a sense of wonderment and gratitude. The hardships that his people had endured for centuries at times seemed unbearable. Much like his ancestors, Hashim took great comfort in his faith and the knowledge that a supreme being would always protect him. That same conviction had bolstered his people from the early days, when seafarers traveled from Arabia and India. They brought with them the mystery of their religion, and sought trade for the new and delightful gifts that sprung from this land. His people, though, held firmly through the ages and fought back the strangers who wanted to push them from their noble earth. The Spaniards and others from the West could not make his people bow, and neither would this new breed of his own countrymen from islands like Luzon, in the north.

Today, however, was different from the past. Hashim and Ilham would sell their cherished farm so that their child could have a better life. Perhaps Malik would return to Mindanao one day as a doctor or lawyer. Their little family would be reunited and their son would serve others.

Hashim heard the chickens rustle. He turned and saw his wife on the porch holding a tray of tea and food for their guests. As the colorful jitney came to a stop, he became concerned: his trusted friend, Eduardo Borco, was not in the car.

* * *

Salipada rolled onto his back and stared at the dingy ceiling of the crew's bunkroom, a foot from his nose on the top bunk. He wondered why he'd allowed himself to fall into this mess. Above him ran thick bundles of wire and iron pipes, their top sides caked in decades of dust, paint chips and crud. The cramped bunkroom held three sets of steel bunk beds, positioned along the room's three windowless walls. The only entryway, a solid door with slatted louvers at its top, had been propped open and lashed in place with a twisted clothes hanger. Day's first light shone through a single porthole outside the compartment, at the end of the passageway.

Sali hacked to clear his dry throat. He swung his body around, carefully contorting himself so not to scrape his head on the overhead, and slithered down from the upper bunk. He slipped on the pair of pants that he'd draped over a bedpost before crawling into the sack. The putrid smell of body odor grew stronger as he crossed the cluttered floor littered with shoes, underwear and sweaty clothing. An unshielded fan bolted to the ceiling whirled at high speed, uselessly churning the same stale air around and around. On his way out the door, he passed another shipmate sleeping naked atop a bare, sheetless mattress. The man grunted something and farted as Sali walked by.

The deck under his feet was steady as the freighter plodded on its northeasterly track at a lumbering ten knots. Based on the smell of grease coming from the galley, Sali surmised that it must be around seven a.m. He was hungry, but breakfast would have to wait; he needed to breathe. He found the closest hatch and walked out onto a weather deck.

Once outside, Sali filled his lungs with clean air: three deep breaths that instantly displaced the human stench from his nostrils. It was a brilliant day. He scanned the empty horizon: not another vessel in sight, only the distant remnants of last night's storm. The angry band of clouds continued northwesterly on their roiling track toward China.

"Mr. Menadun, I will meet with you in my stateroom in one hour," a voice said through the wind noise.

Sali turned his head forward and saw the captain standing on the starboard bridge wing, about fifty feet away. He hadn't noticed anyone else on deck. The Old Man stood with sextant in hand, focusing the instrument on the sun for a morning fix on the ship's position. He looked away from the horizon, faced Sali and repeated bluntly, "One hour."

Sali nodded in reply. Santos returned to his duties: he took multiple sightings from the instrument, and then pulled out a large pocket watch from his trousers.

Confident that it was the right moment, he slung the sextant into position again and slowly called out some numbers. A deck hand at his side wrote the readings on a pad and then read them back diligently. The captain rechecked his watch. Satisfied, he went back inside the bridge to compute the readings and translate them onto a navigation chart. Sali leaned back over the ship's railing, lit a cigarette and resumed his silent gaze across the blue openness.

"Good morning, Mr. Menadun."

Sali rose up and saw Malik approaching him from the stern. He forced a weak smile. "Good morning to you, too, little one." He signaled for Malik to join him. "And I told you earlier, you don't have to say Mister, just call me Sali." Despite his anger and frustration, he had trouble being anything but pleasant to the young passenger.

Malik took his place along the railing. Although the youngster had the luxury of his own living quarters, the space was no bigger than a closet and just as filthy as where Sali and the rest of the crew slept. He'd wanted some fresh air as well.

"You feeling any better today?" Sali asked.

"Yes, I threw up a lot last night during the storm, but the cook brought me some crackers in the middle of the night. That helped."

"Stay away from the greasy stuff for a while, until you get your sea legs," Sali said. "You were spoiled that first day out of Cotabato, when it was nice and smooth. Crackers and water for now. And none of that rancid lemonade the cook mixes up; the acid will make your belly do somersaults." Malik started to grin and Sali stopped himself. "Well, you're old enough to figure it out by yourself, I guess."

"Thank you for the advice," Malik said respectfully. A long silence followed as they both looked out toward the bright sun. Sali reached into his shirt pocket for another smoke.

"The cook told me that we should be there in a couple days. It will be nice to get off this boat, won't it?" Malik said. "What will you do then?"

Sali took a long drag from the cigarette, held it in his lungs for a moment and exhaled from his nose. "Don't know for sure, but I probably won't return with the crew to Cotabato," he said.

"Something bad happened last night, didn't it?"

Sali flashed a sardonic smile at the boy. "Yeah, I guess you could say that," he said, and changed the subject. "What's that under your arm, anyway?"

Malik took the thick book in both hands and held it in front of him. "It's some sort of manual for the ship." He began paging through the tome. "Did you know that the *Jolo* was built in America and the United States Army used it to transport people and supplies during World War Two?" Malik held the book in front of Sali to show him.

Sali kept his eyes on the horizon and said, "Yeah, I heard that somewhere."

"I found it on the bridge this morning. The captain told me that I could keep it for a while if I wanted to. It's pretty boring. I don't know much about machinery." Malik pointed to some diagrams of the vessel's engine room. Sali glanced down at the pages for a second and then back out to sea.

"If you have some time, can you help me understand this?" the boy asked.

"We'll see; maybe later." Sali looked at his watch and decided he should get something to eat before the cook packed things away. He took one last hit from his smoke and flicked it into the water. "Excuse me," he said, and hurried away.

* * *

"You're too late," *Jolo*'s cook said when Sali stepped into the galley. "There's some leftover *lumpia* from last night, but you'll have to eat it cold. I already shut down the stove."

The thought of mushy egg rolls didn't thrill Sali this early in the morning. "How about some bread or something?" he asked. The cook pulled his arms out from a sink full of dirty meal trays, wiped his wet hands across his shirt, and then reached into the cupboard.

"Here," he said, tossing Sali a loaf of bread. "Take what you want." Sali wrapped a few slices in a paper napkin and then grabbed several pickled eggs from a crock mounted on the wall.

"Thanks," he said on his way out.

He returned to the bunkroom. It was empty. Someone had switched on an overhead fluorescent light, which flickered on and off, making the dingy compartment look even more miserable than before. After eating, he rifled through his sea bag for his shaving kit. He found a t-shirt to wear, shook out the wrinkles, and headed to the bathroom to clean up.

Sali knocked on the captain's stateroom door: no answer. He then turned and walked toward the bridge; halfway there, he met the Old Man face to face in the passageway. Santos acted as if Sali were invisible; he never made eye contact and continued walking. Sali followed him.

The captain's stateroom was larger than Sali would have imagined, and much cleaner than the rest of the ship. It was common practice at the shipping line for the freighter captains to swap vessels. Accordingly, the sea cabin had a "bare bones" feel to it, void of any personal effects like pictures or mementoes. The space was painted in dentist-office bright white and furnished spartanly: a single bed, a desk with a high back leather chair, and a ratty wooden folding chair, still lying on its side from the storm.

"Sit down," Santos said, motioning for Sali to pick up the chair from the tile floor. He slid it closer to the desk and took a seat. Santos plopped his ample body down behind the desk. He leaned back, stroked his mustache and sized up Sali. After an uncomfortable silence, he spoke.

"It's pretty simple, Mr. Menadun. Your gross negligence last night nearly cost me my ship and the lives of my crew. As of now, I consider your status on this vessel no different than that of the little Moro boy riding with us: you are a mere passenger."

He pulled a fat cigar from inside his desk, bit off the tip and calmly lit up, all the time keeping his gaze on Sali. After a few big puffs, he slid the stogie to one side of his mouth and continued. "Stay out of my way and don't go near the bridge," he said.

Sali ran a hand through his long black hair and sat up in the rickety chair. There wasn't much he could say to defend himself. Nonetheless, he had no choice but to try and save his tail.

"Skipper, I know I was wrong, but we never got that close to the other ship. I want to…"

"Shut up! I don't give a fuck what you want!" Santos sprang from his seat and nearly leapt across the desk. Tobacco-laden spit sprayed from his mouth as he spoke. With apparent effort, he contained himself and sat down. His face remained purplish-red with rage.

"Eduardo called and warned me about you before we left Sabah. He said he was giving you one last chance to straighten up or else you'd be out on the docks, sweating with the rest of the stevedores. Well, you had your chance and you blew it. There are plenty of hungry first mates in Manila that can take your job."

Santos stamped out his cigar in a tin can, swiveled the chair around and opened a cabinet behind the desk. Inside the cabinet was a large safe. Shielding the combination dial with his body, he spun it a few times and unlatched the heavy steel door. He reached deep into the safe and pulled out a thick money bag. From the key ring on his belt, he found the right one and opened a lock on the bag's zipper. Sali watched as he counted out a stack of bills.

"Here's two thousand pesos. When we get to Manila, you will disembark my ship immediately." He slid the cash across the desk and added, "What happened last night is history. I don't ever want to see your sorry ass again."

Sali stared at the pile of money in front of him; he knew that he had no choice but to keep his mouth shut and take the cash. At sea, the captain had God-like authority, with no room for negotiation. His powers as judge and jury were supreme. Period.

Sali nodded and said, "OK."

* * *

Aside from a couple of short, fitful naps in the bunkroom, Sali remained awake and bored for the entire day. He'd taken on the role of pariah. The crew shunned him at all times, fearful that they might jeopardize their own jobs if they spoke to him. Sali occupied himself hanging out in the galley, alone, drinking coffee and reading old magazines. The rest of the time, he loitered along the rail on the aft part of the ship, far from the bridge. Besides the cook, Malik was the only other person on board to engage him in conversation.

The young Muslim boy finally found his sea legs, albeit on the last days of the voyage. When Sali walked into the galley, Malik was devouring a second plate of breakfast as the cook looked on with amusement. The cook had taken pity on the sick kid and was relieved to see him turned around. He'd already polished off an extra helping of powdered eggs and was now tackling a big mound of garlic rice.

"Nice to see you're doing better," Sali said. He sat down on the bench, next to Malik.

"I don't understand it; all of a sudden, I got hungry. Now, I can't eat enough."

Scattered in front of his tray was an assortment of manuals, maps and notebooks. Sali leaned across the table and saw how Malik had compiled a journal of the trip, printed out so perfectly that, at first glance, the pages appeared to be typed.

"I've read most of the ship's manuals that the captain gave to me. I also found some papers on the bridge about our vessel's history." He wiped some rice from his chin and grabbed one of his notebooks. "Did you know that the *Jolo* was built in a place called Wis-con-sin? Its two engines were made somewhere called... Cleeve-land... they have six cylinders and produce five hundred horse—"

"Whoa, slow down or you'll choke on your food!" Sali said. The youngster's enthusiasm buoyed his spirits and made him feel lighthearted, something he hadn't felt since the near miss. "You're quite a student, Malik. You'll do well at the university."

"I hope so. This mechanical stuff intrigues me, but I think that I will enjoy history and literature more."

"Maybe you'll be a lawyer someday," Sali said. He reached for the neatly stacked collection of navigation charts. On top was one for Manila Bay. "Now, here's something that looks familiar."

"That's my next project, after I finish eating. The captain told me that we'll enter the harbor on the south channel... right here." Malik broke away from his food long enough to trace the route, between Corregidor and Cavite on the western edge of Manila Bay. "You must come up here all the time, don't you?" he asked.

"No, I haven't been to Manila in years. Normally, I work the island ferries down south." Malik listened intently, ready for his new friend to continue talking and maybe tell him an exotic sea story. But Sali didn't; he folded the chart, and then stood up to leave. "We're getting close. Are you ready for port call?" Sali said.

"All I have is my one bag, a few books and clothes. I'm already packed. I have directions to the university. The man in Cotabato, Mr. Borco, told me there are buses that come near the docks."

"How about money?"

Malik grinned and sat up proudly. He glanced from side to side, leaned closer to Sali's ear and whispered, "My father gave me one hundred pesos." His voiced radiated confidence.

Sali grimaced. "How will you live on that?"

"My scholarship provides for one meal a day and a place to sleep." The smile faded a bit from Malik's face, but it didn't disappear. "I can get a job to earn extra money, if I need it. I'm a little nervous, but I know that Allah will take care of me — he always does."

Sali kept quiet as the eager boy rambled on about his exciting future. Malik's irrepressible spirit made him wish that he were seventeen again and could start over.

"Will you be on deck when we enter the channel?" Malik asked. "I'd like to stand by you at the rail."

Sali handed back the chart. "Of course," he said.

Chapter 11

The bright yellow jitney jerked to a stop. A stranger slid out slowly from the passenger side of the battered vehicle. The man was big for a Filipino, nearly six feet tall with long, lanky legs. He never looked in Hashim's direction; instead, he calmly gathered some documents and said something under his breath to another man, seated in the back of the vehicle. Satisfied that he'd collected what he needed, the stranger then turned to greet Hashim.

"Mr. Abbas, how are you today?" the man said, extending his hand. Under his left arm was a thick stack of papers resting on a large leather notebook.

"I'm fine, thank you," Hashim replied, shaking his hand.

"Good. My name is Ramon Dimko and I represent Mr. Gomez," he said while gesturing toward the man who sat quietly in the rear of the jitney. Hashim smiled nervously and peered around Ramon to acknowledge Mr. Gomez. The man was dressed in an expensive white dress shirt; its opened collar exposed a thin gold chain. His dark sunglasses made eye contact impossible and he offered no sign of acknowledgement. He looked to be in his early thirties. Embarrassed by the rebuff, Hashim turned his attention back to Ramon.

"Your friend in Cotabato tells me that you are anxious to sell your land and retire," Ramon said.

"Well, that's somewhat true. My son, Malik, has been selected for a scholarship to study in Manila and I would like to help him live a better life while he's there. But yes, my wife and I are getting older and want to have an easier life, near the city."

Ramon nodded approvingly. He began to speak again when Hashim interrupted. "I thought my friend Eduardo would be here today."

Ramon, apparently sensing Hashim's apprehension, placed a hand on his shoulder and replied, "Yes, I know that Eduardo truly wanted to be here as well, but when my sedan broke down this morning, it caused a delay, and as you can see, we had to hire this jitney in order to get to your place on time. Stopping to pick up Eduardo would have added another hour to the drive. We did not want to be late."

Ramon's sincerity put Hashim at ease. The man looked him in the eye when they spoke and wore common work clothes. His handshake felt firm and coarse, like that of the men who worked the land. Once again, Hashim attempted to acknowledge Mr. Gomez, but the silent man in the car was occupied, diligently studying a large map he'd unfolded across the jitney's back seat. Every few seconds, he'd draw a circle and write notes on the paper.

"If it is agreeable to you, can we proceed without Eduardo?"

Hashim nodded, still a bit uncomfortable with the situation, but willing to go forward. He backed away a few steps and motioned toward his house. "My wife has prepared a *merienda* for us. Shall we all sit on the porch?" he proposed.

The jitney's driver grunted his approval, pleased with the idea of eating. Until now, Hashim hadn't paid any attention to the man behind the wheel. His brown shirt was covered in stains and his body looked filthy. Hashim couldn't help but stare at him. The repulsive character returned his gaze with a dumbfounded expression: one of his eyeballs focused on Hashim, the other looked off somewhere up high and to the right, and what teeth remained in his mouth appeared to be rotting. Ramon glared coldly at him. Realizing that he'd spoken out of turn, the driver pulled a dark wad of something from a pouch by his side, shoved it into his mouth and began chewing. He then slumped in his seat and started picking at his nose.

Hashim looked back at Ramon, who returned his glance with an apologetic frown.

Unfazed, Ramon approached Gomez and asked, "Mr. Abbas has invited us to have…"

Gomez peered over his sunglasses, briefly exposing his eyes. He shook his head "no" and said something in English. Other than some curse words he'd picked up around the docks, Hashim had never grasped the foreign language like his son had done. Ramon got the message and picked up the pace.

"Well then, Mr. Abbas—"

"Please call me Hashim."

"OK, Hashim," Ramon replied. "As you know, Mr. Gomez's development company is building paved roads to connect many of the small villages out here to improve the lives of people like yourself."

"Yes, I see the trucks and hear their noise every morning across my fields."

"Mr. Gomez would like to make you a fair offer for your land so that the project can continue on schedule."

Hashim felt his heart pound faster as he fought to hold back his excitement. Prior to this day, he'd spent a few idle moments in the fields thinking about what things would be like for him and Ilham with money in the bank. Never in his life had he been able to save more than a few dozen pesos at a time, and although his family always had food and shelter, they lived day to day. He loved his land, but it was time to provide for his bright young son in a different way. While in Manila, Malik deserved to wear nice clothing. If he met a pretty girl, he should have money to take her to a movie or go to a restaurant if he wished. When Malik had first told his parents of his scholarship, Hashim hugged him tightly and, with tears flowing from his eyes, had said jubilantly, "Now my gifted son will not have to work like I did. From this day forward, Malik, the heaviest tool you are allowed to pick up is a pencil!"

Ramon continued, "Mr. Gomez tells me that his grandfather in the north was a farmer like you, and that he'd like to reward you for the hard work that you have put into the land."

"Yes, we have worked hard," Hashim said. He proudly turned toward his wife, who remained waiting on the porch, and smiled at her.

"Unfortunately there are some issues that we must discuss before we can complete the transaction." Ramon's mood transformed from the neighborly friendliness that had put Hashim at ease to a somber tone. He retrieved a folder from the pile he'd set down while talking.

"What do you mean by issues?" Hashim said. He glanced again to the porch and saw Ilham put down the tray and sit in one of the rocking chairs. She picked up a book, found her place and started to read.

"During the examination of your property's records in Cotabato, it was discovered that most of what you have considered your land is actually titled to someone else."

"What do you mean?" Hashim asked. His spirits sank at hearing this news. He wished that his friend, Eduardo, were here to explain.

Ramon removed a pair of reading glasses from his shirt pocket, put them on and began reading words that made no sense to Hashim. "Whereas said parcel registered by name to one Juan Tribino of Quezon City, Luzon..."

"Wait, please stop. This cannot be true!" Hashim pleaded. "My father's father and his family before him have grown crops and raised animals on this land. What you say, this cannot be correct. This has always been our land! Ask any of my neighbors." Hashim waved his arms toward the adjoining farms. He feigned a smile at Ramon, hoping to bring reason and order back to the conversation. Once more, he looked at Gomez, who remained detached, intently studying his map.

Determined to make his point, Hashim grabbed the folder from Ramon's hand, pushed him aside and moved toward Gomez in the car. The driver grabbed a shotgun that rested on the front seat and sprung out of the jitney to block Hashim's path. Now face to face with this slob of a human, Hashim was repelled by the man's horrid breath and body odor. At close range, he saw the man's brownish-red teeth, fouled by habitual chewing of tobacco and betel nuts. Other farmers had warned Hashim of these people: what had Malik said they were called? *Illagas*? These "rats" were notoriously evil men hired by some of the wealthy Christians who'd moved from the northern islands. This driver-turned-enforcer was not a big man, but the glare in his eyes made it clear that he'd used the weapon before and wouldn't hesitate to do so again. Hashim froze in his tracks.

"That won't be necessary," Ramon said. He placed himself between Hashim and the driver, who laughed in a bizarre, frightening way.

"I represent Mr. Gomez in all facets of this deal," Ramon said. Hashim looked over his shoulder and saw Gomez had turned his face away; he appeared to be fixated on the road equipment across the fields.

"It's quite simple, really, sir. If you decide to not sell your land, Mr. Gomez will have his people build the road anyway, straight through what you have wrongly considered to be your property. The crops and trees will be ripped out and the small patch of land around your home, which is in fact legally yours, will be near worthless to anyone else. I strongly recommend that you look over this purchase agreement carefully. It is our final and only offer. We will need to have your answer by Monday morning or all terms of the agreement will expire."

Hashim limped back toward his home. He felt as if someone had kicked him in the stomach and then followed through by tearing the heart from his chest. He hung his head and looked down at the papers in his hands. He couldn't make sense of the letters and symbols on the documents; however, he could do simple math and he understood what the bottom line read: barely one-quarter the amount of pesos that he'd figured as a fair price for his family's sacred land. There was no way that he and his wife could live near the city on this amount for more than a few years. And, according to these strangers, the road would be built, destroying his farm, whether he chose to sell or not.

His spirits were crushed; he'd known Eduardo since they were teenagers. His old friend was a "city boy," but they'd developed a special bond as young stevedores in Cotabato, loading and unloading freighters. Every other weekend, Hashim had ventured downriver to earn extra cash. He'd even spent nights sleeping at Eduardo's home, where they'd shared the same bed. *How could Eduardo be friends with these men?* he thought to himself.

Hashim heard Ramon call out, "Thank you, sir. We will return first thing Monday for your decision," but didn't bother to reply. He remembered that he'd hired some workers from the village to help trim the mango trees after lunch. Normally, he'd have the task already completed earlier in the day, before the sun got higher. But now, he didn't care if the limbs of his prized trees became snarled or if their fruit overripened and fell to the ground.

As he shuffled his way up the dirt path, Hashim missed his son and wished that the boy were here, instead of on his way to Manila. Malik was a clear thinker who could make sense of this dizzying mess. Ilham would have to help him decide what to do. The chickens were nowhere in sight when he hauled himself up the steps. He turned to see the yellow jitney fade from view across the fields. It seemed to be moving faster than it had during its arrival.

Hashim's eyes sought out his wife, but she'd disappeared inside. On the table sat the untouched tray she'd so lovingly prepared. Next to the tray, open to the page that she'd been reading, was the Qur'an.

* * *

Sali's body finally gave in to exhaustion. When his head hit the pillowless mattress, just before midnight, it was if someone had clipped the taut muscles and frayed nerves that had held him a sleepless hostage for two days: his entire system went limp.

For the next nine hours it was as if he were comatose. He never heard the comings and goings of his shipmates during the night. Malik tried to rouse him for breakfast with no success.

What eventually brought Salipada back around was the ship's machinery coming to life in preparation for off-loading its cargo. The captain had ordered all booms and winches powered up, and as many freight pallets as possible hoisted from the holds and pre-staged on the forward loading deck. *Jolo* vibrated with activity as the winches and hoisting booms were tested. Sali was jolted awake by the screaming sounds of an electric motor, ten feet above his head. After a quick stumble to the head, he ran into Malik in the passageway.

"I was just coming to get you," Malik shouted over the noise. "We're almost there! I can see Batann, Cavite, and Corregidor already." Still nearly three hours from docking, the ship started a slow turn to the northeast and into the bay's South Channel.

"I can't wait!" Malik exclaimed. In one hand was a notebook; in the other, the navigation chart that the captain had given to him. Malik grabbed Sali's arm like a young child anxiously pulling his father to the circus.

"I think this will be our best vantage point, here on the port side," he said while dragging Sali in tow. *Jolo* was on a track that took her south of the Bataan Peninsula, where the Japanese had brutally "marched" American and Filipino soldiers to their demise during World War II. Closer in were the southern shores of Corregidor and another war fortress, Caballo Island.

A deck hand approached Malik, tapped him on the shoulder and said, "The Old Man wants you to have these." He handed the boy a large set of binoculars. Malik took them with a wide smile. He'd never before peered through a set, but within seconds, he had figured them out and mastered how to adjust and focus them. The first thing he viewed was Caballo Island, less than a mile away. He zoomed in on the steep cliffs of the island's west side, slowly scanning its rugged terrain.

"Look, Sali, that must be one of the gun batteries I read about this morning in my book." He checked the chart and then flipped through the pages of his notebook.

Placing the binoculars back to his eyes, he continued, "I think... that one is the Gillespie Battery. The guns are either twelve or fourteen inch, I can't remember." He hurriedly rechecked his notes for the answer.

"Wow! There's so much to see. Do you think the captain could take us closer to Corregidor? That's what I really want to — here, you take a look." Malik glanced around for his friend, but Sali had disappeared. He turned his head in both directions, and then walked around the stern and forward along the vessel's starboard side. He found Sali, by himself, smoking and staring off toward Cavite, to the south. Malik held out the binoculars.

"No, thanks. There's nothing here I want to look at," Sali said.

"I'm sorry if I was selfish with the looking glasses. It's just that this trip is all I've thought about all summer, and to finally get to see it for real, I..."

"Don't worry about it," Sali said. He pulled out another smoke and lit it from the smoldering butt perched in his lips. He gave Malik a quick, casual hug with one arm. "I'm happy for you, boy. But I won't be returning to Cotabato. I'll be getting off in Manila."

"Great! Maybe we can be together some more in the city," Malik said.

Sali patted him on his head and laughed. "No, little one, you shouldn't waste time with me when we get to port. You'll find your way to the college just fine." He saw the disappointment in Malik's eyes.

"You are smart beyond your years and I know that your Allah will guide you down the right path," Sali went on. "But be careful. There are people who will not always look out for you, people you think you can trust. Pay attention and don't always follow your heart. Not everything that you read in books is the truth."

Malik stared back at Sali as if he were speaking a foreign language. The two of them stood together silently as *Jolo* chugged eastward, into the bay. A few other vessels appeared on the horizon, making their way out to the open ocean. The clean, aquamarine sea started to change color: first, to a blue-gray shade, and then to a murky brown. Garbage and flotsam drifted along the sides of the ship and the air grew dense with a pungent, burning smell. Slowly, out from the haze and smoke, Manila's tall buildings came into view.

Chapter 12

San Angelo's boatswain's mate blew his whistle, signaling flight quarters. Firefighters and aircraft handlers straggled back toward the flight deck after the noon meal, ready to wrap up the leftover cargo transfer from last night's eventful evolution. The glum mood, which had engulfed the crew after learning that the Singapore trip was canceled, began to fade. The anticipation of a port call lifted their spirits.

Olongapo City had become a familiar retreat for the crew during the last several months. Although it didn't have the mystic allure of Singapore, the 'Po, as it was called, would do for now — liberty was liberty. The crew's only bitch was that the carrier and her escort ships would beat them to Subic Bay. The bars would be packed, and some of their favorite Filipino "hostesses" might already be occupied. But that was all a day and a half away. In the meantime, there was a job to do. The old adage, "a working sailor is a happy sailor," still rang true as *San Angelo* prepared to carry out her mission as the fleet's at-sea shopping mall.

When McGirt walked into the hangar bay, the first thing that he saw was the crippled bird he'd almost killed himself in the night before. The helo had been moved from the center of the ship's landing pad to one of the two narrow bays designed exclusively to house an H-46. It'd taken Jenks and his cronies only a few minutes to devise a plan for relocating the aircraft. In typical CPO fashion, their brainstorm consisted of a jury-rigged combination of forklifts, cables and human muscle power. The dark gray machine was now chained in place with its six rotor blades tightly folded within the width of its fuselage.

"Lieutenant, hope you got some dough in the bank, 'cause your repair bill is gonna be a doozy," Chief Jenks said over McGirt's shoulder. The big man had come up behind him as he knelt down to look at the aircraft's mangled underside.

"Looks like we'll have to replace most all of her avionics and some stabilization amplifiers," Jenks continued. "Actually, the only part we don't have on board is the nose gear. Storekeepers sent out a message this morning. Cargo plane is flying one in from Guam, so we'll be in business when we get to Subic."

McGirt stood up and rubbed the deck grit off his hands. "Sorry about this, Chief," he said, shaking his head disgustedly. During his five years as a Navy pilot, he hadn't come anywhere close to scrapping an aircraft, until now.

"Aw, don't worry 'bout it, sir. We got the A team on this; we'll have her up and running ASAP. They're flying over some of those Japanese tech reps from Atsugi to help — some sort of airframe specialists. One of my buddies tells me those guys work 'round the clock, on shifts. Sleep right there in the hangar and cook rice on a little stove. Regular workin' fools!"

McGirt laughed at Jenks' story, most likely a yarn embellished over drinks at the Chiefs' Club. Jenks was the eternal optimist when it came to fixing aircraft. If there was work to be done, he was the first one on the scene and the last to leave. It was not uncommon for him to peel off his khakis, don a set of coveralls and dig into the grease. Whenever things were looking down for him and his crew, he'd remind everyone how good they all really had it.

"Warm bed, three squares a day and a free ride around the world! How can a fella beat that?" he'd often say. "Gotta get a lot worse than this to make me miss Brooklyn."

The other helicopter had been pushed back and "spotted" on the flight deck. Jenks' boys swarmed over it, checking every last detail in preparation for flight. McGirt looked up as he heard the voice of Thomas Rayburn. The Assistant Officer In Charge sauntered into the hangar carrying a stack of logbooks and maintenance manuals. As usual, the ship's boot ensign, Eddie Bishop, was in trail. As the junior officer onboard, "the Boot" had latched on to Rayburn as his "sea-daddy" mentor since the first week of the WESTPAC cruise.

"Yeah, lookie there; that's a fine 'hello-how-do-you-do,' isn't it?" Rayburn said to the Boot as they approached the wreck. "Chief, any estimates on timeframe for repairs?" Jenks and McGirt rose up from their crouched positions.

"She'll be ready when she's ready, sir. Can't predict that right now," the chief said. "Excuse me, please." He walked out to the flight deck.

"How you feeling, Rayburn?" McGirt asked.

Rayburn coughed and cleared his throat. "You know, John, it's the strangest thing. I felt pretty good last night. Then, after I saw you at breakfast, I got this sinus thing." He snorted through his nose, then cringed in pain. "Doc said it'd be best for me to sit this one out. Besides, there's plenty to do here." He held up the books and gestured toward McGirt's wrecked aircraft.

"Hope you feel better. Puker and I got the Tower."

McGirt joined Chief Jenks on deck. Bud, still suited up from last night, was inspecting the cargo being staged for transfer. A cornucopia of items ringed the flight deck: refrigerated and canned food, medicine, paper goods and machine parts. The supplies were piled four to five feet high on square pallets and then tightly wrapped in plastic, like giant Christmas presents. Each mound had been shrouded in a thickly netted cargo sling. A parade of forklifts deposited the freight cubes outside of the helicopter's rotor arc.

"Ready to go, Commander!" a thin voice said above the wind noise. Bud, Jenks and McGirt turned to see Ensign Bright. Despite the olive-drab flight suit, steel-toed boots and layers of survival gear, Brightness still looked out of place, like a kid who'd discovered his dad's old stuff in the attic and was trying it on for size. A huge smile beamed from the diminutive, baby-faced pilot. He'd donned his helmet and leather-palmed gloves in his stateroom and walked through the maze of passageways and ladders in complete battle garb. He was fully rigged for flight: even his shaded helmet visor was lowered into place. Brightness had started this pre-flight routine on his initial day at sea. Convinced that it brought him good luck, he hadn't deviated. At first he'd gotten laughs, but took the gibes in stride, reasoning that it helped him get in the mood to fly.

"Do you think we'll be done by 1500, Commander? I promised some of the enlisted guys that I'd help them study for their advancement exams coming up."

Bud looked at his watch and then at the growing wall of freight around him. "Supply tells me that the tin can placed another order. We're up to fifty pallets now. We can take some as double loads. Yeah, we should be done by then."

Out of nowhere, a white blur streaked overhead and banked sharply to the right. All eyes followed the H-3 helicopter as it flew down *San Angelo's* starboard side, less than fifty feet above the water.

"They're early. Let's go, Brightness," Bud said. Jenks and McGirt watched the H-3 shoot into a steep climb, roll hard left, and then wing-over into a dive, ahead of the ship's bow. Gaining speed rapidly, the antisubmarine helo pulled out at the last second, clearing the wave tops by only a few feet.

"Hotdogs," McGirt said to himself. The pilot yanked into another climb, duplicating the maneuver perfectly in the opposite direction. McGirt grinned; he couldn't keep his eyes off the "flat-hatters." Activity on the flight deck picked up when Brightness fired off the H-46's auxiliary power unit, the first step in energizing the aircraft's systems before starting its engines and rotors.

McGirt turned away from the H-3's air show and headed toward the hangar bay. His bad knee buckled as he started the hike up to the control tower. He grabbed the ladder's handrail and chugged forward, one step at a time.

The H-3 buzzed the ship again. The flight crew was eager to land, dump its passengers and return to the carrier. McGirt made his way across the hangar bay roof to the tower. From below, he heard the helo's second engine light off as the pesky H-3 continued its dance, this time swooping low, directly over his head. Its rotor blast shook the steel deck under his feet. This time, he didn't bother to look up.

***

Paul Uker hadn't slept a wink and he felt like crap. After an hour of flailing, he'd gotten out of his rack and showered. Rather than put on a clean set of khakis, he'd robotically climbed back into his sweaty flight gear and spent the rest of the night wandering around the ship. He'd drifted into a dark, empty wardroom, passed through the Bridge and finally settled in at CIC. He knew Combat's duty officer from NROTC, and they'd spent the last few hours bullshitting about *San Angelo's* surface radar system. Uker wasn't really interested in the ship's radar, but he faked like he was, happy to do anything that kept his mind off what had happened. He'd been sitting alone in the Tower for the past thirty minutes. He'd forgotten to shave.

"Hey Puker, thanks for getting up here on time. I was below with Bud and Brightness," McGirt said as he sat down.

"Yeah, I saw you guys from up here," Puker said.

McGirt scanned the control tower's interior: deck status lights were switched to red; Bridge intercom and UHF radios were tuned up; a logbook and pen were at the ready, perfectly centered on the table. "Looks like you've got everything ready to go," he said.

Puker acknowledged with a faint smirk and a nod. A speaker above their heads crackled, "Tower, Bridge?" McGirt reached for the communication panel, but Puker beat him to it.

"Roger, go ahead, Bridge," he said.

"Wind zero-two-zero at one-five, cleared to engage when ready."

Both men looked up at the Tower's anemometer gauge to confirm what the Bridge had reported. If the relative wind was out of limits while the helicopter spooled up, catastrophic damage could result to its rotor hubs and blades.

"Roger, Bridge, cleared to engage," Puker replied.

McGirt slid back and propped his feet up on the table. He clasped his hands behind his head, balanced the chair on its rear legs and rocked as if he were sitting on the porch back in Michigan.

"Let me know what I can do to help, Paul," he said.

Puker pushed the lime-colored notebook across the table while keeping his eyes fixed on the flight deck. McGirt opened it to a blank page and scribbled the date and time.

"You gonna be like this all day, pal?" McGirt asked.

Puker's eyes dropped to the floor. His jaw tightened and he began to turn pale. "I almost killed us all last night, J. J." Until this moment, he hadn't said those words aloud.

McGirt set down the logbook and put his hand on Puker's shoulder.

"Yeah, but we're still here, amigo," he said. "We've just been demoted to the junior varsity for a while. Not much else we can do except hang in there till it's time to get back in the game." He gave his shipmate a firm pat on the back.

The H-3 pilots had tamed their routine and were orbiting in a lazy holding pattern off *San Angelo's* starboard side. McGirt and Uker followed the aircraft with their eyes as it flew by gracefully, feeling like a couple of benchwarmers.

* * *

The H-46's two General Electric turbo-shaft engines fired up smoothly. Still mechanically disconnected from the transmission and rotor hubs, they whined patiently at idle.

"Tower, request permission to engage," Brightness said over the radio.

"Sideflare Zero-One, wind zero-two-zero at one-two, cleared to engage," Uker's voice said through the pilots' headsets.

"Here we go, Boss," Brightness said to Bud. He reached up and flicked off the rotor brake switch, then took his right hand down to the helo's center console next to his leg. Pulling up and then releasing a T-shaped lever, he "dropped the hammer," allowing the aircraft's two sets of counter-rotating blades to spin slowly. The helo's jet engines were now free to transfer their energy through a complex series of gears, clutches and mixing units. A long drive shaft, traveling the length of the H-46's upper fuselage and linked to the forward transmission, turned in perfect synchronization with the rear rotor hub. The six rotor blades intermeshed in harmony. Even at idle power, the rotor heads generated enough force to set the aircraft into a casual, side-to-side motion. Two landing gear shock absorbers cushioned the movement as Bud and Brightness swayed in their seats.

Brightness inched his right hand farther up the console toward two throttles labeled "engine control levers." He gripped the two levers in his palm and began walking them forward, signaling more fuel to pass through a metering unit and into the engines' combustion chambers. As the turbines' RPM increased, so did the rotor head revolutions. Within fifteen seconds, the throttles were locked in their forward detent and the blades were spinning at full speed. The sluggish rocking motion in the cockpit increased rapidly in frequency, but was now dampened to a smooth pulsation as the blades reached gyroscopic balance. With the machine light on its wheels, Bright held firm on the flight controls, effectively pinning the aircraft to the deck. She wanted to fly.

"Zero-One, you've got a green deck, request that you depart to port; H-3 on the perch to starboard."

"Wilco, Tower," Bud answered. He reached down to a gaggle of switches on the collective and flashed the helo's nose light, signifying "ready for takeoff." The LSE directed the chock runners to do their thing. When they'd dashed clear, the LSE gave the flight crew a thumbs-up and slowly raised his hand wands into the hover position. Brightness pulled up steadily on the collective, increasing pitch on all six rotor blades simultaneously. The machine levitated off the flight deck, suspended in a perfect ten-foot hover. He pushed gently on the left rudder pedal, canting the aircraft's nose at a thirty-degree angle from the ship's heading. The LSE checked that the airspace was clear to his right, swirled the wands above his head and finished the gesture with a throwing motion toward the ship's port side. Brightness pulled in more collective pitch and eased the cyclic stick forward with his right hand. The helicopter accelerated and began to climb. At about forty knots, the fuselage shuddered briefly as the helo passed through translational lift: the phenomenon when the rotor blades produce additional lift as they spin through the slipstream's increasing velocity. More fuel poured into the engines to maintain the rotors at a constant 100-percent RPM.

"Let's drill around off to port while the H-3 lands," Bud said.

"Got it," Brightness answered over the intercom.

They were skimming across the waves at one hundred knots at less than one hundred feet. As they reversed course, Bud saw the H-3 about to touch down and disembark the accident investigation team. The crew took only a few seconds to unload and get airborne again.

"That was fast," Brightness said. "Guess they didn't need any gas and just want to get back to the flat-top."

"And on to Cubi," Bud added. The aircraft carrier had spent two consecutive months in the Indian Ocean and its crew hadn't been ashore during the long stretch.

"Lots of thirsty sailors," Brightness said. "Probably some horny ones too." Both guys chuckled at the thought of the carrier discharging thousands of anxious swabbies out into Olongapo for a well-deserved liberty call. It felt good to get back into the air and away from the remnants of last night's debacle, especially for Brightness who'd spent most of last night melting away in the Tower with Chief Jenks.

Tower broke into their conversation. "You guys ready to go?"

Bud took a final hit of his smoke and crushed it out. "Yup, let's do it," he replied.

Brightness volunteered to take the first ten loads. The two crewmen in the back had opened the hell-hole after liftoff and rigged the cargo hook into position. After hearing Freddy Lincoln's story about the hook jamming up last night, they'd spent an extra twenty minutes pre-flighting theirs on deck.

The Supply gang had quickly positioned a couple of loads in the center of the flight deck while Brightness began his approach. The ship stocked everything from beans to bullets, including a huge supply of spare parts for both the Surface Navy and aviation squadrons. However, unless it was mail, once they knew the cargo's approximate weight, most crews didn't care what they were hauling: a load was a load.

Brightness lined up for the first pickup, a combination of two tightly wrapped pallets shrouded in netting. The lighter loads would go first, and as the aircraft burned down its fuel, the heavier lifts would follow. He set up a constant glide path approach to the pickup spot while maintaining an airspeed of one hundred knots. The ship was traveling forward at twelve knots. That, coupled with a fifteen knot headwind, created a closure rate of around seventy knots — a mere fraction of what the helicopter pilots' tail-hooking cousins dealt with during an arrested landing on the carrier.

Vertical replenishment, however, demanded another set of equally demanding aviator skills to be accomplished effectively. A jet jockey guided his machine precisely down a constant-angle light display under the sharp eye of the landing signal officer. The success of the maneuver, of course, fell squarely on the airplane's pilot, who used a full bag of mechanical and scientific tools to get himself aboard. By contrast, flying a helicopter between ships was a nearly total seat-of-the-pants experience, especially with several thousand pounds of cargo dangling below.

"Let's see how this works today at one hundred knots," Brightness said, more to himself than to Bud. He double-checked some notes on the small clipboard that was strapped to the top of his right thigh, and then eased off on the collective pitch. He kept the airspeed at exactly one hundred knots by pushing forward on the cyclic. The aircraft was in a shallow descent, headed straight toward the pickup point on *San Angelo's* flight deck. The tiny landing spot grew larger in the helo's windscreen as they got closer.

"Forward, forward," an aircrewman said, giving directions over the intercom. From his position peering out from the hell-hole, he judged their proximity to the flight deck by the intensity of bubbling froth churned up by *San Angelo's* propeller. Brightness kept his speed up until precisely the right moment. Then, using experience and instinct, he gradually decreased power, raised the helo's nose a bit to bleed off airspeed, and fed in right rudder. The aircraft continued descending at a constant rate, but was now doing so with its nose cocked sideways, thirty degrees to the right.

"Over the deck, load's in sight," the crewman said.

The helicopter appeared to be on a collision course with the hangar bay and Tower. But at the last second, Brightness applied a series of control inputs that defied most fundamentals of aerodynamics, except those of the H-46: he rapidly pulled up on the collective and lowered the nose; a split second later, he kicked in more right rudder and applied a handful of right bank, thus laying the helo's underbelly in full view of the deck crew.

"Forward... forward... over the load."

With the "side flare" nearly completed, Brightness leveled the wings, added a touch more power and settled in to a perfectly stable hover, ten feet above the load. A pair of gloved hands emerged from the square hell-hole that housed the helicopter's cargo hook. On the flight deck was an assortment of freight, tightly staged in groupings of two or three netted pallets. The nets were gathered at the top, forming a huge, sling-like bundle. Attached to the bundle was a long aluminum pole, or pendant, with a loop on its end.

"Down, down."

Brightness followed the crew chief's commands by easing off slightly with collective pitch, all the time placing his trust in the enlisted man's instructions. The load was invisible to him, directly beneath the helo and twenty feet behind the cockpit. His eyes were fixed on the hangar bay and flight deck for visual cues.

On deck, a sailor known as the hook-up man stood next to the load. Braced against hurricane-force rotor wash, he held the long aluminum pendant. Two helmeted crewmen peeked out from the hell-hole: one of them held his hands out toward the pendant. The hook-up man raised the pendant to him and watched as the crewman grabbed the pole's end and slid it onto the cargo hook.

"Load's on the hook. Up... up... up."

The hook-up man bolted as the slackened pendant and netting drew taut. Brightness held his spot but continued to increase collective pitch. Slowly, the load levitated from the deck. Inside the cabin, the crew heard both transmissions groan under the strain. Rotor RPM dipped below 100 percent briefly, but recovered when the bird's fuel control system compensated by dumping more JP-5 into the engines' combustion chambers.

"Load's off the deck, cleared to go," the crew chief said, signaling that the first phase of the delivery cycle was complete.

"You've got that down pretty good, Ensign," Bud said. "You may have a future in this business."

Brightness smiled like a kid who'd finally mastered pedaling a bike without training wheels. "After six months, it's about time," he said.

Once given the signal, Brightness fed in more right rudder, aiming the helo's nose off to starboard. More up collective, a touch of forward cyclic and they were off. The machine accelerated smoothly despite the three-thousand-pound load streaming beneath it.

Brightness leveled off at exactly two hundred feet above the surface and adjusted power to cruise at an even one hundred knots. "Nice round numbers," he liked to say. Other than a slightly increased thumping of its rotor blades, the added weight had little effect on the helicopter's maneuverability.

The sleek, agile warship was positioned five thousand yards ahead. It was steaming at high speed toward Subic, anxious to rejoin the convoy that served as the carrier's defensive screen.

Brightness bore-sighted the tiny drop zone on the vessel's fantail. Unlike *San Angelo's* roomy flight deck, the area was nothing more than a couple hundred square foot patch of decking, highlighted with white markings. It was too small to accommodate any Navy helicopter for a landing. He followed the crew chief's instructions again, first allowing the load to dampen out its oscillations before gently lowering it to the deck. A crowd of sailors stood off to the side, ready to break down the load and hand-carry its contents below deck.

"Load's on deck, hook's released, clear to go," a voice called over the intercom.

Brightness guided the helo clear of the fantail, then spun its nose around rapidly with a good dose of left rudder. He pulled an armful of collective, pushed forward on the stick. Without a load, the airspeed shot past one hundred in just a few seconds. *San Angelo* reappeared in the windscreen. Its bow peeled back the placid blue waters into snow-white foam as it drifted farther behind the faster destroyer.

"Y'all ready for a triple? Supply tells me she weighs in at a mite over five grand. Milk and ice cream; they don't want it sitting out on the deck too long." Bored with Puker hogging all the Tower Flower duties, McGirt had grabbed the mike to relay the request.

"Stand by," Bud said. He turned to his copilot. "Well, what do you think, professor?"

"You take it for a minute, Boss, while I check," Brightness said.

Bud waggled the stick, signaling that he had control, while Brightness flipped through a stack of charts he'd mounted to his kneeboard.

"Nope... too heavy. I'd feel better if we burn down some more fuel." He then pulled out a thin, plastic computing device the size of a saucer. He spun the "whiz wheel," taking time to line up a series of numbers just right. Satisfied with the results, he looked at his watch and wrote down some figures.

He keyed the intercom switch on his stick while reading from his kneeboard. "Let's see... three and a half minutes per delivery cycle with a fuel burn of... tell 'em that we'll take three more doubles and then do the triple."

Bud transmitted back to the ship, "Einstein says three more doubles, then the triple."

Brightness made three more flawless drops as Bud marveled at the rookie aviator's precision. He was always calculating and making small adjustments for whatever variables the aircraft, wind or sea state threw at him. After a half year of flying nearly every day, Ensign Bright appeared ready to upgrade to aircraft commander.

"Hey, Mr. Bright, when's the last time you done a button hook?" a voice from behind asked.

Brightness turned in his seat to see the two crew chiefs lying prone on the cabin deck. Both were grinning boldly with "I dare you" looks on their faces. He didn't answer, but instead responded by nosing the aircraft over forcefully until nothing but wave tops were visible through the windscreen. Now, much lighter than before, the helicopter took off like a scalded dog. Bud hollered out, "Yeehah!" and folded his arms across his chest, ready for the show.

The destroyer had pulled away another thousand yards, widening the gap to nearly four miles. Brightness sighted *San Angelo* at his one o'clock position and held a track aimed straight at the Bridge. His head bobbed to the beat of throbbing rotor blades as the helo tore through the humid air at its maximum speed, "balls to the wall."

"Perfect," he said to himself, purposefully keying the radio mike for all to hear. He was confident that he could pull this off and wanted everyone to know it. During the deployment, all three copilots — Bright, Uker and even the older Carbone — had struggled to master this tricky maneuver. Uker and Carbone had eventually gotten it down, but Bright, despite his many talents, had consistently fouled it up. The crew chiefs had continued to egg him on, as if they were encouraging their own kid brother who couldn't hit a curve ball when it was his turn at bat.

Bud turned toward his copilot, who sat intently focused on the looming ship ahead. Brightness kept the aircraft frozen on speed and altitude. At the precise moment that felt right in his gut, he dumped the collective and raised the aircraft's nose. Airspeed bled off rapidly as *San Angelo's* bow zipped by off his right shoulder. The aircraft was eye-level with the khaki figures watching from the starboard weather bridge. Slowly, Bright fed in right rudder as the flight deck came into view. The aircraft hugged the ship's starboard side and twisted in a sliding, sideways motion. Raising the nose higher to maintain altitude, he put in more rudder as the hook-up man appeared, pendant raised above his head.

As the flight deck raced toward him, the closure rate was lessened by the ship's relative forward motion. The aircraft's nose was cocked forty-five degrees off *San Angelo's* heading. Bright nudged the stick to the right and added power, essentially using the two rotor heads as massive, spinning airbrakes. He heard an elated shout over the interphone as G-forces pinned down the belly-flopped crewmen. One last control input and the aircraft came to an abrupt stop, hovering directly over the hook-up man.

"Over the load, load's on the hook, up, up, up," the crew chief said. The three pallets sank deep into their netted slings as the aircraft strained to lift the two-and-a-half ton load.

"Arrgh — that's a heavy one!" the crewman said. His body was in tune with every grind and moan coming from the helo's drivetrain.

"Load's off the deck, clear to go." Bright pushed the cyclic forward and accelerated smoothly. "Nice pickup, sir," the crew chief said. Bud looked over at the young pilot. A proud smile showed beneath the ensign's dark sun visor.

Bud took over and finished up the last few loads. The aircraft's fuel tanks were nearly empty, making the job easier at the lighter gross weight. They bee-lined it back to home plate as the destroyer crept over the horizon, eagerly steaming toward Subic Bay. The last hour and half felt like heaven for Bud — no worries or concerns, just flying and watching proudly as the young guy next to him honed his skills. He looked toward *San Angelo*. In the distance, he saw McGirt hobbling down from the Tower to meet them.

"Green deck, Zero-One, cleared to land," Puker said over the radio.

"You've got it, Ace. Bring us home," Bud said, turning over the controls for their final approach. He glanced down to the white envelope protruding from the ankle pocket of his flight suit. He'd carried it with him, planning to reread Jill's letter for the umpteenth time. Every time he opened the envelope, he hoped the words on the paper would change, but they never did. His initial feelings of frustration and anger at his wife had given way to a profound sadness. In the past, he'd done an adequate job of compartmentalizing these sort of personal issues from his job, but that task was becoming harder and harder. They'd always found a way to patch things up, even during the roughest times after the war. This time, however, Bud knew it was different.

As they neared the ship, Bud saw the unfamiliar faces of the investigation team standing in the hangar bay next to Rayburn. The Assistant Officer In Charge's arms were loaded with reams of paperwork and manuals.

Brightness steered the bird on a smooth glide path. He felt as if they'd reached the end of a wild roller coaster ride — glad to be done, but saddened that the thrill was coming to an end.

After they landed, Bud crammed Jill's letter deep into the pocket and zipped it shut.

Chapter 13

Malik craned his head though the narrow bus window and watched Sali fade into the teeming Manila dockside. Within seconds, his new friend was engulfed by the raucous cacophony of honking horns, shouting vendors and the screeching grind of machinery. He strained his eyes to catch one last glimpse, but Sali was gone, his long, dark hair morphing into just another black dot bobbing in a sea of humanity. Malik looked back toward *Jolo*. A fleet of trucks had raced hungrily into position by the small freighter, ready to take on her cargo and get it to market. A platoon of stevedores joined *Jolo*'s crew on deck to hasten the off-loading and make way for bigger, more profitable vessels. *Jolo*'s captain paced the deck anxiously.

The bus was only half full, so Malik had taken a row to himself, halfway back, and set his one bag next to him on the seat. He mustered up his most proper Tagalog, rehearsed the sentence several times in his head and rose to speak. The driver caught Malik's movement in the mirror above his head and shot back an intimidating stare as their eyes met.

"Can you please tell me how long the ride will take to the university, sir?" Malik asked.

"We get there when we get there," the dark-skinned, wrinkle-faced driver replied. He hadn't bothered to look at Malik when he'd paid the fifty-centavo fare and boarded. Now, eye-to-eye in the mirror, the little man's unsympathetic scowl frightened him. Malik blushed nervously but stood his ground. The driver bristled in his seat and slid his palms across the big steering wheel. There was no doubt that this was *his* bus and *he* was in charge. When he glanced back into the mirror, he saw Malik standing patiently, waiting for a more appropriate answer.

"Probably an hour today. There's an accident on Quezon Boulevard and we'll have to go north through Tondo to get around it." Having spent his daily quota of politeness, he settled back into comfortable insolence.

"*Salamat,*" Malik said, bowing his head respectfully.

After a few more passengers got on, the engine rattled and they lurched forward, going only a few hundred meters before stopping again. A throng of noisy riders boarded. Suddenly the bus was jammed. Malik felt lucky to have nabbed a seat early, but now he had company. A perspiring fat lady carrying a baby took the spot next to him and then a man squeezed in beside her, pressing Malik against the window. Malik's bag, now wedged between his chest and the seat in front of him, pinched the skin on his forearm. The aisle was full of bored riders whose bodies swayed and jerked as the bus stopped at every street corner. Malik hoped that the load would lighten up, but it seemed that for every passenger who got off, two more got on. He shifted his body, brushing against the woman and finally freeing his trapped arm. She pushed back, gave him a dirty look, and hugged her sleeping infant.

After twenty minutes of stopping and starting, the bus began to gain speed and traveled several blocks without braking. The morning air was already stifling, but the breeze coming through the gap in the window felt refreshing. Malik peeled off his cap and looked out the dirty window. He could no longer see the bay and guessed that the bus was finally headed east, toward the university. But his hopes were dashed when the driver pressed the brake pedal firmly, squealing the vehicle's tires to an abrupt halt. They'd entered an area congested with cars, motorbikes and pedestrians. The bus grew hotter and Malik sensed a change in the smells around him. At first, he thought that the baby had relieved itself, but soon the odor became stronger and chemical-like. The other riders groaned and reached for handkerchiefs to cover their noses. A man in the aisle yanked at the bottom of his t-shirt and pulled it up over his entire face.

Malik's eyes began to water and burn as the stench grew stronger. He shuffled his weight again. This time the fat lady didn't shove back. She'd draped a thin shawl over her head and extended it over the infant's body. Malik saw that the clear skies had become hazy with smoke.

"Close your windows, it won't be so bad!" the driver shouted in an authoritative tone.

Malik grabbed at the window above his seat. It was stuck open, corroded in place from years of neglect. He rose, peering forward to see what was ahead, but the smoldering air had thickened so that visibility was limited to just a few car lengths. The bus chugged forward as the driver navigated through the mayhem. Malik saw what looked like spotty flames coming from a large mound or hill. He strained to get a better look, but the bus swerved rapidly into another lane, the driver vainly trying to find a clear path.

Everyone on the bus was coughing now. Malik managed to pull a kerchief from his satchel and tied it bandito-style over his mouth and nose. The putrid odor repulsed him, but he couldn't take his eyes away from the scene unfolding before him. Emerging from the haze, he saw what had first appeared to be a small hill, but was in fact a massive pile of garbage. On top of it, looking like insects, were human beings. Men, women and small children were all bent over, picking through the filth like ravenous rodents looking for crumbs. As far as Malik could see, a grotesque wasteland lay before him. Tears dripped though his bandana, his eyes singed from the acrid stink.

The bus lurched again as the driver found an opening and floored the gas pedal, brushing against a bike rider and knocking him to the ground. Malik looked around and realized that, besides the driver, he was the only person on board not crouched low, covering up. The bus continued to move forward, slow but steady. Looking outside again, he saw English words, scribbled in spray paint along a teetering corrugated fence: "Welcome to Smoky Mountain, thank you Mr. President." Plastered below the phrase was a poster of the First Couple: Ferdinand, standing tall in a glowing white *barong Tagalog*; next to him, his glamorous wife, Imelda, wearing a traditional Filipino gown with highly tufted shoulders. She'd chosen her favorite color for the portrait, powder blue. Their smiling faces were marred with the crude graffiti of stitch marks and blacked-out teeth.

A few meters later, the driver slammed on the brakes, yielding to a stream of pedestrians. At first there were just a few. But others joined the exodus with the urgency of a mob about to miss out on something. They were all headed in the same direction — toward the garbage heap.

Malik followed the procession with his eyes. People raced to the base of the trash hill and then slowed to a crawl as they began their ascent. When the bus stopped at an intersection, he heard a loud rumble of diesel engines ahead. A big green truck emerged, followed by another half dozen identical ones with matching logos. The caravan veered in formation to one side of the hill and began a traversing climb up Smoky Mountain.

Malik saw a crowd congregating at the peak, eagerly awaiting this morning's delivery of refuse. Scattered across the mound of waste were small fires that had erupted from methane gas thrown off by the decaying matter.

The last trash hauler passed and the bus started moving again. Malik looked back at the First Couple and saw a tiny young girl standing alone below the poster. She wore a short, soiled dress and her feet were bare. Long, matted hair shrouded her round face and she was crying. In her hands, she clutched a meaty bone of some sort. Her eyes frantically sought familiar faces among the rushing melee of bodies. People streamed by her on their way to the crest, ignoring the frightened child as if she were just another piece of debris standing between them and the treasures at the summit.

From the corner of his eye, Malik saw a mangy dog creeping along the fence toward the girl. She seemed paralyzed with fear as the animal skulked toward her. The dog growled viciously. Its drooling jaws were only inches from her trembling face. An older child would have had the sense to drop the bone — that was what the mutt wanted, not her. But the girl was terrified and hugged the bone to her chest. The dog began to nip at her hands.

As the bus accelerated, Malik pushed violently against the fat lady, who hollered an obscenity at him in Tagalog. He twisted and raised himself on to his knees and forced his shoulders through the narrow gap of the window.

"Someone help her!" he shouted. Everyone, on the bus and outside, appeared ignorant to what was happening. The child had fallen and the dog was on top of her now. "Didn't you see that?" he shouted to the woman next to him. She stared at him blankly. "If you care so much, jump out and save her," she said. A disgusted look covered her sweaty face. Malik sat motionless, as if in a trance. His stomach muscles contracted and he felt nauseous, much as he had at sea during the storm.

The bus leapt forward and traffic moved steadily now. Sighs of relief rose from the passengers as cleaner air filtered inside. The skies began to clear and sunlight pierced through the smoky haze. Malik fell back into his seat, stunned at what he'd just witnessed. Passengers, grateful to finally be on their way, removed their kerchiefs and casual conversation resumed.

"Is everyone OK?" the driver asked over his shoulder. "Did any of the rats crawl onto my bus and bite you?" He cackled an eerie laugh and rambled on about how he'd seen worse while driving through the Tondo district.

The man sharing Malik's seat got off and the fat woman slid over, giving him more room. Gradually, the tension that had gripped Malik's body ebbed and he grew drowsy. As he drifted in and out of slumber, his body twitched from fatigue. It had been seven long days since he'd left the safe peacefulness of his home in Mindanao. His mind drifted to the many scenes that had filled his brain during the voyage. Now, with his final destination a few kilometers away, he placed the bag on his lap, buried his head on it, and began to sob.

The bus's rocking motion helped propel him off to dreamland as his thoughts slipped back to the river valley where he'd grown up. He pictured himself walking lazily up from the river's bank toward the family's hut, through the mango groves and bountiful garden that nourished his family. He could smell fresh fruit and hear his mother's gentle voice from inside. She sang a pretty folk song while going about her chores. Malik emerged from the grove and saw his father seated on the porch. The old man stood up, raised his arms in welcome and smiled at him proudly.

Malik awoke to the fat woman poking him on the shoulder. She mumbled something in Tagalog and pointed in the direction of a cluster of buildings across the street. Malik didn't understand, so she pointed again. This time she spoke louder and in English.

"University," she said.

***

After he'd said goodbye to Malik, Salipada walked quickly away from the crowded docks. He'd had enough of *Jolo* and its captain and really didn't give a damn — he wanted to get drunk.

Before the captain brought the vessel into port, Sali had cleaned up and packed the few personal items he owned into a duffle bag. While the rest of the crew was busy preparing for port, he'd had the tiny head facility to himself. He took a long hot shower and ran a razor across his face. He needed a haircut badly — he never cared much for the long hairstyles that were popular at the time — and made a note to find a barber later in the Big City. For now, however, he brushed the long strands of black hair straight back, where it rested just above his shoulders. Returning to the bunkroom wrapped in a towel, he searched through his bag for something decent to wear. Everything he owned was stained with either grease or paint from a working life at sea. Confident that he was alone, he rifled though the unlocked belongings of his shipmates until he found a clean white shirt and a reasonably new pair of black trousers. He couldn't find a better pair of shoes that fit and had to stick with the only ones he'd brought aboard: a worn-out pair of black sneakers. He took his own soiled things and tossed them in a trashcan.

He'd traveled to Manila a few times while working the ferry runs, but was unfamiliar with the waterfront area where *Jolo* was tied up, just north of the Pasig River. He'd left the ship without saying a word to his fellow crewmen, who were busily working with the stevedores emptying *Jolo*'s cargo holds. All the better for his exit, he'd thought after stealing the clothes that he now wore.

Once dockside, Sali pushed though the throng and flagged down a taxi. "Makati," he told the driver as he slid into the little car's back seat. With a pocket full of pesos, he could afford to head for one of Manila's high-rent districts, gladly skipping the pier-side dives where he usually hung out. After a few minutes of zig-zagging through the crowd, the cabbie found the open road. Crossing the Pasig River on Bonifacio Drive, they picked up speed.

"Any place particular in Makati, my friend?"

Sali made eye contact in the rear-view mirror and answered, "Someplace where I can get a drink, with air conditioning and clean women."

The cabbie raised his left arm from the wheel and ostentatiously checked his watch. "Ah, it's always a good time for a cold beer, eh?"

"Yeah, right," Sali mumbled. He shook his head at the driver's unsolicited chattiness. Manila was nice, but being several hundred miles from his home with no job and nowhere to go wasn't exactly his idea of paradise. The couple thousand pesos he had might be a fortune back in Mindanao, but he couldn't survive on that for very long around here.

"I got just the place for you," the cabbie announced proudly. "My cousin is a waitress there; her name is Gigi." He checked his watch again. "It's still early, but I think they may be open now."

"Sounds great," Sali said. He tried to be more cordial; the farther away they got from the ship, the more relaxed he became. The breeze streaming in through the small sedan's window felt good against his head, still wet from the shower. "How long till we get there?"

"Maybe ten minutes," the cabbie said. "Traffic's pretty light now on Roxas."

Sali settled back to enjoy the ride. As they traveled south, he recognized the United States Embassy off to his right. The grand white fortress stood out majestically against the backdrop of Manila Bay. Around the building, he saw a squadron of gardeners trimming shrubs behind the tall wrought-iron fence encircling the compound. The grounds were pristine.

"Where you from?" the driver asked.

"Does it really matter?" Sali replied.

"Guess not." The cabbie shrugged his shoulders and backed off. Sali figured that the guy feared losing a tip if he continued to press the conversation.

As they wove their way to the Makati district, the buildings got taller and the streets appeared much cleaner than those around the piers. Sali scanned the crowded sidewalks: well-dressed people, light-skinned, affluent looking. He glanced down at his own shabby clothes. He'd been to a few high-end areas in port towns, but this was Manila, his nation's capital and the epicenter of what little concentrated wealth the archipelago possessed. The shirt and pants had looked OK when he'd thrown them on in the dimly lit bunkroom. Now, in the bright daylight, he felt embarrassed about his appearance.

"Here you go, my friend, Makati's world famous Polo Club!" The cabbie extended his arm majestically as if pointing to Windsor Castle. Sali thanked him as he handed over the fare plus a twenty-peso tip.

"Hey, a high roller! Thanks," the driver said. "Don't forget to ask for Gigi. Tell her cousin Manny says hello."

Sali walked into the club and was greeted by a welcome blast of frigid air. His eyes adjusted from the bright sunshine. He saw that the spacious room was empty, except for a lone employee stooped over behind the bar: a small, dark-skinned fellow wearing a white dress shirt and black bow tie. At the far end of the room was a stage with a drum set and a couple guitars propped up against amplifiers. The place was decked out in rich-looking brass, mahogany paneling and large mirrors. British rock music pulsated over the sound system.

Unlike the watering holes that he normally frequented, there were no bar floozies standing by, ready to hawk drinks. Absent too was the rank smell that permeated those dives — the aroma of stale beer, cheap perfume and overflowing urinals. The man behind the bar saw Sali and looked up from arranging drink glasses in orderly rows. Above his shirt's pocket was a shiny nametag. It read "Butchie."

"How much for a beer?" Sali asked. He regretted saying the words as soon as they'd left his mouth. There wasn't a faster way to tag yourself as somebody who couldn't afford it if you had to ask.

"Imports ten pesos, San Miguel five," Butchie said.

"I'll have a Heineken," Sali said. He placed a wad of money on the bar as he sat down. The barstool had a soft, padded leather seat, another perk that he wasn't accustomed to. The beer tasted good. He chugged the bottle in less than a minute. He lit a cigarette, sucked in a deep draw and savored the smoke in his lungs. For the first time since the night of the storm, he started to unwind.

"What time does Gigi come in?"

Butchie laughed and shook his head. "Everybody wants to see Gigi."

"The cab driver who brought me here said she was his cousin and asked me to say hi."

"Four o'clock," Butchie said, unfazed by Sali's statement. "Another beer?" Sali slid the empty bottle forward, signaling "yes." The second one tasted even better than the first.

"So where'd you come in from?"

"Who said I came in from anywhere?" Sali snapped. "I just came by for a drink."

"Well, you just said a cabbie told you about Gigi. Thought that you might have come from the airport or something," Butchie smiled apologetically.

"Yeah, that's it; I came in from the airport. Just flew in from Hong Kong," Sali said. He lit another cigarette, dropped the old one to the polished floor and squashed it with his heel. "You ask a lot of questions, don't you?"

Butchie turned away and said something under his breath. Sali drained the Heineken, tapped the empty bottle loudly on the bar, demanding a refill. Butchie ignored him, feigning some busy work at the other end of the bar.

"Come here, little man," Sali said loudly.

Butchie stopped what he was doing, walked cautiously toward Sali and stood facing him, arms folded across his chest.

"Yes?"

Sali placed his weight on the bar's brass foot railing and rose out of the stool. At five feet six inches, he was taller than most Filipino men. Propped up even higher by the railing, he towered over the little bartender. He leaned over the bar close enough for Butchie to smell his beer and cigarette breath.

"Listen, what's your name — Butchie?" Sali said. He pulled on the man's nametag until it began to tear away from his shirt. "I came in here to get drunk, not tell you my life's story. So you keep to yourself. When I finish one beer, you move your Negrito ass and get me another. Understand?"

Butchie nodded his head and flashed a nervous, toothy smile. Sali patted him on the head, reached into Butchie's shirt pocket and pulled out a couple cigarettes.

"Don't mind, do you?" Sali said.

Butchie walked away without saying a word. He reached into the beer cooler and set down another bottle in front of Sali. When two businessmen came in and sat down a few stools away, Butchie took their order and struck up a jovial conversation as if nothing had happened.

Over the next hour, Sali downed two more Heinekens, using the last one to chase down a shot of American whiskey. The happy-hour crowd ambled in and Butchie turned up the music. Sali tapped his foot and swayed to the beat. The last forty-eight hours were behind him now. He had no idea how he'd make his way back to Cotobato or where he'd find another job, but at this moment, he didn't care: his wallet was full and the night was young.

The click-clack of stiletto heels and the scent of perfume preceded her words. It was a sweet, exotic fragrance that Sali had never experienced before.

"So, you know Cousin Manny?" a raspy woman's voice said from behind him. Sali felt her body heat as she pressed her firm breast against his shoulder. He lifted his head from his hands. After the last beer, he'd propped his elbows on the bar and drooped into a semi-conscious snooze with his head cradled in his palms.

"Yeah," he said. Slowly, careful not to lose his balance, he turned in his seat.

"I'm Gigi," the woman said. She held out a delicate, well-manicured hand.

"Sali. Glad to meet you," he slurred. The brief nap had deepened his inebriation. He struggled to stay upright.

"Whoa," Gigi said, putting her arm around him.

Sali gently removed her arm from his waist and sat straight. He shook back his long hair, straightened his collar and smiled.

"Butchie said that you just flew in from Hong Kong. How exciting!"

"That's right," Sali said, cheerfully following through with his story. He ran his eyes over Gigi's rock-solid body. She wore a lacy white halter top that accentuated her smooth, caramel-tinted skin. Her black leather shorts, like the top she had on, were a couple sizes too small, highlighting every tender curve and crevice. The sexy shoes on her feet brought her nearly eye-to-eye with him. Sali's heart raced and he became aroused instantly.

"I'd like to hear all about Hong Kong," she said. "Too bad I'm so busy. Can you hang around for a while?"

"Sure," Sali answered. He returned her flirtatious smile with a grin. His libido had the waking effect of a stiff jolt of caffeine.

"I'll be back later, Sali, you just stay here and have another drink. This one's on me and Manny, OK?" Gigi threw him another inviting look, got closer and ran a red fingernail down the side of his neck. Behind him on the bar, another bottle of Heineken magically arrived.

Gigi turned and disappeared into the now-crowded club. Sali followed her tight buttocks and slender, muscular legs as she sashayed across the room to take an order. She stood by a table of three serious-looking young men. Like Sali, they appeared slightly out of place in the swanky Polo Club. The music and happy hour banter made conversation difficult, so Gigi leaned in toward the table to be heard. All three men did the same to hear what she was saying. Gigi turned her head to face Sali and made eye contact. She gave him a playful wave. Embarrassed at his gawking, Sali tipped his bottle to her and turned back to face the bar.

Another bartender had joined Butchie. The joint was in full swing as Manila's beautiful people escaped the heat and chaos of the big city for some after-work carousing. Sali glanced out the window. It wasn't even dark yet and he was already several sheets to the wind. He'd have to start pacing himself if he were to make it with Gigi tonight. He looked at the fresh bottle in front of him and took a measured sip. When the new bartender passed by, Sali fanned himself as if he were hot and asked for some ice water. When it arrived, he drank a couple gulps of water, scooped out an ice cube and ran it across his head and neck. After a few deep breaths, he felt more energized.

Gigi came by again carrying a tray covered with empties. Her tip glass was crammed with money. When she got closer, Sali slid his arm around her waist. She responded and pressed up against him. He massaged her trim, bare midriff gently.

"Listen, baby, I want to party with you tonight when I get off." She leaned in closer and put her forehead against his. Her eyes focused on his thigh as she began to rub it. After a couple strokes, she backed off and covered her mouth in mock astonishment.

"Baby, where'd you get those shoes?"

Sali looked down at his tattered sneakers. His face reddened and his jaw went slack as he stared back at her, speechless. At that moment he realized that he'd left his duffle bag in Manny's cab.

"Where we're going tonight, you'll need something better than that. And look at those pants!"

"The airline lost my bags," Sali said. He was feeling his booze, but managed to grasp an alibi. It seemed to work.

"Well, let me call Manny and he'll take you to buy some decent clothes."

Sali nodded and mustered a sheepish, "OK." He'd been seated at the bar for nearly three hours without going to the bathroom. Suddenly, his bladder felt like it was about to explode.

He stood up awkwardly and said, "Where's the... I gotta go."

Gigi waved her arm like a traffic cop in the direction of the restrooms.

"Butchie will save your seat," she said. As if on cue, the little bartender appeared, gave Sali an affirming nod and took the untouched Heineken off the bar for safekeeping.

Sali bumped his way through the crowd and found the door marked "Gentlemen." Swaying into the bathroom, he spotted a small man who looked like Butchie's brother, seated on a stool next to the sinks. Sali ricocheted between the wall and the line of commode stalls, eventually zeroing in on a urinal. He unzipped to relieve himself and discovered that he was still half-aroused. He chuckled out loud. This is all surreal, he thought. Normally, he'd be on guard against a come-on from a bar girl. But Gigi was different: more refined and not like the rode-hard skanks he'd had before. And besides, he'd already met her cousin, Manny, hadn't he?

After what felt like five minutes, his bladder finally drained. He zipped up and swung around to the sink and was greeted by Butchie's lookalike, who started fanning him vigorously with a towel while Sali washed up. The man then handed Sali another towel to dry off. He spotted an assortment of cologne displayed on the counter, reached for one and splashed a handful on his face. He dug into his pocket and flung whatever change he had into a dish next to the sink. Half of it skipped onto the floor.

"Salamat! Salamat!" the attendant said, as he scampered to retrieve the coins. He bowed gratefully.

As promised, Butchie had protected his seat. Sali plunked down feeling weary but more alert after the bathroom break. Butchie hustled over with a freshly opened Heineken and another shot of whiskey.

"If you're Gigi's friend, you're my friend too. No hard feelings?"

Mellowed out and with Gigi in his future, Sali regretted the way he'd treated Butchie earlier. "No hard feelings," he replied. He held up the shot glass in toasting fashion and then tossed the whiskey down. The fiery liquid ignited his senses. His head buzzed and he started to sweat. He grabbed the beer bottle and took a long pull of the icy brew.

Gigi materialized at his side and said, "There's a taxi outside waiting for you. Butchie called another girl in so I can leave when you get back."

"You'll be here?" Sali asked.

"Of course I will."

She snuggled up against him, this time sliding her hand slowly down the back of his pants and gripping a butt cheek. She dug her long nails into his skin — forcefully, but on the nice side of hurt. A rush pulsated through Sali's body. As they parted, Gigi gave him a soft kiss on the lips.

Sali slipped into the back seat of the cab. There was a stranger behind the wheel.

"Where's Manny?"

"Manny's off tonight. New clothes, right?" the driver said as he waited for a chance to merge into the zooming traffic.

Sali let his head fall back against the seat. The sun was setting over Manila Bay, illuminating the sky with vibrant rays of yellow and orange. He felt a little queasy as the taxi swerved onto Roxas Boulevard, and wished that he'd gotten something to eat. The last food he'd tasted was breakfast with Malik; that was twelve hours ago, before they'd sailed passed Corregidor. He sat up straight and started to say something to the driver, but his mouth was out of synch with his thoughts. It took a few tries to get the words out.

"How much farther?" he asked.

"Just a few more minutes," the driver said.

Sali struggled to think. Why were they driving so far, just to buy clothes and shoes? There were shops all over Makati. He sank deeper in his seat as the U.S. Embassy went by in a blur. He caught himself drifting off to sleep, the same way he'd done that stormy night on Jolo's bridge, so he rolled the window down and let the cool evening air hit his face.

Soon they were off the main streets and winding through barren, unlit alleys. The air smelled of burning garbage. Sali had been around long enough to know that this wasn't looking good. He rustled in his seat and again asked how much farther. The driver ignored his question and said, "Buddy, that Gigi is a real piece. You're gonna have a good time tonight."

Any apprehension that Sali had felt disappeared as he pictured the little sexpot and imagined her long fingernails caressing him, this time in bed. He giggled and then mumbled something unintelligible.

"Here we are." The taxi stopped in front of a dimly lit storefront with no sign displayed. The building's windows were so dirty that Sali couldn't see inside.

"Go on in; I'll wait for you. Take your time." The driver pulled out a smoke and slouched in his seat to get comfortable. "Just knock and ask for Ernesto," he said, waving his hand toward the door. "He's Gigi's cousin, too."

"Another cousin?" Sali blurted out. His mouth and brain had miraculously reconnected.

Feeling a bit more alert, he got out of the cab and walked slowly toward the door. He reached to grip the handle, but couldn't hold on to it. His hand was a good foot away from the handle, as if someone had moved the entire building as he got closer. He tried again with the other hand, this time losing his balance and falling backward. But he steadied himself and kept on his feet. He felt as if he were at sea and the ship was taking heavy rolls. The door in front of him began to fade in and out of focus. He lunged at it and grabbed the knob with both hands. But before he could twist it, the door opened and he fell forward, into the arms of someone in the doorway. He struggled to stay upright and tried to face the man who'd broken his fall. He lifted his head and saw four blurry faces spinning like a pinwheel.

"Gi-gi sent..." he slurred. He heard the door click shut as the man abruptly let him go. Bright lights flickered above him and a muffled roaring sound filled his ears.

When he hit the concrete floor, Sali sensed every part of his body crumpling in slow motion — first his knees, then his hips, back, shoulders and arms. His head slammed to the floor. The sound that registered in his ears was that of a person kicking a soccer ball, and the room went black. Muted voices reverberated like echoes in a canyon. He forced himself to take a deep breath as he began to fade. The last thing he heard was the screeching of tires as his taxi sped away.

Chapter 14

After Bud and Brightness landed, *San Angelo's* deck crew wasted no time securing from flight quarters. The thought of liberty call in less than twenty-four hours put a spring in everyone's steps and buoyed morale. The aircraft was post-flighted, its blades folded, and was shoved into the barn. Likewise, the Supply types who'd shuttled the cargo on forklifts for pickup quickly stowed their gear and raced for a front spot in the chow line. Other than a short flight quarters the following morning to launch an advance port-call party to Subic Bay, the flight deck would be quiet for a few days. During that time, the powers-that-be would decide what lay ahead for USS *San Angelo*.

The Bridge sent a messenger to deliver a handwritten note from the XO to Johnny Jack McGirt. Printed in bold, green capital letters, it read: MISHAP BOARD INTERVIEW 1600. SKIPPER'S STATEROOM.

McGirt readied his best-looking khaki uniform, shined his shoes and stood by in his compartment. Too nervous to eat, he'd turned down noon meal, choosing instead to nibble on some of his sister's cookies. He'd put on some music and tried to relax by reading a magazine. After ten minutes of absently thumbing through a couple of stories — his eyes saw the words but nothing seemed to register — he tossed the magazine in his locker and stretched out on the lower bunk in his skivvies. During flight school he'd never received any unsatisfactory grades, or "downs." Once assigned to a squadron, he'd never come close to busting the proficiency check flights every naval aviator must endure annually.

Staring at the underside of Bud's bunk, he retraced the events from a couple nights ago and rehearsed what he'd say to the Mishap Board. How would he explain what had happened? It had all transpired so quickly that he wasn't even sure. Finally, he fell back to what his mom had always told him to do whenever he faced a difficult situation: just tell the truth. Comforted by those words, he set his alarm clock and took a nap.

Later, on the way to Lugansky's stateroom, McGirt crossed paths with a few of the other officers in the passageways. One blackshoe lieutenant commander, whom he barely knew, stopped and wished him luck. Like the news of the cancelled Singapore trip, news of the Mishap Board had traveled from bow to stern within minutes.

As he approached the skipper's cabin, McGirt was confronted by *San Angelo's* XO, Tom Latimer, standing guard next to a sign that read, "Silence! Meeting in Session."

McGirt was ten minutes early; nonetheless, the XO instinctively checked his watch.

"Lieutenant..." Latimer said sternly. His lips started to move as if to say something more, but he held back. The man normally displayed about as much empathy as a crowbar. But, as he reached to push open the stateroom door, he gave McGirt a reassuring nod and a pat on the shoulder.

Once inside, Johnny Jack snapped to attention and sounded off: "Lieutenant McGirt reporting as ordered, sir." Before him were the same quarters he'd visited the other night, except this time, the space had been converted to a conference room. The big table had been expanded and the Old Man's bunk was shrouded behind a curtain. The rolltop desk, typically smothered with clutter, was sealed tightly. Absent too was the skipper's crusty coffee maker.

McGirt stared down the barrel of four senior officers and a chief yeoman, seated in a row on the opposite side of the conference table. Centered on the table were a stainless steel water pitcher and a stack of drinking glasses. In front of the chief was a reel-to-reel tape recorder and microphone. From the corner of his eye, McGirt saw the end table that concealed Lugansky's hidden stash, now draped in green Naugahyde that matched the conference table. The sterility of the scene reminded him of the operating room where he'd had his last knee surgery. There would be no "kicking back" this afternoon.

"Lieutenant McGirt, please be seated," said the officer in the middle, a captain in the Judge Advocate General Corps. McGirt took the lone chair that had been placed squarely in front of the Mishap Board's senior member. He couldn't help but notice the black patch that covered the officer's right eye. He found himself unconsciously staring at it.

"Lieutenant, you know why you're here so we'll skip the pleasantries," the JAG said. "But allow me to digress for a brief minute." The captain raised an index finger to his face, pointing to the patch.

"In case you're wondering, this is from when I punched out of an F-4 off the coast of North Vietnam. As a consolation, the Navy was nice enough to send me to law school. That's my story."

McGirt glanced from the patch to the man's decorations — several rows of brightly colored ribbons, piled so high over his left breast pocket that the officer's aviator wings over them were pinned on a level with his collarbone. On the other side of his starched khaki shirt was a plain black nametag that read "RIGGS."

"You're the last link in the chain, McGirt. We've taken statements from Uker and the two aircrewmen, and interviewed Bridge and Tower watch standers. Maintenance and training records have been perused." Riggs folded his arms across his chest, leaned back and waited. After a long pause he asked, "So let's hear it. What happened?"

His one eye focused like a rifle's high-powered gun sight, straight through McGirt, whose mouth suddenly went dry. He looked at the untouched water pitcher, dripping with condensation. He wished that someone would offer him a glass, but no one did. He cleared his throat and hoped the words would come out when he spoke. He cleared his throat a second time and began.

"Well, sir, we were finishing up a long night of VERTREPing when the ship's formation entered some bad weather. Rain was coming down pretty hard and my aircraft was getting bounced around real good from the gusty winds."

"Who was at the controls?" Riggs asked.

"I was, sir. Uker had made the last pickup and drop so I took over for the landing at home plate."

"Then what happened?"

"Our OIC, Lieutenant Commander Lammers, and his crew had just landed and were going to call it a night. They'd actually launched before us, earlier in the day."

"Yes, Lieutenant, we know that," Riggs said. He tapped his pen on the table.

"We were holding off the port side when we passed through another nasty rain squall. It took an armful of collective to break one of the descents we got in. We were at about two hundred feet and in an instant we got hammered down to below a hundred — I'd estimate seventy-five feet — before I recovered."

The officer to Riggs' left interrupted. "Lieutenant, please repeat who was flying at that point."

"I was, sir."

"Were you on the flight controls when the aircraft impacted the water?" Riggs asked.

McGirt looked down at the table. His mouth went dry again. "No sir, I was not. Ensign Uker was flying the helicopter when we struck the water." He inhaled a deep breath and stared straight into Riggs' good eye.

"I see..." the JAG said. He jotted some notes. "May I ask, Lieutenant McGirt, why you turned over the controls of your aircraft to a far less qualified pilot when you were penetrating such severe weather?"

"Ensign Uker is a qualified second pilot, sir, and he..."

The officer to Riggs' right spoke up. "Lieutenant, are you aware that Uker failed his last proficiency check because of shoddy airmanship during instrument conditions?" The officer opened a folder and began reading from it: "...unable to maintain altitude plus or minus one hundred feet while performing steep turn maneuvers, it says here. This was less than a year ago and signed by one of the squadron's senior flight instructors."

"Sir, I'm aware of that report. Uker has made significant strides while on cruise. He's worked very hard to improve his instrument flying."

"Are you telling us that, in this situation, you turned over the controls of your aircraft, knowing full well that the guy on your left was a marginal instrument pilot?"

"I had no choice, sir." All five men, including the chief, leaned forward in unison. Before any of them could ask "why?" McGirt continued.

"My left knee cramped up real bad and my leg was locked against the rudder pedal, putting us in a steep, skidding turn. I couldn't free my leg without taking both hands off the controls. I think that during the long flight I became dehydrated and that's what brought on the cramp."

Riggs picked up a magnifying glass and read from the notes in front of him. "Yes, we have the medical officer's statement saying that he treated you for mild dehydration. What happened next?"

"Ensign Uker assumed control while I freed up my leg. We were at two hundred, maybe two-fifty feet. From there, I'm not sure what happened. We entered an area of very heavy rain. It was coming down so hard on the airframe that the noise drowned out the rotor and engine sounds. I felt us take a big dip and our angle of bank increased to about sixty degrees. About the time I reached for the controls and hollered "pull up!" over the interphone, we impacted. I pulled full up collective and recovered. The aircraft was pretty wobbly and we lost our radio. I was able to follow the ship's TACAN back to home plate and eventually landed."

Riggs leafed through Chief Jenks' salty-worded statement of how he'd devised the pallet and mattress nose pedestal. "There were plenty of witnesses for your recovery on the ship, Lieutenant. I see no need for us to go into those details." Riggs put his hands out and turned to both sides, beckoning a response from other board members. They agreed.

Riggs pressed on. "OK, let's move forward. What can you tell me about Petty Officer Lincoln nearly falling from the aircraft through the rescue hatch, or 'hell-hole' as it's called?"

"I believe that LaRue had told Lincoln to work on the cargo hook release that had been giving us fits all night. He must have isolated that conversation on the interphone, because I never actually heard him say it. When it came to my attention, I gave the order for both of them to secure from VERTREP and prepare for landing."

One of the other officers spoke up. "Any reason to believe that LaRue had been intimidating Lincoln during the flight, which forced Lincoln to put himself in jeopardy, untethered and hanging over the hell-hole?"

McGirt recalled how the boisterous Cajun had a history of some issues in that area, especially with Negroes. LaRue was a product of his environment and hadn't adapted well to the Navy's diversity. McGirt decided to keep his opinions to himself and replied, "No, sir."

Riggs looked to the officers at his side and said, "Unless any other members have questions, that concludes the interview. Lieutenant McGirt, you're dismissed."

McGirt stood up, saluted and turned toward the door. A bolt of pain shot like a bullet through his knee and thigh. The Darvon capsule that Doc had handed him "off the record" four hours ago was wearing thin. He forced himself to walk upright and with a steady gait. He winced with every step. As he opened the door to leave, McGirt wondered if he could find a job at the auto plant back in Ypsilanti.

Chapter 15

Salipada drifted in and out of slumbering nausea. He'd regained his senses temporarily and raised his head off the ground a few inches, only to get dizzy and pass out again. This cycle went on for over an hour until finally he was able to open both eyes. He stared straight up at the hazy, early morning sky. His body ached. Limb by limb, he started to move and managed to roll onto his side. As he did, he felt a piece of paper stuck to the side of his face. He swatted at it as if it were a fly, but it was matted tight against his skin. He pulled at it again and it broke loose in pieces. He focused on the shreds between his fingers. The brown-colored paper was soaked in his dried blood. It hurt like hell when he tried to peel the rest of it from his cheek, so he laid his head back down and left the itching, crusty mess alone.

It didn't take long for Sali to figure out what had happened: he'd been rolled. The nausea returned, this time brought on more by the realization that he'd fallen for the ancient scam. It had been a classic set-up, one that he'd cautioned the young sailors about when the ship pulled into port: with money in your pocket, be wary of free-flowing booze and the allure of climbing into bed with a pretty woman. He cursed himself for being so stupid.

He really didn't have to check his pockets, but he did anyway. Confirming the facts only made him feel worse. He'd been picked clean. His wallet and the two thousand pesos that *Jolo*'s skipper had paid him were gone. Surprisingly, he still had his watch. Apparently it wasn't worth enough for the bandits who'd "welcomed" him to Ernesto's haberdashery.

He held the Timex to his ear: still ticking. The watch's scratched crystal and the dim surroundings made it difficult to read, but after hearing the hawking of morning *balut* vendors, Sali guessed that it was around six a.m. He'd been unconscious for nearly ten hours.

He took a few deep breaths and sat up by propping his back against the side of a building. He was in a narrow alley, obscured behind mounds of wadded up packing paper and cardboard boxes. He tried getting to his feet. After some swaying, he kicked the boxes from his path and pointed himself in the direction of the congested street at one end of the alleyway. He lowered his eyes and noticed brownish-red flakes of crusted blood splattered across his white shirt. He never saw the truck as it rounded the turn. The driver swerved through a line of trashcans, scattering them over the papers and boxes. Sali froze in his tracks as the careening vehicle came straight at him. The driver slammed on the brakes, but the truck's fender glanced against Sali's hip. He fell back to the pavement.

The truck wasn't moving fast when it hit him, but in Sali's weakened state, a strong breeze could have knocked him over. The driver sprang from the truck and ran to his side.

"You OK, fella? I didn't see you until it was too late. What are you doing back here at this hour, anyway?"

Sali struggled to his feet. He stood several inches taller than the middle-aged man. Fueled with anger and adrenaline, he instinctively doubled his fists to strike the driver, but as he swung, he lost his balance and crumpled like a pile of bricks into the trashcans. On the way down, he scraped his head on one of them, causing his wound to reopen.

The driver took a knee beside him and bent over to speak. "You're messed up, fella." He put an arm around Sali's torso and guided him toward the rear of the truck. He unlatched the double doors and helped Sali rest on the edge of the empty cargo bed.

Sali checked his rage and hung his head in disgust. "I got rolled last night. Where the hell am I?"

"Metro Manila, just east of the Tondo district," the man said.

"How far is that from Makati?" The matted paper on his face was damp with sweat and trickles of new blood. He swiped the last bits away and flicked the sticky shreds from his fingers.

"Ten or twelve klicks. You need a lift somewhere?"

"Nah, I'll flag down a PC. Maybe they can help me."

The driver became agitated and looked nervously from side to side. "No, no, you don't want to do that. You look like a drunken hobo; you'll get arrested. I'll help you sort this out." He patted Sali's shoulder and gave him an encouraging smile. "I've got to make a pickup and drive down to the airport. You can ride with me if you like until you feel better."

Sali accepted the offer. Penniless, with no identification, he wouldn't have much credibility with the strict Philippine Constabulary. What would he tell them, anyway? That he'd just been booted off his ship and was on his way to buy new clothes so he could get laid? His tale sounded too dumb to be true, even though it was.

"Hop in and rest for a while. We'll figure something out after I make my drop," the driver said.

Sali's eyes drooped from the waves of drowsiness. He found a couple of old packing blankets and built a nest for himself in a corner of the cargo compartment. The driver cranked the vehicle's engine and drove a few blocks before stopping again. The hum of the motor quickly lulled Sali back into a snooze. He awoke when the truck's rear doors opened and a crew of noisy workers began sliding large boxes across the deck toward him.

"Hey, Rolio, who's this guy?" one of the loaders asked.

"Ah, don't mind him. Just a buddy sleeping one off after a bad night." Rolio's comment sparked a string of ball-busting jibes about drinking, cockfights and women. Sali untangled himself from the dusty blankets, got out of the truck and helped load the remaining boxes. When one of the guys asked about the crusty gash on his face and the blood-stained shirt, Sali kept his head down and muttered, "Bar fight."

Ten minutes later they were twisting through Manila's early morning traffic, en route to the International Airport. With the cargo compartment jammed full, Sali joined the driver up front.

"Thanks for pitching in. Everyone calls me Rolio," the driver said.

"My name's Salipada. Thanks for pulling my ass out of that alley," he said as they shook hands. "I'll help you unload. What's in the boxes?"

"Women's clothing: blouses, bras, you know, that kinda shit. Most likely on its way to the U.S. You want some for your ladies?"

Sali laughed cynically as he remembered Gigi and her voluptuous body packed into the skimpy top and leather shorts. "Thanks anyway."

The two men sat quietly as Rolio picked his way through the busy streets. After several minutes, he broke the silence. "I've got a lot of work this week. You need some cash to get back on your feet?"

"That would help," Sali answered. "I started out in Cotabato City. I'll need money for the ferry home."

Rolio slapped both palms down on the steering wheel and sat up straight. "Mindanao? No shit!" He gave Sali a curious stare. He'd never been farther than Baguio in northern Luzon, a few hours from Manila. The big island at the archipelago's southern tip seemed like the end of the earth to him.

"You're a long way from home, pal," he said. "That must have been a hell of a bender, from one end of the P.I. to the other."

Sali frowned, embarrassed by his predicament. He wasn't up for revealing that he was actually a professional seaman, busted from his job. Nonetheless, he felt obligated to at least hit the high points of his story.

"I came in on a freighter yesterday. Let's just say the captain and I didn't see eye-to-eye."

"What'd you do, get caught hosing his wife or something?" Rolio asked gleefully, anticipating some juicy details. He reached for a pack of smokes on the dash, lit up, and offered one to Sali. The soothing warmth of nicotine made Sali's head feel surprisingly better.

"Yeah, his fat old lady and three daughters too," Sali shot back.

Rolio let out a bawdy howl and raised a thumbs-up sign. "I like your style, man. Hey, look, my place is a dump, but it's got a roof over it. You're welcome to camp out on the floor till you get things straightened out."

"I could use a place to crash. Thanks."

"If you're up for it, we can do a couple more truckloads today. With an extra body, I can squeeze in another airport run. I'll split the take with you. How's twenty pesos sound?"

"That's twenty more than I've got in my pocket. You're on."

Rolio held out the cigarette pack. Sali took the final drag from the one in his mouth and chain-lit another. His stomach began to roil with hunger pangs. He hadn't eaten in over a day.

"Don't say much when we're unloading. These airport dickheads know me pretty well. If someone asks, tell them you're my cousin."

"Right," Sali replied.

"Let's stop at this roach coach," Rolio said, motioning toward a luncheon truck parked along the airport fence. "I usually don't eat breakfast, but I'm hungry today."

Sali's gut began to growl again with the anticipation of eating. The smell of fried eggs and rice greeted them as they got out of the truck. The warm meal was just the thing that he needed to get over the hump. He suspected his attackers had slipped him some dope last night, but it seemed as if it had finally passed through his system.

Sated and alert, he climbed back into the truck, ready for work. Rolio backed into one of a long line of loading dock slots at Manila International's air cargo terminal. The facility was swarming with activity as other larger trucks came and went. When Rolio shut off the engine, Sali heard some laughs from the crew inside the cavernous hangar. The beat-up looking truck's cargo deck sat a good two feet below the loading platform.

"Don't pay any attention to those pricks. Let's get this off-loaded and back on the road for another run."

The two men emptied the truck in less than fifteen minutes. As they stacked the boxes, a massive 747 freighter sat parked on the other side of the open hangar doors. The bird's nose cone was unhinged and pointed skyward, allowing a parade of shiny cargo containers to be slid inside the fuselage. Sali stood in awe as the loading vehicles cleared a path for two black limousines. The cars drove across the tarmac and ascended a steep ramp into the enormous flying airship.

"Never seen a jumbo jet?" Rolio asked as he deposited the last crate of goods on the hangar deck. Sali shook his head "no."

A fidgety Caucasian holding a clipboard appeared and handed Rolio a copy of the signed invoice. He tapped his watch. "She's taking off in three hours. Better get your butts in gear and bring me those last two loads," he said.

The mid-morning sun beat down on the truck during their drive back to the garment district. Sali's shirt was soaked from the exertion, but it felt good and had pushed the last molecules of toxins from his system. He glanced across the cab at Rolio, who looked cool as a cucumber. The man was at least fifteen years older than Sali, but appeared as if he could work circles around him. Maybe all those years standing idly on the bridge had made him soft, Sali thought.

"Will we have enough time to make two more runs?" he asked as Rolio weaved through the snarled traffic, traveling down alleyways and up over sidewalks.

"Yeah, we'll do it." The corners of his mouth twitched a grin. "And then we'll go back to my place and get high."

By the time Rolio and Sali had made the last run, Manila's skies darkened with thunderclouds and erupted into an explosive downpour. Rolio navigated the empty truck through wet streets, flooded ankle-deep by the torrent. After an hour and a half of short cuts, many of which were on unpaved muck-filled paths, the two men arrived at a small, boxy, two-story structure. The rain had tapered off to steady showers as Rolio pulled into a single carport. The building's warped clapboards looked as if they hadn't been painted in decades.

Dime-sized droplets pelted the shelter's corrugated steel roof. Rolio shouted something and pointed to a rickety outside staircase that led to the upper level. Both men were soaked when they reached the top.

"Not much, but it's high and dry," Rolio said while unlocking the door. The place was dark and dingy, but surprisingly neat — not what Sali had expected to see. The building, nothing more than a two-story shack, was in the center of a slum. Rolio's one-room apartment consisted of an unmade bed and one end table with a lamp. In a corner was a propane stove and several door-less cabinets, scantily stocked with a few plates and glasses. A tiny refrigerator rattled and hummed next to an industrial-looking, cast iron sink. Rolio pulled back a curtain to reveal a broom closet-sized bathroom.

"It might take a couple of flushes to get everything down," he said. "Water pressure's pretty weak," he said.

Sali eyed the sagging single bed. "What about sleeping?"

"I'll find some blankets," Rolio said. "Maybe you can pad up the floor so it's a little softer."

Sali looked down at the chipped white tile. He tapped a shoe on it. The temporary euphoria he'd felt while working today faded. Even *Jolo*'s clammy bunkroom had offered him a mattress.

"Here, get out of your wet clothes," Rolio said. He tossed Sali a set of dry trousers and a t-shirt. He'd already peeled off his own dripping garb and was standing naked next to the bed. He took the wet shirt and pants, hung them each on a hanger, and then suspended them from a thin metal wire that spanned the width of the room.

"They should be dry by morning." Rolio reached up and pulled a chain that switched on an oscillating fan that he'd mounted to the ceiling.

"What the hell happened to your arm?" Sali asked. He pointed to a curving, coarse scar on Rolio's shoulder.

"Aw... drunken dare with some fools and a branding iron. We were dumb-shit kids then." Rolio slipped on a black t-shirt and walked over to the fridge. The little box was empty except for a half dozen San Miguels. He popped two open, handed one to Sali, and walked over to a window.

"Doubt if this rain will let up soon," Rolio said. He pulled back the curtains for a better look. "We might as well stay in tonight and drink."

Sali looked around and didn't see a place to sit, other than on the bed, so he leaned up against the sink and finished his beer. "Hey man, I appreciate your helping me today, but you don't have much room here," he said.

Rolio stared at the rain outside. He took a long draw on the beer, belched, and then wiped some foam off his upper lip. "The way I see it, Sali, you don't have a lot of options today. Unless you're handing me some line of bullshit." He tempered himself and forced a warm-hearted smile.

"I don't give a damn what happened to you last night — that's your business. But I could use another strong back. I own that truck outright and have connections to get use of another vehicle. This is my busy time of the year, and there's tons of merchandise to move around Manila and up to Angeles City. Maybe some runs over to the Navy base at Subic as well. I usually work alone, but you seem like a straight shooter. This could be a win-win for both of us." Rolio turned away from the window to face Sali. "You got a driver's license?"

"Sure, but it got ripped off with my wallet last night."

"We can take care of that," Rolio said confidently. "I know some people."

Sali was suspicious. He'd met the guy only a few hours ago. "How much do you think I can make in a month?" he challenged.

"Four, five hundred pesos, if you're willing to bust your tail. Enough to get you back on your feet, eh?"

Sali ran some figures through his head. That amount would buy ferry passage to Mindanao and he'd still have some cash left over. Maybe he could bribe Eduardo for some stevedore work on the docks and eventually get a job at sea, where he belonged.

Rolio came closer. He held up his bottle, ready for a toast. "So whaddya say?" A few seconds passed until Sali nodded silently. They clanked their bottles to seal the deal.

Rolio's dank apartment didn't look so grim after a few beers. Lubricated with alcohol, Sali opened up a little more about his job on *Jolo*. He stopped short, however, of revealing that he'd fallen asleep at the helm. A light breeze filtered in through the windows, devoid of the oppressive humidity after the clouds had drained. The air was cooler now, but laced with a pungent, smoldering aroma.

"What's that smell?" Sali asked.

Rolio looked up from his sprawled position on the bed. "There's a couple of big trash dumps down the road. Sometimes fires break out from the decomposing garbage. You'll get used to it."

The malodorous air filled Sali's nostrils, reminding him of last night, just before he'd passed out. He walked to the window and gazed across the endless ramshackle huts below. Through the faint twilight, he spotted flickering flames, dotted across the outline of low-lying hills.

Rolio sprang from the bed. "I think we need to properly celebrate our new partnership," he said. He slipped on a pair of flip-flops and grabbed the truck keys. "I'll be back in half an hour. Take a snooze on the bed, if you like."

Sali couldn't take his eyes off the smoking mountain out the window. He thought that he could see people wandering like nervous ants on the hillside. He watched as the truck's taillights disappeared from view as Rolio sped away down the muddy alley. He felt a little creepy about lying on the man's bed, but between last night's events, a full day of physical labor and the beers, he gave in. He lay down and rested his head against the pillow, still damp from Rolio's wet hair. Within seconds he was asleep and dreaming. He saw Gigi, standing by the bar at the Polo Club. Her earrings sparkled like stars on a moonless night. She smiled at him. His mind continued with its fantasy as his shipmates from *Jolo* filtered in one by one. The last to appear in the doorway was young Malik, looking clean and innocent in his freshly pressed work clothes. He held his *kufi* in one hand and approached the others slowly, as if he were afraid. *Jolo*'s skipper was behind the bar. He held a large, chrome mixing cup and was pouring shots from assorted bottles into it. The Old Man covered the cup and began shaking it vigorously. He then lowered it and tapped it on the bar to settle its contents — gently at first and then more forcefully, pounding it harder and harder, all the while staring angrily at Sali.

"Wake up! I'm locked out!" Rolio hollered. He'd been knocking on the door for over a minute before Sali came to his senses. Sali jumped from the bed and weaved to the door, still dizzy from the nap and alcohol. He heard female voices laughing. When he opened the door, Rolio was standing with a girl under each arm.

"Look what I found!" he blurted out. His eyes were glazed over and his voice was filled with silliness. The girls each carried a paper bag: one filled with quart bottles of beer, the other with a fifth of whiskey. Rolio steered the girls straight toward the bed, where the three of them fell into a twisted heap of arms and legs.

Rolio grinned and asked Sali, "Which one do you want?" He sat up, pulled a joint from his pocket, and lit up. The girls pawed through his shirt, like squirrels hungry for a nut, and found a reefer for themselves.

A veil of marijuana smoke soon surrounded them. Sali stood in the middle of the room, baffled. His head still hurt from the mugging last night and he was groggy from the brief nap. The scene was playing out like a comical dream.

"Come on, man, let's have a party," Rolio sang out. He got up, shoved a cold beer into Sali's palm and held out a fresh joint to him.

"I got a great idea," Rolio said to the girls. "But first we need complete privacy!" He choked back giggles, which only made the girls laugh more. He stood at attention and waggled a finger at them in mock admonishment. He walked over to the window, slammed down the sash and cranked up the ceiling fan another notch to keep the air moving.

Sali took a couple hits of weed and chased it with a slug of whiskey and a big chug of beer. He sized up the two women. One was very young. She was thin and petite with her hair piled atop her head. Her face was covered with heavy makeup, giving the appearance of a little girl who'd broken into her mother's cosmetics and wasn't sure how to put the stuff on properly. The other one seemed about Sali's age and was quite large. Her face was just on the pleasant side of homely and rolls of fat bulged from the waistline of her tight-fitting skirt. She wore dark-rimmed glasses.

Rolio rummaged through a box under the bed and came up with a small reel-to-reel tape player. He plugged it into a wall socket. The young girl looked at the older one and said, "Are we going to dance now?"

"That's right, sweetie, we're all gonna dance now," Rolio said as he pressed the play button. The girl got to her feet, shook down her hair and waited for the music.

But instead, what came from the machine's speaker were the muffled sounds of a man's voice singing a native Philippine folk song.

"I don't know this one," the young girl said. Embarrassed, she shied away and sat down on the bed, close to her friend. Another voice, that of an English-speaking female, urged the man to sing on.

"That's President Marcos!" the heavy-set girl said. She covered her mouth. "I heard this on the college radio station a few years ago. How'd you get this?"

Rolio grinned proudly as the tape played. It was a bootlegged copy of the president and his mistress, an American-born actress by the name of Dovie Beams, who'd secretly recorded her adulterous tryst with the president, inside her Manila penthouse. Miss Beams had been hand-picked by Marcos to play the heroine in a movie about the president's dubious exploits during Japan's occupation of the Philippines. The film, entitled *Maharlika*, had been a ploy by Marcos to gain favor with voters during an election campaign. After the filming, he'd kept the B-movie starlet from Nashville sequestered in a posh flat against her will. As protection, Dovie had hidden a recorder under her bed and made tapes to confirm the affair, eventually going to the press. Students at the University of the Philippines who despised the president had obtained a copy and played it over the campus radio station. As payback for her public humiliation, Marcos would later grant First Lady Imelda nearly unlimited power to spend money on herself and on dozens of wastefully decadent projects around metro Manila.

Sali found himself laughing along with the others. The man on the tape, unmistakably Marcos, sang like a love-struck teenager. But the tape's quality was poor. The sounds of sexual teasing between Dovie and the president deteriorated into muted groans and squeaking bedsprings.

Rolio quietly slid his body between the two women and began groping the younger one. Within a few seconds he'd peeled away her flimsy sundress and was on top of her. The older girl took her cue, came across the room and sat next to Sali on the floor.

"Do you want me to be your girlfriend tonight?" she asked. Her breath reeked of booze and smoke. She was stoned. She slid her hand to his groin as Sali sighed and relaxed against the wall. She pressed her body hard against his. His hands glided along her hips, then across her belly and up to a set of big breasts. Her neck and chest were moist with sweat as the temperature in the tiny room rose.

Rolio reached across his girl's naked body and turned up the volume of the recorder. "Fred," as the president insisted on being called by his mistress, was now moaning loudly with delight as she pleasured him.

Sali's woman began to undress herself. Her flesh smelled of cheap perfume. The tape reached its end and flapped freely from the spinning reel. A faint stream of moonlight flowed through the parted curtains, illuminating the glistening nakedness of Rolio and his bed partner. The small apartment filled with the wet, earthy aroma of sex.

Sali closed his eyes and fell back onto the cold ceramic tile as the woman finished removing her clothes and started to loosen his belt. His mind flashed back to the lovely Gigi and her slender, curvy body. Aroused by the crude pornographic recording, he knew this encounter wouldn't take long at all.

Chapter 16

Salipada awoke to the sound of nature's alarm clock: a crowing rooster.

He'd slept for more than eight hours after passing out on the floor. His "girlfriend" for the night had lost interest in him after their brief coupling, choosing instead to join Rolio and her friend in bed. On their way out, the two girls had pulled the sheet off Rolio's spent body and covered up Sali on the floor. It was more an act of pity than affection.

Sali's head hurt like it had the day before, when he'd been beaten and drugged and dumped in the alley. But at least this morning he knew where he was: somewhere in the bowels of Manila's slum lands. Finding his bladder stretched to its limit, he got up and headed for the bathroom. After stubbing his toe on the toilet, he steadied himself, took aim, and launched a loud, splattering stream into the darkness. Finished, he spun around and walked straight into Rolio's naked body. The two men snaked past each other in the tiny water closet. Rolio grunted something and took his turn over the bowl. Sali fell back down into the nest he'd made from the sheet and his clothing. It was still dark outside.

"Let's go," Rolio shouted and kicked Sali's backside as he walked by. "We need to be at the warehouse when they open the doors." Sali turned over and watched as Rolio filled the sink with cold water, then dunked his face. He shook his head like a dog after a swim and wiped off with a nearby rag.

"I'm not kidding. If you want work, get your ass moving." Any camaraderie from last night had evaporated like raindrops on scorching pavement. Rolio dressed in a flash and was already in the truck waiting as Sali lagged behind.

"We'll stop for food after we drop the first load," Rolio said as they backed out into the muddy alley. He grabbed the last smoke from the pack on the dash. After lighting up, he offered Sali a wake-up toke.

"Here's the plan: we get you a new driver's license later today so you can start making some runs on your own."

"But I don't know my way around the city," Sali said.

"Don't worry. You'll ride with me the first few days until you get your bearings. After that, I'll get you some easy routes, you know, on the main streets. I've got a friend who can rustle up another truck for you to drive."

They left the cluttered slums, turned onto a four-lane boulevard and accelerated. The stink of burning garbage receded as they got farther away from Tondo and Smoky Mountain. Sali tilted his head into the breeze and took in a deep breath. The cool morning air helped lessen his feeling of grunginess. With Rolio pushing him like a drill sergeant, he hadn't had time to even splash some water on his face, and his shirt and pants were still soggy from yesterday's downpour.

A few places looked familiar along the way. Sali recognized the gated U.S. Embassy, where a throng of workers was already busy manicuring the compound's lush landscape, and the pier where he'd said goodbye to Malik.

"Thanks for last night," he said.

A grin crept over Rolio's face. "We had some fun, eh? Too bad you crashed so early. That young one was a little machine in bed. She didn't know how to stop. Here, you finish."

Sali took the cigarette, sucked in the last drag and tossed it out the window. They turned into a wide parking lot next to a one-story, windowless steel building. Rolio sped up to cut off a bigger truck that had entered the lot from across the street, and then zoomed forward, straight for the building's loading bay. Whipping the steering wheel through his hands with the dexterity of a juggler, he did a quick direction change, then backed up to the dock, stopping within a few inches of it.

"We made it. Those assholes will have to wait." He faced the driver of the other truck and flipped him the bird. "Bastards." Rolio reached into his pocket and handed Sali a twenty-peso note. "That's for yesterday. Now go get us some coffee and a pack of smokes." He pointed to the lunch wagon parked in the back of the lot.

"And see if he's got some aspirin, will you? My *pistola* hurts from last night." Rolio held his crotch and feigned a painful look. Sali laughed at the aging hustler and got out. For the first time in days, he felt like things were looking up.

Later, after Rolio had hooked Sali up with a vehicle and sent him on his way, Rolio drove across town and picked up a load destined for Angeles City, north of Manila. His white, mid-sized truck was registered in his name. The papers inside its glove box matched perfectly with the truck's plates and description. But the documents were all bogus, compliments of Rolio's "friend" at the motor bureau. The weaselly clerk had demanded an extra bag of grass in exchange for Sali's shiny new driver's license.

The truck meshed indistinguishably with the rest of Manila's late afternoon traffic — just another tattered noisemaker creeping through the sweltering smog. Rolio reached for the bill of lading tucked inside the sun visor. He held it up with one hand for examination: a few native Filipino clothing items, knick-knacks and a whole lot of foreign-made stuff headed for department stores and neighborhood *sari-saris*. After the convenience store goods and novelties had been packed, Rolio had checked out a crate of Japanese transistor radios while the workers had loaded him up at the warehouse.

The straight-line distance between metro Manila and Angeles City is less than sixty miles. Today's journey, however, would take Rolio over three hours, through crowded streets and shabby country roads littered with livestock drifting between unfenced parcels of farmland. He'd make a handsome profit from this run, but that fact paled in comparison to what would lie ahead for him later, after he'd made his drop.

The sun was sinking over the mountains when congestion finally thinned out north of Manila. Rolio checked his watch and pressed the accelerator to make up some time. He hunched over the steering wheel in an effort to stretch his knotted back muscles, still aching from that tunnel-crawling gig last week. Once on an open stretch of highway, he popped a couple aspirin into his mouth and reached down to massage the two knobby pelvic bones at the base of his spine. *Someday, when my work is done, I won't have to drag my body around and do this shit*, he thought. He spent the rest of the drive concentrating on how quickly he could empty the truck and take on his new cargo.

The off-load crew must have read his mind about the radios. While lugging the crates, one of the four turned to Rolio and said, "Oh, I think I'm losing my grip!" The other three snickered and followed his lead, letting the big box crash to the concrete floor. The sound of cracking wood and plastic echoed through the deserted warehouse as four sets of greedy hands tore into the fractured box. Within seconds, they'd scattered a half dozen of the busted radios, and then dug deeper for the good ones. They each tucked one of the palm-sized devices into a pants pocket. The crew's leader found three more and handed them to Rolio. He then took an empty soft drink bottle lying nearby and smashed it to the floor, next to the radios.

"Did you see that? I could have broken my leg when I tripped over that bottle! The son-of-a-bitch janitor ought to do a better job cleaning up around here. The least that dolt of a store manager could do is offer us a little token before I turn him into the constable for unsafe working conditions."

The crew roared their approval and burst into laughter as they turned to leave the building. Rolio handed them each ten pesos for their time and climbed back into the truck.

The ruse was complete: he'd made his rounds with plenty of witnesses. He'd led them to believe that he was driving back to Manila before curfew. After saying his goodbyes, he got back on the highway and headed south until out of view of the warehouse workers. It was much easier this time, tracing a contorted route through the neighborhoods in daylight, without a hysterical female crawling over his back. After a half dozen turns, he was headed exactly in the direction he wanted: toward the outskirts of Angeles City, west of the U.S. airbase. He paralleled the mountain range along a one-lane dirt road for about twenty minutes and checked his odometer for the right distance. The instructions he'd written down said that he should almost be there. Had he been driving any faster, he would have missed the small gap in the brush. Just as they'd told him, there were two dead tree branches placed in a haphazard but recognizable "x" marking the turnoff point.

Two youngsters on a motor scooter whizzed by in the opposite direction as he sat idly on the side of the road. When their dust settled and he was confident no one else was around, Rolio maneuvered the truck into the gap, backing cautiously, deeper into the foliage. Twenty meters into a thicket of smaller trees, the jungle canopy grew dense, smothering the dwindling daylight. Rolio opened the driver's side door and looked straight down at the faintly visible path for guidance. The truck's back-up lights and rearview mirror were of little help in the darkness, but he edged the vehicle farther, straining to hear the prearranged signal above the racket of fronds scraping against the truck's sides. He stopped and turned off the engine. On cue, four sharp whistles rang out. To the unsuspecting ear, it sounded like a wild bird's call, but Rolio recognized it. He heard some rumbling in the bush followed by muffled conversation nearby. Relieved, he bent over the steering wheel again, but the stretching didn't help much. Likewise, the pills he'd taken did nothing to dull the pain.

"Right on schedule, Comrade Rolio."

Rolio recognized the voice as someone from the Movement, but he couldn't place the name. The man, visible only as a shady silhouette, extended a hand and introduced himself.

"You probably don't remember. I'm Cornelio, but everyone calls me Nelly. It's been a while, hasn't it?"

Rolio smiled in agreement and shook his hand. He recalled the after-curfew raid they'd partnered on, four years ago, outside the perimeter of military housing at Subic Bay Naval Station. They'd dragged an officer's motorcycle partially through a hole in the security fence when a night watchman had spotted them. Unlike the dopey fool he'd dealt with during the recent heist at Clark, however, the Navy MPs were reasonably effective that night. He and Nelly had managed to retreat safely back to their jungle hideout. The bike had stayed behind.

Nelly put his mouth next to Rolio's ear and whispered, "We have six of them ready to go — four university dropouts and a couple of field workers. No *pukis* this time, thank God!"

"Yeah, that's good," Rolio said. He gave a quick laugh, unsure if Nelly knew about his unfortunate escapade with the young girl in the pickup last week. The two of them went around to the back of the vehicle. Nelly held a flashlight and aimed it at the truck's bifold gate.

"OK, let's go," Nelly said in a soft voice directed off to one side. There was more rustling, followed by the shadowy image of a half dozen men being marched out from the darkness toward them. The group wore hoods over their heads. They were linked together by each man placing his hand on the shoulder of the individual in front of him. Nelly, just like the times before, had prepared the recruits by reciting a short homily:

There are no chains or bondage holding you here. You are free to leave at any time. But, as soldiers in the Movement, we must all faithfully show blind allegiance before we're allowed to see the true light of freedom.

His comrades were convinced that Nelly had plagiarized those lines from one of the old heroes, either Luis Taruc or the late Juan Feleo, but Nelly swore that the words were his own. A stoic-faced guard carrying a rifle took the first man by the arm and led him toward the truck.

With Rolio's and Nelly's guidance, the gaggle stumbled into the windowless cargo van and sat down. One by one they scooted along their backsides and found a sidewall to lean against for the journey.

"We're ready," Nelly said to Rolio. With the aid of headlights, navigating out of the jungle was much easier than the trip in. As if on a train bolting from a dark tunnel, suddenly they were in the clear. The day's sunlight faded over the Zambales Mountains.

"This is a good group we have," Nelly said as he rolled down his window and fanned some fresh breeze on to his face. "But keep an eye on the tall one with thick glasses and big teeth, Vaccaro. He seems like a wild card. Real wise guy and smart as a whip. I think he spent a few years at the university and he's good with history."

"Sounds like Julio will have some competition from another college boy. He could use a little humility," Rolio said. The two laughed at the thought of their haughty leader taking a bite of humble pie for a change.

Rolio took a circuitous route to avoid Clark Air Base and headed to the farm where he'd been a week earlier. The workday was winding down; nonetheless, a smattering of traffic still lined the two-lane paved road north, toward Tarlac. They'd traveled a few kilometers on the highway when Rolio glanced into the side mirror.

"Aw, fuck!" he said. "We have to...Pork adobo! Pork adobo!"

Hearing the code words, Nelly spun in his seat and pounded his fist three times on the thin sheet of aluminum that separated the truck's cargo box from the cab. He shouted out the code words. The guard responded with two raps and repeated the words back. Rolio and Nelly heard a clunk when the guard, as he'd been instructed to do, pushed his weapon through a concealed compartment and into a dummy gas tank which Rolio had capped off to store contraband.

"Let me do the talking, Nelly. Only speak if they ask you a question directly." Nelly nodded that he understood. Rolio guided the truck to the road's edge and shut off the motor.

The dark blue Datsun sedan coasted to a stop a few feet off the truck's bumper. Two Philippine Constabulary got out of the car and strutted forward like a couple of arrogant roosters who owned the barnyard. They wore tailored, dark green uniforms consisting of pressed trousers and short sleeve, open-collared shirts. Their straight black hair was styled crisply. Apparently they'd decided to leave their caps in the car.

The pair sauntered forward, one on each side of the truck, stopping just aft of the driver's and passenger's side windows. As they did, two low-flying military jets thundered overhead, making a formation approach to the airbase. The officers tilted their heads back and took in the sight. The officer on Rolio's side held out an open hand without saying a word. Rolio had already retrieved his license, registration and shipping invoice for inspection.

"Where you going?" the officer asked while he thumbed through the documents. He peered below the rim of his dark, aviator-style glasses, squinting to read the small print.

"Just made a drop-off at a warehouse in Angeles City, sir. We picked up some workers who needed a lift to a farm in Concepcion." Rolio looked over his left shoulder and pointed his thumb toward the back of the truck. The constable motioned his head in that direction, signifying that he wanted to look inside.

Rolio got out and walked to the back of the truck, followed by both officers. Before he could unlatch the doors, the guard had already pushed them open, revealing himself and the six now bare-headed young men. The recruits, as previously instructed, had crammed the hoods down their pants and arranged themselves, three on each side of the truck bed.

"We have IDs, sir, if you need to see them," the guard said respectfully. He stepped slowly out on to the pavement and held out an appropriately tattered identification card, the same kind the rest of the crew had in their possession — all expertly forged by Rolio's accomplice at the motor bureau. The officer looked at the guard's ID and handed it back. He frowned and appeared bored with the entire ordeal.

"It looked like one of your brake lights was out at that last stop sign, but I guess the sunlight played a trick on me," he said. There was hint of an apologetic tone in his voice. He handed Rolio the documents and returned to the sedan with his partner.

The guard hopped into the truck and closed the doors behind him. Rolio climbed back into the driver's seat and found Nelly sitting at attention, sweating profusely.

"*Hesukristo!*" Nelly said, blowing out a deep breath and wiping down his soaked brow.

"Get used to it, my friend; it's bound to happen again."

"I thought we were goners when those PC looked inside. We were lucky."

Rolio gave him a nonchalant smile and merged back onto the highway. The rest of the ride was uneventful except for the normal delays caused by errant livestock meandering across the road and street merchants hawking their wares at every corner. Both men kept a watchful eye on the truck's side mirrors.

A couple of shirtless workers wearing wide-brimmed straw hats met them at the gate of the farm that was their destination. They took a spot on each side of the truck, walking along as Rolio guided it though the chickens and dogs that seemed to come and go at their leisure on the property. He parked in one of the three barns, the same one where he'd hidden after evading the PC with the stolen machine gun. The *telyadora* machine had been moved off to one side to make room. In the spot that it had occupied, a six-inch layer of dirt and rotting hay had been peeled away, exposing a two by four-foot hatchway that led to an underground bunker. The two gatekeepers stood by the hatch patiently while the guard, with rifle slung over his shoulder, led the hooded men out.

"I smell chicken shit. Let me guess, we're on a farm, somewhere north of Clark," one of them said through the cloth sack. He followed the deduction with a mocking laugh.

"Enough, Vaccaro!" Nelly hollered. He turned to Rolio and said under his breath, "See what I mean? The kid is too smart for his own damn good."

The guard put his face an inch away from Vaccaro's hood, spat a string of profanity and then slapped the neophyte firmly on the side of his head. Vaccaro's shoulders slumped and his chin sank in submission. Nelly nodded to the gatekeepers who reached down in unison and raised the thick wooden hatch cover.

"You'll be walking down ten steps. Use the handrail on your left," Nelly instructed. He led the crew step by step into the pit as Rolio followed. When the last of the procession dipped below ground level, the gatekeepers lowered the hatch with a thud and rapidly shoveled the dirt and hay back on top. Rolio heard the muffled creaking of the threshing machine as the two men pushed it back over the sealed opening.

The bunker had been resourcefully constructed with scrap wood and metal that members of the Movement had gathered from dumps and ditches. Long sections of Marsden matting from the big war had been used as part of a collage, which, when puzzled together, made a shabby-looking but incredibly solid subterranean fortress. Measuring about ten by twenty feet, the shelter had a string of electrical cords and outlets dangling from above. There were two bare incandescent bulbs hanging down, one in the center of the room and another directly over a beautifully built mahogany podium. Folding chairs, "borrowed" from a school or government building, had been arranged neatly in two rows. Between them, a slide projector had been set up on a small table. Across from that, suspended from the ceiling, a white sheet served as a screen. The men stood obediently in place, silently fidgeting but keenly aware that something important was about to follow.

Nelly spoke first. "Comrades, you may now remove your hoods."

Instantly, the group pulled the black sacks from their sweating heads. They breathed a collective sigh and quietly joked amongst themselves, except for Vaccaro. He calmly wiped his face, tossed the hood aside and surveyed the surroundings, much like a prospective buyer inspecting a property for sale. With no intended sarcasm, he said, "Well, I guess we really have gone underground, haven't we?"

The group filed into their seats as Rolio and the guard stood in the background. Nelly walked forward and took his place alongside the podium.

"Gentlemen, our esteemed speaker will be here in a moment. Like your driver, Comrade Rolio, he has a long history with our Movement, dating back to the days of Japanese occupation. Both of these senior members have worked on an intimate basis with our forefathers: Taruc, Feleo and the rest. The two of them have fought their entire lives for the honor of our country."

The young men had turned in their chairs to face Rolio. They'd received many lectures during their training in the mountains, but only from fighters like Nelly, who wasn't much older than them. Rolio was the first authentic member of the Rebellion any of them had ever met.

The guard remained at the back of the bunker as Rolio joined Nelly, who'd left the podium to stand near a doorway. Until now, no one had noticed the alternate entryway. Its bleached-out, marred wooden panels were undistinguishable from the bunker's other ramshackle materials. Two loud knocks came from the door's other side. Nelly checked his watch again, returned the signal with two knocks of his own and said, "Enter. Comrade Julio, we are ready."

The door swung open and a balding, elderly Filipino man walked in. He stood erect. His steps were measured and confident. He was dressed in dark trousers and a clean, but inexpensive looking, off-white barong. The man appeared so ordinary that he could have easily passed for a clerk selling tickets at the village bus station. The room remained silent. The door swung shut behind him, but not before the recruits got a glimpse of a long, dimly lit tunnel that led off into darkness. Rolio closed and latched the door, then slid a thick plank across the opening in barricade fashion.

Julio stood quietly by the podium with his arms folded casually across his chest. A faint, peaceful smile edged its way to the corners of his mouth. Tension grew as the recruits anticipated his words, but he said nothing. Instead, he walked slowly from the podium and strolled between the rows of chairs, deliberately making eye contact with every man. As he passed Vaccaro, the funny-boy smirk disappeared from the youth's face. He stared back unflinchingly through his thick glasses. Julio stopped and returned the gaze. After several uncomfortable seconds, Julio laughed and walked back to the podium.

"Young comrades, on this final day of your indoctrination, you've been transported to this secret place, not far from Mount Arayat, where our heroes began their noble quest nearly a half century ago. Our surroundings are far from elaborate, but we hope that you understand why you are here." Julio removed his wire-rimmed spectacles and tucked them in a shirt pocket. "We could only accomplish a limited amount from the Zambales mountain camps. So you are here with your mentor, Cornelio, and my dear friend, Comrade Rolio, who've prepared a setting where you may better experience the purpose and gravity of what we are about."

Julio reached for the cord that led to the projector and switched it on. Displayed on the screen was a map of the Philippine archipelago. A bold red star signified their location in central Luzon. He began flipping through a series of black and white slides depicting old Spanish governors, American military men and Filipino leaders who meant very little to the young men who sat before him. When he came to the slide of the current president of the Philippines and his wife, he paused and walked away from the podium. Some chuckles and vulgarities seeped from the group as they took in the image of the First Couple.

"I won't spend much time talking about these two," he said. "But I find it intriguing how a convicted murderer and a dim-witted beauty queen could have risen to the powerful positions they now hold." Julio shook his head with dismay.

He removed the slide of the Marcoses and put up a more detailed map of Luzon Island. "Like many things that start out as a worthy cause, they may not end with the hoped-for result. For example, in the 1940s, when Filipino peasants directed their struggles away from abusive landlords and targeted the Japanese aggressors, those who'd been labeled romantic vigilantes suddenly became heroes to the world. Unfortunately, these heroes would not only be a threat to the occupying forces of the Rising Sun, but were ultimately despised by our American liberators, who considered them an impediment to their goals of capitalism and colonization. And yes, even our own countrymen would turn against our movement."

Julio sped through a series of slides until he found one that showed a line of Filipino men and women. They wore odd-looking baskets over their heads. Thin slits had been cut into the baskets, allowing them to see others without their own identities being revealed.

"Look familiar?" The group fidgeted in their seats, confused. "Some of you may have heard the term *Makapili*," Julio said. "These are your countrymen who were used by the Japanese to identify dissidents among your ancestors. You probably had a relative who suffered as a result of these low-life informants." Julio lowered his head and said, "Traitorous cowards. How sad."

He clicked on another slide, this one a blurry image of dungeon-like holes cluttered with emaciated bodies bound in shackles. It was difficult to tell the living from the dead.

"Because of the Japanese and those *Makapili* rats, freedom fighters like our own Comrade Rolio endured these conditions at Fort Santiago, in Manila. By the grace of God, he survived." Julio clicked the next slide. "Unfortunately, those on the lower levels of his prison were drowned when the tides rolled in, trapping them like dogs." The group gasped at the sight of more grotesque bodies, these floating like trash in the submerged corridors. All heads turned again to face Rolio, who stood stoically in the back with Nelly.

"But this brings us to why you are really here today. You may ask, *What does all this ancient history have to do with our cause, Julio?* Well, let's bring this talk into terms that your young minds may absorb more effectively."

Another slide appeared on the screen. At first, this one looked to be a hunting party, proudly standing over their fallen prey — except these were uniformed Filipino soldiers, weapons in hand. Before them were the bloated and beheaded bodies of their own countrymen. The soldiers' uniforms bore a skull-and-bones insignia on their sleeves. A flag bearing the same logo hung behind the platoon.

Vaccaro was unable to contain himself any longer. He growled through clenched teeth, "Nenita Death Squad!"

Julio calmly cleared his throat and said, "Very good. Would you like to tell everyone what you know?" He'd set out the bait, and as Nelly had predicted, Vaccaro pounced on it with a vengeance. Without hesitation, Vaccaro leapt to his feet. The look of fierce lunacy filled his eyes. "This is when it really started! Manual Roxas, that traitorous Jap-lover and a greasy pawn to General MacArthur and his band of thieves. They've denied us our place as an independent government of the people!" He pointed to the slide, still looming over them on the screen.

"All that, so they could cram their so-called Parity Act down our throats and enslave us forever to the United States and the rest of the Western world. Robbing our resources and forcing their poisonous goods on us." Vaccaro paused to catch his breath and wipe at his mouth. His fellow recruits stared at him in awe. They had no idea what he was talking about. Although a few of them had a sanitized knowledge of their country's checkered history, they didn't share their comrade's maniacal enthusiasm.

"Luis Taruc was never given his due!" Vaccaro had unconsciously edged closer to the podium where he stood shoulder to shoulder with Julio. "Peaceful methods will no longer work," he said while pounding his fist on the hardwood stand. "The U.S. bases make us sitting ducks for nuclear attack. We must make a statement to the world. We must..."

Julio cut him off. "Thank you, young man. We need vigor like yours within our ranks." He leaned against the dais and lowered his voice as if he were gently scolding one of his children who'd unknowingly made an error. He looked at Vaccaro as he returned to his seat. "You are obviously a student of history, but I'm sure that you can appreciate the wisdom of timing and moderation.

"What will make our movement successful this time is discipline." He focused directly on Vaccaro now as he went on. "As some of you may recall, many of the *Hukbalahap* went astray and brought discredit upon the noble cause of our people. One of the first such acts was the assassination of First Lady Quezon in 1949. A senseless act that only alienated us from the very citizenry we claim to represent.

"More recently, the selfish actions of former *Huk* Faustino Del Mundo — posing under his silly alias Commander Sumulong — further impeded our progress. He and his ilk, supplying their dope and *putas* to the GIs in Angeles City, only denigrate the accomplishments of Taruc and Feleo."

Julio turned to Nelly and gave a nod. Nelly opened the door into the tunnel, where two men stood behind a rusted wheelbarrow that held a smoldering pile of burning logs.

Julio pulled up the left sleeve of his shirt. Nelly and Rolio did the same. The three men bore identical scars on their upper left arms, just below their shoulders. As Julio traced the symbol with his index finger, he said, "This marking represents the head and horns of the water buffalo, better known as the *carabao* in our culture. The *carabao* is a powerful, plodding animal of great strength and enduring patience. It is gentle and submissive — until it is angered. Then it becomes a dangerous, destructive force, nearly impossible to control."

The heat and smoke from the embers permeated the bunker. Everyone's eyes began to sting. One of the recruits moaned and fell forward, hitting his head against the man's back in front of him. He gagged and then slumped to the floor. The two men who'd pushed in the wheelbarrow ran to his side. He struggled and began screaming as they dragged him down the tunnel and out of sight. His moans faded and the room grew silent. Only the hissing sound of the fire was heard.

"Young comrades, I invite you to join the ranks of our group who have persisted for half a century," Julio said. He reached into the wheelbarrow and grabbed the wooden handle of a rod that rested deep within the coals. He withdrew it slowly and held it over his head. The white-hot figure at its end matched the branding on his shoulder.

"By wearing this symbol, you swear your allegiance to the cause of freeing your repressed countrymen, once and for all!"

Vaccaro exploded from his seat and ran for the podium. Both Nelly and Rolio went after him as Julio reflexively stepped back and pointed the glowing iron at the charging youth. Before anyone could grab him, Vaccaro had pulled off his shirt. Beads of sweat popped from his lean torso. He stood rigid: his face mere inches from the hot steel. Rolio braced his forearm against Nelly, signaling him to hold off.

Vaccaro pivoted ninety degrees and presented his bare shoulder to Julio. He lowered his head. With closed eyes he whispered, "Yes!"

Chapter 17

USS *San Angelo* continued her high-speed run toward Subic Bay, Philippines. Skipper Lugansky had received his orders to enter Subic at 0900 hours the next day. The ship would be met by two tugboats dispatched to guide her safely to a mooring spot at the colossal naval base. From that point, Lugansky's vessel would be on standby while awaiting further orders. The crew was ablaze with speculation over what would lie ahead for the big supply ship. She wasn't scheduled to return Stateside for another month. Rumors said that if the Japanese mechanics could fix McGirt's crippled aircraft in less than a week, the Singapore sojourn would be back on.

With the mishap investigation team's work concluded, its senior member, Captain Riggs, had paid his respects to Lugansky, and then led his enclave to the ship's stern for pickup and return to the aircraft carrier. McGirt had tried to relax by lounging in the wardroom. However, upon hearing the beat of the H-3's rotors approaching, for some reason he was drawn aft to watch the recovery and launch event. He stood in the back of the hangar alongside the wrecked helo, out of view, as the H-3 made its approach and landing. There was no air show this time. Riggs and his team paraded single file through the narrow hangar bay's open door and out onto the flight deck's edge.

While the fueling gang topped off the helo's tanks, a lone sailor charged through the hangar toward the group. It was Thomas Rayburn, who saluted Riggs and handed over a file. He leaned in toward the senior officer and said something as the H-3's idling rotor wash thundered. Riggs smiled gratefully, patted Rayburn on the back and handed the file to the chief yeoman who, in turn, stuffed it inside his overflowing briefcase. Rayburn bowed deeply and then stood at attention as the team boarded. With nothing more to see, McGirt headed back to his stateroom. Rayburn had stood by while the aircraft lifted off and departed.

* * *

The mess decks were abuzz with anticipation of port call. Despite having just left Subic Bay a few days ago, the crew always welcomed the chance to get away from the crowded confines of shipboard life and make their way into Olongapo City, the legendary sailor town on the other side of the naval station's gates.

Those not on watch stood along the rails as the shores of Luzon Island loomed and the mouth of Subic Bay appeared dead ahead. The smaller cousin to vast Manila Bay, forty miles to its southeast, Subic had been a strategic port since its discovery by Spanish conquistador Juan de Salcedo in the 1500s. Over the centuries, it had been occupied by native Filipinos, Spaniards, Americans and, for most of World War Two, the Japanese. The Bay now served as a vital U.S. naval facility in the Pacific theater, most recently as a critical staging point for ships and aircraft during the Vietnam conflict. Besides its military importance, Subic offered an unparalleled spot for rest and relaxation. The towns of Olongapo and Subic were fleet favorites, presenting sailors and Marines with scores of pretty girls, cheap booze and handmade crafts to carry home as souvenirs.

Adjoining the huge Subic port facility was Cubi Point Naval Air Station. The brainchild of Chief of Naval Operations, Admiral Arthur Radford, the post-Korean War construction of Cubi had been led by the Navy's Construction Battalions, better known as the Seabees. The massive earth-moving project rivaled the building of the Panama Canal, eventually making space for a ten thousand-foot airstrip and support buildings carved out from the inhospitable Zambales Mountain and jungle. An entire town, Banicain, was relocated to nearby Olongapo in the wake of this colossal project. Subic Bay Naval Station and Cubi Point airfield were linchpins to the United States presence in the Pacific and the counter-threat to world communist expansion.

Bud Lammers found McGirt with the troops manning the rails. "Yup, smells like the P.I.," Bud said as the pungent scent of land merged lazily with the salty sea breeze. "Rayburn and Brightness are going to fly in the advance team. You want a seat onboard?"

McGirt stared at the craggy tropical landscape in the distance. "Nah... I'll ride in on the boat with you guys. Anybody call ahead for rooms at the BOQ?" he asked, referring to the Bachelor Officer's Quarters on a plateau high above the airfield.

"Jenks is already on it. He cornered that chief yeoman from the Mishap Team and made him swear to reserve rooms for the Detachment. Says they go way back to boot camp and the 'pencil pushing puke' owes him a favor."

"Leave it to Jenks," McGirt said. "One way or another that sumbitch always gets it done, doesn't he?"

"Guess it's a chief thing." Bud threw up his hands. "I don't want to know." Both men shared a laugh at the tight bond that existed between the Navy's chief petty officers, who inevitably found a way to fix things, procure a spare part or solve complex problems. Bud had learned early on that after giving an order, it was usually best to steer clear and let the pragmatic enlisted leaders do as they saw fit.

"Hey, almost forgot to give this to you," Bud said. He reached into his back pocket and handed over an envelope. "The H-3 dropped some mail when they came back to pick up Riggs." It was a letter from McGirt's sister in Michigan. The powder-blue stationery was adorned with brightly colored seashells, leaping dolphins and palm trees.

"Must be visiting Mom in Florida," McGirt said. He tore open the letter and began to read happily.

"I get a kick out of seeing her letters and packages," Lammers said. "It's always something different."

"Yeah... she's that way. Nothing gets between her and the things she loves. I can't remember how many times she got spanked for drawing on everything — walls, desktops, even her white sneakers one time." He read a few more lines and smiled. "Anything from Jill?"

"Nope, and to tell the truth, I don't really give a damn. I'll try to call when we check in at the Q. Getting an overseas line is always a pain in the ass, though, and expensive as hell. She's probably already packed up and left town." Bud's anger at his wife had resurfaced. *Why the hell did Jill decide to drop this bombshell on me now?* he thought to himself. *Doesn't she know I have more than the marriage to worry about? What the hell does she expect from me, anyway?*

The boatswain's whistle blew over the ship's 1MC, followed by a call to flight quarters. "I'll help Carbs in the Tower," McGirt said as he refolded the letter and tucked it away.

"Good. Lugansky wants to see me before we make it abeam Grande

Island. We have to go over plans to get your aircraft craned onto the pier and flat-bedded to a hangar at Cubi."

McGirt lowered his eyes and gazed absently at the wake spreading out from the ship's bow. He spit and watched it disappear into the sea foam. "Right," he said. "See ya later."

* * *

Rayburn and Brightness manned up Sideflare Zero-One for the short hop to Cubi Point. The ship was less than twenty miles from the harbor's entrance; however, steaming at barely twelve knots, it would take her a couple hours to rendezvous with tugs, be guided into a mooring and lower the gangplank. The helicopter would set down at Cubi in less than fifteen minutes.

The aircraft was jam-packed with aviation mechanics and toolboxes. Among the passengers were Freddy Lincoln and L. C. LaRue, both still grounded after the mishap. Once ashore, the crew would set up shop at the detachment's land-based facility while the damaged helo was repaired. After a foothold was established at the transient hangar, they'd be free to get some rest, go into town or start drinking at the enlisted men's club at the top of the hill. With the carrier's huge air wing already in port — the floating airport and her escorts had arrived a full day ahead of *San Angelo* — the naval base and Olongapo would be swarming with sailors hell-bent on cramming as much fun as possible into the port call.

Rayburn was the helicopter aircraft commander, or HAC, for this short transport mission. Although he outranked Bright by nearly five years seniority, during their long deployment Bright had logged triple the flight hours. Rayburn had spent the majority of his time on the Bridge, cuddling up with the blackshoes in pursuit of his shipboard Surface Warfare qualifications.

"Hey, Bob, I haven't flown for a while. Mind if I take this one?" he'd asked during their pre-flight briefing. After the storms had passed and the Mishap Team had departed, Rayburn's sinus problem had miraculously disappeared.

"I feel great today," Rayburn had told the doc earlier that morning. "Guess I just needed a good night's sleep." The physician examined him and then scribbled an "up chit" signifying that he was fit to fly. As he'd handed over the slip, the doc had simply said, "Interesting..."

Early morning clouds had built up steadily over the lush jungle that surrounded Subic Bay, promising the predictable band of afternoon thunderstorms. A strong wind blew from the east, tumbling over the mountains and causing whitecaps on the typically placid harbor. Rayburn lifted the helo into a hover, initially ignoring the LSE's guidance and doing a pedal turn in the wrong direction.

"Right, right, right!" Brightness hollered over the intercom.

"Oh, yeah, that's what I meant to do. Thanks, Bob," Rayburn said. He laughed nervously at his error and maneuvered the aircraft into a wobbly, yawing climb. He leveled off abruptly at one thousand feet, switched on the autopilot and pulled out a notebook from his helmet bag. After a couple minutes of writing, he spoke. "Bob, when we shut down, fill out the logbook and make sure that everybody gets things squared away."

"What do you mean?" Brightness asked. The runway was straight ahead at about five miles.

"You know... make sure the guys secure everything before they go into town. Jenks is on the ship to help off-load McGirt's wreck and I've got business to tend to up on the hill. Sorry."

"Sure, Lieutenant, I'll cover for you," Brightness said. The dark helmet visor obscured the fact that his eyes were seething. "Must be something pretty important."

Rayburn served up a smarmy smile and put down the notebook. He raised his visor and said with deadpan seriousness, "As a matter of fact, it is quite important." He then continued writing. Brightness saw some neatly written paragraphs intermixed with columns of numbers resembling a ledger.

"Mind if we make a low pass over Grande Island?" Bright said. "I want to get some pictures of those disappearing guns I've been reading about."

"OK, but just one turn, that's all we have time for." Rayburn slipped the notebook back into his bag and pointed to his wristwatch. "Don't want to waste the taxpayers' dollars drilling holes in the sky." He left on the autopilot and guided the bird down to five hundred feet over the water while Bright dug out a small Instamatic camera from his flight suit pocket.

"What the hell's a smart M.I.T. grad doing with a pathetic-looking thing like that?" Rayburn asked.

"Well, I'm saving up, sir. Hope to see if there's any thirty-five millimeters on sale at the Navy Exchange."

Rayburn shook his head. "Next time, I'll let you borrow one of my Nikons. That thing you've got is an embarrassment. Here, I'll drop down lower so at least something recognizable will be in the snapshot."

Rayburn turned off the auto-flight controls and let the helicopter settle into a slow descent, stopping at two hundred feet. They made a wide circle around the rectangular-shaped island that guarded Subic Bay. The tiny outpost, formerly a garrison known as Fort Wint, had a long and colorful history. After being defeated during the Spanish-American War of 1898, more than one thousand Spanish soldiers had fled nearby Olongapo, seeking refuge on Grande Island before surrendering. At different times, the Spanish, American and Filipino forces had manned the small patch of earth with armament, protecting the harbor's entrance. The Japanese held it during their three-year occupation of the country during World War II. In 1975, Grande Island had served as a relief camp for hundreds of Vietnamese who'd been rescued by American ships as communist forces overran their nation. Absent any conflicts, the island was now used as a rest and recreation facility for picnics, camping and softball games.

"Darn, I'm having trouble finding those gun batteries," Bright said as he squinted into the camera's thimble-sized viewfinder. "You know, I read an article about them last year; maybe they're not here any more. Let's go. I'll ride the motorboat over tomorrow and take a look."

"Good idea, we're wasting time," Rayburn said. He jerked the controls, causing Bright to fumble the camera and drop it on the cockpit floor. He then nosed the aircraft over and added power to accelerate, but he failed to compensate for the big pitch over. Within seconds, they'd dropped to fifty feet off the water while still a couple miles from the runway. Rayburn sheepishly eased the cyclic back, climbed and found the autopilot switch.

"Tower clears us to land, sir. Wind is right down runway seven at twenty-five knots. With this heavy load aboard, we're set up perfectly for a roll-on landing and a trip through the wash rack," Brightness reported. It was standard procedure for aircraft returning from salt-laden, at-sea operations to taxi between an array of nozzles that drenched the fuselage in fresh water.

"Not today, Ensign. Tell the Tower that we'll fly down the runway and land at the helo pad by the hangar."

"But with all due respect, sir, Chief Jenks wants us to go through the wash rack before we park. He asked me specifically to do that."

"Is Jenks the aircraft commander?" Rayburn said harshly. He tapped a finger on the leather name tag Velcroed to his flight suit. Rayburn lowered his voice to emphasize the point. "Ensign, have the crew give her a good hosing when we shutdown."

Bright nodded that he understood. LaRue came up from the back and wedged himself between the two pilot's seats. Despite being officially off the flight schedule, he'd donned his gear for the ride and surreptitiously plugged into the intercom while Sartelli readied the cabin for landing. He bent forward and found Bright's Instamatic hiding beneath the ensign's seat.

Cubi's control tower cleared Sideflare Zero-One to make a low pass down the runway and then fly east of the field, over the bay. From there, Rayburn planned to reverse course and land on the painted helicopter spot adjacent to the maintenance hangar, performing a land-based version of the button hook maneuver that Brightness had mastered the day before.

Rayburn's ham-fisted flying smoothed out as they zipped down the runway at one hundred twenty knots and fifty feet above the concrete. "Watch this," he said confidently as they crossed over the runway's upwind end and raced low level over the bay. He then made a hard right turn and pointed the nose at the helo pad. But the friendly headwind he'd enjoyed while flat-hatting the tower now became his nemesis, causing the aircraft's track and closure rate to change dramatically. Like an overbearing mother-in-law, the strong tailwind pushed them off-course from behind. The machine was zooming perilously toward the hangar.

"Too fast!" LaRue and Bright shouted in unison. With no way to salvage the approach, Rayburn pulled an armful of collective and full back stick, propelling the aircraft into an extreme, nose-high attitude. The helicopter rocketed skyward, overshot the landing pad and came to a clumsy, dangling hover two hundred feet in the air. Bright looked down through the helo's chin bubble below his feet and saw a working party of Marines scattering for cover. Rayburn edged the bird backwards, sighted the landing spot and settled cautiously to the ground. He taxied close to the hangar and set the parking brake.

"Shut 'er down, will you, Bob?" he said. His voice was shaky, but still full of the forced baritone that the crew loved to mock. Bright dutifully pulled back the two engine control levers and switched on the rotor brake. In a few seconds, all motion and noise stopped. Rayburn was first to peel off his helmet and unstrap.

"Boy, that wind really shifted at the last second, didn't it?" He grabbed his flight gear and unlatched a suitcase from the cabin. Sartelli and the rest of the group had already bolted down the rear ramp and began unloading. Rayburn high-stepped through them and across the tarmac. He found a private having a smoke next to a faded gray government pickup. Rayburn heaved his bag into the truck and said a few words to the young Marine. The private saluted, then hopped in behind the wheel. They drove out the hangar complex and onto the steep road that led up to the BOQ.

Bright finished powering down the bird's electronics. LaRue climbed into the vacant cockpit seat and wiped his sweat-soaked face with the leather palm of a flight glove. He squeezed a stream of tobacco juice out from his lips into a styrofoam cup.

"Sir, what... was that?" he asked.

Bright stowed the shutdown checklist and slouched back in his seat. "I don't know, Petty Officer LaRue, I don't know."

Chapter 18

Bud, McGirt and Jenks were the last ones to leave the building after they'd coordinated moving the crippled helicopter into place at the transient squadron hangar. Once again, Jenks came through in the clutch. This time he'd finagled a deal with his Marine counterpart whose squadron was also occupying the hangar. Within five minutes of the gunnery sergeant barking out a string of fierce orders, one of his own unit's helicopters had been towed onto the tarmac and a space was cleared for McGirt's aircraft. The Japanese technicians, five of them, had arrived the night before. They'd set up their gear neatly in the corner.

When Bud had approached the team leader and introduced himself, he respectfully offered the only Japanese greeting he knew, *ko-nee-chee-wah*, meaning hello, bowed at the waist and extended his hand. The slight, middle-aged man, dressed in slacks and a sport shirt, dutifully returned the greeting. He got closer to Bud and whispered in perfect English that he was an American citizen and had graduated from UCLA with a master's degree in engineering. "Yoshihiro Ogawa, call me Yoshi," he said. He confided that, after living most of his life in southern California, he'd returned home to help his aging parents and began working with the Kawasaki Company. The corporation had a contract to handle field repairs for the Navy when the job was beyond the squadron's own expertise. His team was comprised of seasoned experts who'd been turning wrenches before the majority of Bud's mechanics were born.

Bud couldn't resist confirming the rumor that Jenks had been spreading. "Do you guys really camp out in the hangar and cook your own food?"

Yoshi laughed heartily. He pointed to a couple of folded cots by the wall and said, "Yes, we'll be working around the clock in twelve-hour shifts. Occasionally, one of us will need a nap." He went on to say that the men also had private rooms at the BOQ, and that it was easier for them to prepare their own food to save time. Bud glanced over at Jenks, who'd befriended the other foreigners and was huddled beneath the aircraft's damaged nose section. The four mechs wore spotless white coveralls and listened intently, muttering rapid-fire *hais* while Jenks spoke in Brooklyn-laced aviation lingo and recreated the crash with his big hands. McGirt squatted in a crouched position nearby, preferring to let the senior enlisted man do the talking.

The sun was getting low on the horizon and Bud sensed that the Japanese were anxious to be left alone. They'd rested while waiting for *San Angelo* to dock and would work at full strength this first night. Confident that there was nothing more to discuss, Jenks, McGirt and Bud headed for the parking lot and climbed into a bulky gray passenger van that Jenks' Marine buddy had commandeered from the motor pool. As they tossed their bags into the back, they heard the whine of air-powered tools. The Japanese workers had begun disassembling the mangled nose section, rivet by rivet.

"Well, sir, let's keep our fingers crossed that them fellas can get it done pronto," Jenks said. "The longer we sit here in port, the more I worry about my boys getting into trouble. They're all tapped out from the last liberty call and were looking forward to saving up some dough on the way to Singapore." Bud and McGirt agreed: there was nothing more harmful to a unit's morale than young sailors with idle time and no money in their pockets. Whenever work assignments were doled out, the detachment's youngsters felt obligated to complain like teenagers asked to take out the trash. Nonetheless, after years of running maintenance shops, Jenks trusted the adage: a busy sailor is a happy sailor.

"It'd be helpful, sir, if we could schedule some flights to keep the kids busy."

"I agree, Chief," Bud replied. "The air station can always use an extra aircraft with their runs up to Clark and the Embassy in Manila. I'll check in with Base Operations in the morning. At the very least, we can schedule some training flights."

"Thanks, Commander," Jenks said. "Mind if we give these guys a lift, sir?" He pointed to a handful of sailors making their way up the hill on foot. Their dungaree shirts were darkened with perspiration.

After dropping off their passengers at the enlisted barracks, Jenks turned into the BOQ's circular drive, where Bud and McGirt got out. The complex at the top of the hill was tightly clustered on a lush verdant plateau, high above the airfield. Like the runway below, the facility had been a massive project painstakingly carved from the jungle. Every building looked the same: blunt, concrete-block walls and flat roofs designed to withstand the onslaught of a typhoon's wind and rain. The fortress-like structures were painted white to reflect the intense, ever-present Philippine heat.

Bud and McGirt heard whoops and hollers from behind the building when they got out of the van. The poolside bar at the center of the billeting complex was jammed with partying aviators grateful to be back on terra firma. Bud and McGirt ignored the revelry and dragged their gear into the Q's lobby.

"Mee-ster Lammers?" said the cute Filipino woman behind the desk. "I have message for you." She handed Bud a small yellow piece of paper that had been folded over and taped shut. Bud opened the note and read: "Call Colonel Jacobs. IMPORTANT." He reached for the phone that the woman had hoisted up from her desk to the countertop before she discreetly disappeared to an anteroom. McGirt grabbed a couple of registration cards and began filling them out.

"Yes sir, Lieutenant Commander Bud Lammers, returning your call." The senior Marine launched into a tirade, reaming Bud loudly enough for McGirt to overhear. For the next two minutes, the only words that Bud could get out were "yes sir," "no sir," and "OK."

"Absolutely, Colonel. Yes, sir," Bud said solemnly. The Marine got in the last word and hung up. Bud's face was ashen as McGirt slid a card across the counter for him to sign.

"Apparently Rayburn scared the living shit out of some Marines outside the hangar today. That was the C.O. of the Air Group. Guess you could tell he wasn't inviting us over for dinner."

McGirt had deplored working with Rayburn during the cruise. He felt like saying something, but figured he'd only make matters worse. After all, his mishap was the only reason that the Detachment was here at Cubi Point anyway. If it weren't for his and Uker's screw-up, *San Angelo* would be halfway to Singapore by now.

The cheerful, smiling clerk reappeared with their keys. "Sorry, sirs. You have to share room tonight. Air Wing here and we full. I put you on third floor with Mr. Blight and Mr. Carboni."

"That'll be fine," Bud said. He heard McGirt chuckle at the woman's earnest but failed attempt to pronounce the names correctly. They thanked her and headed up the stairs to their room. On the way, they passed by a window overlooking the pool area. The patio was jammed with dozens of male bodies and a handful of daring females who'd joined the crowd. In the pool's shallow end, a game of basketball was underway. "Animal rules" prevailed, which meant there were no rules. Organized sides didn't seem to exist as the mob wrestled and flailed in a splashing swirl of motion. Occasionally someone tossed the ball in the vicinity of the backboard and net rigged to the pool's edge, a couple feet above the water. At the far end of the deck was a shallow wading pool normally reserved for children; however, with families nowhere in sight, it now teemed with sprawling sailors gulping beer from plastic cups.

"Looks like everyone's got a head start on us," Bud said as they looked down from the third-floor railing. "I was gonna try and call Jill tonight, but screw it… let's change and get over to the club. I need a drink."

Bright and Carbone had already unloaded their bags, showered and left. The space that would house the four pilots for the next several days looked identical to every other room in the building: ten foot ceilings, two sets of metal bunks, one chest of drawers and a small desk. A tiny bathroom comprised of a commode, shower stall and sink was located off to one side and shared with the adjoining room. With up to eight sailors using the same austere facilities, it wasn't uncommon for your neighbor to hop in the shower while you sat on the toilet and your roommate brushed his teeth two feet away.

The rooms exuded the warmth of a hospital ward with their concrete block walls painted in a glossy, pale shade of green. To a civilian, the place would be graded as a low budget motel. But to a weary sailor fed up with cramped life at sea, it felt like the Ritz. Bud and his crew would gladly pay the five dollar per night rate for the opportunity to get ashore and spend time in a quasi-normal setting.

The Cubi Point Officers' Club was in full swing when Bud and McGirt stepped through its ornately carved mahogany doors. Happy hour prices had just ended without anyone noticing; the revelry carried on without missing a beat. The multi-tiered building was packed with officers, wives and girlfriends. Its more formal upper level contained a dining room, a bandstand and a sunken parquet dance floor. To one side was a cozy barroom adorned with squadron plaques, which covered nearly every inch of its wall space. The plaques displayed unit logos and names of pilots who'd deployed before, during and after the Vietnam War. In effect, the plaques chronicled unique chapters in naval history through images of growling tigers, screaming eagles and scantily clad women in provocative poses.

A staircase led to the club's lower level, better known as the "ready room" or "flight suit bar." Because flying garb was prohibited upstairs, this was the favorite spot for aviators, especially the young, single ones. Loud music, a shuffleboard table and sassy Filipino waitresses greeted the officers as they shook off their sea legs and enjoyed time ashore.

"Looks like the bar's pretty crowded," McGirt said. "Want to sit in the dining room?"

With the air wing in port, there wasn't a vacant stool or table in the topside bar as jet jocks huddled together telling sea stories. Many of them were dressed in loud, colored jumpsuits commonly know as "sierra hotels" or "shit-hots." McGirt had derisively tabbed the off-duty wear as "Bozo-the-Clown-suits." He and Bud were each attired in their usual O'Club garb: short-sleeved sport shirts, dark dress slacks, and penny loafers.

"Yeah, circus is in town," Bud said after seeing the throng of pilots. "Dining room tonight." The two found a spot overlooking the stage where a trio of Filipinos was setting up their instruments to play.

"Is that Rayburn?" McGirt asked. He pointed across the dance floor to a large table by the windows.

Bud squinted to see in the room's dim lighting. "Yup. I'll be right back." He stood up and walked down the steps to the dance floor. "Order me a double scotch, will ya?" he said over his shoulder.

Still smarting from the ass-chewing he'd gotten over the phone, Bud approached Rayburn. "Thomas, I'd like a word with you," he demanded. The table talk subsided as Bud took Rayburn by the arm and guided him out of earshot of the group.

"What the fuck happened when you and Brightness landed today?"

Rayburn looked back at his friends. The group had turned their sights outside to the panorama overlooking Subic Bay and the airfield. An F-14 Tomcat had just lifted off the runway. Its afterburners lit up the sky like two fiery rockets. Rayburn smiled at the group as they resumed conversation. "It's under control, Bud. See that guy at the end of the table?"

Bud eyed the fellow, a tough-looking jarhead in civvies. Whenever in Subic, Rayburn snubbed staying in the austere BOQ, choosing instead to bunk with his married friend in base housing. The Marine sported a no-nonsense "high and tight" brush cut. His upper body was chiseled like McGirt's, except he was taller and at least thirty pounds heavier.

"Classmate of mine at the Academy. He works for the colonel you talked to." Bud was stunned that Rayburn knew about the phone call that had taken place less than an hour ago. "They play golf every week and the colonel's daughter baby-sits my buddy's kids. Trust me... it'll go away."

Rayburn headed for his seat, but Bud grabbed him by the shoulder. "Listen to me. I'm not finished." Rayburn stopped in his tracks and glanced toward the table, where a waiter had appeared with a tray full of shots.

"Listen, Bud, I know where you're going with this, but believe it or not, I'm your best hope. You know my connections back in San Diego."

Bud loosened his grip. Although he'd only been aboard HCS-30 for a year, it hadn't taken him long to figure out who the squadron's movers and shakers were. Lieutenant Thomas Rayburn III and his wife, Madeline, were kingpins in the unit. They lived on the same street as the commanding officer and his spouse, and the two women were close friends. Wherever the skipper's wife went, it seemed that obsequious Maddy Rayburn was close behind.

Bud felt powerless in the presence of the smooth-talking golden boy. Word around the squadron always led to the same conclusion about Rayburn: nothing bad stuck to his Teflon-coated reputation. Stay out of his way or you'd get squashed like a tortoise trying to outrun a steamroller.

The big Marine shouted out, "Hey, Thomas, hurry up! We're itching to light off these shots."

Rayburn waved back and then placed a hand on Bud's shoulder. He got close enough for Bud to smell the alcohol on his breath. "I know it's tough on you, Boss — getting passed over, trouble with your wife, and now McGirt's crash. If there's something that I can do to help out, just let me know."

Bud stood speechless, stunned at the junior officer's arrogance. There was nothing constructive for him to say, so he just walked away. A raucous howl erupted from behind him as he crossed the dance floor. Rayburn's posse had downed their drinks and broken into a chant. A few couples drifted onto the parquet as the trio played an upbeat instrumental version of a popular tune. As he picked his way through the dancers, Bud wondered how Rayburn knew about Jill leaving him. Her letter had arrived less than a week ago and McGirt was the only person he'd told.

"Boss, here's your scotch. Lurch brought us some warm rolls too," McGirt said with a mouth stuffed full of bread. "You look like you've seen a ghost. What happened over there?" McGirt guzzled the last of his coke, and a tall, stone-faced Filipino quickly appeared with a refill.

Bud was mesmerized by the happy faces on the dance floor. "What... what was that?"

"Rayburn," McGirt repeated. "What gives with him?"

"Uh... said he's got it under control. Apparently, the goon at the end of his table is tight with the colonel who ripped me on the phone."

The waiter returned with pad and pencil ready for their order. Although his name tag read "Jimmy," for as long as anyone could remember, everyone had called him "Lurch" based on his resemblance to a well-known character on television.

"Lapu lapu, please," McGirt ordered.

"Same for me, Lurch," Bud said. He sipped his drink and gazed over at Rayburn's table.

"That son of a bitch has got you by the short hairs, doesn't he?" McGirt said.

Bud nodded slowly and rubbed the top of his head. A burst of light reflected off the picture window as the rowdy group torched off another round.

McGirt felt badly about the quip. "Hey, Boss, I was out of line. I got no room to judge, especially after what went down with me and Puker the other night."

Bud stared into his half empty glass. "Oh... I didn't want to ruin the evening any further, but since you brought it up, Paul stayed on the ship instead of joining the rest of us. He turned in his wings today. XO called me to his office this morning and said Uker came to him late last night. Apparently he was too embarrassed to approach one of us."

"You talk with him yet?" McGirt asked.

"Sure, first thing I did after leaving the XO. But honestly, can't say that I blame him for pulling the plug. His heart hasn't been in the cockpit for a long time. He'll be happier reassigned to a non-flying billet, or as a civilian. He seemed like a different guy when I talked to him. First time I'd seen him smile in weeks. Like a big weight had been lifted off his shoulders."

Lurch delivered two steaming platters of locally caught fish complimented with vegetables, rice and a fresh basket of rolls. Bud noticed that the meticulous server had also brought him another scotch. He looked up to say thanks, but Lurch had already disappeared to another table.

"XO's working on some orders for him as we speak. He'll probably be off the ship before we get underway."

"Damn," McGirt said, dropping his fork to the table. Until now, he'd made it his mission to stay upbeat since the crash. After hearing the news about Uker, however, he couldn't help but get down on himself. He fought back the urge and started to eat. "How's your fish?" he asked.

"About the same as it's been the last six months. Not bad, but I'd rather be eating some Pacific snapper back home."

The crowd swelled at the O Club. Bud and McGirt were lucky to have snagged a table for the night. By the looks of the dance floor, several of the carrier's pilots had flown their wives in for the port call. Bud thought about Jill spending months alone at their San Diego condominium. When he'd nixed their plans to rendezvous in Manila, it had seemed like the right thing to do. The deployment had been going so spectacularly well that he'd been hesitant to take leave and entertain his wife. Now, seeing the joyful couples swaying to the music, he regretted that decision. He'd tell her so, later, when he called home — not that he expected it to make any difference. Lurch materialized again with dessert menus. Both men declined. McGirt ordered coffee; Bud chose another scotch.

"J. J., I don't know how any of this will pan out. My career's pretty much on the ropes." Bud took a healthy swig from his glass. "You haven't said much about the Mishap Board. How are you getting along with all of this?"

McGirt was taken back by Bud's directness. Despite the fact that they'd shared a tiny bunkroom and worked closely together for months, it wasn't like Lammers to delve into the "touchy-feely" side of things.

McGirt sat back in his chair and said, "Out of my hands now. Riggs and his guys have got all the dirt on me. Reckon I'm in for a good whuppin', so to speak." He chomped on a toothpick and looked across the dance floor at Rayburn and his disciples. All eyes were on Thomas, who was deep into telling a yarn.

"Guess we're not part of the in-crowd tonight," Bud said as he and McGirt watched the party on the other side of the room.

"Yeah, well, if that's what it takes, count me out. That's not my kind of crowd." McGirt looked away and sipped some coffee. Bud drained his scotch in a single swallow.

"Hey, Bud, not to sound like the pain in the ass that I am sometimes, but it'll be a long haul if I've got to carry your drunk ass up to the Q." McGirt forced a chuckle to convey that he was only half serious.

"I'll be all right; just feeling sorry for myself." Bud paused and shook his head dolefully. "Man, I really blew it with Jill, didn't I?" He swirled his drink and stared into the glass. "You know McGirt, she's never let me down. Always been there for me. Guess I started taking her for granted. I should've seen this coming, you know?" The thought of living alone was finally setting in on Bud. He'd known Jill most of his life and wasn't sure how he'd get along without her — probably not too well.

"Maybe you can call her later tonight. It'll be morning on the coast," McGirt said, checking his watch.

"I'll try and get an outside line when we get back to the Q, but I'm not getting my hopes up. She's probably back in Virginia Beach by now." Bud raised his hand to signal Lurch he was ready for another. Freed from inhibition, he asked, "I never thought it was my business, J. J., but why is it that you don't drink?"

McGirt reddened and laughed. "Yeah, I get asked that from time to time. I used to, that's for sure. Me and my buddies liked to sneak six-packs into the woods when I was in high school. Then one day I had to quit."

Bud raised his eyebrows, anticipating more. McGirt's gaze drifted down to the tablecloth. He cracked a weak smile and fiddled with his silverware. "You really don't want to hear this shit tonight, do you, Bud?"

Lammers hoisted his glass in a mock toast and took a swig of the smoky-flavored liquid. He then leaned forward sternly, expecting an answer. McGirt fidgeted a bit more in his chair, put both hands together in front of him and sat up straight.

"I had an uncle who worked at the B-24 bomber plant in Ypsilanti during the war. Later, when General Motors converted it over to making car parts, he helped my daddy get a job on the assembly line there. So many of us southerners came into town, folks started calling the place Ypsi-tucky. It wasn't a term of endearment. We were thought of as white trash." Bud ignored the commotion around them, captivated by his roommate's revelation.

"Anyway, from the time I was a young 'un in Kentucky, seemed like the old man was always drunk. After coming up north, he settled down for a while, but by the time I was in high school he was back at it pretty hard. Never laid a hand on me, Sis or Mom, but there weren't many nights that he didn't pass out in his easy chair, too sloshed to climb up to bed."

Bud set down his drink and listened intently. McGirt paused, cleared his throat and continued. "Then it all ended one October night. It was a Thursday, I remember, the day before a big game. He and some UAW buddies stopped at a roadside bar after work. On the way home he ran a stop sign on Michigan Ave and t-boned a lady and her three little ones. Killed her and one of the kids. Not that it matters, but her husband was a prominent doctor in Ann Arbor, a surgeon at the University of Michigan hospital. The press made it a huge deal. My dad was brought up on charges of vehicular homicide."

"How long was the sentence?" Bud asked. A sick look came over McGirt's face, and Bud wished he'd never asked the question. "Listen, I'm sorry I..."

"No, that's OK, might as well finish it up. The case didn't even make it to trial. He put a shotgun to his chest out in the back yard the day after his brother posted bond and got him out of jail." Bud sat speechless and let him continue.

"The hell of it was, he had enough control not to drink on the days I had a football game — never. From pee-wee league on up through high school, he'd show up at games stone-sober. Win or lose, he'd go home and toe the line that night too. After we buried him, my teammates congregated out in the woods for some beers. I drank half a bottle, but it tasted like skunk piss to me. Haven't had an ounce, or even cared to, ever since. That was ten years ago."

The music picked up tempo as a gorgeous Filipino songstress joined the trio on stage. Her long raven hair was pulled across one shoulder, draping to the waistline of her flowery turquoise sarong. She moved gracefully to the beat and sang a cheery tune that drew more people onto the floor. Both men welcomed a break from McGirt's tragic story.

"She's beautiful, isn't she?" McGirt said as he tapped a foot. "Pretty good voice, too." The place was alive with joyous partiers who wanted the night to go on forever, refusing to accept that in a few days the wives would fly home as their husbands headed back out to sea. The band rocked on, building to a crescendo that led the audience to clap enthusiastically. Lammers and McGirt joined everyone in a standing ovation when the entertainers went on break. Lurch cleared their plates and left the bill. "No hurry, sir," he mumbled.

McGirt sensed that Bud was at a loss for words, so he volunteered, "Want to sit tight and listen a while longer when the band returns?" Bud marveled at how McGirt had put away the glum details of his father's demise and moved forward. By comparison, his own upbringing in Virginia had been as uneventful as an episode of *Ozzie and Harriet*.

"Sure." For some reason—probably the scotch—Bud blurted out, "You ever wonder why I got passed over?"

"I only heard the rumors, Bud. Never had a cause to ask you." McGirt picked up the check and reached for his wallet to pony his share. "How much you want to give Lurch? I think he was exceptionally good tonight."

"Naw... you need to know the facts, J. J." A mild slur had crept into Bud's speech. His face was flushed from the alcohol.

"Not necessary, Boss. You know, on second thought, I'm pretty tuckered out. Think I might just call it a night." McGirt got to his feet but Lammers reached across the table and shoved him back into his seat.

"Sit down, Lieutenant, that's an order." McGirt's jaw tensed as he slumped down into his chair. He'd never seen the Detachment's Officer In Charge this way and he wasn't enjoying it. What had started out as a relaxed dinner was rapidly turning ugly. He crossed his arms over his chest and sat expressionless, waiting for Bud to speak.

"Sorry about that, but I think you need to hear it from the horse's mouth. You told me about your pa, now it's my turn." His words were slow and deliberate. He knew that he was inebriated, and if he were to tell the story, he'd have to do it soon.

"I was a brand-new lieutenant commander, attached to a Huey gunship squadron in Vietnam. I'd volunteered for combat duty while stationed in Norfolk. Jill stayed there while I went through some training with the Army at Fort Rucker, and then I deployed overseas. Our primary mission in-country was to provide air cover for the Navy's river boat squadrons."

"Yeah, Operation Game Warden," McGirt said. "Some of my instructors in Pensacola had spent time over there and told me a little about it. Said that whoever controlled the waterways controlled South Vietnam."

"You got it," Bud said. "The country's road and rail systems were rudimentary. Nearly everything travels on the river to get where it needs to go. The quickest way for the Vietcong to transport their weapons was on the rivers and canals, the same waterways that the merchants and rice farmers moved their goods on. Our PBRs patrolled the waters and interdicted when they found weapons smuggled on sampans."

McGirt leaned back in his chair and nodded.

Bud rolled the glass between his palms. "We'd inserted a half dozen SEALs deep into the bush, about thirty klicks up the river from our camp at Binh Thuy. They'd joined up with South Vietnamese Regional Forces and were looking for some bad guys out there who'd been hassling the villagers. On his way out the door, the SEALs' leader comes up to me. He's a young officer, no older than Brightness. He smiles, taps me on the shoulder and says, 'See you later, sir. Don't forget us.' I tell him not to worry, that we'll be back. About eight hours pass. When we went back to retrieve them, a line of weather had moved in. Big-assed thunderstorms like the ones you see around here all the time. We'd been given a briefing on the radio that we could expect good conditions for the duration of the mission. It must have been some hung-over, eighteen-year-old weatherguesser with his head up his ass. Man, did he get it wrong. Halfway there, my escort gunship has a transmission failure and has to land in a rice paddy. As fire team leader, I pressed on alone, like John fucking Wayne.

"We get within few kilometers of the pickup zone and start to lose sight of the ground. It's coming down in buckets and we can't see to find our way, so I change course and try to do an end run around the weather. But that track puts me directly over a hot zone. I'd flown through the same spot the day before and taken heavy fire, wounding one of my door gunners. It's no different this time. At such a low altitude, we're getting pelted with small arms fire, so I turn tail. By now, there's a solid wall of storms between us and the SEALs. With nowhere to go, I head back to Binh Thuy. The SEAL team's boss at headquarters has already radioed our base and he's going ape-shit. Thirty minutes had elapsed since our rendezvous time and his boys are under ambush, wondering where the hell I am. By the time we're able to get back, all but one of them is dead. The lone survivor is the young platoon leader — the one I promised we'd be back. I'll never forget the look on his face as we hauled him aboard. One of his legs was tore up real bad, barely still attached. He didn't need to say a word; his eyes said it all. He and his team get slaughtered while I'm sitting on my yellow ass waiting for the sun to come out." Bud stared angrily at his drink. "After the war, I looked him up at the hospital. Found him alone in his room, sitting in a wheelchair and missing a leg. His head was hung low. I didn't have the guts to face him and left without him knowing that I'd ever been there."

"It would have been suicide pressing through that hot zone," McGirt said.

"Well, guys flew through that stuff every day. Some got shot down in the process and others got through. I made my choice and it's been following me around like a dark shadow ever since."

"It's easy to be a Monday-morning quarterback. Sounds like you did the best you could under the circumstances. You had to protect your own crew," McGirt said.

"Yeah? Well, who the hell knows?" Bud downed the last of his watery drink. "Let's go," he said.

On their way out, they passed Brightness and Carbone, who'd just arrived. "You sissies turning in for some beauty rest?" Carbone shouted at them. He and Brightness were wavering down the hallway, bumping into each other as they walked.

"Jenks invited us over to the Chief's Club, so we had a few," Bright added. The two junior officers were an odd couple: Carbone nearly six feet with the physique of an aging wrestler and Bright with the innocent look of an altar boy. Ironically, despite the fact that Carbone was the Detachment's second oldest officer, he'd formed a special kinship with Bright and his childlike enthusiasm.

"Looks like all the snobs are topside tonight, Bobby." Carbone drifted toward the staircase leading to the Ready Room.

"You seen Puker or Rayburn?" Brightness asked. Carbone was already at the bottom, engulfed by the rowdy mob in the lower bar.

"Paul had some business on the ship," Bud said. He skipped the news about Uker turning in his wings. The Det would find out soon enough. "Rayburn's in the dining room."

"See you guys tomorrow. Don't wait up," Bright said. On that note, he stood at the top of the stairs and raised his arms up like an Olympian preparing to make a dive. He let out a screaming whoop and hurled himself forward in a tip-toeing flurry. When he stumbled on the last few steps, a mass of green flight-suited bodies caught him before he hit the floor.

Once back at the Q, Bud changed his mind about calling the States and went to bed.

* * *

Carbone and Bright found their way to the Ready Room's shuffleboard table. They'd run off a streak of victories — with each win, garnering a draft beer from their opponents. Most of Bright's drinks sat on a window ledge, going warm and flat. The same couldn't be said for Carbone's. The stout Bostonian delighted not only in defeating his rivals, but chugging down the twelve-ounce drafts and toasting the losers to rub it in.

"Bobby-boy, explain to me again the finer points of Sir Isaac's theory, will you?" Carbs hollered for all to hear. "They didn't talk much about that where I got my degree."

The baby-faced M.I.T. grad launched into a rehearsed performance of the nutty professor, replete with waving arms and eyeglasses cocked askew. Standing on a chair, Brightness spewed strings of multisyllabic words expounding on the famed scientist's hypothesis of energy, mass and motion. The setting of chrome-plated pucks skidding over sawdust and hardwood was the ideal laboratory for the young engineer/pilot to hone his teaching skills. By contrast, his sidekick had earned a college degree via correspondence courses and night school. In Carbone's neighborhood, the term "Newton" was more commonly associated with a fig-filled cookie. Over the last several months, the duo had perfected their Abbott and Costello-style routine.

Finally, after an hour and a half, they'd had enough and decided to deliberately throw a match. They climbed the stairs to the dining room level and joined the throng of patrons exiting the building and walking back to the Q. Spotting Rayburn and his entourage, Carbone charged ahead and grabbed hold of him from behind, hoisting him up in a sweaty bear hug.

"Rayburn, you dip-shit, how you doin'?" he said in his thickest Northeastern brogue. He held tight and bounced Rayburn in the air as if he were on a pogo stick.

"That's enough!" Rayburn said with a condescending laugh. Carbone squeezed harder, let out growl and dropped him to the floor like an empty cardboard box. Rayburn brushed off his shirt and slacks as if Carbone had just given him fleas.

"You and your girlfriends too good to drink with the rest of us downstairs?" Carbone said. Sensing an impending disaster, Brightness wedged himself between the two.

"Uh... Lieutenant, we were just passing through. You have a good evening, sir." Bright extended his hand apologetically. Carbone brushed him aside without malice, but hard enough to convey that he wasn't going anywhere.

"Why'd you leave Bobby flapping in the breeze the other night when McGirt crashed? Huh?" His tone had changed from playfully teasing to hostile.

Rayburn stepped back cautiously. "You're drunk, sailor," he said. "Stand down." He glanced back at his friends and shrugged, as if bored with it all. Carbone inched closer and stood nose to nose with him. Dressed in shorts, Carbone's tanned, muscular legs resembled oak pillars.

"You know, you're right, Tommy-boy. I am drunk. But tomorrow, when I wake up, I'll be sober. Unfortunately, you'll still be a dip-shit."

Rayburn's Marine pal stepped forward. "You need some help here, Thomas?" He puffed out his chest, ready for action. Rayburn gave the jarhead a reassuring nod. "I can handle this," he said to him. "Lieutenant Junior Grade Carbone, I caution you to check your demeanor when addressing a senior officer."

Carbs giggled and contorted his face in mock terror. "You gotta be kidding me. We're at the fucking *O'Club*! What you gonna do next, Rayburn, write me a bad fitness report and go crying to the Old Man in San Diego?" Carbone gave up on suppressing his rage. "Go ahead, asshole, I'll just go back to working the fishing boats. You wouldn't last a day where I come from."

The remainder of Rayburn's crowd closed in around him. Carbs collected himself and stepped away, all the time maintaining eye contact with his adversary. "I'm on to you, Rayburn," he said calmly. "Watch your step."

Chapter 19

Salipada was glad to have a job and to be making money again. It had been nearly two weeks since the morning Rolio had rescued him from the alley. As promised, Rolio had managed to get him a new driver's license and use of a vehicle to make deliveries. The wheezing pickup truck looked like hell, but it met the most important requirement for its mission: it ran. Within a few days, Sali had gotten his bearings on some of Manila's major streets and was gaining confidence maneuvering around the bustling metropolis alone. He'd joined Rolio each morning, getting up with the roosters and hurrying to be among the first in line at the shops and warehouses where his partner had prearranged the pickups. They'd meet up after dark back at Rolio's place in Tondo, where his new boss would diligently pay him for his day's work. Other than indulging in a few beers and an occasional joint, the twosome was all business and stayed out of trouble. The one time that Rolio traveled to Angeles City and spent the night, Sali ventured into the neighborhood in hopes of finding the two hookers who'd partied with them the first night. After encountering a sea of squalor and begging children, he gave up, returned to the apartment and fell asleep on the air mattress he'd bought with his first handful of pesos.

Sali had made a couple of solo runs to the airport, where there always seemed to be action. The planes provided an endless stream of rumbling overhead entertainment while he sat in traffic awaiting his turn at the loading dock. Once inside the freight hangars, the display continued to amaze him: crates of clothing, wooden handicrafts and what-nots stacked high on the concrete floor, waiting to be flown to some far-off place thousands of miles away.

Today, however, he'd been given a different set of marching orders. Using a hand-drawn map, Rolio had directed him to a corner of town near the university. He was to load up with automobile parts and deliver them to various repair shops in Tondo, a few blocks from their apartment. When Sali seemed confused about the last part of the drive, Rolio became irritated, thrust the map into his hands and said cynically, "Don't worry, stupid. You'll know when you get close — just follow your nose."

Traffic crept along the avenue by the University of the Philippines. Young people scurried between the idling vehicles, going to and from class. Above the din of road noise and blaring horns, Sali heard the crackling sounds of a bullhorn followed by a series of muffled explosions. Ahead, he saw a plume of smoke erupt into the humid air. Hordes of students fled from the billowing haze, scurrying among the logjam of cars and trucks. Some were screaming. Most had covered up their mouths and noses from the noxious fumes. Soon Sali realized what was going down. The blasts he'd heard were detonated canisters of tear gas; there must be a riot or something going on nearby, Sali thought. The penetrating chemicals engulfed the stalled procession. Sali's eyes and nose burned and he began to cough.

Thankfully, a breeze funneled through the buildings and carried the vapors away after a few minutes. Sali struggled to see the traffic light ahead through his weeping eyes. He squinted at the vehicle directly ahead and hugged its bumper as they inched forward into cleaner air. Most of the students had left the scene except for a few stragglers. Sali saw a young boy and girl lingering behind on the sidewalk. The girl had one arm over the boy's shoulder and was hobbling painfully. He held her around the waist and dragged a sign along the ground with his free hand. Sali wiped his eyes with a kerchief and strained to see the boy's face. It was Malik Abbas.

Traffic surged forward, but Sali refused to move. He dropped the kerchief and hollered out the boy's name. Malik looked over a shoulder, but kept going in a hopscotch jog with the girl clinging to his side.

"Malik! Malik! Over here!" Sali called. He eased the truck to the curb, and got out to follow the couple as cursing drivers swerved around him in the road. He grabbed Malik's arm from behind, but the youngsters refused to stop. Sali persisted and took hold of both of their shirt collars. The two kicked and squirmed to break free.

"Stop! It's me, Salipada, from the ship." Malik recognized him then and relaxed. The girl, however, continued to resist.

"It's OK, I know him," Malik told her.

"What are you doing here?" Sali asked. The tear gas had winded him and he struggled to regain his breath.

"We were part of a demonstration," Malik said. "The PC came and began to threaten us to make us leave. When some students refused, they shot tear gas at us."

"Take a few deep breaths and calm down," Sali said in a fatherly voice. The air was clearer now and traffic was moving freely. Malik dropped the sign to the ground.

Sali looked down to read it. "'Remember Jabidah'? What's this all about, anyway?" he asked.

Malik and the girl looked at each other again, confused and hesitant to speak. "I... I can't tell you here," Malik finally said. His eyes followed a platoon of Philippine Constabulary filing down the sidewalk, on the other side of the street. Sali picked up the sign and flung it into an alley, away from them.

"Well, come with me. I'll drive you out of here." He put a hand under the girl's elbow as they walked back to his delivery truck.

"I think I turned my ankle a little bit," she said. "Thank you."

Sali cleared some papers and food wrappers off the passenger seat. He reached back into the cab and found two cans of soft drink. "It's warm, but should help you clear your senses," he said. They opened the cans and drank thirstily. Sali scanned the area, found a small parking lot next to some campus buildings and drove to it. Malik and the girl had settled down and seemed more at ease. Sali looked at the two of them and smiled, attempting to lift their spirits. "So tell me, little one, how's the big city treating you? Are you ready to go home to Mindanao?"

Malik's bottom lip quivered, but he kept his composure. He slid the *kufi* off his head. It was smeared with grime.

"It's been a nightmare, so far, my time at the university. I should never have come here." He pulled off his glasses wearily and rubbed his eyes. "I learned from a friend, who arrived after me from Cotobato, that my parents may be in trouble. They've been swindled off of our land. I think they're living in the Muslim slums in the city." Malik lowered his head. The bright-faced prodigy whom Sali remembered fondly from *Jolo* appeared totally defeated.

The girl spoke. "It's that tyrant Marcos' fault. He's ruining our country. We have to—" Malik gently touched her knee, signally her to be silent.

"What about all of this?" Sali asked, motioning toward the littered plaza where the protest had taken place. A few students were picking up scattered signs while most simply walked over them on their way to class.

"I volunteered to help with what I thought would be a peaceful information session. We didn't want any trouble, just to tell other students about what the government is capable of doing when it doesn't look out for the interests of all its people."

Sali looked at the signs on the ground, identical to the one Malik had been carrying. "What's this Jabidah?" he asked.

"I didn't know about it until I talked to some of the older Muslim students. They told me that in 1968 a couple dozen army recruits were executed on Corregidor Island. They were all Muslim soldiers who'd signed up to defend our country."

Sali nodded vaguely, remembering the details now. "Malik, that rumor's been circulating for years," he said. "You shouldn't believe everything that you hear, especially around this college. I heard something about that five or six years ago when I sailed into Sulu — a story that Marcos was training a group of Philippine Moros to reclaim territory in Malaysia. That legend's come and gone."

"Of course it did, after martial law was proclaimed," Malik argued defiantly. "But one of the soldiers survived and was picked up at sea. He told the story of how his fellow Moros had questioned the nature of their mission and stood up to mistreatment during their training. For that, they were marched down to the shore and massacred."

The girl interrupted again. "We have to spread the word about this and other atrocities against our people! Professor Misuari tried to when it happened, but he's been stifled and forced into exile." She pounded her hand on the dash. "Christians and Muslims must unite to…"

"That's enough, girl!" Sali said sternly. He looked in the rear-view mirror to see if any Constabulary were still nearby. "I think that you should be on your way now. I'd like to speak with my friend alone."

The girl checked her watch. "Fine. I have a pottery class in ten minutes anyway." She shot Sali a bored, disgusted look and then leaned over and placed a kiss on the smooth skin of Malik's cheek. Sali watched as the little warrior glided through the plaza, her sore ankle obviously much better. Her looks reminded Sali of the underage prostitute that Rolio had dragged up to the apartment. Despite the girl's insolence, she appeared to come from a family of means, and not from a place like Tondo. Malik sank down into the seat, embarrassed by his girlfriend's actions.

"So I see this has not *all* been a nightmare for you, has it, boy?" Sali grinned and gave the youth an affectionate pat on the shoulder.

"No," Malik said softly. "She's nice. Her father's a doctor in the city and she wants to be a politician."

Sali bristled. "Well, if you ask me, she needs to learn some manners if she expects people to listen to her." Malik laughed in agreement, but the day's events seemed to weigh on him. Soon he covered his eyes and began to cry.

"I don't know what to do, Salipada. It wasn't supposed to be this way. My parents worked so hard to get me here. After my sister died, I was all that they had. They did everything to help me. But now, what kind of a man am I if I can't help them in return?"

Malik wiped his tears and took a deep breath. "The government gave me a scholarship, but my parents were selling our farm to provide me with living expenses in the city. Now they have nothing. They wouldn't be in this position if it weren't for me." He lowered his eyes. "Without their help, I don't have enough money to live on, let alone buy a ferry ticket to go home."

Sali stared at the droves of students moving between academic buildings. "I don't know what to tell you, other than you shouldn't do anything when you're in a panic." A long silence followed. A twinge of guilt shot through Sali's body. He felt like a hypocrite giving advice to the boy after what he'd brought down on himself recently — his negligence on the ship, not to mention his recklessness at the Polo Club. Malik turned his deep brown eyes toward his elder. "What should I do, Sali?" he asked.

Sali reached for a cigarette. "Well, you don't know for sure what happened to your parents. Is there any way that you can communicate with them?"

Malik tugged on the sleeve of his t-shirt to wipe his face. "Yes, there is. We had agreed to send each other letters through my old school in Cotabato. One from my mother arrived the day I moved into my dormitory. She said that a man was coming later in the week to buy our land and there would be plenty of money for them to live on. They were going to get a place near the city and maybe open a small business, a grocery store or something. But when my friend telephoned his parents in Cotabato, they told him they'd seen my mama and papa living on the street. They said they'd been duped into selling the land for next to nothing."

Sali checked the time. He was already late from the traffic and still had to deliver the car parts in Tondo. "I have a good job," he said. "The man I work for pays me a lot of money to drive this truck – almost as much as I can make as a seaman. I wanted to earn enough to buy passage back to Mindanao, but I may just stay here and live." He turned and looked the youngster in the eyes. "If I had someone to help me, I could take on more work and make more money."

Malik looked anxiously at Sali. "Are you offering me a job?" His eyes came alive at the prospect.

"I can't pay you too much at first, but yes. Maybe it will help you and your parents."

Malik sat up excitedly. "I'm a good worker, you'll see! I have classes today and tomorrow, but nothing on Friday. Can I start then?"

"Let me see what I can do," Sali said. "My partner told me that sometimes there's merchandise to deliver farther from the city at the end of the week, so merchants have their goods on Monday. I'll try to get some work for you soon. Do you know how to drive?"

"Of course," Malik said proudly. "I learned on our neighbor's tractor when I was little. I don't have a license, though."

"Let's have you start by helping me load and unload. We'll see how it goes from there, OK?"

Malik nodded and extended his small hand to seal their partnership. He clamped on hard. Sali looked at their clasped hands and smiled at the kid's resolve.

"OK, you go do your homework. I'll come by tomorrow and let you know if I have any news." He handed the boy a ten peso note.

* * *

When American ingenuity is combined with Japanese diligence, miracles can happen. In just over six days, less than half the original estimate of two weeks, the Kawasaki mechanics were on the verge of wrapping up their work on McGirt's wrecked aircraft. Yoshi and his team had been working the last thirty-six hours straight, foregoing their beds at the BOQ, while functioning on cat-naps and food from their rice cooker and hot plate. All that remained to be done was the inserting of a few rivets and reinstalling the avionics that had been wiped out when the helo smacked the water. Those components were en route from Guam aboard a C-9 jet transport.

Bud Lammers put in a quick phone call to Captain Lugansky, informing him of the good news. If all went as planned, *San Angelo's* skipper had said that the ship would get underway in forty-eight hours and continue its trek to Singapore, completing the cruise on a high note. Then, by bypassing a stop in Hawaii and steaming directly from Malaysia to the States, the ship's company and Detachment 110 would return home on schedule.

Jenks was present when Bud had gotten the afternoon situation report from the Japanese-American supervisor. The chief immediately began preparations for a test flight. In addition, Bud had received a call from Captain Riggs, who'd directed the Mishap Board. Both McGirt and Uker had been absolved of any serious wrongdoing and were reinstated to full flight status. The cause of the crash would be officially recorded as "pilot error." However, the report would detail extenuating circumstances of severe weather, which had contributed to Ensign Uker losing control and not recovering from the helicopter's rapid descent. The investigators concluded that McGirt's aircraft had most likely encountered a phenomenon known as a severe downdraft, or microburst. The team referenced a string of similar accidents that had occurred recently in the States involving commercial airliners. Recognition of a microburst as a causal factor was a reasonably new concept. There were only a handful of weather scientists around the world who were able to fully understand or forecast a microburst with any degree of accuracy. Navy meteorologists carried a limited bag of tools when it came to predicting these violent downdrafts.

Also included in Riggs' analysis was a mildly scathing commentary questioning why, in fact, the replenishment event had been allowed to take place during such inclement conditions. Although the carrier and her escorts could have accomplished a large share of their resupplying while docked in Subic, the group's commander had decided otherwise. The at-sea replenishment had been given a "go" in hopes of maximizing liberty time for all hands after a grueling extended period in the Indian Ocean.

When Bud didn't find McGirt at the BOQ, he went to the only other place he could think of — the base gym. Unable to complete any activities that stressed his bad knee, McGirt had resorted to doing double sessions at the Cubi Point weight room during his free time in the early morning and late afternoon. Bud found him alone, lying flat on his back doing bench presses.

"Hey, you'll want to add a few more pounds to the bar when I tell you what I just found out," Bud said. McGirt racked the bar and sat upright on the narrow bench. His face dripped with sweat and his chest muscles stood out beneath a faded black jersey. Its sleeves had been cut off, fully exposing his biceps.

"What's that, Boss?" he asked while patting down his arms with a towel.

"Dust off your gear, sailor, we're going flying tomorrow."

"What?"

"You heard me. I just talked with Riggs on the phone. Final ruling: 'Pilot error with extenuating circumstances of severe weather.' You'll have to swallow a below-average grade for airmanship on your next fitness report, but you'll recover from that. Congratulations!"

"What about Puker?" McGirt asked. He tossed his towel over the weight bar, stood up and tucked in his shirt.

"Uker's off the hook too, but I guess it doesn't matter at this point. XO gave him the news. He still wants out of flying. He's manifested on a cargo bird back to the mainland tomorrow. He'll finish out his service in some staff job, I guess."

McGirt frowned and shook his head. "Staff puke Puker. That just doesn't seem right, does it?" A few days earlier, McGirt, Carbone and Bright had taken Uker out for a night in Olongapo, hoping to talk him into finishing the cruise. But even after a few San Miguels and Carbone's animated haranguing, Uker had held firm to his decision.

"Breaks of Naval Air. He made his choice." They shared a quiet moment over the loss of their squadron mate before Bud went on, "Jenks is working things up with the Japs for a test flight tomorrow. How do you feel about flying with me on that one? We'll get you a 'back in the saddle' warm-up and check-ride to keep the squadron happy. I called the skipper and he's onboard with the plan."

"Sounds good to me. What are the other guys up to? Thomas hiding out with his buddies again?"

"Surprisingly, no. He's scheduled to take a passenger run up to Baguio tomorrow as well. He practically got on his hands and knees begging for the mission because he's on the verge of going noncurrent. He needs the flight time or else he's grounded."

McGirt rubbed some chalk across the calloused palms of his hands. "Guess it's time to hop back on the horse that bucked me, huh?" An impish smile spread across his face. He grabbed the towel off the bar and gave his flattop a vigorous rub.

"Oh yeah," Bud continued, "Jenks wants to go with us to double-check the rotor blade tracking or something. I think it's just an excuse to breathe some cool, fresh air up at altitude."

"Smart move. It's like a sauna bath in that hangar. Don't know how those Kawasaki fellas keep going." McGirt sat down on the bench. "Anything from Jill?"

Bud's face slackened. "No answer when I called San Diego, so I tried her mom in Norfolk. Made up a story that I was wondering how she was and asked her to take a drive by our rental house in Virginia Beach. She said she hasn't heard from Jill in over a week and she's worried. I told her to tell Jill I was trying to reach her, if they talk."

"Yeah, don't wanna upset the old gal," McGirt said. "Thanks for hunting me down and delivering the news."

"Well, look, we can talk more about the flight over dinner. I've got to find Brightness. The ship needs to send an officer out in town for Shore Patrol tonight and he's junior man."

"Check the library first," McGirt said. "And tell him not to forget his I.D. He'll have to prove he's old enough to get into the bars."

Bud laughed in agreement and hustled out the door. McGirt slid back onto the bench, ready to bang out another set. When he gripped the bar, he saw a geeky looking face wearing glasses, staring at him from above. The fellow's gym gear appeared new, as if he'd just taken it out of a box. With his sparkling white sneakers, he wore khaki uniform socks. The man said, "Pardon me, but I couldn't help overhearing your conversation. Are you Johnny Jack McGirt from Ann Arbor, Michigan?"

McGirt sat up. "Actually, it's Ypsilanti, but, yup, that's me." He extended a friendly hand.

"I knew that was you!" The man took McGirt's hand and pumped excitedly. He introduced himself as Jerry Saunders, and said he was one of the JAG officers assigned to the Naval Air Station.

"I was in law school when you were a player on the Michigan football team. Man, you were something: Mad Dog McGirt! We even had a cheering section for you." Saunders inspected the amount of weight McGirt was pressing. "Still looking pretty strong," he said approvingly. "But based on the way you used to crumple ball carriers, I thought you'd be bigger."

Uncomfortable with the conversation, McGirt decided that his workout was finished. He got up and began edging toward the door. "That was a while back. I've lost a few pounds since those days." He turned to walk away, saying over his shoulder, "Nice talking with you, pal. Gotta go."

Saunders followed him, refusing to take a hint. "I always wondered why you didn't come back to play your senior year. I know that you got hurt before the Ohio State game, but we never saw you around campus after that. You just disappeared." He noticed the lettering on McGirt's jersey. "Long Beach State?" he asked, incredulous. "Where's your maize and blue?"

McGirt eyed the exit. "Gotta go now, really." He hurried out of the building, leaving behind the bewildered Wolverines fan. The swelling was down today, so he tested his knee with a slow jog back to the Q. After a couple dozen strides, it loosened up and seemed almost normal.

Chapter 20

The farmhouse near Angeles City was dark and deserted when Rolio approached. Without the usual greeters to open the gate, he was suspicious. He turned around and drove back along the one-lane road through rice paddies, parking a quarter-mile away. For a moment he just sat and watched the house. He turned on the truck's radio and found a strong signal: the Armed Forces Radio station from Clark. A female voice was reading sports scores in a droning monotone. Mercifully, she segued into some popular American music. Rolio tapped his foot to the song. He wondered why his own countrymen couldn't produce music with a decent beat. There were *some* things that he did like about the Americans.

Rolio turned down the volume. Other than a light breeze rustling through the fields, it was silent. He craned his head outside the window to check whether anyone was approaching from behind. It was clear. When he turned back around, he saw that a single light had come on at the farmhouse, exactly where he'd been told — a window at the far right corner of the building. He put the truck in gear and drove cautiously forward. This time, a lanky shadow emerged from the darkness and unlatched the gate.

Rolio parked near the same barn where he'd deposited Vaccaro and the other recruits two weeks ago. He looked over his shoulder again. The gate had been latched shut and its keeper had vanished. He walked onto the farmhouse porch and knocked softly on the edge of the screen door. A sliver of light from an adjacent room illuminated the foyer. He heard a familiar voice before the face materialized before him.

"Good evening to you, sir, or should I say, *Mr. Rolio*." Both men chuckled as the elderly gentleman stepped from the darkness and opened the door. "It's a lovely night, isn't it?"

"And it's a pleasure to be here as well, José, or should I say, *Mr. Julio*." Another round of laughs at the pseudonyms they'd chosen for the mission. José shuffled across the foyer and led Rolio into a modest study. Bookcases covered three of the room's four walls. A colorful, well-worn braided rug sat atop the room's wide plank flooring. In the study's center sat two leather parlor chairs. Between them, a simple reading lamp and a framed picture rested on a small table. Rolio paused by the window and pulled back the curtains. He looked across the barnyard toward the gate.

"He's out there. You just can't see him," José said. "It's Vaccaro, that enthusiastic one you brought to us. Quite a fellow — very smart and knows his history. He has an insatiable thirst for anything to do with the *Hukbalahap*. We made a good choice."

José held two cups and gave one to Rolio. "Hot tea. If it's not strong enough, I probably have something that will liven it up for you. I don't drink anymore, myself."

"No, this will be fine." Rolio raised the steaming cup to his lips. His street-wise edginess melted away in the presence of his mentor.

"Tell me, what's new in the big city?" José asked, settling into his chair.

"We've been moving many goods from warehouses and garment shops. Much to the airport, a few to Subic and up here. I made a delivery of office equipment onto the Air Force base today." Rolio knew that he hadn't been summoned to engage in chitchat. He set down his cup.

"I think it is time," José said. "We were planning for a period closer to the holidays, but everything is pointing to now — as early as this week." He set his drink on the table. He sighed and rested his head against the chair back.

Rolio fixed his gaze on José's eyes. "I agree," he said.

"We've come across some valuable information during the last few days. Like most things of great value, it is elementary and uncomplicated. I've decided to proceed."

Rolio picked up the picture frame and studied it. It held a faded snapshot of six smiling Filipino men. Their hands were joined together above their heads in a sign of unity. Surrounding them was a crowd of joyous people, waving their arms and pumping their fists. He held out the picture like a priest offering up a chalice to his congregation. He took a deep voice and recited, *"Democracy, freedom and lasting peace for all, including the common men who feed a nation when it is starving and fight for it when it's in danger."*

"Yes, Luis Taruc had a way with words, didn't he?" José said. "Can't say that I hold him in such esteem now, though. A dozen years caged like an animal will break most men's spirit."

"Everyone looks so happy," Rolio said, bringing the picture closer.

"Of course we were happy! We had elected our friends and neighbors to represent us in Manila. We put our trust in that Democratic Alliance. They were our best hope to finally get the nation out from under oppression, once and for all. Four hundred years is long enough." A spark of fire ignited inside the old warrior. "And we thought that we had such a great model to follow," he went on. "We even honored them by declaring July fourth our own Independence Day." José pointed to the faces in the photo. "There's Lava, Cano, Padilla, Amado Yukon, Simpauco, and, of course, Luis."

"Is that you?" Rolio asked, touching his finger to a smiling young face in the background.

"Yes, it is," José said with a grin. "Young and strong."

"Where's my uncle, Juan?" Rolio's eyes searched the photo like those of a child seeking a hidden treasure.

"Your uncle took this picture," José said solemnly. "A few months later, he was gone." A hush fell over them as they recalled how the revolutionary, Juan Feleo, had met his demise. While traveling to a meeting with the new Secretary of the Interior Zulueta, he'd been kidnapped and murdered. Along with his wife and several others, the group had been ambushed by what was widely believed to be henchmen of wealthy landlords in central Luzon.

José reminisced, "The tensions actually began in May when Manual Roxas was sworn in as president. He refused to seat our six members in the new congress."

Rolio knew the facts, but he let his elder continue uninterrupted.

"We all knew that passage of the Bell Trade Act would pour huge sums of money into the country for post-war reconstruction. With that would come jobs, many of them high-paying ones on the U.S. military bases." José waved his finger. "But Taruc and your uncle knew what the long-term effects would be. America would have unchecked access to our resources and markets. As long as that existed, we could be no more than a nation of lackeys. Those six brave men would have blocked the trade act vote had Roxas allowed them to be seated."

Rolio set down the picture. "Some people say that money always wins," he said. "But I'm not so sure of that. Our country has fallen into a trancelike stupor under martial law. It needs an awakening."

"How true," José said. He gave a tired laugh. "It's probably just my fantasy, but had we been able to stand firm in the beginning, perhaps our nation would have advanced like the Japanese or South Koreans. Instead, we've been puppets on a string, controlled by power brokers thousands of miles away. That lying poseur, Marcos, and his wife living in their palace think they're in charge. But they really aren't." He lowered his head sadly. "I wish I could have done more."

Rolio stood up and toyed with a book protruding from the volumes lining the walls. It was a leather-bound tome, in English, about the American Revolutionary War. He slid the book back into its place.

"You shouldn't feel guilty about anything, Comrade José. By providing us with use of your farm, you've more than made up for your inactive years." Rolio stepped over and took the older man's hands. "These are extraordinary times," he went on. "And with that, we have no choice but to carry out extraordinary measures." Tears began to well in José's eyes.

"You and your humble colleagues planted the seed," Rolio said, gesturing to the picture. "That seed has laid dormant for decades, but it still can sprout and grow into the movement that you, Taruc and Feleo envisioned. You can't blame yourself. The forces were much too strong: the fruit and sugar companies, the logging interests, the lure of jobs on the military bases. Where could citizens have made the kind of money they can at Clark or Subic? Sweating in the fields chopping cane or working the paddies?" José sank deeper into the chair. Rolio saw that he'd gone too far with his rant.

"I apologize, Comrade. But I have trouble holding back my rage. I, too am guilty of not doing enough. I left the land and hid in the cesspool of the city." The room grew quiet again. Rolio could tell that that José was tired. It was time to leave. "So where do we go from here?" he asked.

José rose slowly and walked his protégé to the door. "You'll be informed by the usual means. I've delegated the rest of the details for you to decide. I trust that you'll use good judgment."

"Thank you," Rolio said. "Besides the young fellows we've brought aboard, I have others in the wings. Our numbers will grow."

"I know that I'm getting melancholy in my old age," José said, "But when I see fresh faces like Vaccaro, and this new army of the people, it rekindles the fire within me! I have a renewed enthusiasm that you and the others can pick up where we left off."

"We'll only need to know the time and the place," Rolio said.

"Of course," José replied. "You'll have at least a day's notice." He paused in the hallway and looked up at a portrait of his children. "After it happens, I'll leave here. The life of a widower is a very lonely one. My children both live with their families in Cebu. I'd like to spend the rest of my days with them. Unless someone in Manila doesn't want me to."

"What about this farm?" Rolio asked as they walked onto the porch. "It's valuable land."

"Yes, it can be, but it wasn't mine in the beginning. Why should it be mine in the end? I've left it to the workers. They can farm it, or sell it if they wish. We turned them loose after the last harvest. When you brought your idea to me, we told them we wanted to let the earth rest for a season. Their *kutiwala* is one of us. He'll call them back when it's over."

The men shook hands. "So this is it, isn't it?" Rolio said. José took off his glasses and rubbed his eyes. At first, Rolio thought the old man was about to tear up again. But a penetrating glare took the place of sadness on José's face. He raised his hand and pressed a finger to Rolio's chest. His jaw tightened with a fierceness that Rolio had never witnessed.

José stared him in the eye and said, "This is our chance to make history. Be ready!"

***

Whenever an aircraft carrier tied up at Subic Bay, it was a big deal in the town of Olongapo. Its arrival kicked off a celebration on the level of Mardi Gras or New Year's Eve. Merchants packed their shelves and a caravan of San Miguel delivery trucks paraded down Magsaysay Boulevard in anticipation. Thousands of sailors and Marines rushed into town, fueled by pockets full of money they'd saved up during extended periods at sea. They were overwhelmed from the moment they arrived. Throbbing lights, blaring music and strange smells assaulted their senses. Busloads of "hostesses" were transported in from the countryside. The young cuties knew that the men had more than drinking on their minds, and they were eager to provide companionship and relaxation – for a price.

Ensign Robert Bright wasn't a big fan of Olongapo. During the last six months, *San Angelo* had docked in the Philippine port on three separate occasions to take on fuel and supplies. Bright had been "out in town" only twice: the day before — when he, McGirt and Carbone tried to convince Uker to stay — and the first time, when three of Detachment 110's enlisted men had advanced in rank. They were throwing a bash at the Det's favorite hangout, the Rufadora Club. He'd stuck close to Carbone's side as they'd braved the onslaught of hawkers and hookers on Olongapo's main drag. He'd had one beer and then bee-lined it back to the BOQ. Carbone had stayed until closing time.

When Bright drew Shore Patrol duty, he naturally turned to his burly running mate for advice. "Bobby," Carbone had said, "Don't walk anywhere alone. If things get rough, call in the AFPs." The Armed Forces Police were the pros. Unlike the SP details from the ships, they carried weapons and were trained to deal with drunken derelicts and scorned bar girls. "Keep your head down. Don't be a hero," were Carbone's parting words.

Bright joined the swarm of revelers heading out the gate. He pulled up short when he reached a bank of turnstiles surrounded by American and Filipino guards. A blue and gold lettered sign reading "Shore Patrol muster here" directed him to a courtyard where he joined up with a couple dozen other personnel. The group was comprised mostly of enlisted men dressed in traditional white bellbottoms.

A whistle blew from behind them, followed by a gravelly voice. "Listen up!"

The detail turned to face a brutish-looking guy wearing olive-drab fatigues. His face was darkened by a five o'clock shadow that appeared to have the consistency of forty-grit sandpaper. A green helmet sat atop his head. Stenciled across it were white letters reading "AFP."

"OK, we don't have much time, so pay attention," he barked. "Number one rule: don't get hurt. It's gonna be a goat-rope out there tonight with the carrier in port. Everyone just got paid and the locals know it. We'll pair you up in three-man teams: two petty officers and one khaki. You'll have a radio. If you observe anything that don't look right, you'll call one of us. My boys will take it from there."

Bright noted a black billy-club hanging from the man's belt. On his other hip were a revolver, handcuffs and a canister of mace. "Unless acting in self-defense, do not — I repeat, *do not* — lay a hand on any Filipino citizens. We work closely with the Philippine Constabulary. If there's trouble with the locals, they'll handle it." He pointed to a platoon of PC gathered around a Jeep nearby.

"OK, I'm gonna read some names. When I call yours, answer up. Ensign Robert Bright?"

"Here," Bright said. He raised his hand and stepped forward.

"Sir, you're senior man." The MP coughed to stifle his laughter when he saw the pint-sized officer. He lowered his voice a few decibels and held out the clipboard for Brightness to see. "Just CPOs and Warrants tonight, sir. You're up first," he confided. "Pick two men to go with you."

Carbone's words stuck in his brain. "Grab the two biggest guys," he'd said. Bright scanned the group and settled on a tall, sinewy black sailor and a bulky, pale-skinned redheaded guy. The rest of the detail paired off by seniority and awaited further instructions.

"Next thing we gotta do is choose your beat." The MP held up a large map of Olongapo. "We got the main drag, Magsaysay Boulevard; also Jet-jockey Row; Hillbilly Heaven, and VP Alley." He pointed to various parts of town that had evolved into their own unique districts, attracting sailors from various communities. There was no special spot for Marines — they went everywhere. "Oh yeah, can't forget the Ghetto," he added.

Again, Carbone's advice rang in Bright's ears: "Stay out of Hillbilly Heaven." Comprised of country-western bars, the area was a magnet for every redneck rowdy in WESTPAC. Its clientele was a mixture of airdales, blackshoes and grunts, all embarked on the same mission: to drink themselves stupid and raise havoc until curfew cleared the streets at midnight.

"Ensign, you get first choice again," the AFP said to Bright. The black sailor stooped down and whispered, "Sir, take the Ghetto, take the Ghetto. Never any trouble there." Bright looked to the redhead, who shrugged that he didn't care. "The Ghetto," Bright said. The remainder of the detail picked their districts. They slid "SP" armbands over their biceps and marched out of the courtyard.

The black sailor introduced himself first. "Petty Officer LaMont Young. South side Chicago." The redhead followed with, "Name's Gilbert. Grew up on a farm outside Omaha." Bright shook their hands and shared that he hailed from upstate New York, near Syracuse. They fell in line with the throngs exiting the gate.

"Come see this," Young said. "This is some funk-ee stuff." He led them to the center of the bridge that crossed an irrigation canal separating the base from Olongapo. The canal's murky waters carried a flow of garbage and raw sewage out into the bay. It was not uncommon to see a dead dog or pig float by. A crowd had gathered along the bridge railing. Below, two shallow canoes known as *banca* boats rested idly on the surface. Inside each was a pretty adolescent girl dolled up like a princess, complete with long gown and a glittering tiara. The girls stood up with baskets in their hands, ready to snare coins tossed down to them. Next to the girls were boys wearing swimsuits. A loud group of servicemen teased the kids from above. Finally, some sailors heaved pesos in the air. The boats rocked as the girls stretched to catch the coins. Then the boys dove into the polluted water to retrieve the ones that the girls had missed. After a few seconds they surfaced, proudly displaying coins in their hands and between clenched teeth.

"Aw, man, that's sick," Gilbert groaned.

Young tapped his partners on the shoulders. "Follow me. I know a short cut." He led them down an alley, through an open-air market and onto a side street off Magsaysay.

"Here we are, gentlemen. Welcome to the Ghetto!" A few black sailors strolled the sidewalk, inspecting racks of brightly colored clothing. Young broke ranks and jogged across the street to greet a friend. They shook hands in an elaborate way and hugged. His friend was wearing a natty jumpsuit and matching fedora. Young jogged back, saying, "Sorry, sir. Just had to say howdy to one of the cats from my ship."

The trio spent the first few hours carrying out the instructions given to them at the Shore Patrol headquarters: cruise the streets, restaurants and clubs; inspect bathrooms and look there for passed-out servicemen. There appeared to be no trouble. Young was right; the Ghetto was a peaceful place, at least for the time being.

Olongapo's streets swelled with activity as darkness crept over the town. Bright quickly realized that, if not for their Shore Patrol insignia, he and Gilbert would never have ventured onto these streets. They were the only whites around.

Soulful sounds drifted out from the clubs, prompting Young to rub his hands together and do a fancy shuffle. The neon signs flashed names like Little Harlem, Blackjack's, and the Apollo Club. Scantily clad Filipino girls posed provocatively in front of the bars, urging men to join them inside. Bright took a deep breath and led his detail into the smoky confines of the Apollo. Psychedelic murals covered the walls, colors vibrant under black lights. A dark-skinned hostess with her hair curled into an Afro cuddled up to Bright.

"Hey, handsome boy. You come back to see me when you not do Ess-Pee?" she asked. She stood eye-to-eye with Brightness, wearing thick-heeled platform shoes that raised her dainty frame six inches off the floor. Her kinky hair was puffed out to the size of a beach ball. Young and Gilbert chuckled as Bright politely shied away from her. The girl tossed her head back and cackled before slapping him on the rump and slinking into the mob of sweaty bodies.

"Mr. Bright, Mr. Bright, over here!" The unmistakable voice of Irvis Jenks cut through the din. Bright looked across the room and saw Jenks seated at a table in the corner. He turned to Young and Gilbert. "Fellas, take a peek around. Make sure to check out the head," he said. The twosome split off to inspect the joint. People on the dance floor parted as they crossed it.

Bright picked his way toward Jenks. The big sailor engulfed him with a warm bear hug. A posse of older guys, all black, had joined him at the table. They seemed happy to be off by themselves drinking, without the women. Had Bright not recognized the voice, he wouldn't have known the chief. Jenks was wearing a long, intricately embroidered shirt called a *dashiki*. The garment's billowy sleeves hung below his elbows. His friends were decked out in similar fashion. The rest of the table stood up to greet Bright.

"Sir, I want you to meet my buddies," Jenks said. He hurled out names that Bright couldn't hear over the music. Bright recognized one of the men; he was Jenks' counterpart, the Marine gunnery sergeant from the hangar. Bright found himself sandwiched between him and Jenks.

"Big Willy here really helped us out," Jenks said. "Got us the extra tools and parts so those Japanese boys could turn to." The men pressed in closer. Bright felt their body heat and smelled liquor. Jenks stooped down, speaking closer to his ear. "Understand that you and Mr. Rayburn are scheduled to fly some dudes up to Baguio tomorrow." Bright nodded. "Well, after we recover you guys and all goes well with the boss's test flight, we're back in business. Singapore, then home sweet home: good ol' USA."

Jenks and Big Willy shared a laugh and exchanged some sort of ritualistic handshake, the same kind that Young had performed outside with his friend. Young and Gilbert snaked through the crowd and found Bright. It was time to go. "See you tomorrow, Chief," Bright said loudly. "We have to finish making our rounds." Jenks gave him another hug. Bright looked up to the Marine and said, "Thanks for all the help, Gunny." He extended his hand. Big Willy grabbed it with a crushing grip and backed off a little when he saw the young officer wince.

Over the course of an uneventful evening, the only problem the trio encountered was an inebriated sailor throwing up in Little Harlem's bathroom. Young and Gilbert carried him out to his buddies, who promised that they'd get him back safely to their ship.

Back at the Shore Patrol base, they turned in their armbands and radio. Bright looked behind him at the crowd thinning out on Magsaysay.

AFPs guided the mob, slowly corralling everyone toward the main gate as the clock counted down to curfew. The PC joined in, essentially sweeping the streets like a riot patrol. Bright saw some commotion break out between a Filipino teenager and a drunken sailor walking back from Hillbilly Heaven. The sailor was furious. He accused the boy of stealing his wallet. Within seconds, an AFP was on the scene, followed by a PC paddy wagon. The Constabulary promptly took charge. The boy shook his head, emphatically denying his guilt, but the two PC persisted. One of them gave the boy a slap across the head. The other stepped in and ransacked the kid's trousers, ultimately retrieving the billfold from inside his underwear. The satisfied sailor took it and headed for the gate. The Constabulary shoved the thief into their van and sped away.

Bright crossed the intersection known as "last chance corner." Scores of women flirted with the retreating servicemen, hoping to find a bed partner for the night. Bright shrugged off their advances and hoofed it over the bridge. Relieved to walk onto U.S. government property, he boarded a bus for the ride back to the Q. He looked forward to his flight with Rayburn tomorrow. Hopefully, it would go better than the last one had.

Chapter 21

Salipada had worried all night that he would oversleep, but the roosters crowed at dawn and wakened him as usual. He'd spent the dark hours alone in the apartment. Prior to going to Angeles City, Rolio had offered him the opportunity to earn more money than he'd made since arriving in Manila — three hundred pesos. Sali had jumped at the chance, and had invited Malik to ride along. He rolled off his air mattress, eager to get started.

After two weeks of living in the Tondo flat, he felt at home. On several nights, he'd had the place to himself. He'd concluded that life as a truck driver wasn't that bad. In some ways, it was better than his routine at sea: no long celibate periods; no need to sneak booze or dope aboard; and it was easy money. Rolio gave him his daily orders. He got paid when the work was done. Period.

A run to the mountaintop town of Baguio would be his first venture beyond the city's confines. Rolio had left a detailed itinerary, complete with driving times and a hand-drawn map. "Just follow my instructions and you'll have no problems," he'd said. "But don't be late. My customers pay a premium when we're on time."

The task at hand was to take his empty pickup from Manila to a warehouse in Angeles City. From there, he'd switch vehicles with Rolio, who'd drive Sali's truck back to metro Manila. In turn, Sali would load Rolio's larger vehicle and travel another five hours north to Baguio. After making the delivery, he was free to do as he pleased: spend the night or continue back down the mountain and return home. It had sounded a little complicated when Rolio first explained the job. Nonetheless, considering the amount of money on the table, Sali didn't want to jinx the deal by asking too many questions. When he inquired what they'd be hauling, Rolio told him, "The usual shit — clothes, electronics, you know."

Early morning traffic was light. He made good time from Tondo to Malik's dorm at the University of the Philippines. The sun was cresting over the horizon when Malik hopped in.

"Assistant truck driver Abbas reporting for duty, sir," the youngster said, saluting as he sat down.

"Something smells pretty good. What'd you bring us for breakfast?"

"Left over *lumpia* from the cafeteria. I snuck four of them in my pocket last night. I went to my friend's room earlier and she warmed them on a hot plate. You remember her — the girl with me at the demonstration." Malik handed a spring roll to Sali.

"Ah, very nice," Sali said as he took a bite. "Perhaps she'll make a good wife someday." He reached over and pulled Malik's *kufi* over his eyes.

"So, we're off to Baguio?"

"First Angeles City, and then Baguio. Did you bring your things in case we have to sleep over?" Malik held up a small sack and pulled out a map from it. "I borrowed it from the library," he said. His mouth was stuffed with food. "Do you want another one?"

"No, you can have it. I figured it'll take us about two and a half hours to get to Angeles. Speak up if you need to take a leak; otherwise I'll keep going," Sali said. "We're on a strict timetable and have to be at the drop-off point in Baguio before two o'clock."

Malik nodded and sat back to enjoy the scenery, still chewing. He'd unfolded the map neatly across his lap and quickly pinpointed their position. His index finger traced their route as Sali drove. They made slow but steady progress through metro Manila's northern suburbs. There wasn't anything appealing on the radio, so eventually Sali struck up a conversation.

"Tell me about your girlfriend. What's her name?"

"Nina. We met when I signed up for the Muslim independence awareness demonstration last week."

"Is she a Muslim?"

"I don't think so. If she is, she's unlike any of the girls in my village. From the way that she talks, I assume that she's a Catholic, like everyone else in Manila."

"Now that you're living in the big city, you must be careful who you choose to call your friends, little one," Sali offered.

"I know. She seems nice," Malik said.

"A lot of things in life seem nice. Just remember who you are and where you came from."

"What do you mean?"

Sali saw an open stretch of road ahead and mashed down the accelerator, hoping to make some time. The pickup's engine rattled and pinged as it gained speed.

"You're young and have been protected from it, but there are many who don't like your people."

"You mean *our* people," Malik said. Sali turned his head away from the boy, embarrassed by what he'd said.

"I don't have anybody's religion. I'm my own man," Sali countered. He squirmed nervously in his seat. "Your people — OK, *our* people — have been under attack for a long time. Just because I don't practice the faith doesn't mean I don't care what's going on."

"You don't have to sound defensive when we talk, Sali. I'm not angry at your choices."

Sali was amazed at the boy's brazenness. "You speak arrogantly for someone so young,"

It was Malik's turn to be embarrassed. "I don't know everything, but I do know how our brothers and sisters are being mistreated and thrown off their land. Nina has opened my eyes to things you don't read in the newspaper." He paused, then asked, "What about you?"

"What about me?" Sali replied.

"Tell me about your family. Where do they live?"

Salipada laughed. "Who cares?" Malik's eyes zeroed in on him. The kid refused to let him off the hook; he expected more than that for an answer.

"I was raised to be a good Muslim, like you, back in Mindanao. I had a brother and a sister, both older, but I never fit in. When I was old enough to defend myself, I ran away. Never been back."

"Never?"

"No. I found a job on the wharf unloading freighters. Remember Eduardo, the man who booked you passage on *Jolo*? He let me sleep in one of the dockside buildings. That was twenty years ago."

"Don't you wonder about your family sometimes? Where they are or how they're doing?"

Sali stared ahead. His hands squeezed the steering wheel. "If you knew about my family, you'd understand. It was not a pleasant life in my household. Not like yours."

Malik refolded the map and set it on the dash. "You're right. I've been fortunate."

"Do you have brothers and sisters?" Sali asked.

"I had a sister, but she died at four years old, before I was born."

"Oh. What happened to her? Did she contract a disease?"

"I only know what my parents told me. My father had walked down to the river to fish for dinner. He took my sister with him because my momma was sleeping. Nothing was biting, so he decided to move to another spot. His hands were full with his fishing gear, so he told her to follow close behind him. He'd walked twenty or so meters along the river's edge when he heard her scream. He turned to see my sister's body inside the jaws of a crocodile."

"My god!" Sali gasped. He looked over at the boy, expecting to see some emotion, but there was none.

"My father ran to save her. The animal was much bigger than him, but he is a brave man. He jumped on its back and tried to free her. The beast began to slide back into water with both of them. He tore out the croc's eyes with a knife and it finally released her. As my father climbed up the bank, the croc lunged up and bit him. It took out a hunk of flesh from his leg, the size of a mango. He hobbled back to the house with her in his arms, but it was too late. It had crushed her to death."

A minute passed before Sali responded. "So you are quite special to your parents, aren't you? The only child."

"I guess so. They sent me to a good school in Cotobato. That prepared me to receive a scholarship as a Moro student in Manila. Allah has always laid out a safe path for me."

Two hours into their journey, they'd entered the farmlands leading to Angeles. Sali got confused at an intersection on the city's outskirts. Malik unfolded the map and got his bearings. When a fighter jet zoomed overhead, he assured Sali that they were headed in the right direction.

"See, that's the roof of the big warehouse over there, on the east side of the Air Force base," Malik said. The large storage facility looked just as Rolio had described. Sali recognized the white panel truck parked across the street from the loading dock. He parked next to it and jumped out, glad to have arrived on schedule.

"Rolio, I want you to meet my friend," he called out.

A stranger stepped out of the truck. "Rolio ain't here today. I'm filling in," he said. He wore a filthy work shirt and a pair of military-looking green pants. On top of his head was a frayed ball cap, crusted with sweat stains. "Here's gas money and directions to Baguio. I'll drive your truck back to Manila." The man climbed inside and gave Malik a disgusted look.

"But where do we load up?" Sali asked. He looked around the warehouse's bustling parking lot.

"Everything's already packed. There's a seal on the door so you don't steal anything. Just drive it to Baguio like you said you would."

As soon as Malik got out of the truck, the guy dropped it into gear and sped away. Sali looked at the envelope in his hands. Inside was another homemade map and a wad of cash.

"Here, count it," he said and handed the bills to Malik. He pulled out the directions. At the top was a note. It read: "My friend. You've made it this far. Good! It's very important that you arrive at the destination by two p.m. We will exchange vehicles again there. Don't be alarmed when you reach the rough terrain. My truck is sturdy and can make the journey. There will be a bonus when you arrive."

"One hundred pesos!" Malik said. He played with the bills, fanning them out like a deck of cards.

Sali reread the note. He was confused at the change in plans. He was expecting to see Rolio.

"Give me that," Sali said. He yanked the cash from the boy's hand. "Come on, let's get going. We don't have much extra time."

They followed Rolio's instructions onto Manila North Road. "Aren't you concerned about what we're carrying back there?" Malik asked. "That man didn't look very trustworthy and he stunk like a pig. Maybe we should make sure everything is tied down."

"Nah," Sali said. He waved his hand nonchalantly. "Rolio knows what he's doing. What time do you have?" The boy held up two naked wrists.

"It's all right, I set my watch to the radio before I picked you up."

Malik turned on the radio, bypassed the Armed Forces station and settled on some Filipino music. He hummed along to the tune and held a hand outside. The wind made his palm rise and fall like an airplane.

"Thanks for giving me a job," he said. "So far, though, all I've done is eat and read the map."

"Don't worry, you'll earn your keep later," Sali said. "This truck holds a lot and Rolio always packs it tight as sardines in a can."

The next few hours passed quickly as they continued on the highway toward the only major intersection in Rolio's directions: Kennon Road near the rural town of Saitan. Other than a few slow-downs for carabao and goats crossing the road, the drive went smoothly.

Malik squinted through his glasses. "Saitan, thirty kilometers. That's where we turn," he said, pointing to the road sign ahead. He searched the map. A long period of silence passed as the radio station faded into static. Malik was the first to speak.

"How come you're not married? Do you have a girlfriend?" Sali shook his head and laughed. "You ask too many questions." Again, Malik sat patiently, expecting an answer. Sali turned to see the boy's eyes focused on him like laser beams. "I had a woman once. Someone fiery and smart, like your friend Nina." Malik sat up, eager to hear the details.

"It was when I worked the ferry boats, on the other side of Mindanao. She had a job in a *sari-sari* store, near the passenger terminal. We developed a friendship. One day when I had some time off in port, she invited me to join her at a protest march inland of Davao. Something like you and Nina went to at the university."

"What was it about?" Malik asked.

"A big company from the north had built a lumber mill on the coast. They wanted to drag timbers from the highlands and float the logs several kilometers downriver to the mill. To do so, they'd have to carve out a staging area. A shantytown of squatters lived where they wanted to set up their business."

"Were the squatters Muslim?"

"Yes, they were," Sali said. "When we got to the site, the company's bulldozers had been stopped by a blockade of villagers. They were shouting and throwing things at the construction workers. It got pretty ugly. My friend helped lead the charge as people hurled everything imaginable at the intruders: rocks, dirt, even buckets of crap. I stood back from the melee, but my friend jumped right into the middle of it."

"Then what happened? Did the workers back down?"

"Initially they did. But after a while, their foreman gave the signal for the convoy to move forward. The villagers had no choice: they had to move or be trampled. A few minutes later, their flimsy town was destroyed. The machines pushed their huts and possessions into the river. That was the end of it."

Sali saw that one of the truck's fuel gauges indicated a quarter tank. The other had read zero since they'd left Angeles. "We'll have to get some gas before making the climb," he said. "I'm not sure how much we have in the tanks. One of these gauges looks busted."

"What happened to the girl?"

"We got split up in the chaos. I had to get back to the city and catch my ferry. When I returned to Davao a week later, I sought her out at the store. She wasn't there. The owner said that she hadn't been to work since that day. I don't know what became of her."

"I'm sorry," Malik said.

A filling station came into view, where the road split off to Baguio. Sali pulled in and parked next to a pump. Malik went inside to relieve himself while Sali filled one of the tanks. He attempted to fill the other, but couldn't twist off its cap. It looked like it was corroded shut.

"There's plenty in that one tank. We'll be OK," Sali concluded. They took the cutoff onto Kennon Road. "Rolio told me that this would be the hardest part of the drive." The roadway paralleled the Bued River valley. Water flowed through the gorge, dark and thick with mud that had eroded from the mountain slopes. Within twenty minutes, the highway narrowed into a dizzying series of climbing switchbacks. Sali let the truck's big engine do its work and checked his watch: 12:30. Rolio had said it would take another hour once they'd entered the steep zigzagging climb.

"This truck seems to be doing well with such a heavy load," Malik remarked. They'd caught up with a tourist bus that was barely making headway. After a few moments Sali got frustrated and started honking.

"Pull over, you idiot!" he yelled out the window. Mercifully, the bus drifted onto the shoulder, allowing them to pass. He checked his watch again. "We can't afford to lose time like that."

"Its only 12:50. The last sign said twenty kilometers to Baguio." Malik noticed that his friend had broken out in a nervous sweat. He studied the map to double-check. "We're OK."

Sali lit a smoke to calm himself. "You're right." He forced a smile. "No need to get excited." The road ahead was clear so he pressed the accelerator. Malik leaned his head out into the sunny, cool air.

For the next half hour, the view was spectacular. Sali relaxed and took in the sights. On one side was a sheer drop-off into the river valley. Foaming waters gushed through a labyrinth of rocks, cascading into waterfalls. Above, they saw verdant stripes of multi-tiered gardens and rice paddies hugging the mountain's contours.

"This is wonderful!" Malik exclaimed.

Sali's eyes returned to the road just in time to see a jumbled pile of scrap metal on the pavement. He pulled hard on the wheel, but the truck's left front tire hit the junk head on. They heard a loud bang followed by the unmistakable *thunk, thunk* of a flat.

"No!" Sali yelled. Malik froze in his seat and braced himself. The truck surged into the other lane as Sali struggled to regain control. He lifted his foot off the gas pedal. Using all of his strength, he pulled hard to the right. The steep grade helped by acting as a braking force. The truck jerked to a stop.

"We have to unpack and find the spare," Malik said as he jumped outside, headed for the rear door.

"Wait, don't open it up," Sali said. "I think it's under here." He got down on the pavement. The spare was mounted beneath the chassis.

"Do you think the jack might be up front somewhere?" Malik asked.

"Yes, yes, go look for it now. Behind the seats." Sali crawled under the truck. He unwound a rusty chain that held the spare in place.

"Found it! I found it!" Malik cried out. He'd never changed a tire himself, but recalled seeing it done along the road in Cotobato. He quickly surmised where he thought the jack should be placed, assembled the apparatus and began pumping furiously. Sali joined him with the tire.

"Here, let me do that," Sali said. In a few seconds, the damaged wheel was suspended off the pavement.

"I think we're going to get wet soon," Malik said as he caught his breath. He pointed to a line of towering clouds rolling in from the west. Sali loosened the lug nuts and glanced at his watch. It was 1:30.

"Damn...Malik, we don't have time to store the flat. When I pull it off, roll it into the ditch. We can retrieve it on the way back." With the good wheel in place, Sali lowered the truck.

They felt a rumble under their feet. At first, they both thought it to be thunder from the approaching storm. But the sound grew into a steady, pulsating beat — *womp, womp, womp.*

"Wow, I've never seen a real one of those." Malik pointed to a dark speck maneuvering between the clouds. The sun's rays reflected off the helicopter's windshield.

"I think we're good to go," Sali said. "Come on."

A few hundred meters up the road, they saw the sign pointing the way to a landmark that Rolio had annotated on the map. "Camp Four," they both read out loud.

"OK, about another five klicks and we should see a dirt road on the left leading up to a ridgeline. Rolio said he would mark it with a pile of empty San Miguels on the roadside, at the base of a tree. Brown glass with white letters," Sali explained.

"I know what they look like." Malik had never tasted a drop, but he was familiar with the national brew. As they rounded the next turn, a wall of black exhaust and flashing taillights flooded their view. It was the bus they'd passed nearly an hour ago. Like the tortoise catching the hare, it had passed them unnoticed while they'd changed the tire. Sali pounded on the horn, but here the road was narrow with no shoulder. The bus had no room to pull over. With a stream of oncoming traffic ahead, Sali and Malik were trapped.

Sali read his watch: 1:55. He wasn't sure why his boss had been so emphatic about being on time. What he did know, however, was that Rolio was tight with his pesos. He feared that their big payout was lost.

Malik rallied to bolster his friend. "It's all right if we're a little late," he said. "Besides, you did all the work. I don't need any money this time." His words helped Sali center his thoughts. The tension ebbed from his forearms. He relaxed his grip and eased off the bus's bumper. They'd done their best. Unfortunately, there had been too many obstacles today.

A light drizzle filled the air and the road became slick, forcing the bus to drive even slower. Sali checked the truck's odometer: just under three kilometers since they'd passed the Camp Four sign. At this rate, it'd take at least fifteen minutes to go the rest of the distance. Minutes passed like hours. Finally, the road leveled out and the bus accelerated.

"Beer bottles, straight ahead, left side!" Malik called out. Sali sighted a gap in the pine trees that led up a gentle rise, exactly as Rolio had drawn on the map. "That must be the ridgeline up there," Sali said.

Malik adjusted his eyeglasses. "Why would someone put a store out here?" he asked. "This doesn't look right."

Sali was so focused on driving that the boy's concerns went unheard. He turned off the highway. The truck bounced and shook as they crept up the narrow dirt road. It weaved upward for another kilometer, eventually widening at the crest.

"I see Rolio. We're here, Malik, we made it!"

Ahead in a clearing, Rolio stood, waving them forward. Three men were at his side. Sali parked between two other vehicles.

"You're late. I told you two o'clock." Rolio's dark eyes were cold as ice.

"We ran into some trouble," Sali began apologetically. The truck rocked as more men exploded from nowhere and ripped open the rear hatch. The truck's passenger door flew open. Sali watched as Malik was dragged out. A chill ran through his body.

"What's going—" A roundhouse punch struck him from the side. He felt his nose begin to bleed. Someone opened the door and slugged him again before he could react. He fell onto his back in the dirt.

Sali heard a voice. "You didn't say anything about the kid. What should we do with him?" He rolled to his side and saw the boy's legs kicking while being dragged across the gravel.

"Forget him," Rolio said. Sali looked up and saw men clamoring onto the top of the truck. He heard the sound of boxes tumbling out, followed by the clanking of metal. "Quick, get it up here, now. I can see them lifting off the runway," another voice said.

Sali felt his eyes swelling shut. His nose was numb with pain. He saw the blurred image of arms and legs slipping around on the truck's wet roof. "Don't hurt the boy," he mumbled. "Please."

Rolio hollered, "Screw down those mounts like I showed you yesterday!" Sali heard another voice, standing above him. "What about the boy, and this one on the ground?"

"Do what you have to do," Rolio said. Sali turned his head. He saw that Malik had broken free and was stumbling across the boxes that Rolio's gang had flung from the truck.

"Run, boy, run!" Sali yelled.

Two rifle shots rang out as Malik disappeared into the trees. Sali watched as a pair of muddy boots walked around the truck toward him. He rolled to his side and tried to prop himself up, but he was too groggy. Gradually, his vision cleared, allowing him to focus on the face above him. The man had long, scraggly hair and wore thick glasses that made him look bug-eyed. He raised his rifle and held the barrel an inch from Sali's nose. Sali's heart raced as he lay in the dirt, paralyzed with fear. The man growled at him, then laughed and slung the weapon over his shoulder. Sali gasped a sigh of relief. He pushed the blood-soaked strands of hair from his forehead and started to get up. But a boot crashed into his chest and shoved him back down. The man hovered over him again.

The final image that registered in Salipada Menadun's brain was the sight of a rifle butt descending into his face.

Chapter 22

The Japanese mechanics began packing up for their flight home. They'd successfully reattached the helicopter's nose gear and repaired its mangled underbelly. Together with Jenks' crew, they'd installed new wiring and electronics.

McGirt and Bud pulled up into the hangar parking lot as the aircraft was being towed onto the tarmac. "She looks pretty good, even with just the primer," Bud said to Jenks and the mechanics' supervisor, Yoshi.

"Don't have time to spray a coat of Navy gray on her now, sir," Jenks said as he nursed a mug of black coffee. "We'll do that after we fly aboard."

McGirt crouched below the aircraft and ran his palm along the yellow-green primed section of new aluminum. The repair was flawless. Supporting the nose section was a shiny chrome strut with two new tires.

"We'll do some abbreviated ground checks, Chief, to verify engine trimming and flight controls," Bud said. A slew of black boxes affecting the aircraft's stabilization system had been replaced, prompting the control check. "Then the same in a hover. Assuming everything's OK, we'll fly out over the water and bend her around a little."

"Sounds good to me, Commander," Jenks acknowledged. No longer assigned to regular aircrew duty, he'd made a trip to Cubi Point's para-loft, where flight gear and survival equipment were maintained. The young female sailor who'd fitted him with a loaner zoom-bag had apologized, "Sorry, Chief, this is the biggest size I've got – fifty-two extra long." The bottom of the green flight suit's legs barely touched the top of his boots. In order to get it on, he'd held his breath while she'd fought with the zipper. He looked like a giant pickle.

Earlier that morning, Bud and McGirt had driven to Base Operations to take care of pre-flight paperwork. A pimply-faced petty officer had diligently shown them some charts depicting a front moving in from the South China Sea. "You should be OK, sir," he'd said. "Try and get back by mid-afternoon. After that, I predict we'll get dumped on dang hard." After the briefing, they filled out the standard military flight plan, leaving a copy with the operations duty officer.

They would depart to the west under visual flight rules. In addition to the cockpit's required checks, Jenks would do a scan of the helo's rotor blades as part of a periodic check to confirm that the six airfoils were tracking properly. Once the functional checks were complete, Bud and his crew would be on their own, free to do what they wanted. McGirt had been grounded for over two weeks, and Bud wanted to give him some extra stick time before setting out to sea on *San Angelo*. Accordingly, they planned to motor up the west coast of Luzon, skim over the Zambales Mountains and then descend to a spot on the Lingayen Gulf for a fuel stop. From there, they'd fly an inland route back to Cubi, with practice approaches and another fuel stop at Clark. Total mission time: four and a half hours.

McGirt strapped himself into the aircraft commander's seat. "Nice to be back in the saddle," he said to Bud. Pre-flight and engine start were uneventful, as were the myriad ground checks they were required to perform.

"Taxi's real nice," McGirt commented as he steered the helicopter up an inclined taxiway that led from the hangar to the airfield's runway. Jenks had recommended that the crew make a rolling takeoff to further verify the new nose gear's integrity.

"Those Kawasaki boys did some fine work. She feels smooth as glass," Bud said as they scooted down the long strip of concrete. "Guess they do more than just build fast motorcycles over there."

They lifted off and whizzed by Grande Island. Nothing but open, unrestricted blue sky lay in front of them. McGirt wasted no time. He pressed the cyclic forward and pulled up on the collective. Unloaded, the aircraft accelerated rapidly. The two pilots performed more controllability checks while Sartelli and Jenks readied the test equipment for rotor blade tracking.

"Controls feel nice and tight. Plenty of engine torque, too. Maybe a slight beat coming from the forward rotor head," Bud said. "Chief, you rigged for blade tracking yet?"

"Yes, sir, ready to go," Jenks replied.

As McGirt kept the aircraft straight and level, Jenks held up a boxy-looking lantern attached by an electrical cord to an outlet behind the aircraft's cockpit. He stood by the open entry door and pointed it at the bird's forward rotor blades whirling above. Two-inch wide, rectangular metal flags had been screwed into the ends of the blades. The small flags were each painted with a distinguishing set of reflective markings. Jenks triggered the lantern and aimed its strobe light at the spinning blades. The three flags became visible, superimposed as a single image by the pulsing beam. Jenks focused on the blinking display frozen in space. Sartelli was ready to log the readings.

"Yup, just as I'd expected," Jenks said. "Number two blade's down an inch. Number three's up a half. One's OK." He faced aft to check the other head. "Commander, aft head looks good to me. Whadya think?"

"That's exactly what it feels like up here, Chief. Do you want to go back right now and make the adjustments, or can we press on?" Jenks squeezed his thick frame between the two pilot seats, gave a thumbs-up and waved his hand forward, signaling they should keep going. Upon return, a mechanic would climb up to the helicopter's forward head and adjust the errant blades' pitch links a few clicks to bring them into sync. The result would be a smoother ride and less stress on the helicopter's moving components. The readings that Sartelli had recorded were acceptable by the book. During the cruise, however, Jenks had insisted that the blades track perfectly — not just "within limits."

McGirt made a series of turns, climbs and descents. He waggled the stick and keyed his mike. "You want some, Boss?" Bud took over and continued putting the machine through some paces: high banked "rotor-overs," rapid ascents and auto-rotating dives. After a few minutes of yanking and banking, he turned the controls back to Johnny Jack. McGirt swooped down to a hundred feet above the water and hugged the lush tropical coast. They flew past a group of fishermen casting their lines from the sandy shore. The natives waved as McGirt added power and pulled the helo into a steep climb — one thousand, two thousand, three thousand. The aircraft's altimeters spun like pinwheels in a storm. The humid air thinned out, replaced by a cool, clean breeze throughout the cabin.

"Yeeee-haaaa! God damn, it's great to be back!" McGirt hollered. They flew inland, passing abeam the town of Santa Cruz. McGirt continued on a northeasterly course toward the Lingayen Gulf and their fuel stop, Wallace Air Station, on Poro Point. Sartelli sat down to gnaw on the box lunch he'd brought along while Jenks stretched out on a troop seat and fell asleep.

***

Two hours after Bud and McGirt launched, DET 110's ground crew readied their second aircraft for its flight to Baguio. With Jenks airborne, supervisory duties fell into the hands of a crusty, twenty-two-year First Class named Dobbs. Jenks had delegated the role to Dobbs before, with varying results. The sailor had been busted a few times and seemed hopelessly trapped in his present rank, unable to advance into the vaunted world of chief petty officers. Nonetheless, Dobbs had done a decent job as second-in-command during the cruise. Jenks felt comfortable turning over the reins to him while he went flying. He'd scribbled out some pass-down instructions for the sailor. At the bottom of the list were his encouraging but succinct words: *Don't fuck up.*

Thomas Rayburn had leapt at the opportunity to make the Baguio run. He would drop off a cadre of blackshoes from *San Angelo* who'd won a lottery for the chance to spend a couple nights in the cool mountain resort. Rayburn, as usual, showed up at the last minute. He'd left all the flight planning duties to Ensign Bright.

"Bob, I have some personal business off base this morning," Rayburn had told Bright. "Why don't you fly the legs up to Baguio?" He handed Bright a blank flight plan, which he'd already signed. The passengers and crew were already onboard when his Marine pal dropped him off on the tarmac.

"Thanks for doing everything," Rayburn said to Bright after he'd tied down a suitcase in the cabin.

"Planning on spending the night?" Bright asked.

Rayburn forced a belly laugh and said. "No, no, no. Just brought some things to drop off with some friends up north." He turned to face the dozen passengers and gave them a hearty, airline-style greeting. "Gentlemen, welcome aboard." The apprehensive group smiled nervously. On Dobbs' orders, they'd been strapped in their seats for twenty minutes already and were miserable cooped up in the sweltering cabin.

"Sir, how long will this take?" one man asked.

"Well, son, probably no longer than a couple hours, total. The ensign here has informed me that we'll need to refuel once," Rayburn said.

"Good," the guy replied. Rayburn gave him a reassuring pat on the shoulder and said, "Relax, you're in good hands today."

The two crewmen for the flight, L. C. LaRue and Freddy Lincoln, had been reunited for the first time since their fateful night at sea. As a result of the Mishap Board, LaRue had been sent to Captain's Mast where Lugansky had awarded him a two hundred dollar fine and a suspended reduction in rate. Lugansky had told him, "You so much as fart upwind of me and you're busted." Lincoln's leg had healed well enough for the doc to sign his up chit. Despite being paired with the uncouth Cajun, he was glad to be flying again.

Bright held out the paperwork for Rayburn to see as the lieutenant strapped in.

"Our clearance is on request, sir. The weather office says we'll have strong headwinds en route. Chance of storms later today, but I think we'll beat them if we don't loiter in Baguio."

Rayburn gave the documents a cursory glance and said, "Let's go."

The thirty-minute trip up Luzon's central valley went as planned. They taxied into Clark's hot fueling pits to top off their tanks for the climbing jaunt to Baguio. Lincoln and LaRue got out and handled the refueling evolution while the aircraft's engines and rotors kept spinning. With a relatively light load onboard, the helicopter climbed easily to eight thousand feet for the leg to Baguio's Loakan Airport. Once dropped off there, the passengers would hire a jitney to shuttle them a few miles to their destination, Camp John Hay. The facility was named in honor of President Theodore Roosevelt's secretary of state, John Milton Hay. The recreation complex was a treasured getaway for servicemen and U.S. government employees. The pine-shrouded mountain resort offered them an escape from the harsh temperatures of the lowlands.

"Aren't you tired of hand-flying this thing?" Rayburn asked on the interphone.

"Nope," Bright said. "Every chance I get to work on my stick and rudder skills, I take it." He'd ignored the aircraft's auto-flight system since departing from Cubi.

"Ensign, at some point in your career you'll realize that there's more to being a naval officer than flying." Rayburn reached across the cockpit and tapped on Bright's helmet. "That's what will get you ahead in this man's navy, not your hands and feet."

"Probably so," Brightness said. "But I sure as heck enjoy doing this while I can." Rayburn checked his navigation chart to confirm that they were still tracking the designated course. Bright was holding a sizeable crab into the stiff, crossing headwind.

"Don't know why I even carry this anymore," Rayburn said, referring to the map in his hands. "It's quite elementary: follow the roads and don't hit the mountains." Bright looked down at the detailed itinerary he'd drawn up. On his kneeboard was a point-to-point breakdown of their route. He'd spent an hour computing the data. Each flight segment was laid out neatly by distance, time, and fuel burn. Rayburn saw the columns and waved a hand dismissively. "Looks like you wasted a lot of time there, Bob."

The crew enjoyed the ride over Luzon's luxuriant terrain. Green peaks jutted up more than ten thousand feet above sea level. Rayburn was more than happy to let Brightness do the driving this afternoon. "Wish I had more time to put my mind at parade rest like this. It's a nice change of pace," he said. "But with everything going on — my duties as assistant O-I-C, and writing the flight schedule, and my job on the ship! — these short runs to Baguio and the embassy in Manila are about all that I can squeeze in."

"Yes, sir, we've noticed."

Rayburn bristled. "Oh really – what do you mean by that?"

Sensing the conversation was going down a path he didn't want to follow, Bright back-pedaled and quickly moved on to something less volatile. "Like you said, sir, you've been busy. Someday, I'd like to spend a few days up here treasure hunting."

"What for? Did pirates get shipwrecked and bury their doubloons in the hills?"

"Pretty close, sir. I've been reading some local history. The Japanese hid much of the war booty they'd gathered from around Asia here in the Philippines. Legend has it that a good deal of it is holed up in tunnels right up there." He pointed to the steep terrain ahead as the city of Baguio emerged in their view.

"That so?" Rayburn said. He reached for his notebook. "Where is it?"

Bright laughed. "If I knew that, I'd probably be sailing my yacht to Martha's Vineyard right now! Supposedly, in tunnels and caves carved out into the mountains. People call it Yamashita's gold, after the general who commanded the Japanese army in the P.I."

"Did he take some of it back to Japan with him?" Rayburn asked.

"Unfortunately for him, no. He was executed by hanging after being convicted of war crimes."

Rayburn jotted some notes. "Yam-a-shee-ta, got it. I'll have to read up about that gold."

The hook was set and Bright couldn't resist. "Or you can get a private audience with the Philippine president; maybe he'll give you some clues. Apparently he's tapped into the treasure. Some folks suspect he's got it hidden below his palace."

"Yeah, right, like that's going to happen." Rayburn smirked and tossed the notebook back inside his helmet bag. LaRue and Lincoln prepared the cabin for landing, and Bright lined up for an approach to the runway. Considering the airport's elevation, close to a mile high, he decided to do a running landing. After touchdown, they rolled the length of the five-thousand-foot strip to a small terminal at the airfield's western edge. A handful of workers appeared to greet them.

Bright looked west, toward the Lingayen Gulf. "Looks like those clouds are moving in faster than they thought," he said and looked at his watch. "Those headwinds made us a little late." The passengers hustled off to a couple of awaiting jitneys, grateful to be out of the rumbling aircraft and on their way to liberty.

Rayburn was quickly out of his seat. "Got some business to do, Ensign." He grabbed his suitcase and walked out the aircraft's aft ramp. "Make sure everything gets done," he said over his shoulder. Bright followed behind. LaRue had already hooked up the hose. A fuel truck had parked next to them when the rotors had stopped.

Lincoln climbed down from the helo after inspecting its engines and rotor heads. "Shouldn't need that much gas, Mr. Bright. We're just going back down into the valley, to Clark, aren't we?" he asked.

LaRue interrupted, "The lieutenant told me to fill 'er up. Said he wants to go straight to Cubi." He waved a hand at the fueler, telling him to speed it up. The truck wheezed and rattled. "Damn, this thing's pumping slower than I piss," he commented.

Bright spotted Rayburn standing with a group of Filipino men by the side of the terminal building. Rayburn reached into his bag and extracted four packages wrapped in brown paper. One of the men tucked them into a canvas sack and walked to a car. Another gave a thumbs-up signal. Three pickup trucks eased forward and onto the tarmac. Bright met the convoy as they approached the aircraft's aft ramp.

"What's up?" he asked the lead driver. The guy shrugged and pointed behind him. Bright peeked under the tarp-draped bed. He saw cases of strawberry wine stacked inside. He went to the second vehicle; it held a load of rattan furniture. The third truck carried a variety of furniture, more wine and a mound of wooden crates. The crates were stenciled with the words "Thank you for shopping at the Saint Louis Silver Store."

Rayburn jogged back across the tarmac. "Hey, Bob, I forgot to mention it, but I'm helping out some P-3 guys and hauling some gedunk that they ordered. The usual touristy stuff."

Bright surveyed the freight. "Any idea how much this weighs?"

Rayburn held up his palms reassuringly. "Not an ounce over three thousand pounds. My friend said they put it on the scales this morning. We can punch the charts. If the numbers don't add up, then I'll have them take some of it back." The drivers got out and started hauling the gear into the aircraft.

"What about the fuel? You told LaRue to top off the tanks," Bright said. "That's going to make us pretty heavy for this density altitude."

Rayburn reddened. "Yeah, well, that's another thing. My buddies are getting airborne for Guam in about an hour and a half. We lost time on the way up here. I think we'll be OK with the tailwind and can skip the fuel stop at Clark."

Bright frowned and walked back into the aircraft. He grabbed the helicopter's operating manual and sat in his seat. He paged to the back of it, where the performance section was located. Rayburn came aboard and helped the two crewmen secure the cargo. The merchandise seemed to have multiplied while it was being carried off the trucks. The cabin was stuffed full, or in loadmaster's lingo, "cubed out." Bright wrote some numbers on his kneeboard. He turned to Rayburn, held up the flight manual and pointed out graphs that cross-referenced temperature, altitude and aircraft weight.

"Follow me, please," he said. "Twenty-five hundred pounds of fuel, another three thousand of cargo. At a temperature of seventy-five degrees and an elevation of forty-three hundred feet, that puts us at a density altitude of over seven grand." Bright guided his index finger along the graph: right to left, along a curved index, back left and down. "According to this, we're barely legal, even if we make a rolling takeoff." Lincoln and LaRue were wedged into the cockpit's entry, hanging on his words. "We'll get airborne, but this thing's going to climb like a pregnant sow."

LaRue laughed and then spit into a cup. "No sweat. Why can't we just fly through the valley, like we always do? It's downhill all the way." He slapped Lincoln on the back, sat down and cracked open a fresh can of Skoal.

"Looks like that storm's brewing fast, Mr. Bright," Lincoln observed. A grayish wall of water was falling from a bank of clouds to the west. Bright looked up and noted the approaching weather, then turned his head to the left and noticed that the three pickups were long gone.

Rayburn checked his watch and buckled up. "I'll take full responsibility, Ensign," he said. Brightness sat defiantly, arms folded across his chest. The thick blue flight manual remained on his lap.

"Let's get goin'!" LaRue shouted. "I've got a hot momma-san waiting for me out in town."

Rayburn could see that Bright wasn't going to budge, so he offered, "Listen, if you don't want to go, we won't." He rapped his knuckles on the top of the instrument panel impatiently. "Well?"

Bright set the manual down to his side. "OK, but you can't get slow in the climb. We're right on the edge." He pinched a forefinger and thumb together.

The crew went through the pre-flight checklist. The engines and rotors spooled up while Rayburn called the tower for taxi clearance and asked them to change the flight's destination from Clark to Cubi Point. The helicopter rolled lethargically to the far east end of the runway. Bright noted two airplanes standing by to land after the helo departed. A small Cessna and another bigger twin-engine — most likely a commuter from Manila — orbited lazily over the mountaintops. Rayburn did a one-eighty on the runway as Bright called the tower for takeoff clearance. The airport's orange windsock hung limp. No words were spoken as Rayburn pulled up on the collective slightly and pushed the cyclic stick forward. The counter-rotating rotor heads tilted down and pitch increased equally on all six blades. The aircraft began to gain speed. A third of the way down the airstrip, Rayburn applied a little aft stick, raising the nose gear off the deck, the same as any fixed-wing pilot would do. Slowly, the helicopter's main wheels lifted free and they were flying. Airspeed increased through fifty knots. The airframe shuddered as the rotors passed through translational lift. Rate of climb increased.

"I'll make a left turn at the end of the runway to stay away from the weather," Rayburn said.

"Speed looks good and we're climbing five hundred feet per minute," Bright said.

"Engine temps below limits." Both aviators breathed easier. Rayburn rolled into a steep left bank and followed the canyon. The aircraft lost airspeed in the turn, but now over the deep ravine, he was able to trade off some altitude and accelerated past one hundred knots.

About three miles from the airport, LaRue unstrapped and came forward. "See, I told you, Mr. Bright — piece of cake," he said. He stepped to the right side of the aircraft, behind the cockpit, and enjoyed the view out the main entry hatch. A half-mile ahead, he saw a cluster of vehicles huddled together on a ridge. A man was standing on the roof of one of them. LaRue raised a hand to wave when he saw a puff of smoke erupt from the vehicle. "What the…? They're shooting at us!" he screamed over the intercom. A second later the forward rotor head buffeted and the aircraft started shaking violently.

Rayburn looked up and saw one of the forward blades hopping wildly, out of sync with the other two. He fought with the controls and managed to maintain course and speed. "We... got... to... set... down!" he said. His vibrato voice was barely understandable. LaRue leaned out of the hatch and watched the ridgeline as it disappeared behind them.

"Forward head out of track. RPMs OK," Bright reported.

Rayburn searched frantically for a spot to land. He saw a dirt road below, but ruled that out because of thick pine trees on both of its sides. A few miles to the east, the topography flattened out, so he aimed for that. The helicopter bucked like an angry bronco, but stayed in one piece. Then the second wave of fifty-caliber shells hit. The first round tore through the right fuel tank's lower section and exited cleanly out the top. Miraculously, it missed all six rotor blades as it sailed upward between them. But the crew's luck didn't hold. Whether through marksmanship or blind luck, the shooter found the aircraft's right engine, scoring a direct hit on the motor's turbine section, just forward of its exhaust. The engine's precision-milled turbine blades disintegrated instantly. Its combustion chamber erupted and the engine burst into flames.

"Engine failure, number two. Fire, number two," Bright called out. He stretched forward over the center console and pulled an illuminated red fire handle. Fuel and oil were shut off to that engine, but the molten-hot, damaged turbine continued to burn. Bright followed up by pressing two buttons located below the handle he'd pulled. An electrical signal was sent to a set of bottles that released chemical agents into and around the burning engine. After a few seconds the fire was extinguished.

"Going for the open area up ahead," Rayburn said. His eyes were glued on a clearing. The operating engine, sensing that its twin had died, automatically triggered its fuel control to open wider, providing full military power. A complex set of gears and clutches allowed the lone engine to drive both rotor systems at reduced power. The aircraft shook badly, but was still maintaining altitude.

"Watch your turns," Bright commanded, referring to the rotor system's revolutions. "And keep your airspeed up."

The 50 percent loss of power quickly drained the aircraft's rotary energy. Airspeed sank precipitously below fifty knots. Rotor turns decreased below 100 percent and drooped dangerously toward the minimum safe level to remain airborne.

"Lower the collective to get some turns. Lower the collective! Right rudder, right rudder!" Bright hollered as if he were instructing a primary flight student. He tried desperately to coach Rayburn through basic emergency procedures, but the pilot was unresponsive. "We can't fly this slow, Lieutenant. We don't have the energy!"

The aircraft continued its path down the winding valley. The only way for the rotors to regain their speed was for Rayburn to decrease blade pitch by lowering the collective and pushing forward on the cyclic. Both were counterintuitive moves as the aircraft skimmed over the treetops. But it was their only way out.

Airspeed continued to bleed away. "You're too slow!" Bright screamed. "Arm the emergency throttle."

Rayburn poked around on the top of the collective, searching for the correct button. The emergency throttle would allow him to completely bypass the engine's automatic fuel control and regulate fuel flow manually, free from any governing limits. Bright activated the throttle himself. He then remembered a step he'd missed and commenced dumping fuel to lighten their weight, but it was too late. Rayburn had frozen up. Bright tried to overpower him on his set of flight controls, but Rayburn was stronger. Airspeed and rotor turns decayed rapidly. The aircraft wobbled in a gyrating hover as the crew of Sideflare Zero-One ran out of rotor turns, altitude and ideas. Generators dropped off-line, cutting electrical power to the helicopter's stabilization equipment. They were no longer a flying machine, but rather a big, free-falling mass of moving parts. The aircraft plummeted into a canopy of dense pine trees. The thick vegetation cushioned its descent rate as the machine ripped through tightly knitted branches and rolled to its left. On its way down, flailing rotor blades shredded trees like giant machetes.

The aircraft fell unimpeded the last twenty feet and slammed to the earth.

Chapter 23

The helicopter came to rest on its left side, tilted at a fifteen-degree, nose-down angle. Rayburn was in mild shock, but physically unscathed on the upside of the wreck. He looked to his left and saw Bright slumped against the instrument console. A bundle of pine boughs had smashed through Bright's side window, shrouding his helmet and shoulders. Rayburn pushed against Bright's side and called his name, but received no response. The left engine was still running and whined sickly, despite being disconnected from the mutilated rotor system. Rayburn shoved the motor's control lever to the shutdown position. The turbine wound down and hissed to a stop.

Rayburn heard garbled hollers and cries from behind him in the cabin. He craned his head below the forward transmission area to look for Lincoln and LaRue, but his view was blocked. The furniture and crates had broken loose from their tie-downs and had flung forward after impact. He was isolated from the two crewmembers in the cabin, so he reached up and sprung the escape door to the right of his seat. He braced himself against the cockpit's center console and heaved the Plexiglas and steel door away from the aircraft. He shimmied out the opening and jumped six feet to the ground. The wreckage was ensconced in a heap of tree limbs, twisted rotor blades and assorted debris, causing him to lose his balance and stumble as he walked.

From ground level, through the trees, Rayburn could see the small clearing he'd been heading for before things turned bad. The aircraft had traveled just a few miles from the populated airport area, but he saw no sign of people in the remote surroundings. He moved farther away from the crash site until he was able to see some activity on a ridgeline a quarter mile above. An automobile had appeared and three men got out. Rayburn shouted and waved his arms for help. One of the men motioned to his companions for them to join him as he began to descend the steep embankment. Rayburn heard the men arguing in Tagalog. One man was ranting about something and started hollering at the other two. The group disappeared briefly into the thick woods. When they reemerged, two hundred yards away on the hillside, one of the group stared down at Rayburn, drew up his rifle and took aim. The other two became agitated and yelled at him, but the shooter ignored them. Whatever thoughts Rayburn had of being rescued vanished as a volley of shots rang out. He dove for the ground as the bullets whizzed over his head and ricocheted off a formation of boulders behind him. He stayed low, scampered behind the rocks and took cover.

The trio continued arguing. One of them cursed the other two and started back up the hill toward the car. Rayburn saw his chance and bolted out from behind the barricade. He ran deeper into the dense forest.

When the aircraft had rolled to its side, an untethered case of wine had caught Freddy Lincoln squarely in the midsection. The crate had knocked the wind out of him, preventing him from answering Rayburn's calls. The last thing he remembered was hearing LaRue's voice on the intercom. After that, his mind had been saturated with noise, vibrations and the jolting crash.

The cabin load had shifted forward and to aircraft left. Lincoln thought that he heard LaRue moaning from under the freight. He called out the Cajun's name, but there was no response and the moaning had stopped. Lincoln unlatched his seat belt and started pushing through the loose freight, forward toward LaRue, but his path was blocked. He turned around and spotted a gap between the aircraft's ramp and aft transmission. He began clawing his way to the daylight. He gripped the sides of the narrow opening to hoist himself out, but his gloves slipped on the wet metal. The distinctive aroma of JP-5 jet fuel filled his nostrils. Freddy got a better grip and pulled his way clear, out from the back end of the helicopter.

Fuel poured from three locations: the two dump nozzles at the bottoms of the tanks, with another stream gushing from the top of the right tank, where a shell had exited. Lincoln crawled along the outside of the wreckage and went forward toward the cockpit. He looked through the helo's chin bubble and saw that Rayburn's seat was empty. He crouched down and looked into the copilot's section. Bright was still strapped in. Lincoln tore off his bulky flight gear and hoisted himself up into the opening on Rayburn's side. His ribs ached. The flying case of wine had struck him harder than he'd thought.

"Mr. Bright, Mr. Bright, you OK?" he called. He turned the pilot's head to one side and placed two fingers along Bright's jugular, finding a faint pulse. Lincoln unstrapped him from his seat and attempted to raise the pilot's sagging body up and out of the aircraft. But the cockpit was too cramped for him to get any leverage and he didn't have the arm strength to manhandle Bright through the opening. The smell of aviation fuel grew stronger as the tanks continued to drain. Fuel seeped into the rear cabin and began to pool in crevices around the aft transmission and engine bays.

Lincoln looked back into the cabin, hoping that LaRue's face would rise from the rubble. "LaRue, LaRue, I need you up here, man. I need your help!"

Suddenly he heard a loud pop, followed by a wave of heat against the skin of his face. Flickers of orange flames flashed through the cracks of open space in the dim cabin. Lincoln's worst fears had come into being: the fuel had found a path to the hot transmission and engines. The fire spread quickly through the shattered pieces of wooden crates and rattan furniture. In less than a minute, the aluminum tunnel was a raging inferno. Lincoln had to make a decision: try again to get Bright out, or save himself. His eyes searched frantically around the lopsided cockpit. He gripped and yanked hard on the pilot's survival vest, hoisting him partially from his seat. He then hooked a loose strap on Bright's gear over the top of the other pilot's collective stick, which protruded straight out like a short yardarm. With Bright's body suspended from the collective, Lincoln slid across Rayburn's seat and dangled feet first, halfway out Rayburn's open escape hatch. He grabbed Bright's vest with both hands, held tightly and jerked until the strap that he'd hooked over the collective was free. He started kicking in a jack-knife fashion from his waist, like a swimmer does while doing the butterfly stroke.

"LaRue, LaRue, I need you!" he hollered.

The fire roared forward, licking at the cockpit entryway. Lincoln saw flames touch the bottoms of the ensign's spit-shined boots and the polished leather began to smolder. Searing heat scorched his skin and singed his eyebrows. He jack-knifed harder and pulled as the twosome teetered over the hatch's edge like a human seesaw. Desperate, he cried out, "Sweet Jesus, help me!" His forearms ached from the strain and his ribcage hurt terribly, but he refused to quit. He threw back his head and gave a violent kick, then another. A third convulsive kick was the charm. Bright's head and shoulders emerged from the hatch. Gravity took over and did the rest as the two men fell to the ground. Bright's unconscious body landed smack-dab on top of Lincoln, and the pilot's helmet slammed into Lincoln's forehead, splitting open a nasty gash. But the stubborn sailor from Alabama was unfazed. He rose to his feet and dragged Bright a dozen yards away before tripping over some tree branches and aircraft parts. Pumped with adrenalin and thankful to be alive, Lincoln sprang back to his feet. He slung Bright over his shoulder fireman-style, the way he'd learned in boot camp, and trudged to the nearby clearing. As he walked, he searched the area for Rayburn, but the lieutenant was nowhere in sight. He deposited Bright's body on the ground and then collapsed next to him. He rolled over to his back and gasped from the smoke and fumes he'd ingested. A black mushroom cloud blotted out the sunlight above them. He prayed that LaRue had somehow gotten out of the helo before the fire had erupted.

* * *

Initially obscured by high terrain, the evil-looking black smoke had risen several thousand feet, straight up above the peaks. Once the strong wind got hold of it, it flattened out the plume like the head of an anvil.

"That doesn't look good, does it?" Bud said. He and McGirt were thirty miles south of the Baguio airport, on their way to Clark. The wall of weather west of Baguio provided a curtainlike backdrop for the dark, ugly smoke cloud.

"Only one thing I know makes that color smoke," Jenks said. He and Sartelli had heard Bud's comment. Without saying a word, the rest of the crew knew exactly what Jenks meant. He'd seen enough grisly accidents in his time to recognize the portentous sight of burning aviation fuel.

McGirt had just asked Jenks what time Rayburn was due at Cubi when they heard the distress call: "Zero-One under fire!" There was a period of silence, a burst of static, and then the words "shot down." Bud switched their UHF radio to preset channel "G" or Guard: frequency 243.0 megahertz.

"Go ahead Zero-One, this is Zero-Two. Say again," Bud transmitted. A garbled response followed. "Somebody's on their Prick 90," McGirt said, referencing the handheld radio all crewmembers packed in their survival vests. The PRC-90 had a range limit of fifty miles when its beam traveled line-of sight, without obstructions. McGirt started to climb higher for better reception.

"Let's turn back toward Baguio," Bud said. The black cloud was now obscured from their view as the rainstorm barreled eastward. Bud repeated, "Zero-One, this is Zero-Two, say again please."

"Five miles... south... attack, aircraft down."

"We've got to get over there, fast," Bud said. "Sartelli, Jenks?"

"We're on it, sir," the chief answered. "Standing by."

McGirt stayed on the controls while Bud coordinated with the crew. "We'll look for a spot to set down. It doesn't look too promising, though, this far up into the mountain range. Be ready with the hoist."

Sartelli replied, "Chief and I are rigging it as we speak, sir."

Bud had focused all of his efforts on the radio call and had ignored the storms they'd skirted after leaving Poro Point. After reversing course, however, they were headed directly at them.

"Bud, we're driving right into this crap," McGirt said. The aircraft entered some moderate turbulence and rain as they nibbled on the storm's leading edge. McGirt had spent most all of the last three hours flying. His hands were tired, so he'd turned on the autopilot.

Bud reached down and turned off the switches. "I've got it, J. J." The weather was rapidly getting worse and it became more difficult to see the high terrain around them.

"Coming over from Poro, I'm pretty sure that I sighted a road to the west of the smoke," Bud added. "That's got to be it, over there." He pointed to the meandering swatch of pavement. "Can't be too many other highways out here." He dipped down to follow it. The crew could smell the smoke as the hazy visibility decreased to less than a mile. A steady rain started to pelt the windshield and the turbulence got worse.

"We've got to get down lower or we'll never see them," McGirt said.

Bud slowed the aircraft and descended to treetop level above the highway. Rainfall grew more intense. He fought with the machine as it rocked from the downdrafts; they were directly beneath a thunderstorm. With visibility near zero, Bud cautiously brought the aircraft to a hover over the road. He resumed a slow forward flight and followed the twisting road up the mountain.

"Jesus Christ, we've got nowhere to go!" McGirt said. He saw steep terrain on both sides; they were boxed in. He turned on the aircraft's wipers, but the rain was falling so hard, they were useless and just added to the noise. He switched them off.

"Just keep us in the air until this weather passes," he said to Bud. Forward visibility was nil so the pilots looked out their side windows for reference.

Jenks keyed his mike. "Commander, I think I see something to the right, about our two o'clock position." Bud pushed on the right rudder pedal and pointed the aircraft in that direction. A burning pile of debris materialized before them. The deluge was suppressing the black smoke, but the inferno still raged. The HCS-30 logo on the aircraft's tail confirmed their fears. Jenks stood by the cabin doorway, stunned by what he saw. Bud kept the helo at one hundred feet above the wreck. Even at that height, they could feel the intense heat. He backed away from the crash and did a methodical three hundred and sixty degree pirouette to survey the site. His heart sank at what he saw.

"Somebody musta made it out to call us like they did," Jenks said.

Sartelli had joined him in the doorway. "Commander, look over there, farther to our right. I see somebody in that clearing. I'll go down on the hoist to check it out if Chief can operate the winch."

Bud air-taxied to the spot where a crumpled form in a flight suit lay on the ground. There was a break in the weather as the wind let up and the showers petered out to a drizzle. "Hold on, Guido. I think I can set her down. It looks level enough."

"We'd better do it now, Bud," McGirt said, "Before the next cell rolls in."

Bud centered the helicopter over the landing zone and gingerly lowered the collective. By now it was evident that they were looking at a fellow crewmember. The limp body buffeted from the rotor wash as they descended. "Looks clear on my side," McGirt said. "You've got least ten feet."

The ground was more sloped than it had appeared from the air. One wheel contacted the ground first. Bud compensated with side stick and lowered the other set of tires. The aircraft settled at a manageable ten-degree list — no worse than when landing at sea during moderate swells. Sartelli and Jenks were out the door before the rotors came to a stop.

Bright, now conscious, rolled onto his back as Sartelli approached him. "They took Freddy," he said as he gripped his left forearm and tried to get up.

"You ain't looking too good, sir," Sartelli said. Bright's sleeve was soaked in blood and there was a large hole in his flight suit, near the shoulder. Sartelli gently examined the tear. Beneath the fabric, he saw that a jagged bone had ripped through the skin. "Better stay down, sir. Your arm's busted up pretty bad." He raised the pilot's helmet visor. Bright's eyes were open, but his pupils were dilated wide in a thousand-mile stare.

"They got Lincoln... in the woods," Bright slurred. "Dizzy..." he turned his head and vomited.

The two pilots came out of the aircraft. Bud knelt down and asked, "Robert, where's Rayburn and LaRue?" Bright shook his head. His eyes rolled back and he drifted off.

There was a rustling sound from behind them. The group turned in unison to see Thomas Rayburn appear slowly from the trees. Rayburn ran the last few yards to join them. He took off his helmet and hurled it to the ground.

"They shot at us, those bastards!" He proceeded to tell what had happened and how someone had chased him with a rifle. But the words didn't make sense to Bud. *Where the hell was Rayburn after the crash?* he thought. *Why hadn't he stayed with his men?*

"Rayburn, where's LaRue? Was he with you?"

"I heard some sounds from the cabin after we crashed, but I don't know if he made it out. I only saw them take Lincoln."

"I'm goin' to look for LaRue," Jenks announced. "Maybe he got tossed out when they hit."

"Chief, stay away from the fire!" Bud shouted as Jenks double-timed it across the clearing.

Bright came to his senses again. He was more alert this time. "Boss, two guys with rifles took Lincoln. I saw them start toward that hill over there." He raised his good arm and pointed to the opposite side of the valley.

"OK. Rayburn, you make some more calls on the radio and stay here with Sartelli." Bud looked back at the fire again and added, "Maybe LaRue will show up. The two of us will go after Lincoln."

Lammers and McGirt dropped their gear and started jogging in the direction that Bright had pointed. A thick grove of pines led up to another ridgeline. They'd traveled only a few yards when Sartelli hollered, "Commander, up there! I see them!" Bud looked up the hill and saw three men. Lincoln was in the middle, being dragged along.

McGirt had sprinted ahead and was already fifty yards up the hill. Bud followed him but couldn't keep up. The air was thin and the ground was still wet. Bud became winded and kept slipping as McGirt disappeared from his view.

McGirt closed in on Lincoln and his captors. He heard a voice shouting in broken English for Lincoln to get up. The sailor screamed that his leg was hurt and he couldn't. The voice cursed and threatened to kill him if he didn't get to his feet. McGirt was now close enough to see their faces — two young Filipinos dressed in rag-tag paramilitary garb, carrying rifles. One was quite short; the other was taller and wore eyeglasses with thick lenses.

"Get up and walk, dog. I kill you now, black dog. I kill you..." the one with glasses said. He turned and saw McGirt. "And we kill you too." He swung his weapon around.

His accomplice seemed confused, unsure of what to do. He pointed his rifle unsteadily at Lincoln and then jerked it toward McGirt. He spewed some words at his partner and then lowered his weapon slightly. At that instant, a bullet ripped through the air, so close to McGirt that he felt it go by. He instinctively hit the deck and took cover next to a fallen tree.

The short rebel collapsed in a heap and Lincoln started to move away, crawling on his backside. The other rebel turned toward him and laughed sadistically. He raised his rifle and took aim. But before he could fire, a second round whistled by. The bullet struck him squarely in the back, between his shoulder blades. He spun around and his knees buckled, but he managed to raise his rifle, prepared to shoot at his attacker. But he never got the chance. The next bullet penetrated the center of his forehead and he fell straight back.

McGirt got to his feet slowly. He heard the sound of other people making their way up the hillside. A few soldiers came into view, weaving between the pines. He recognized their uniforms: they were Philippine Special Forces. Confident that they were friendly, he pivoted in the direction the bullets had come from. To his surprise, a familiar figure emerged from behind a tree. Bud Lammers held a gun still aimed at Lincoln's kidnappers, ready to fire again.

Chapter 24

The job of commanding officer carries with it many perks, but head-of-the-line privileges on the San Diego-Coronado Bridge isn't one of them. Commander Rex Reeder sat stuck in traffic, halfway across the majestically curved bridge that connects the city of San Diego with Coronado, where Reeder's squadron, HCS-30, was located.

When the phone rang at 4:15 that morning, the veteran pilot picked it up after just one ring. He'd grown accustomed to the after-hours calls from squadron watch officers, his XO, and Detachment OICs, a dozen time zones away. The message from his wing commander, a two-star admiral and former POW, was blunt: "My office as soon as possible. Pack for a week." Reeder's wife, Louise, was up and making coffee before Rex had hung up the receiver.

Reeder checked his watch: 5:45. Not bad considering the short notice. Earlier, as he'd descended from his upscale Highlands neighborhood, he'd noted that Maddy Rayburn's house lights were on. Most likely, she was up with a sick youngster, he thought. Louise had mentioned something about that over dinner. With their only child, Rex Junior, a sophomore at the Naval Academy, he and Louise served as surrogate grandparents for the Rayburns' two kids while Thomas was deployed. Louise's friendship with the effervescent Maddy had blossomed into a sisterly relationship, and Maddy was at Louise's side during most officers' wives' club events. Rex, on the other hand, had kept a professionally safe distance from the ambitious Thomas Rayburn. As HCS-30's skipper, playing favorites with any of his officers would only diminish his authority as the unit's commander. He was responsible for thirty helicopters, more than four hundred sailors and several detachments scattered around the Pacific. Reeder couldn't afford to be too chummy with anyone.

He tapped his big Class of '58 ring against the car's wooden steering wheel. The Triumph TR-3 had been a graduation present to himself after tossing his cap in the air at Annapolis, nearly two decades ago. The lanes were crammed with "sand crabs" hurrying to punch in for the early morning shift at Naval Air Station North Island's huge aircraft rework facility. The operation employed thousands of civilians who worked around the clock overhauling the Pacific Fleet's helicopters and airplanes. He switched on the car's radio, hoping to kill time while the sea of red taillights ahead of him crawled toward the tollbooths.

Reeder tuned to his favorite drive-to-work station, where two morning shock jocks were deep into an animated skewering of California's futuristic young governor and his latest proposal: a state-funded Space Academy. The duo began chirping in alien-like voices, *"Earth to Moon Beam, earth to Moon Beam. Come in please, Governor!"* The skit distracted him from dwelling on what news — obviously not good at this hour — awaited him in the admiral's office. The word of McGirt's mishap had arrived in a more routine fashion: via the squadron duty officer who'd retrieved the "immediate" message from North Island's communication center. The ensign had delivered the dispatch to Reeder while he'd been seated comfortably at his desk.

Reeder saw a break up ahead. He swerved around a motorcycle and joined the file of cars for the far right booth. He coasted through without stopping as the attendant plucked the ticket stub from his hand. The rest of the drive went quickly. He chose the Base's less-used side gate, by the carrier piers, and cruised along the waterfront road that led to Air Wing Headquarters. A handful of other vehicles had already arrived. He parked and grabbed his khaki cap. Two armed Marines greeted him at the door.

"I.D. please, sir," one of them demanded. Reeder took out his wallet and handed over the laminated card for inspection. "Thank you, sir," the grunt said as he and his partner snapped to attention and saluted. Reeder heard one of them discreetly announce over a walkie-talkie that he was here. He double-stepped up the stairs and strode to the admiral's office at the end of the hallway. On the way, he passed a tall coffee urn percolating the first of the day's many brews. Two more guards saluted and then opened the door into the anteroom that led to the two-star's office.

No one stood up when Reeder entered the darkly paneled room, and rightly so. He was the junior officer on board. Seated at the long conference table was his boss, the two-star rear admiral. Across from him was a pair of glum-faced civilians: a well dressed Asian gentleman, and an American attired in a boxy looking dark suit, white shirt and narrow tie. At the head of the table sat the two-star's boss, Vice Admiral Edgar Harrison, Commander, Naval Air Forces Pacific.

"Have a seat, Rex," Harrison said. Reeder had met with the admiral a few times at change-of-command ceremonies and other official functions. Nonetheless, he felt awkward being addressed by his first name by such a high-ranking officer. "Thank you, Sergeant," Harrison said in an aside, signaling the Marine to close the door. "Let me introduce you to Mr. Agustin, deputy director of the Philippine Consulate in Los Angeles. Next to him, Agent Davis of the Central Intelligence Agency, Western District."

Reeder had steeled himself for bad news during the thirty-five minute drive from his home in the South Bay. He'd played out a few scenarios in his mind, rehearsing a response for each of them. Another mishap like McGirt's? One of his sailors arrested for a capital crime? He'd even considered that the brass might tell him what every skipper feared above all else: that someone under his command had lost his life. But none of those tragedies would have prompted this urgent a response or the summoning of the two civilians at this early hour.

Despite the gravity of the situation, Harrison's reputation for short meetings held true. The former World War Two ace facilitated dissemination of the facts, issued his marching orders, and concluded the forum in less than ten minutes. In outline form, Rex jotted down some notes:

> Helo shot down
> At least one death
> Highly sensitive
> Situation changing by the minute
> Fly to Cubi
> More info later

***

An unmarked twin-engine business jet was fueled and ready to go when Reeder and Agent Davis arrived. The Wing Commander had personally shuttled them to the flight line at North Island, bypassing the normal check-in and manifesting rigamarole and parking his government sedan ten feet from the aircraft's entry door. The two-star offered Reeder the uninspiring sendoff of a firm handshake and the assurance, "We'll be in touch." Reeder and Davis were the only two passengers on board. They strapped in for the first leg of their journey, a six-hour flight to Hickam Air Force Base on Oahu.

Reeder was eager to pump the agent for more details once aboard, but within five minutes of their departure from Coronado, both men had fallen asleep. After a twenty-minute, jet-drone-induced coma, Reeder awoke. He gratefully accepted a freshly cooked plate of ham and eggs, which the flight's male steward had prepared after already serving Davis. Reeder cut to the chase.

"So what can you tell me?" he asked Davis, who was seated across the aisle.

"Not much at this time, Skipper," Davis said.

"Thought you spooks knew everything," Reeder persisted. "While we're at it, who really killed JFK, anyway?" He cracked a grin, hoping to break the ice. The no-nonsense G-man loosened his tie and laughed. Even a hard-core like himself found it impossible to be cooped up in a tiny jet without making small talk.

"No one in Langley has filled me in on the grassy knoll, if that's what you're asking. I do, however, have my own theories," Davis said. He'd polished off the last of his breakfast and covered the plate with a napkin, signaling that he was finished. The flight attendant quickly picked up the plate and returned to his station in the rear of the aircraft. "Concerning the present incident, you should know that it's being monitored at the absolute highest levels in both D.C. and Manila."

"Presidential?" Reeder asked.

"If that's not the highest level, then I don't know what is."

"Wow" was all Reeder could muster for a response.

"What I can tell you, Commander, is…"

"Rex — please call me Rex." They shook hands for the first time since their abrupt meeting in the Wing Commander's office.

"Dan," Davis replied in turn. He opened a note pad and paged through his briefing."Sad as it is to lose your guy, LaRue, that tragedy pales in comparison with the political implications this event carries."

This was the first time Reeder had heard who had died. The admiral hadn't been specific. "What about the rest of the crew?" he asked.

"At least one serious injury that we know of at this time, an Ensign Bright. Our office in Manila will have an update when we arrive."

Reeder did some quick math: about eighteen hours of flying time, two or three fuel stops and a fifteen-hour time change. "Early Saturday evening, their time," he said. With his detachments halfway around the world, he'd mastered the calculations. Davis checked his itinerary. "Yup, that's right," he said.

"Can I assume that a lid's been put on this so it doesn't get much attention from the news media?" Reeder asked.

"Correct again," Davis replied. "That's why two guys relatively low on the totem pole are on this government plane right now. Every effort is being taken to have this appear like nothing more than an unfortunate accident over an allied country."

Reeder frowned. How could this be viewed as nothing more than "an unfortunate accident"? The steward appeared and topped off their coffee mugs. Davis continued, "If this thing goes mainstream, there could be major implications affecting national security and world affairs." He took a sip and sat back. "That's about all I can tell you, Rex."

Reeder was flabbergasted at Davis' revelation. He looked aft. The steward was putting away the breakfast dishes. He tilted his head toward Davis and whispered, "Aren't you a little concerned about making that kind of a statement around him?" He raised his eyes toward the back of the plane.

"No. He's Agency," Davis said indifferently. "Top Secret clearance, same as the two pilots."

"Oh," Reeder said, and put on his best game face.

"I understand that you have a son at the Academy?" Davis asked. Reeder belatedly realized that Davis would have all the details of his own background, personal life, and service record — small town upbringing in Oregon; Eagle Scout; track star at the Academy; graduated number one in his flight school class and promoted early to his present rank. His Academy nickname, Rapid Rex, wasn't derived solely from his days racing around the quarter-mile oval. Career-wise, he was on the fast track and some said he was likely to be the helicopter community's first homegrown admiral. "That's right, he's in his second year," he replied.

Conversation tapered off, and Reeder's thoughts returned to the briefing. He jotted down some notes for his executive officer back at North Island. His second-in-command would see that LaRue's next of kin was notified. *I can't believe that I lost a man on my watch,* he thought sadly.

The one-hour fuel stop in Hawaii would allow him adequate time for phone calls to tie up loose ends at the squadron. Neither of the two admirals, nor Davis, had mentioned the details of the crash. Absent most notably were the names of the men who'd been on the aircraft with LaRue and Bright.

Davis had reclined his seat and fallen asleep, but Reeder wasn't ready for another nap. Unable to quell his nervous energy, he gazed down at the Pacific's deep-blue waters, inventorying the faces of Detachment 110's personnel. His mind kept flashing back to the lights having been on at the Rayburn house. He hoped that it hadn't been an omen.

* * *

Twenty straight hours of air travel is no picnic. Reeder and Davis were exhausted when their jet set down at Cubi Point just after sunset, Saturday evening. After a flight crew change in Hawaii, they'd made fuel stops on Wake Island and Guam. By the time the aircraft shut down at Cubi, everyone on board was ready for a hot shower, a meal and a bed.

Bud Lammers and Assistant Officer In Charge Thomas Rayburn were standing by on the tarmac. Rayburn scooped up both men's bags and hustled off to the van that he and Lammers had driven down the hill. Davis declined an invitation to dinner. He made some calls to Langley and turned in for the night. Reeder, on the other hand, showered and changed into civvies. He met Lammers and Rayburn in the BOQ lobby.

"Fellas, I'd like to bypass the O' Club and take a drive over to the Chuck Wagon," he said, referring to the country-western hangout on the Naval Station side of Subic Bay. Rayburn drove while Lammers and Reeder sat in the back.

"Skipper, how was the flight over?" Rayburn asked.

"Long" was all Reeder cared to say about that. He went on, "It's my understanding that we'll be attending a classified briefing at 1000 hours tomorrow. As much as I'd like to discuss what's on all of our minds, I'm prohibited from doing so until then."

During the last hour of his flight, more information about the incident had been transmitted to the aircraft via encrypted data-link. Agent Davis had gone over the details with Reeder. "I'd like to get a status report, however, on personnel and equipment," he added.

Lammers filled him in on the facts: LaRue had died in the aftermath of the crash. Bright had been transferred from a clinic at Clark and was now in stable condition at the Naval Station hospital. His prognosis was good; however, his left arm and shoulder were badly damaged. Navy doctors feared that he might have permanent loss of motion and not be able to fly again. Lincoln, though shook up by the ordeal, was uninjured, as was Rayburn.

Lammers also gave a status report on the rest of the Detachment. He had corralled everyone and imposed a gag order while the mishap investigation was being conducted. After he'd left the hangar, Jenks had followed up with his own edict: "Keep your damn mouths shut." Everyone knew that rumors would be flying in the enlisted barracks and onboard *San Angelo*.

As Rayburn parked, Reeder tapped him on the shoulder and said, "Pick us up in an hour."

Erected from war-era Quonset huts, the Chuck Wagon was actually two separate structures, bolted together. At one end was a stage for musicians, and on the far side was a grouping of tables, which made up the dining area. Between the two venues was a string of slot machines.

"Let's get away from the noise so that we can talk," Reeder said. They passed the stage where a band of Filipinos was belting out their rendition of a Johnny Cash song. The group's front man, barely five feet tall and dressed in black, held a huge guitar. His deep baritone voice sounded odd coming from someone of such small stature.

"These guys can copy just about anything, can't they?" Reeder remarked as they walked through the clanging casino area and settled at a table away from the smoky hubbub. A waiter appeared, ready to take their order.

"Steak, medium rare, with all the fixings. And a round of beer," Reeder said. He didn't bother to read the menu; he'd been here before.

"Same for me," Lammers said.

They enjoyed the music without speaking until their beers arrived. Reeder took a long gulp. "Ah, San Miguel — no two bottles taste the same," he joked. Lammers took a sip. He was a scotch man, but obligingly followed Reeder's lead. He wasted no time getting to the matter at hand.

"Skipper, I don't have much to say, except this isn't what any of us expected. I'm in uncharted waters and not sure where this is going."

Reeder stopped him cold in his tracks. "Commander, we can't change what's already happened. Tomorrow we'll be receiving a highly sensitive briefing from the State Department and CIA. Based on what the agent dished to me on the way across the pond, this thing goes way beyond what any of us can imagine. You and I have to be prepared for the consequences."

"What do you mean, sir?"

"We can't get into it here, but I've got a hunch that what really happened up in those mountains may not be what comes out in the final report. You'll see what I'm talking about tomorrow. Right now, it's crucial that we keep a solid grip on our men. Bright will receive a private briefing after we do. Likewise for the other crewmembers."

"There'll be no problem with Bright in that regard. I spoke with him this afternoon and he's onboard. He's too smart not to know something's in the wind. As for the others, Jenks has assured me that he's got it under control."

"I'm sure he does," Reeder said, grinning. He'd known Irvis Jenks when the big man was a teenager, fresh out of boot camp. The steaks arrived and they dug in.

"How's Jill?" Reeder asked between bites.

Lammers set down his fork. "We're separated now, sir, just recently."

"Sorry to hear that. Is there anything Louise and I can do?"

Bud's face reddened. "No, sir, I don't think so."

"I haven't had the opportunity to speak with her often, but she seems like a charming girl. You're East Coast folks, aren't you?"

Lammers nodded and kept his head down while he ate. Reeder read his body language and graciously moved on. "How are your pilots holding up?"

"Well, you know about Uker; he's probably Stateside by now. Bright seems in good spirits, all things considered. I think the morphine has a lot to do with that. McGirt's returned to flight status and Carbone's ready for upgrade to aircraft commander."

"Let's do that ASAP," Reeder said. "You'll need him for the rest of the cruise."

Lammers continued, "Rayburn was shook up pretty bad after what happened the other day — who wouldn't be? That being said, he's spent most of the last six months working on his Surface Warfare quals, and has done the bare minimum VERTREPing at sea. He's had to rely on short runs to Manila and Baguio to stay current with his flying." He was aware of the neighborly connection between the Reeders and Rayburns, so he chose his next words carefully. "Skipper, Thomas is a very capable officer. But frankly, I question his priorities. He doesn't bond well with the rest of the detachment. He requested that he be assigned a stateroom with a ship's company officer on *San Angelo*. Whenever we're in port, he always seems to be occupied with other issues. He avoids the Q and stays with a friend here in Cubi." He waited for a reaction from his boss.

Reeder waved to their waiter for another round. "Yes, I know all about Thomas," he said flatly.

They directed their attention to the band at the far end of the building. The miniature "Man in Black" had launched into a twangy guitar solo that had the crowd stomping its feet. Reeder and Lammers joined the ovation. They finished their beers, paid their tab, and headed for the parking lot, where Rayburn was already waiting.

Bud stopped as they walked through the door. "Thanks for letting me tag along, Skipper, I needed that."

Reeder rested his hand on Lammers' shoulder. "Let's get some rest. We're both going to need it."

***

Rapid Rex Reeder was up before dawn. He put on his running gear and quietly strode out of his BOQ room. He walked past the swimming pool and then behind the Q's dining room, where he could smell the early stages of today's breakfast special wafting from the galley's griddle. Outside the kitchen door was a Dumpster, where he could hear some critters rummaging inside as he passed. A cool breeze coasted through the jungle foliage as he began his jog. A cadre of curious monkeys emerged from the green darkness to escort him along the highway. The animals tag-teamed him from atop a high fence that bordered the pavement, screeching and howling as Reeder intruded into their domain. After following him for a couple dozen yards, they'd lose interest, jump to a tree and disappear. Soon, another one of the pack would scoot up the fence and repeat the challenge.

By the time Reeder chugged up the last peak, the sun was up. He'd arrived at the end of the road, where the Naval Hospital was situated. He walked into the lobby and identified himself to the Navy nurse on duty at the front desk. She balked at first, but reluctantly carried out Reeder's request to check whether Ensign Bright was awake. She returned, tossed him a towel to dry off and led the way to a private room. He found Robert Bright propped up in bed, reading a *Scientific American* magazine.

Bright smiled broadly at the sight of his squadron commander. "How you feeling, Robert?" Reeder asked.

"They've got me doped up pretty good, sir. No complaints." Bright set down the magazine as Reeder closed the door.

Reeder eyed the heavy cast around Bright's shoulder, which stretched over his hand and down to the fingertips. "Glad we didn't lose you, son," he said quietly and pulled a chair up to the bed. "Do you feel well enough to talk for a bit?"

"Yes, sir."

"Ensign, you'll be meeting with some heavy hitters today. The crash was enough in itself, but that's not all of it. Turns out there's a lot more involved with this whole thing."

"We were shot at, sir," Bright blurted out. Apparently the drugs muted his pain but not his memory. "We should have been able to set down safely, though. We were shaking real bad after the first shot to the rotor blades. When the right engine torched, I got the fire out right away. But it wasn't anything that we shouldn't have been able to pull out of, and make an emergency landing."

"Who was flying?"

"Lieutenant Rayburn, sir. With all due respect…" Bright choked back tears. "With all due respect, sir, other than the shaky ride, it wasn't much different from the procedures we practice all the time. We were heavy, but we should've made it. LaRue shouldn't have died. I thought this was a friendly country! Why would someone want to shoot at us?"

"The Philippines is one of our staunchest allies, Robert. But it appears that some elements don't agree with the majority of the population. That's about all I can tell you right now. The men you'll see later today will have to take it from there."

Bright glanced at the H-46 flight manual that he'd asked Carbone to fetch from his stateroom. "The doctors said that there's a chance I may never regain full use of my arm."

"We'll deal with that in good time, Ensign. I want you to know that, as your commanding officer, I'm proud of you." He took hold of Bright's good hand.

"You know, sir, I have a confession. I never intended to make the Navy a career. I took an ROTC scholarship because I couldn't afford the tuition. When I got my aerospace degree from M.I.T., I thought being a pilot for a few years would be a good way to see firsthand what I'd studied. I always wanted to get out and go back to school, maybe teach someday. But during the last six months, I've had so much fun flying the 46, I've thought about staying with it… until now."

"Son, either way, you've got a lot of living ahead of you. Be patient."

Bright winced and shifted in his bed. The medication was wearing thin. "Sir, I'm onboard with whatever comes out of this. I've always been a team player."

Reeder gave his hand a firm squeeze. "Good luck, Robert. We'll talk again soon."

He took his leave, making sure to thank the nurse on the way out. He felt his age on the run back to the Q. The early morning tropical sun beat down on the asphalt, making the return trip hot and sticky. He forced himself to keep going the last half-mile, even though his body wanted to quit. He didn't see a single monkey on the way back.

Chapter 25

If not for its tall flagpole and circular drive outlined by white rocks, the Base Administration Building would have looked like every other bland structure on the hill. Bud Lammers parked in a spot in front marked "Visiting Commanding Officer." Reeder, McGirt, Rayburn and Jenks were with him.

A dozen armed Marines loitered by the glass doors that opened into the building's lobby. Jenks said under his breath, "Looks like something big's going down." Reeder said, "Get used to it, Chief."

The senior jarhead, a stocky major, approached and saluted Reeder. "Good morning, sir. We'll need to check I.D.s before entry — orders from above."

The group was escorted into a windowless conference room in the center of the first floor. Half of the guards followed while the others remained outside, encircling the building's perimeter. Reeder and his men were the first to arrive. The stark room contained two long tables, folding chairs and a blackboard.

"The rest of your group should be here shortly, sir," the major said to Reeder.

Reeder directed his men to take their seats in the front row. Rayburn had brought along a briefcase. He opened it and retrieved a brand-new notebook labeled "Briefing."

"Lieutenant Rayburn, put that away. This is a classified brief. There will be no taking of notes," Reeder said.

The major opened the door again and led three more men into the meeting: Agent Dan Davis, another American civilian and a Filipino man. Davis shook the Marine's hand and said, "Thanks. I'll let you know if we need anything." The Marine left the room and joined his fellow grunts in the hallway as everyone took their seats.

"Gentleman, let's get started. I'm Agent Dan Davis of the CIA, Western District. With me this morning are Agent Mike Morris of the Naval Investigative Service and Mr. Jim Posadas, attached to the U.S. Embassy in Manila. This briefing is classified Top Secret. Please handle information accordingly."

Jenks began to stand up. "Skipper, I don't have a Top Secret clearance," he said.

Davis said, "You do now, Chief. Trust me." He gave a reassuring smile and motioned for him to sit down.

"The last few days have been very hectic for us all," Davis began. "I thought that it might serve our goals best to get a historical perspective, so I've invited Mr. Posadas to join us today. Jim is first generation Filipino-American. He was born and raised in Hawaii after his parents emigrated there in the 1930s. We met at Stanford University several years ago while attending graduate school. Jimmie, it's all yours."

Davis took a seat next to the NIS agent while Posadas inserted a tray of slides into a projector and pulled a viewing screen down from the ceiling. He was a medium-height, light-skinned Asian with movie-star good looks. His styled black hair rested just above the collar of his linen, short-sleeved barong. The first slide displayed a four-word phrase: *Hukbong Mapagpalaya ng Bayan.*

"That's Tagalog for People's Liberation Army," he said. "After World War Two ended, this group changed its name from something slightly different: *Hukbo ng Bayan laban sa Hapon*, or People's Anti-Japanese Army. In the next several minutes, I'll explain how what started out as a noble organization, devoted to fighting Japanese invaders across the countryside, eventually degenerated into a band of thugs." He advanced the slide tray to display a map of the Philippine archipelago.

"As much as I love my Big Macs and Oakland Raiders, I volunteered for this assignment in Manila because of my fascination with the Philippine nation. As you can see, the P.I. is comprised of many islands, over seven thousand actually, sprawled over several hundred miles. Like its geography, the history of the Philippines is equally unique. The rise and fall of the *Hukbalahap*, or Huks, has been a startling chapter in Filipino history." The next slide was a faded snapshot depicting a group of shabbily clad rebels. Their rifles were hoisted high in the air.

"This photo was taken in early 1942, after the Japanese occupation. Most likely, this platoon of Huks was celebrating a conquest of some sort. These freedom fighters originated not far from here, near what is now Clark Air Force Base. They sprung from angry peasant farmers who'd united to seek better working conditions from their landlords. When war broke out, most of the landed elite abandoned their farming businesses and fled to the safety of the cities. Many of them collaborated openly with the Japanese. When the war ended, the landowners returned to reclaim what they'd left behind. The peasants, who'd continued to maintain the farms, protested and wanted a larger share of the profits in return.

"In simple terms, it was a struggle of rich versus poor. When the landlords formed private armies to protect their investments, the Huks naturally sided with their own people, the farmers, and took on the role of vigilantes against the landowners.

"We could spend a couple of college semesters dissecting the Huk Rebellion. In the interest of time, though, I'll be concise. From the beginning, communist interests from outside the Philippines had made attempts to inject their anti-American agenda into the Huk movement. When the new, democratically elected administration emerged in 1949, a campaign was initiated to disarm the Huks. It failed. The movement grew in size and strength into what became the Huk Rebellion. With massive aid from the United States, the revolt was suppressed in the early 1950s. Surviving rebels fled to the hills. Most of them ultimately assimilated into Philippine society, but many became outlaws and criminals. But if you think that these folks have quietly gone away, I've got a bridge in San Francisco that I can sell to you. Survivors of the original Huk leadership inspired the creation of a present-day group of agitators: the New People's Army, or NPA. This conglomerate of radicals is the guerrilla wing of the Philippine Communist Party. They're pledged to oppose all American and foreign interests in the P.I., and they're everywhere: in the mountains, the villages and the cities. They are fearsome in their beliefs and their numbers are growing."

Rayburn threw his hand in the air. "Yes, Lieutenant?" Posadas said.

"Sir, can you address the ongoing negotiations between the U.S. and the Marcos administration regarding lease agreements for our military bases over here?"

Rex Reeder stood up before Posadas could answer. "There will be no questions from this group today," he announced, and glared at Rayburn as if he'd just passed gas in a crowded elevator.

Posadas continued, "Let's move to the present. I've prepared a two-page character summary of Ferdinand Marcos and his wife for you to read at a later time. I'll summarize it by saying they're an enigmatic couple, who, despite the odds, have maintained a fascinating grip of power over the country. Not bad for a self-proclaimed war hero and former bank teller. Feel free to a take copy when you leave. The document is unclassified." Posadas paused and poured himself a glass of water from a pitcher on the table.

"As I said, it would take much longer than we have today to analyze the complexities of the modern-day Philippine nation. The NPA is growing rapidly in numbers. Additionally, there's a major uprising of Muslim separatists taking place on the island of Mindanao. This rebellion has prompted Marcos to dispatch the majority of his armed forces to that region. Leaders of the Arab world, spearheaded by the premier of Libya, have repeatedly spoken out on the Muslim issue, accusing the Philippine government of genocide against its own citizens and have threatened to give assistance to the militant separatists if conditions don't improve for all Filipino Muslims. And of course, there's the bargaining chip of oil, which the Arabs are never shy about tossing on the table. You won't read much about any of this in *Stars and Stripes*," Posadas said, referring to the daily newspaper printed for servicemen abroad.

"In summary, the present Philippine government is held together by U.S. aid and duct tape. The country is safer now, under martial law. Clark and the Subic complex continue to thrive because their presence offers a deterrent to communist expansion in Asia."

Agent Davis rose from his chair, looked at his watch and said, "Thanks, Jimmie. We need to move on." Posadas headed for the exit. Before he turned the handle, a Marine guard pushed the door open. Walt Lugansky and his executive officer, Tom Latimer, stepped in and took seats in the back row.

With Posadas gone and the room secure again, Davis took over. "OK, men, let's cut to the chase," he said, and inserted a new carousel into the slide projector. "Excuse me if my language is terse, but I've had very little sleep in the last two days. Agent Morris and I have been on the phone with the Pentagon, the Philippine ambassador and my people at Langley. Please hold your comments until the end.

"First of all, Lieutenant Rayburn's helicopter absorbed a series of fifty-caliber shells, which were shot from a weapon that had been smuggled from the armory at Clark Air Force Base in Angeles City."

Rayburn pounded his fist on the table. "I knew it!" he said through clenched teeth.

"This man was the ringleader of the operation." The mug shot of a chubby Filipino flashed onto the screen. "Vincente Angara. This photo is dated. We believe that he's lost weight and possibly had facial surgery since it was taken. As a teen, Angara was a member of the Huks, the good ones who fought the Japanese. He was captured by the Japs, tortured, and imprisoned. After the war, he faded into the countryside and lived a life of obscurity. After interrogating one of his accomplices, we learned that Angara resurfaced in Manila under the name of Rolio Riberra. Probably worked some menial jobs with forged I.D.; we're not quite sure. But one thing that we're convinced of: he's been instrumental in forming a splinter group of the NPA, focusing its efforts against U.S. military operations in the Philippines. With limited advanced weaponry, what better target than a slow-moving aircraft such as a helicopter?"

Another slide appeared, this one of a smiling, elderly gentleman. His image appeared to have been cropped from a family snapshot. "José Cantador, one of the organizers who helped get some former Huk kingpins elected to the Philippine Congress after MacArthur's forces liberated the country. The Philippines' president at that time, Manuel Roxas, never allowed those six men to take their seats in the newly established democracy. That's a confusing story that I don't have time to go into right now.

"Cantador married into wealth and oversaw a large plantation in central Luzon, near Clark. We believe his farm was the staging ground for this covert operation. Philippine intelligence was a few steps behind all the way, unfortunately. When a laid-off worker rode his bicycle past the farm, the day before Rayburn's shoot-down, he saw a man with a gun outside a barn. He reported it to the local constabulary. The dots started connecting. Witnesses who'd seen Angara's truck change drivers in Angeles City came forward. The best we can ascertain, a couple of mules were hired to drive the vehicle, which carried the fifty-caliber machine gun concealed in a compartment connected to one of the truck's gas tanks. The group had specific knowledge of where Rayburn's aircraft was going, and when. Not difficult to find out, really, once you print a flight schedule, days in advance, and post it on the wall in Cubi Point Operations. With hundreds of locals employed on the base, that info wouldn't be hard to discover — a janitor, secretary, whomever. Or maybe a sailor with loose lips from your detachment, out in town."

Davis paused to loosen his necktie and take a drink. The room's two air conditioners were losing their battle against the midday heat. Another face appeared on the screen. "Manuel Vaccaro, college dropout and former mental patient. He was a confirmed hater of any foreign presence in the Philippines, basically a crazed nut, looking for a spot to create chaos. He was one of those who took Lincoln hostage; we don't know the name of his accomplice." The next slide showed Vaccaro lying flat on his back with a blood-crusted hole in the middle of his forehead.

"Nice shot, sir," Davis said to Bud Lammers. Davis reached into a canvas sack and pulled out a plastic evidence bag. It contained a Glock nine-millimeter pistol. He inspected the weapon admiringly and said, "I've read that Glock is developing a lighter model for law enforcement. Should be out soon." He walked over to Bud and handed him a letter-sized envelope. "The leader of the Philippine unit that arrived on the scene sends you a personal message," Davis said. "Allow me to share its contents with the group. He commends you for your heroism and regrets that he was required to seize your weapon." Everyone turned toward Lammers as Davis tucked the gun away in the sack. "Sir, you can claim it at my office when you return Stateside."

Jenks turned to Rex Reeder and said, "Skipper, this place is more dangerous than the snake pit where I'm from back in Brooklyn! Why are the rest of us flying around unarmed?"

Reeder shook his head and said, "Chief, we're considered non-combatants operating over a friendly country. According to directives, we're not permitted to be armed."

Davis went on, "As you've all undoubtedly gathered by now, this incident is a tinderbox. When the Filipino forces arrived at the crash site, another group had been dispatched a few miles up the canyon, where the shots had been fired at your aircraft. They uncovered boxes of anti-American pamphlets condemning everything from Marcos to the U.S.-owned fruit and lumber companies in the Philippines. The Filipino soldiers captured or killed everyone except Vincente Angara, who managed to flee. He's an expert at living undercover. It's doubtful that we'll ever track him down."

Davis dragged a chair to the front of the room. He plopped into it, folded his hands behind his head and leaned back. "Now comes the delicate part. The prime reason that the Marcos administration was able to implement martial law five years ago was under the pretense that doing so would protect the nation from this kind of mayhem. For the regime to admit that it's failed in that regard would only serve to reignite forces calling for Marcos' removal. Those forces exist, believe me."

Rex Reeder folded his arms across his chest defiantly. "I see where this is going. My squadron's going to take the rap, isn't it?"

"Hold on, Rex," Davis replied. "Let me finish — it's not that simple. One of the mules driving the truck to Baguio was a Muslim college student from Mindanao. The kid was wounded when the Special Forces unit arrived and started shooting at everything that moved. He's in critical condition at a Baguio hospital." Davis took a deep breath and continued. "His girlfriend is a rabble rouser on campus at the University of the Philippines — very vocal on human rights, especially when it comes to Filipino Muslims. She knew that the boy was going to Baguio and, when he didn't return, she organized a group of activists who drove to Baguio to find him. They'd like nothing more than to have a martyr to help bring attention to their cause. As Jimmie said, the Philippines has been on thin ice with the Arab world for a long time because of the country's treatment of its Muslims. The harm caused to this student, although it may be tangential, could have serious consequences. In short: Muslim student relates to Arab world; Arab world relates to oil, the same oil stored in those big tanks down the hill that fuel your ships and aircraft." Davis leaned forward and rubbed his hands together. "Questions?"

"Yeah, I got a bunch," Reeder said. "What the hell are you telling me, that this will be spun as a crash, and not actually what it was — a terrorist act?" Reeder appeared ready to explode, but he managed to contain himself.

"That's exactly what I'm saying, Commander," Davis replied. "With the free flow of Arab oil to this part of the world hanging in the balance, coupled with our need to have an ally like Ferdinand Marcos in power, the U.S. has its you-know-what in a ringer. That fox sitting in the presidential palace never misses an opportunity to gain the upper hand. Our leases at Subic and Clark are valid for a few more years, but he's always maneuvering for additional U.S. aid. Let me remind you, we're talking about a leader who, among other things, signed on to a fake assassination attempt against his own defensive minister to help him usher in martial law. He's holding all the cards on this one."

"I've got to talk with my boss in San Diego," Reeder said. He got up and headed for the door.

"Rex, we have a secure line set up for you," Davis said. "I also have some immediate messages that arrived this morning." He held out a folder. Reeder took it, gave the classified notes a quick scan and sat back down.

"I guess you do," he said as he paged through them. He slumped in his chair, deflated. The messages had been sent directly from his Wing Commander and were endorsed by Vice Admiral Harrison. He slid the folder over for Bud Lammers to read. Rayburn, McGirt and Jenks sat speechless. Lugansky and Latimer quietly departed. The NIS agent joined Davis up front.

The classified messages said it all: The investigation of Rayburn's crash would be handled from higher up the chain of command. Reeder was instructed to comply with all directives from Agent Davis and the State Department rep, Jimmie Posadas. When his duties were completed in the Philippines, Reeder was ordered to return to San Diego immediately. Additionally, Lieutenant Commander Bud Lammers was relieved of his duties as Detachment 110's Officer In Charge.

"Chief Jenks, you're excused," Davis said. "Lieutenant Rayburn, please take a seat in the hallway. Gentlemen, I remind you again of the sensitivity of this subject matter." The two men left the room. Reeder, Lammers and McGirt sat nervously, unsure of the next step.

"Fellas, I want you to know that, like you, I'm playing this by the seat of my pants," Davis said. "Prior to this meeting, I was on the phone with our embassy in Manila. I spoke directly with the ambassador, who's been in close contact with the Philippine president and our State Department." He motioned to Lammers and McGirt. "Looks like the three of us will be joining Jimmie for a little ride across Manila Bay."

Reeder jumped up again and thrust a finger at Davis. "Dan, that's it! I insist on accompanying my men."

"Stow it, Skipper," Davis said. "Those are my orders; the four of us and no one else. Agent Morris has a new line of business for you, here in Cubi." Davis removed his reading glasses and massaged his brow.

Morris came forward and said, "Commander Reeder, there's another matter we need to talk about."

Chapter 26

Lammers and McGirt followed Davis outside, where a Navy sedan was waiting. They rode down the hill and got out at Base Operations, where a Philippine Armed Forces H-1 Huey helicopter sat ready to fly them to Manila. Its twin engines spun at idle while its two rotor blades remained braked and still. Jimmie Posadas was already strapped in. He gestured for the threesome to join him. Within a minute, rotors were turning and then the aircraft was climbing above the rugged mountains to the east.

The four Americans wore soundproofing headsets, which allowed them to speak to each other over the intercom. Davis approached the two pilots and made a couple hand signals to them. They acknowledged and flicked a toggle switch on the aircraft's communications panel, which allowed Davis' conversation to be isolated between them.

"OK, guys, here's the drill," Davis said. "Ferdinand Marcos, president of the Philippines, has requested the pleasure of your company at his private residence in Malacanang Palace." He sat stone-faced, waiting for a response. Lammers and McGirt looked at each other, dumbfounded.

"What in the hell does he want with us?" Lammers asked.

"Well, he has a thing about meeting people when he seeks their trust," Posadas answered.

"What about the others in the crew: Rayburn, Jenks and the rest?" Bud said.

Davis keyed his mike. "Rayburn is being dealt with separately; same with Jenks, Sartelli, Bright and Lincoln. Marcos specifically requested to see you two. State Department tells me that we have no choice but to play along with the guy. Too much is at stake not to."

Lammers looked outside. They were already over Manila Bay, about halfway there. Davis reached below his seat and pulled out two duffle bags. Each had a handwritten tag, labeled with the two naval officers' names.

"Sorry that I can't offer a private dressing room." He tossed each man a bag. "Put these on. For the record, the two of you represent an Ohio steel company. You've been invited to the palace to discuss a large contract with the Philippine government."

Lammers and McGirt opened the bags. Dark-colored business suits were inside, complete with white shirts, ties and wing-tipped shoes. Everything was their correct size.

"Forget the jackets for now. Just carry them with you to put on when you meet the president. It's too damn hot," Davis lamented. The officers removed their headsets, stood up and began undressing, fumbling around in the tight cabin. Davis and Posadas turned their sights forward, out the window, in an attempt to offer a modicum of privacy.

One of the pilots spoke up over Posadas' headset. "About ten minutes to go, Jimmie," he said in perfect English. Posadas gave him a thumbs-up. They were cruising at one thousand feet above the water. Manila's cluster of skyscrapers loomed ahead through the haze. Once dressed, the officers tucked their khaki uniforms inside the bags and slid them under their seats.

The eastern edge of Manila Bay looked familiar to the two Navy pilots. During port calls to Subic Bay, detachments were routinely dispatched on flights to the U.S. Embassy helicopter pad to pick up and drop off Filipino-American sailors. The twenty-minute flight to see their families in metro Manila was much quicker and more enjoyable for them than a three-hour Victory Liner bus ride from Subic. The men sighted the U.S. Embassy to the south as the aircraft began flying up the Pasig River. Another three miles inland was Malacanang Palace, the official residence of the president and first lady. The grand white building crowned with red roof tiles was unmistakable. Built in 1750, its ornate Spanish Colonial architecture distinguished it from everything nearby. The aircraft decelerated and turned back into the wind as the pilot commenced an approach to a landing area adjacent to the riverside palace. As the rotors coasted to a stop, Davis removed his headset and said, "I'll wait here for you with the pilots. Jimmie will take you inside."

Posadas led them along a walkway through a thick, lush garden. They were met by two guards, who escorted them into the palace's entrance hall. Lammers and McGirt slipped on their suit jackets.

"Please wait here," one of the guards said. He went to an alcove located at one side of the entrance hall and made a phone call while Lammers and McGirt took in their surroundings. They were standing on a floor of beige-colored Philippine marble. The walls of the high-ceilinged room were constructed of the same glossy stonework. A grand staircase rose dramatically nearby. At its base were two matching statues of lions, which straddled the red-carpeted steps.

After a few minutes, a short Filipino woman appeared and introduced herself as the president's secretary, Camille Bantay. She shook the hands of all three men with a surprisingly firm grip, confirming her no-nonsense position within the administration. She was dressed in a casual blouse and slacks outfit. Wire-rimmed glasses rested on her bosom, held in place by a colorful jeweled strap.

"Please excuse my appearance, gentlemen," she said in halting but correct English. "It's Sunday and we don't normally do business on the weekends." As she led them toward the staircase, she turned to Lammers and said, "I so love the Midwest. My sister lives in Sarnia, Ontario, not far from Ohio. Have the leaves started to change colors there?"

McGirt spoke up, "Yes, ma'am, they have. Their colors should peak in another week or two." Camille touched McGirt's arm in a friendly way and said, "So beautiful." Despite her tiny legs — she stood less than five feet tall — the men nearly broke out in a trot to keep up with her.

At the top of the stairs they passed through a vestibule leading into the Reception Hall. Farther down the hallway, along the walls, were portraits of past Filipino presidents and United States civil governors who had lived in the palace. Bud paused by a case displaying a collection of Ferdinand Marcos' military decorations and medals.

"This way please, Mr. Lammers," Camille said sternly, but with respect.

She turned down a short passageway and stopped. "Mr. Posadas, you may wait here, please." Jimmie sat down on an elaborate Queen Anne-style chair. Bud noted two plain-clothes security men watching them from the end of the passageway.

Camille disappeared for a few seconds and returned with a broad smile on her face. "Mr. Lammers and Mr. McGirt, the president will see you now." She knocked, then pushed open a hand-carved wooden door that led into the president's study. A huge crystal chandelier hung from the center of its high ceiling. At the far end of the spacious room was a large desk and an empty executive chair. To one side of the desk sat the bicolor flag of the Philippines; on the other side was a royal blue flag displaying the gold presidential emblem. Above, attached to the top of elegant gold-colored drapes, was a round crest. Embroidered around its edge were the Tagalog words: *Sagisag ng Pangulo ng Pilipinas* — Seal of the President of the Philippines.

The secretary stepped back and gently closed the door. The room was silent except for rhythmic, tapping clicks that came from a corner, behind Lammers and McGirt. They turned in unison and saw Ferdinand Marcos hunched over a string of golf balls. He putted three more balls across an oriental rug, aiming them at a coffee cup placed on its side. The first two found their mark: dead-solid-perfect. The third nicked the cup's lip and glanced to one side. Marcos sighed after the miss and leaned the putter against a chair. When he turned toward them, they saw the face of a tired, almost sickly looking man. His features were more Asian than the mixed-blooded mestizo look of many Filipinos. He wore bright yellow trousers and a light blue sport shirt.

Marcos extended his hand and flashed a warm, magnetic smile that made Lammers and McGirt feel more relaxed. The weariness had drained from his face. He appeared jubilant and energized by their presence.

"Ah, my good friends from Cleveland," he proclaimed. "Welcome!"

* * *

Rex Reeder took advantage of Davis' offer and called his boss in the States. As commanding officer, he'd committed the admiral's home phone number to memory. It was Saturday evening in San Diego. After a series of operators and handoffs — the final one through a switchboard at CIA headquarters in Virginia — he was connected. The admiral confirmed everything that Dan Davis had said: Comply with Davis' and Posasdas' plan, and then catch a flight home. Bring Lammers with you.

Reeder and Agent Morris were alone in the conference room when he made the call. "Davis was right; this is way out of my hands," Reeder said. Morris sat on the edge of the table and held up the thick portfolio that he'd brought with him before handing it to Reeder.

"Now what's *this* about?" Reeder asked, taking the packet. "Davis already mentioned something about Rayburn inappropriately selling some items out in town." He knew that, because of the two "accidents" — McGirt's and now this mess — his own career was on the brink. He'd lost all patience for matters he filed in the "chicken-shit" category.

"Skipper, it's a lot more than that. Take a look," Morris replied.

Reeder opened the packet. On top of the pile of papers was a table of contents chronicling a series of events that had taken place during the last six months. Farther down in the stack were copies of invoices from *San Angelo's* ship store, along with similar records from the Cubi Point and Subic exchanges.

"Your boy Rayburn has been running quite a wholesaling racket over here," Morris said. "This is the most recent photo that I have, from two days ago." He pulled out an eight-by-ten glossy of Rayburn handing over packages to a group of Filipinos. "Loakan Airport, Baguio. Approximately thirty minutes before the crash."

Reeder tossed the pile of documents back at Morris. "What the hell are you trying to tell me?" he demanded. The news was coming at him faster than his brain could currently process. Morris did away with the cat-and-mouse routine and laid it on the line.

"Commander, Lieutenant Thomas Rayburn is part of a smuggling operation that we've been tracking for some time. Together with storekeepers onboard *San Angelo*, plus some Filipinos on base, he's been distributing high value, discounted items on the black market around WESTPAC — cameras and jewelry primarily, sometimes American cigarettes. Your squadron's helicopters were the pony express to get the goods out on the street. In Olongapo, he simply carried the merchandise though the gate. To doctor up their ledgers, the storekeepers were using the names of sailors who'd transferred off the ship as the purchasers of record. Tedious work, but not hard for my people to debunk. Rayburn fronted the money to make the buys, and then got the goods to connections off base. There's a huge markup for the items that he was pedaling. The prices he paid were, at times, below cost. The Navy Exchange system isn't as profit-driven as outside enterprises. Frequently, they'll practically give away merchandise in order to clear inventory."

Reeder's head was spinning. "Why'd you wait so long to tell me? Goddamn it, I'm his commanding officer!"

"My orders were to let the ruse continue for as long as practical. We wanted to nab as many players as we could."

"Does the Wing already know about this?"

"Our North Island office will brief your superiors first thing Monday morning."

"Good. I'm not making any more calls to the admiral. At least give him a few hours to recover from the news about the shoot-down. This pales in comparison." Reeder knew what he had to do, nonetheless. There was no way to candy-coat Rayburn's wrongdoing, even in light of the tragedy at Baguio. "Is he still outside?"

"Should be," Morris said. He went to the hallway and brought in Rayburn. Morris then left the room.

Rayburn stood at rigid attention. "Yes, sir?"

"Mr. Rayburn, I've received orders to return to San Diego," Reeder began. "Bud Lammers is going with me. I've relieved him of his duties as Officer In Charge of Detachment 110."

Rayburn's posture became even more erect. "Skipper, I'm ready to assume the duties of Officer In—"

"Shut up, you son of a bitch!" Reeder screamed. He flung Morris' portfolio in Rayburn's face. Its content scattered over the floor. "Did you really think that you could get away with something so stupidly reckless?" Rayburn lowered his eyes to the deck and saw the picture of him on the tarmac in Baguio. He broke out in a cold sweat.

"Of all the infantile schemes! You'll be court-martialed for this!"

Rayburn's voice cracked as he spoke. "But, sir, my family in San Diego..."

"You should have thought about them earlier, Lieutenant. You've shamed the whole squadron with your conduct. On top of this mess, I got the lowdown on how you bolted from the crash site, leaving your crew to die. You spineless coward!"

Sweat dripped from Rayburn's face, but Reeder wasn't finished. "I always gave you the benefit of the doubt, figuring that, with your Academy training, you'd eventually come around. Even stood up for you a few times because of our wives' friendship. But this is indefensible."

"Sir, request permission to speak?"

"Go ahead."

"I acknowledge my indiscretion and respectfully ask that, as a fellow Annapolis shipmate, you reconsider. I promise that I'll make amends to all concerned and pay back whatever I've taken wrongfully."

Reeder was flabbergasted. Unconsciously, he doubled his fists. "How dare you wave the Naval Academy in my face! You don't get it, do you? You're a disgrace to the institution that we were so honored to have attended. Get the hell out of here before I kick your ass."

Rayburn pivoted, and halfway to the door he stopped. "Sir, one more thing. There's the issue of the crash. As the CIA gentleman said, this is a highly sensitive matter. There could be serious repercussions if word gets out of what really happened."

Reeder was stunned by the words. "You pompous prick! You're threatening blackmail, aren't you?" Rayburn said nothing, but raised his chin arrogantly. Reeder felt his blood boil and knew that he was approaching his limit of restraint. He had to conclude the meeting now.

"Mister Rayburn, as your commanding officer, I hereby restrict you to arrest in quarters. You'll remain there until further notice. I strongly advise that you seek counsel." Reeder walked up to him and got nose-to-nose. "And Rayburn, I swear to God, if you even think about leaking any of this to the public, you'll wish that you'd never been born."

* * *

Lammers and McGirt were with President Marcos for nearly an hour. During that time, Marcos' secretary took pity on Jimmie Posadas and struck up a conversation with him over a cup of tea. Like many Filipinos, Camille had a direct connection to the United States. In addition to her sister in Canada, her cousin was a retired Navy cook living in San Francisco. She'd visited him several times over the years and shared her countrymen's fascination with all things American.

When the pair finally emerged from the president's study, they were escorted with Posadas back to the helicopter. They found Agent Davis and the two pilots lounging in the shade beneath a mango tree.

The pilots flew down river, turned south and hugged the shoreline that led to the U.S. Embassy helo pad. Posadas said goodbye to the Americans, exchanged some words in Tagalog with the pilots and shared a hearty laugh before deplaning. Few words were spoken during the hop back to Cubi Point. The officers began to change back into their uniforms. When Bud retrieved his khakis from the duffle bag, a small, heavy leather bag fell out. He looked up and saw that McGirt was already stripped down to his skivvies and had his back to him. Davis was looking out the window at the water below. Bud carefully untied the bag's drawstring and examined the contents. It was stuffed with shiny gold coins. On top was a handwritten note that he unfolded. It read: *Brave and loyal men should always be rewarded.* At the bottom of the note were the initials *F. M.*

Bud's hands began to shake violently as he looked up. McGirt was still occupied and tying his shoelaces, but Davis' eyes were focused squarely on Bud. The CIA man had a faint grin on his face. Bud resealed the leather bag and shoved it deep inside the duffle bag.

"Gentlemen, the civvies are yours to keep if you'd like," Davis said over the intercom. "Otherwise, we'll just throw 'em away."

McGirt shook his head and declined. Bud, however, spoke up. "Yeah, might as well. Thanks." He took a deep breath and sat back. Davis acknowledged with a friendly nod and returned his gaze back outside.

Chapter 27

After two days, Malik Abbas was able to sit up for the first time since he'd been rushed to the Baguio hospital. The doctors had deliberately kept him in a doped-up, nearly comatose state so that he'd lie still enough for his leg wounds to stop bleeding and begin to heal. Two bullets from the rebel's rifle had found their mark: one had glanced his hip and only required cleaning and a few sutures; the second round, however, had struck him squarely in the thigh and shattered his femur. Malik had lost several pints of blood, but the prognosis was good for a full, albeit lengthy, recovery. His entire right leg was encased in a cast, which was elevated a few inches off the hospital bed and suspended from the ceiling by a chrome cable and pulley contraption.

Malik heard the door to his private room creak. He opened his eyes and saw a young man clad in a white coat standing at the foot of his bed. The man picked up the clipboard hanging from the bed's metal frame and studied it.

"How are you feeling today, Mr. Abbas?" he asked without looking up from the notes. "I'm Doctor Tomaseo."

Malik looked intently at him. "Are you really a doctor?" he asked in a groggy voice. "You don't look old enough."

Dr. Tomaseo chuckled softly and said, "Yes, I can assure you that I'm qualified. I've been at this hospital for over three years." He smiled warmly. "The staff was correct when they warned me that you are a very inquisitive fellow. That's a good sign.

We can begin scaling back on your medication now that you're thinking more clearly." Dr. Tomaseo scribbled some notes on the clipboard, hung it back in its place, and then slid a chair close to Malik's bed and sat down.

"I requested to be assigned your case because we have much in common. In fact, we were nearly next-door neighbors at one time. Like you, I grew up in a small village outside of Cotabato City, on Mindanao Island."

Malik perked up at the mention of his native province. "Why are you here now, in the north?" he asked.

"After medical school in Manila, I did an internship in Baguio and fell in love with the place. Never left," Dr. Tomaseo said.

"Are you..." Malik said, pausing in mid-sentence.

"Yes, we share the same faith, if that's what you're asking. That's the other reason I requested to be your physician. I thought that I might help you feel more at ease in these new surroundings."

"Oh," Malik said. "Why aren't you wearing your *kufi*?"

Dr. Tomaseo glanced at the soiled skullcap on Malik's nightstand, but ignored the question. He said, "You had a couple of bad nights which necessitated keeping you heavily sedated. Are you aware of what has happened to you?"

"All that I remember is when Salipada hollered and told me to run. Before and after that, I recall nothing. Where is he? Can I see him?"

The doctor leaned in closer and lowered his voice. "Mr. Menadun died before we could treat him. He sustained a fatal head trauma and never really had a chance of survival. I'm sorry. Was he your friend?"

"Yes," Malik said. Tears began to stream down the boy's face.

Dr. Tomaseo continued, "The authorities told us that it was an ugly scene on the hilltop where they found you. You were lucky that the soldiers found you before you lost any more blood." He inspected Malik's cast approvingly. "I do have some good news, though. There's someone waiting in the hallway that I think you'll be happy to see. She tells me she's your girlfriend from college." Doctor Tomaseo stood up and opened the door. Nina bolted into the room without even acknowledging the physician.

"Malik! How are you? Are they treating you properly?" she said. She turned and gave Dr. Tomaseo a disdainful glare.

"They are. I'll be OK," Malik answered. "You shouldn't worry."

"Well, the hospital administration has been far too uncooperative. I came all the way up here with half a dozen students to protest the way you're being mistreated. The moronic floor nurse would only let one of us at a time in to see you." Nina spun around and pointed a finger at the doctor. "Go tell that woman she was out of line," she demanded. "Tell her to let my friends into the room now."

"No, please," Malik waved his hand signaling Nina to stop.

"He doesn't know what he's saying. He must be delirious," Nina said to Dr. Tomaseo. "Now you'll have to leave us alone; we have private matters to discuss."

"Doctor, please stay here with me," Malik said.

Nina refused to back down. "How soon before he can leave this place?" she asked sharply.

Dr. Tomaseo approached and stood eye-to-eye with her. "Young lady, Mr. Abbas will require extensive care for several more days, maybe weeks."

"That's unacceptable. He must be moved to a better facility in Manila. There are people who need to hear his story. They need to learn how our oppressive government is hunting down people like wild game. I've set up an interview with a foreign news reporter who's promised to expose this atrocity to the world." Nina pawed through her purse, searching for her notebook. "His name is…"

Malik forced himself upright and shouted, "No! Stop it, now! Doctor, please make her leave. I don't want her in here anymore." He felt far too weary to tolerate Nina's obsessiveness. At the moment, politics was the least of his concerns.

Dr. Tomaseo touched Nina's arm lightly and motioned toward the door. She jerked away. "Keep your hands off of me!" she exclaimed. "You haven't heard the last of this!" she added while stomping out.

"Hmm, I guess that would explain all the commotion I saw outside when I came to work," Dr. Tomaseo said. He parted the blinds to get a better look at the scene below. There, clustered on the hospital's lawn, was a group of students waving signs and chanting something that he couldn't make out. Nina emerged from the building's entrance, pumped her fist and joined in with the demonstration.

"*Stop religious persecution… Free Malik Abbas…*" the doctor read aloud from the posters. "*Down with imperialism.*" He shook his head slowly and sighed. "Your friends would be wise to tone down their activities before the P.C. arrive."

"They're not my friends," Malik said. "And they'll have to find someone else to be their martyr. I just want to go back to my family – back to Mindanao where I belong."

The doctor returned to Malik's side. "Young man," he said, "you have a difficult path to travel before you'll be able to return home. But when that time comes and you're completely healed, I promise that you'll get there, even if I have to drive you myself." He took Malik's hand in both of his and held it tightly. "Now try and get some rest."

Malik sat back and stared at ceiling. His thoughts drifted to Salipada Menadun, the friend he'd known just briefly, but whom he already missed. He thought to himself how much his life had changed since he'd left Mindanao. The jubilation that he'd felt upon arriving in Manila had faded, along with his dream of going to college. Perhaps he'd return one day and finish school, but not now. He wanted to be with his mother and father again.

* * *

When Bud got the word that he and Reeder were departing for the States that very day, he scrambled in order to get ready for the flight. Most of his gear was still onboard *San Angelo,* so Chief Jenks gave him a lift to the other side of Subic Bay where the ship was moored. Bud crammed two suitcases full of his personal things, figuring that whatever he missed, McGirt would pack up for him later. He doubted that he'd need his flight gear or any of his professional Navy items, so he chose to leave them behind. He'd claim them in a few weeks when the ship tied up in California.

Neither Lugansky nor the ship's XO was aboard when Bud arrived, so he checked out with the ship's Officer of the Day and left behind a copy of his change-of-duty orders.

"Chief Jenks, I'd like to swing by the helo ramp and say a few words to the men," Bud said during the drive back to Cubi Point.

Jenks checked his watch. "Plenty of time for that, sir. Skipper told me that your ride to Manila isn't leaving for another hour."

The pair found the detachment's enlisted crew scattered across the tarmac working on the unit's single remaining aircraft. Once again, Jenks had delegated supervisory duties to the next man in line: Dobbs. Unfortunately for the crusty petty officer and his crew, the Marines had reclaimed both sides of the transient hangar, prompting the Det to work outside on the unsheltered pavement. Though it was early in the day, the tropical sun had already transformed the ramp into a blistering concrete sauna. Most of the crew had shed their t-shirts and wore cutoff working dungarees in an effort to stay cool.

Jenks put two fingers to his mouth and whistled loudly to get the group's attention. "Fall in!" he barked. The men straggled quietly into a cluster on the aircraft's shaded side where Bud and Jenks were waiting.

"All present or accounted for, sir," Jenks reported. He leaned toward Bud and added in confidence, "I sent Sartelli and Lincoln on a parts run 'bout half an hour ago."

Bud wondered if Jenks had deliberately isolated the two sailors from the rest of the detachment because of what they'd seen in Baguio. "Very well, Chief," he said matter-of-factly.

The men stood solemnly in anticipation of their boss's parting words. They'd learned that he'd been relieved of his duties within minutes of the CIA briefing the other day and had spent time speculating about the "hows" and "whys" of what had happened to Rayburn's helicopter.

Bud caught a whiff of the group's alcohol-laced body odor as they surrounded him and Jenks. "Smells like you guys had a good time out in town last night," he said to break the ice. The men burst into laughter and commenced joking and grab-assing about their exploits in Olongapo the previous evening.

Bud laughed along with them and said, "Well, that's all right. I'm confident Chief Jenks and Petty Officer Dobbs will sweat it out of you before the day's over." The revelry settled down as his expression turned serious.

"Gentlemen," he went on, "I'll be frank. This wasn't exactly the way I'd expected our deployment to end. I'd stay on for the last month if I could." The men stood silent and motionless, listening respectfully. "But you'll be in good hands as you travel down the last stretch and head home." Bud reached up and patted Irvis Jenks on the shoulder affectionately. He craned his neck and looked over the group. "Anybody seen McGirt?"

A young sailor in the back piped up. "Sir, I saw the lieutenant at morning chow. He told me that Brightness, er...Mr. Bright's already gone through every book and magazine in the hospital. Said he was going to fetch some more reading material for the ensign and run it up to him."

"No big surprise there," Bud said as the crowd chuckled in agreement. "Men, I ask that you give your new OIC the same respect and diligent effort that you've afforded me during the cruise." He started to say more, but an unexpected lump rose in his throat and he choked on the words. The men lowered their eyes and fidgeted in place while he collected himself.

Bud took a deep breath and scanned the group, making eye contact with each and every sailor. With all the activity that had occurred since the fateful day in Baguio, he'd neglected to prepare emotionally for this moment. But the words came straight from his heart when he said, "These last six months have been the highlight of my career." He instinctively drew his right hand slowly to his temple and said, "It's been an honor and a privilege. I salute you." The detachment snapped to attention and returned the salute, holding it respectfully until the officer lowered his arm.

"At ease," Bud said. "I'd like you to huddle in good and close while I say this." The unit pressed around him tightly as he spoke barely above a whisper. "Whatever those federal agents told you at your briefing this morning, that's the way it all went down." Conviction filled his voice and he stabbed a finger in the air as he spoke. "Lieutenant Rayburn's aircraft experienced a catastrophic engine failure and the crew was unable to recover from the malfunction. That's the story, and that's all you need to know. Period." Bud signaled Jenks that it was time to go and began walking away. After a few steps, he hesitated and turned to face the group again.

"And one final thing," he said. "Remember to say a prayer for your fallen shipmate, Lipton Caleb LaRue."

* * *

A pair of tugboats guided USS *San Angelo* away from the pier. Once under her own power, the bulky freighter cruised through Subic Bay at a cautious eight knots. Captain Walt Lugansky had treated himself to the pleasure of having the con as his vessel got underway. Abeam Grande Island, Lugansky called out, "All engines ahead, flank. Navigator, give us a course for Singapore!" A round of applause erupted on the Bridge as the ship rumbled forward, accelerating to her maximum speed. Black smoke belched from *San Angelo's* stacks. Lugansky turned over control of the ship to the Officer of the Deck and retired to his stateroom. Shortly afterwards, flight quarters were set as two helicopters appeared on the horizon. The lead aircraft, Sideflare Zero-Two, was piloted by Detachment 110's two remaining aviators — Johnny Jack McGirt and Ron Carbone. In loose trail off their right side was another CH-46 on loan from Naval Air Station, Cubi Point. Lugansky had politicked for the extra workhorse in anticipation of VERTREP missions en route to Singapore. A flight crew assigned to shore duty at the air station leapt at the chance to make the trek. Bored with land-locked flying around Luzon, they were itching for some "yanking and banking" at sea. They'd hitch a ride aboard an oiler back to Cubi after their services were no longer needed.

The helos landed uneventfully. Chief Irvis Jenks supervised the recovery detail as the aircraft were folded up and secured in the hangar. He found McGirt with the other pilots as they put the finishing touches on the aircrafts' logbooks. "Lieutenant, Skipper wants to see you ASAP." McGirt signed his name to the logbook's "yellow sheet" and headed topside.

Lugansky heard the clunk of McGirt's flight boots in the passageway.

"Come in, Lieutenant, door's open," he said. McGirt found the skipper at his rolltop desk. It had returned to its normal state of organized clutter; empty styrofoam cups and paperwork littered the big mahogany surface. "Coffee?" Lugansky asked. He motioned to a fresh pot on the corner of his desk. McGirt helped himself.

Lugansky reached overhead and triggered the lever on his intercom. "XO, I've got the OIC, Lieutenant McGirt, with me in my stateroom. I'd like to see you in about ten minutes when we're finished." McGirt watched as the Old Man walked across the space and peeled back the covering from his private fridge. As he opened it, McGirt saw a full bottle of Jack Daniels hiding in the back behind a row of soft drinks. Lugansky stooped over and opened a can of diet soda. He gave McGirt an innocent grin. "Too early," he said.

"Well, Mr. McGirt, a lot of water has passed over the dam since the last time we had a sit-down, hasn't it?" McGirt could only nod in agreement. He took a sip of java and set down the cup. "You ready to go?" Lugansky went on. "Looks like we'll be pretty busy the next several days. Just got a message that you'll have a two hundred pallet lift tonight. Kick-off's scheduled for 2100 hours."

"We'll be ready, sir. The guys from Cubi will need some pink time and then cycle through some landings to get their night qualifications up to speed."

"Sure. Let my ops officer know what you need. We'll man the Tower with our guys before sunset. How's the knee?"

"Feeling fine, sir. The doc at the Cubi clinic took a look and said it's healin' up right nicely. I'll get it checked out good when we return Stateside."

The skipper drained the last of his soda and heaved the can across the stateroom. It swished squarely in the center of a metal trashcan. "I made some calls back home during our extended stay in Subic and spoke with my brother-in-law in Michigan. Not sure if I ever told you, but he's a huge Wolverines fan. He hasn't missed a game in Ann Arbor for more than twenty years. He recognized your name soon as I mentioned it." McGirt began to feel uncomfortable. He sensed what was to follow.

"He wanted me to ask why you never came back for your senior year. He said you were a real legend during your playing days. 'One tough son of a bitch,' to quote him."

McGirt started to laugh. Normally, he'd bypass telling the story, but he figured that, after what they'd just been through, Lugansky deserved the straight skinny. "Well, sir, I walked on without a scholarship. Had some offers from smaller schools, but wanted to know if I was good enough to cut it in the big leagues. I had pretty good grades, so Michigan accepted me on my academics alone."

"Kind of small for the Big Ten, weren't you?"

"Yeah, probably, but I practically lived in the weight room back then. Played on the junior varsity and fought my way up the depth chart. Finally got a starting position at linebacker third game into the season of my junior year. Held onto it until I tore up my knee a week before the Ohio State game."

"Then what?"

"Had surgery, a long rehab and missed spring ball. But I got myself in shape over the summer and was ready for two-a-days in August. After the long layoff, the head coach put me down on the JVs. Can't say that I blame him. Competition is really fierce at U of M and I'd missed a lot of practice. Anyway, I was taking a bad pounding on the scout team and got into it with an assistant coach during a blocking drill."

"What happened?"

McGirt shuffled nervously, embarrassed by what he had to say, but it was too late to turn back. "Skipper, I guess you could say that I sort of lost it. They'd recruited a fast running back from Chicago. Real pretty boy, if you know what I mean. He had a lot of fancy moves, but shied away from contact when the ball wasn't in his hands. My job that day was to stand between two tackling dummies and take pretty boy on, half speed, while he blocked me. But I couldn't hold off. I wanted my job back on the varsity, so I flattened his ass three times in a row. After the third time, the backfield coach grabbed me by the face mask and made, let's just say, some disparaging remarks about my family."

"About your dad?" Lugansky asked. "My brother-in-law knew about what happened to your father." Lugansky had gotten so caught up in the story that he'd inadvertently crossed the line. He quickly switched gears. "Sorry, Lieutenant. We've got a busy night ahead. Get some rest."

"That's all right, Skipper." McGirt took another slug of coffee and continued. "The coach said something like 'Didn't you understand what I said, hillbilly? Half speed. Stupidity must run in your family.' That's when I came unglued. I hauled off and cold-cocked him. It took half the team to pull me off. I wanted to strangle him to death." McGirt lowered his eyes. "I'm not proud of what I did, sir. I walked off the practice field and never went back. The head coach called me that night and wanted to broker peace between me and the assistant, but I refused."

No further words were necessary. Lugansky stood up and extended his hand. "Good to have you guys back aboard," he said. "One more thing, McGirt. What happened in Baguio is just the tip of the iceberg, in my opinion. XO and I received a more thorough briefing from the Intelligence boys after we left you folks on the hill. There's some real angry folks over here. Beside that New People's Army, the Muslims in the south are barking pretty loud. *San Angelo* is my last set of sea duty orders and I'll probably never be over here again. You youngsters better be prepared for more of these threats. Be careful out there."

McGirt replied, "Yes, sir," and started for the door. Lugansky added, "And I don't blame you for going after that coach. The bastard deserved it."

Chapter 28

Commander Rex Reeder carried out his orders. He'd proceeded to the Base transportation office first thing Monday morning to make arrangements for the trip home. The Filipino clerk made a few phone calls. In less than five minutes, Reeder walked out with airline tickets for himself and Bud Lammers. Their flight left Manila International in three hours. He then touched base with Cubi's operations officer and successfully begged a helo ride across Manila Bay to the airport. The pilots did "buster" and got them there a few minutes prior to scheduled departure. Once dropped off, they'd dragged their bags across the tarmac to the Northwest Airlines 747 parked at the gate. It was sheer luck that a mechanic had noticed them while doing his final inspection of the plane. The man took the pair in tow and led them directly to the podium for boarding passes. The two officers fell into their economy class seats just as the gate agent slammed shut the jumbo jet's door.

The four-hour flight to Tokyo passed quickly. Despite the devastating events of the last few days, the men were pumped with adrenaline and ready to get home. They made a smooth connection at Tokyo's Haneda Airport and boarded another crowded Northwest jet for the long transoceanic flight. At over three quarters of a million pounds, the big, red-tailed airplane had used nearly every foot of runway to get airborne. The aircraft banked gracefully over Tokyo Bay on the first segment of its five thousand mile flight to Los Angeles.

Reeder and Lammers lucked out with tandem aisle seats in coach. On the leg from Manila, they'd been sandwiched smack in the center section with crying babies and foreigners all around them. During climb out, a tall blonde stewardess appeared at their side.

"Gentlemen, the captain would like to offer you a different seating arrangement," she said. "Please follow me." She led them forward and pointed to a spiral staircase. The roomy upper section was only half full. The officers chose two seats in the compartment's last row. During the next couple of hours, they were treated to something that neither one was accustomed to: first class service. After dinner they ordered another round and finally began to mellow out.

"So what happened in Manila?" Rex said in a low voice. During the chaos of the last twenty-four hours, he hadn't had the opportunity to ask Lammers about his trip to see the president. Bud went on to describe his flight with McGirt, the clothing change and the grandeur of the Malacanang Palace.

"I think the guy just wanted to meet the two of us," Bud said. Reeder looked around them. Confident that no one could hear their conversation, he said, "Did he ask about what happened up north?"

"No, not a word. Nothing. Someone must have given him the background on the two of us though. He knew where we were from and what colleges we'd gone to. He even knew the details of my service in Vietnam. He must be tapped into some pretty good intel, especially on such short notice."

"That's a little scary," Reeder said.

"When we got back to Cubi, I asked Davis about it. He said the guy has near total recall. When he took the bar exam after the war, he scored so high on the test that the law school was sure that he'd cheated. But when the professors put him through an oral examination, he scored even higher." Lammers started chuckling. The alcohol and fatigue were making him giddy. "And then, according to Davis, at the end of the oral, to emphasize his point, he recited the Philippine Constitution — backwards!"

"Christ's sake," Reeder said. "What else happened when you were inside? Did you see his wife?"

"No, but after he showed us pictures of his kids, he told us that she'd left earlier in the day to visit 'Muammar in Tripoli.'"

"Gaddafi? The president of Libya?" Reeder nearly came out of his seat. People in front of them turned around when they heard his words.

Bud lowered his voice to a whisper and continued, "Apparently this thing with the Muslim kid really caused some waves. To paraphrase his words, 'I think Muammar is sweet on her. She can smooth things out with the Arabs better than I ever could.'"

"Damn. Davis was right on." Rex said. "He warned us about everything going on in the southern islands, and how pissed the Arabs were about it." Reeder thought about what Lammers had said. "Why the hell do you think he'd share that with a couple of guys like you and McGirt? What would he have to gain from that?"

Bud shrugged. "Don't know. Like I said, I think he just wanted to feel us out and gain our confidence. We were the only two who actually saw what went down with Lincoln and those two dirt-bags who tried to kidnap him."

"What else?"

"Not much, really. He showed us some pictures of him with a bunch of other world leaders. He said that he felt sorry for LBJ and that Vietnam had ruined the man. Then he told a few more stories and bragged about being the best golfer of all the Asian heads of state. But when we were leaving, he said something that I don't think I'll ever forget. Let me see if I can get this right: 'Remember men, leadership is the other side of the coin of loneliness. He who is a leader must always act alone. When you act alone, you must accept everything alone.'" Bud swirled his glass of scotch. "I thought that was rather prophetic; painfully so." Both men silently pondered Marcos' words for a moment.

"What do you think will happen now?" Bud said.

Reeder tapped his empty beer bottle absently on the console. "Well, I wasn't planning to drop this on you until we got back, but I can't see what difference my timing makes. You deserve the truth." He turned to face Lammers. "Bud, you'll be asked to submit your letter of resignation when we arrive. For the record, it will be because of the two crashes that occurred during your tenure as OIC. A handful of us will know the real reason."

"Better that I just fade away into civilian-hood, huh?"

"You got it. What do you think you'll do?"

Bud paused and looked up at the ceiling. "Flying is all that I've ever known. Maybe take a shot at the airlines, if I'm not too old."

"Oh, jeez, that reminds me. Davis asked me to give this to you." He dug through his briefcase and pulled out a large envelope. Bud tore it open and found a note that read, "The Agency is always looking for good people. If interested, please return the enclosed job application directly to me. I'll hand carry it to Langley." Bud handed the papers back for Reeder to see.

Rex smiled. "Well, I think you've already validated their marksmanship requirements." The tired officers quietly chuckled to themselves.

"What about you, Skipper?" Bud asked.

Reeder was quick and unequivocal with his reply. "End of the road for me. After the mishaps and Rayburn's shenanigans, C.O. of HCS-30 will be the high point of my career. Louise and I will probably get some bullshit orders to D.C. where I'll be an errand boy and make coffee for the admirals. With our son in Annapolis, though, not a bad twilight tour, all things considered."

"What's your take on Rayburn?" Bud asked. Reeder's face reddened at the sound of Thomas' name.

"The Cubi Point admin officer told me that Rayburn's already contacted the JAG office and lawyered up. He'll probably cut a deal for his silence. That mess will be front-and-center on my desk when I go to work tomorrow. Hey, I never had a chance to see Bright before we left. How's he doing?"

The corners of Bud's mouth turned up in an affectionate grin. "Robert J. Bright — now there's a talented young fellow. When I spoke with his doctor before we left, he told me that he'll have a long row to hoe with the rehab on his arm. But despite his wimpy looks, I sense that he's tough as nails inside. There's got to be a spot for a smart kid like him: teaching, research, that sort of thing. Maybe the Navy post-grad school in Monterey."

Reeder agreed, "He's a good man. The Navy can't afford to lose him."

The aircraft entered some mild turbulence. The bumps soon flattened out to a gentle rocking motion, similar to when *San Angelo* was going through a patch of light swells. It was a black, moonless night over the northern Pacific. Bud reached up and switched off the reading lamp above his head. With eight more hours still remaining in the flight, he and Rex Reeder drifted into their own thoughts.

The snug confines of the jet's upper deck provided Bud with a long overdue chance to evaluate his future. He was slowly coming to grips with the fact that his military career was ending. In the past, he'd never had an inkling what that day would feel like. Now it was here. Without the burden that had weighed him down for the last decade, his mind turned to Jill. *How can I get her back?* he thought. *Has she already filed for divorce?* Bud knew one thing for sure: he had to find his wife and talk with her. It was time for him to see their relationship more clearly, without the veil of military service or remembrance of his dreadful time in Vietnam. He still loved Jill with all that was in him, and had to tell her so. He now looked at his firing as an opportunity for a fresh start. Furthermore, for the first time in his life, money wasn't a major concern. Sure, the "gift" from Marcos would certainly help, but also, Davis had all but offered him a job on a silver platter. He was anxious to see his wife and start making plans for their new life together. He prayed that she would see it in her heart to reconsider.

Chapter 29

The rumble of the 727's engines startled Bud from a deep stupor as the pilot applied full power and executed a missed approach at San Diego's Lindbergh Field. He looked down from his window seat and saw nothing but a layer of haze and fog covering the ground. They may as well have been flying into Bangor, Maine during a snowstorm rather than sunny Southern California.

"Christ, will this trip ever end?" Rex Reeder mumbled. Sitting next to Bud in a center seat, Reeder rubbed his bloodshot eyes. Both men had been in constant motion for over twenty-four hours and were punchy with jet lag after hurtling across a dozen time zones. Other than short periods of time while rushing between gates in Tokyo and Los Angeles, they'd spent the majority of the last day cooped up in an aluminum tube. The luxurious comfort of the L.A.-bound jumbo jet had long since faded from their memories.

Bud surveyed his crumpled khaki uniform. The double-knit polyester fabric was normally indestructible, able to be worn for days on end and still bounce back with sharp military creases. But this marathon voyage had pressed such ugly wrinkles into the outfit, he wondered if it was beyond repair and destined to be deep-sixed. Likewise, his whole body felt clammy, as if he'd been swimming in the ocean and hadn't showered afterwards. Bud hadn't felt this lousy since he'd pulled an all-nighter during a spring break binge in Florida with his fraternity brothers.

"Folks, some of that annoying coastal fog has crept in over the airport and we'll have to give it another shot, this time on a different runway," the captain announced over the P.A. in a reassuring voice. The plane made a gentle course reversal over the cloud-covered water as the crew lined up the aircraft for another try.

Bud could see the inland mountains in the distance, where the skies were clear and bright. Closer to the shoreline, though, only the peaks of the tallest buildings were visible. The jet engines began to unwind and slowly the airliner sank back into the thick fog. In less than a minute, the familiar sight of runway lights and striped concrete came into Bud's view. The pilot eased the throttles to idle and raised the aircraft's nose slightly to cushion their descent. The Boeing's landing gear touched the pavement with a gentle *thunk* as a smattering of applause broke out from the crowded cabin. Bud glanced to his left and exchanged a "thank God" look with Reeder. But the welcoming feeling was short-lived for Bud. He became anxious again and resumed worrying about where his wife might be.

As they made their way to baggage claim, Reeder waved his arms and let out a shrill whistle to get the attention of the enlisted man that the squadron duty officer had dispatched to meet them. The pencil-necked youngster, dressed in crisp, white bell-bottoms, came to a rigid attention and saluted when he sighted them.

"Good morning, sirs. May I help you with your bags?" the kid asked respectfully.

Reeder nodded and motioned toward the baggage carousel where a stream of suitcases trickled out one at a time. He scanned the terminal as if he was looking for someone else.

"I need to make a beeline for the squadron and start untangling this Rayburn mess," Reeder said to Bud. "After the driver drops me off, I'll have him take you home. You live in Bonita, right?"

"Yes, sir. Bought one of those Murdoch condos, down the hill from your neighborhood," Bud answered. Reeder shifted his eyes toward the open doors that led to the parking lot. Suddenly, an ear-to-ear grin shot across his face.

"Hey, hey, there she is!" he exclaimed.

Bud turned and saw Jill as she walked tentatively into the baggage claim area. She clutched her purse tightly to her side. Her eyes darted to Reeder and then back to Bud, who was staring at her in disbelief.

"Hi, Bud. Do you need a ride?" she asked with a hesitant smile. Rex patted Bud's shoulder and said, "Welcome home, sailor! Don't hurry in to work; take a few days off." He shook Bud's hand heartily and added, "I'm sure you two have some catching up to do."

Jill looked up at him gratefully and said, "Thank you, Commander."

Reeder volunteered the driver to help with Lammers' suitcases, but Bud politely declined. The skipper handed the driver his attaché case and took hold of his own luggage. The youngster had to break into a jog to keep up with Rapid Rex as the lanky officer charged like an eager racehorse from the gate.

"We need to talk," Jill said flatly. Bud felt a slight chill down his spine. He'd heard this tone before in his wife's voice. He could tell that she was dreadfully upset.

"OK. Where are you parked?" he asked. She pointed to the door and they began walking. She carried Bud's small valise while he lugged his two big suitcases outside and into the airport parking lot. He quickly spotted his blue Corvette.

"Ah, she still runs!" he said happily.

"Yep, I've started it once a week and drove two laps around the block, just as instructed," Jill replied. Bud wedged his luggage into the car's tiny trunk and climbed in behind the wheel. His sudden cheerfulness disappeared as Jill sat down and turned to face him.

She wasted no time. "Listen to me, Charles T. Lammers. I mean really *hear* the words that I'm about to say. Otherwise, I'm marching right back into that airport and getting on the next flight to Norfolk."

Bud pulled the keys out of the ignition and sat back. He took a deep breath and lowered his head.

"We can't go on like this anymore," Jill said. "I'm tired of always being second in your life. It's been ten years since you got back from the war and it's the same old song: if it's not your job you're worrying about, it's our money. I'm sick of it! Our wheels keep spinning, but you and I never get anywhere in life, Bud. And worst of all, I'm tired of being alone."

Bud glanced outside and then turned in his seat to face her. Jill's lower lip was trembling, but her blue eyes were locked on his with steely resolve. He knew she was absolutely right, and he knew he should have done something about the situation long before now.

"I am so sorry for everything," he said. "You've never let me down, Jill, and you deserve better than the life I've given you." He took her hand and continued, "Coming back on the flight, I had no idea whether or not you'd still be here. You sure had enough reason not to be. Thanks for coming to meet me." Bud's eyes began to water, but he caught himself and added, "I missed you terribly."

Jill tried desperately to stay firm, but her lip continued to shake and she began to cry. "I missed you, too, so very, very much," she said. The anger drained from her face and she squeezed his hand lovingly. They were quiet for a moment.

Bud broke the silence and asked, "Your last letter said you were leaving. Where'd you go?"

Jill brushed back a long strand of hair from her forehead and said, "I started driving back to Virginia after you canceled my flight to Manila." She looked down and shook her head. "I couldn't believe that you put being with your men above seeing me."

"But that's not what it was, honey! I couldn't wait to see you. It was just that I was afraid that it would look bad if I took leave, like I was a no-load or something."

Anger returned to Jill's face and she started to cry again. "Haven't you given enough to the Navy? When will it stop?"

Bud thought of all the times when he'd been in harm's way. He'd faced down death more than once. Nothing, however, got straight to his soul like the words of his wife—and her tears. "You're right," he said. "I may as well tell you now. I've been asked to resign. My military career is over."

Jill gasped and instinctively put her arms around him. "It's OK," he went on. "It's the best thing for both of us. I already have a lead on a new job, something that will keep me home more." They sat for a long moment and hugged quietly as Jill's crying tapered off.

"So, what else do we need to talk about? The picture?"

Jill smiled weakly. "Well, that certainly didn't help," she said. "Maddy Rayburn had a nice time with that during one of the wives' club meetings I'd dragged myself to. She giggled smugly and held it up for everyone to see, then said something like, 'Poor Thomas must have mistakenly sent home the wrong pictures. You know how he's been under such stress, doing so many jobs on the ship.' The girls all had a good laugh at my expense."

"Rayburn's got more than a little stress on his plate right now, trust me," Bud said. "You know that picture was just a gag, don't you?"

"Yeah. After all these years, I knew it was just a bunch of rowdy rotorboys blowing off steam. After you nixed my trip, though, it just rubbed salt into the wound. I quit my job, loaded up the car and headed east. I got as far as the middle of nowhere in Texas, someplace called Shamrock, when I turned around. I had a lot of time to think while alone on the road and decided that we'd both worked too hard for me to run out like that. But I can't be the only one. You have to promise that you'll make me more a part of your life."

Bud peeked outside again and slid his palms absently over the 'Vette's steering wheel. He said firmly, "I promise." The tears had smeared the makeup Jill had so painstakingly put on this morning. Bud reached over and ran his fingers gently across her cheek.

"I wanted to look nice for you today," she said. "After Louise Reeder called last night and told me you were coming home, I was so excited that I could hardly sleep. Now look at me; I'm a mess."

"You look beautiful," Bud said as he stroked her hair. "Things are going to change for us in a big way," he said. "We have a lot to talk about."

Bud started the car's engine and peered out at the sky. "Looks like it's breaking up," he said. He undid a couple of latches above the windshield, and then pushed a button to lower the Corvette's convertible top. As they drove onto the freeway ramp, he floored the accelerator and merged with the heavy traffic traveling to the South Bay.

"Hey, honey, do me a favor and reach into that small bag for my sunglasses, will you?" he said.

Jill unzipped the valise that Bud had carried with him on the plane. As she did, the leather bag from Marcos fell to the floor with a jingling thud.

"What's in the sack?" she asked as she handed him the sunglasses.

Bud slipped on his Wayfarers and laughed. "Just some shiny souvenirs. I'll tell you about it when we get home." He gunned the motor again and swung into the left lane. Jill tossed her head back and let her hair blow wildly in the breeze. Bud watched her from the corner of his eye; she was still a beautiful woman and he felt lucky to have a second chance with her. Leaving the Navy suddenly seemed like a blessing in disguise. He felt like the weight of the world had been lifted off his shoulders. Jill glanced over at him and smiled. The warm California sun felt great on their faces.

Acknowledgements

I'd like to thank the following people for their contributions to my research: Allen Conrad, Dennis Dolfie, Curt Hingson, Ken Hollett, Lonnie Kinderman, Chip Lancaster, Casey Mangine, John Mann, Mike Murphy, Matt Schramm, Jess Springfield and Bill Ungvarsky. A special thanks goes out to Mac McLaughlin, president of the USS Midway Museum, for giving me an open gangway to his wonderful ship and its library. I'd also like to recognize the two "Godfathers of Vertical Replenishment," Joe Gardner and Mike Reber, for their invaluable knowledge and endless supply of sea stories.

I would be remiss to not mention my editor, Lee Lewis Walsh, for her friendship and professionalism. Thanks, Lee.

And finally, a heart-felt "thank you" to my wife, Connie, and our daughters, Katari, Anna, and Mary for their unwavering love and support.

I hope you enjoyed reading ***Rotorboys***. If so, I'd appreciate your feedback on Amazon.com and I invite you to visit my website at www.LarryCarello.com.

— Larry Carello

IT WAS NOT JUST ANOTHER HOSTAGE RESCUE...

LARRY CARELLO

They called themselves Abu Sayyaf, the *Bearer of the Sword*.

www.braveshipbooks.com

THE WAR AMERICA CAN'T AFFORD TO LOSE

GEORGE GALDORISI

THE CORONADO CONSPIRACY

NEW YORK TIMES BESTSELLING AUTHOR
GEORGE GALDORISI

Everything was going according to plan...

www.braveshipbooks.com

CUTTING-EDGE NAVAL THRILLERS
BY
JEFF EDWARDS

SEA OF SHADOWS

THE SEVENTH ANGEL

SWORD OF SHIVA

www.braveshipbooks.com

THE THOUSAND YEAR REICH MAY BE ONLY BEGINNING...

ALLAN LEVERONE

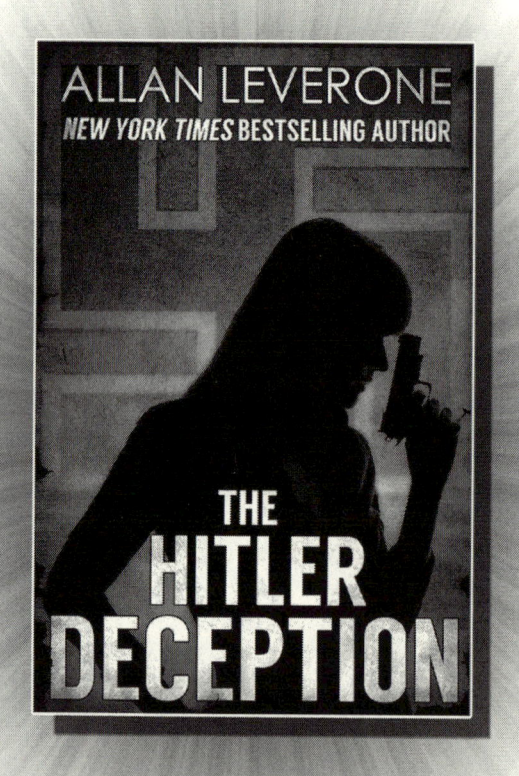

A Tracie Tanner Thriller

www.braveshipbooks.com

Made in the USA
Middletown, DE
27 March 2025